10672749

The Secret-Keeper

a novel — *Nov.08*

© 2005 by Chris Zimmerman

All rights reserved. No part of this publication may be reproduced, utilized in any form or means electrical, mechanical, including photocopying, recording, information storage, retrieval systems or film making without written permission from the publisher.

ISBN: 0-923568-69-7

Cover photo: Round Island Lighthouse, Mackinac County Michigan

Fifth edition, published by:

Joker's Conundrum LLC
Post Office Box 180
Shepherd MI 48883

Visit the author's website:
www.authorchriszimmerman.com

Send electronic correspondence to:
setterindebtor@yahoo.com

This book is fictional and intended for entertainment purposes only. The characters, names, governmental agencies, settings, dialogue and plot are products of the author's imagination and should not be construed as authentic. Any resemblance to actual persons or events is purely coincidental.

Printed in the United States of America

The Secret-Keeper

Chris Zimmerman

Also by Chris Zimmerman:

INTENTIONAL ACTS

One

A FUNERAL HARDLY SEEMS like a good place to begin a story. A funeral by most accounts is the end of life, the final chapter. My wife Carrie's funeral came way too soon, way too premature. She was young when she died, with many goals yet uncharted, with many challenges to prevail. But while all of us grieved the end of her life, Carrie had taken steps to ensure that her dreams would not soon be forgotten.

Carrie was one of those people who always planned ahead, who wouldn't take no for an answer. If a door closed ahead of her, she'd figure out a way around it. If she didn't get the answer she was looking for, she'd ask somebody else. She was determined, motivated. Sincere. And now, tragically, gone.

There'd be lots of hugs from well-wishers, friends, and family—both mine and hers. There'd be scores of her pals from college and friends from her young career. And church. Many from the congregation would come out of the woodwork to see Carrie off—some of them were genuine in their intent; others had nothing better to do. Still more came to the funeral because they somehow needed to reaffirm the fact that they were mortal. Whatever.

1

I had to be strong in my grief.

I had to keep a stiff upper lip, as they say.

It was a sad day.

The saddest.

She was my everything—my world—and today I would say goodbye.

But despite my despair, life goes on. I still had to shower, shave, and get ready for the day. Even though I had a broken heart, I still needed to get dressed and get on with things. When I opened the door to our closet, I noticed Carrie's business suits hanging next to mine. They were nice and orderly, all facing the same way like a row of soldiers. What was I going to do with her clothes now? I pulled a suit out of the closet, hung the hanger on the hook behind the bathroom door, and watched it hang there, lifeless and still. My, how she had filled out that suit, made it come to life! I took it off the hook and held it in my arms. I closed my eyes and held it against my chest; her subtle perfume and dainty scent still permeated the delicate fibers. I could almost feel her in my arms, sensing her in my grasp; wishing that she wasn't gone.

Just then, Curtis, her brother, rang the doorbell to the back door. I went downstairs and waved him inside, even though I was only wearing a bathrobe. He gave me a hug, and his eyes looked as red as mine. I asked if he wanted coffee, then realized that I hadn't gotten that far in the morning ritual. He brushed me off, directing me back upstairs to the bedroom, while he started a pot to brew. I put away Carrie's suit and put on my own, slowly but surely. From there, I scoured the sock drawer for a clean match but there was none. Damn, I let the smallest details of life get away from me. I had an excuse, after all. A sudden, severe illness has a way of doing that, but so does a bad accident. I had both to deal with.

It started out so simple. Another check-up, another green light from her family doctor. But there was more. Three months after our wedding she came home from the doctor's office and said that the doctor wanted to remove a mole from her back, "just because it doesn't serve any purpose," she smiled. A week later she came home with a small band-aid stuck to her back and a promise that the doctor would call her if there were any problems. To our surprise, the doctor called, and she wanted us to come to her office as soon as possible.

Both of us?

Curtis had the coffee brewed when I finished tying my necktie. "How are you holding up?" He asked.

"Aw, Curtis. I don't know. This sucks, the whole damn thing. I can't believe it," I said. He gestured with the coffee pot and I pulled the last mug from the cupboard. I looked inside, and blew a small plume of dust from the bottom. All the other coffee cups were either collecting food scraps in the sink or were in various stages of cleanliness in the dishwasher. I had trouble dealing with the smallest parts of life—like doing the dishes.

Curtis filled my cup and told me, "This will pick you up. It'll make your hair stand on end if you're not careful."

"Thanks, Curtis," I said. "But my hair already stands on end." We stood for a few pregnant seconds, stirring creamer into our coffee, trying to come up with something apropos to say to one another.

"Got any cordovan?"

"I beg your pardon?" I asked.

"Cordovan...for my loafers," he said, barely smiling. "Did you think I wanted some sort of liqueur for my coffee?"

"Not a bad idea, either," I told him. "Sure, give me a second. I could probably use a pat or two myself."

I made my way upstairs to the bedroom and found the cedar box with all the polish, brushes and supplies inside. Curtis did have a good idea. He was full of them, just like his sister. I met him downstairs at the kitchen table, where he had carefully cleared a path through the stacks of mail to cobble a makeshift workbench for a couple of men with heavy hearts.

"Who's going to be the pallbearers?" I asked him.

"Me, three cousins from Ohio, one of her professors and Uncle Jim."

"That should be fine. She would be pleased."

"I suppose," he replied in a tone that sounded a lot like Carrie. He handed me the tiny jar of cordovan, the brush shaped like an oversized toothbrush, and a mottled cotton cloth. "You have a nice view here," he said, gesturing toward the hanging thistle feeder outside. He did have a point. The feeder was coated with goldfinches, decked in their summer suits of brilliant yellow. Cardinals and mourning doves sifted through a small mound of discarded sunflower shells on the earth, under the outstretched limbs of a hundred-year-old spruce. Our spruce was the bookend for the row of two dozen. They were tall and stately—like a row of guards at Buckingham Palace. When the winds blew through the needles they made a haunting, whistling sound.

"Thanks," I said. "There are certainly worse places to live, that's for sure." Curtis looked back from the window, took a sip of coffee, and fidgeted with one of the plotted plants our local flower shop delivered. "Carrie and I used to sit here on Sunday mornings drinking coffee and reading the newspaper. Sometimes it took us till noon before we got out of our bathrobes and pajamas. Those were great times."

"Strange…what you remember," he said. "Do you want me to let Toby in?"

"Sure…yeah. I forgot all about him." Curtis pushed himself from the table and disappeared down the hallway to the back door. I heard the heavy oak door open and Toby's tail whack the jamb. He trotted inside, nails clicking the hardwood floors, tail swishing behind him. Toby is a good dog, ever cheerful and affectionate. He came from a long line of English setters that had the looks to be in the show ring and the drive to hunt, too. He's dappled white and black, called a "blue Belton" among aficionados. The spots are easy to see on his snout and legs, but where his coat is long, the spots meld together to form a smear of black and white. But the best part about Toby's appearance is his face. His jowls are enormous and covered in drizzled spots. When he shakes his head they smack together, making a fleshy, clapping sound. His jowls also pull at his bottom eyelids and make them look sleepy, almost sad. English setters look good even when they're bad, maybe that's why Al Capone kept an English setter in his limousine, just for show. "Toby liked Sundays, too, the afternoons at least." I gave Toby a little scratch behind the ears, and he shook his head, sending a wad of saliva over his muzzle.

"You'd take him for walks?" He asked.

"Sure. The three of us walked all the time." I smiled, then lowered my head to Toby's. He licked my ear, gently nibbling on the lobe. Strange, I never heard him bark when the doorbell rang, or figured out how he made it outside. Curtis must have taken care of that chore. "That was our routine, around the grounds of the Centre. I kept Toby on the leash until we made it to the woods on the far end of the property, then I turned him loose. He chased after squirrels, and pointed rabbits. Carrie said she missed our walks most of all when her health really began to fail. Toby missed our walks too. Since she's been gone all he does is sit in her recliner and bow his head. I've never seen a dog so sad."

"I see," Curtis frowned and rummaged through the cedar box for the horsehair brushes.

The doctor didn't mince any words when she gave us the results of the toxicology report: Carrie's mole was malignant. She'd have to go through a battery of tests to find out if the cancer had spread to other parts of her body. So we scheduled the blood tests, the ultrasound, and the MRI. Shortly after the first round of hospital visits, we turned in a claim to our temporary health insurance carrier, Atmantle Health & Casualty. We bought that policy several months before, to cover us until my employer's benefit package was activated. Oh sure, we could have gone without it; we were young, and as healthy as a couple of Belgian draft horses. The whole idea behind paying two hundred a month in premiums was that it would keep us from getting into financial trouble in the event something major happened. We both thought it made sense, but never anticipated how badly it would backfire.

Just then the back door opened, and Carrie's mother Virginia marched in wearing a short-sleeved, black suit, shouting, "Good morning, gentlemen!" She was always upbeat, good-natured, and a bit of a busy body. She put her arms around me and gave me a hug, a long one, as well as her son, who was now wearing his loafers on his feet instead of his hands. "Now there, you boys look so nice," she said, scuffing imaginary flecks of dandruff from Curtis' shoulders. "Please, help me load these flowers into my car; we've got to drop 'em off at the church before everyone arrives."

Curtis walked to the bar at the kitchen and left the same way that his mom had come in. She saw him off, as if he were a still a Boy Scout, then jumped right after the dishes piled in the sink.

I gathered the horsehair brushes, the cordovan, and polishing cloths from the kitchen table and set them back in the cedar box. Virginia stood at the sink, watching the suds overcome the saucers, plates, and cups. "Here, leave those dishes," I warned her. "I'll do them later…Really." She kept her head down, hands jumping from plate to saucer, splashing watery suds left and right. My hand eventually found the small of her arm, just above the elbow, "Really," I said, "let me do that." She stooped over the sink with her head bowed sadly. All I could do was watch her wring the grief from her pores the way only a mother can.

"Oh, Jim," she cried, and hugged me again. "I'm so sorry."

An hour later, we were inside the church at the rear of the sanctuary; the altar was surrounded in Carrie's favorite flower—daffodils—on frail, metal tripods. Reverend Erik Robinette came all the way from Carrie's hometown in Ohio to orchestrate the funeral and procession. He was her preacher growing up—the man who counseled and married us. He was a likeable guy, humorous, humble, and had an inner peace about him that was contagious. But what I liked best about him was his speaking ability. He commanded attention with his deep voice, catchy one-liners, and lively sermons that were relevant and interesting. I couldn't think of a better man for Carrie's funeral.

Our church in Mt. Pleasant, Michigan wasn't like the church of Carrie's childhood. When Carrie's mother came to church with us, she said that we had the music from a local "Seven Eleven" convenience store. Her contention was that our hymns had "seven" words, sung "eleven" times. She was right. A lot of churches have abandoned their musical roots in favor of simplistic lyrics and monotonous scores. Reverend Robinette ordered the music—the contemporary "On Eagle's Wings," and a couple of classics: "Amazing Grace," and "How Great Thou Art."

Everyone was gathered around Carrie's casket at the back of the church. It wasn't much of a casket, just a gleaming hardwood box with polished brass banisters bolted to the sides. I never paid much attention to caskets and wouldn't have known an expensive one from a cheap one until I had to choose one out of the parlor's gallery. When the funeral director showed me the models I tried to think of Carrie and of what she might like. It was mental anguish: realizing that Carrie was gone, and would never have a say in what was going on. I played it safe and chose neither a casket that was the cheapest nor the most expensive.

Reverend Robinette welcomed everyone inside the sanctuary with a smile and a few kind words. Carrie's mother was propped between Uncle Jim, her second husband, and Curtis, their white gloves clenching each forearm. Beyond them, I recognized some vaguely familiar faces of people that were at our wedding, from her side of the family. There were lots of them, from all over the country—many with tissues at their noses. Across the aisle were the folks from my familial contingent—Mom, my frowning older brother, his miserable wife, and their adorable children. Mixed between them all were dozens of friends from work, college, church, and the community.

"Ladies and gentlemen," the reverend started, "This is the day the Lord has made. Let us rejoice and be glad in it." He paused for a moment, either for dramatics or to collect his thoughts. "Today, we join together in God's presence in his house of worship to say goodbye to Carrie Nunnelly. Some would say that we 'lost' Carrie, like she was 'lost' in the woods, but we really didn't lose her after all. We know exactly where she is, don't we?

"If I knew Carrie," he continued, "and I'd like to say that I did, she loved Jesus from the time she wore pigtails and patent leathers." Another pause. "And by now the two of them must be getting along marvelously." He turned, clutching a Bible to his chest, and walked toward the altar, adorned in a thousand flowers. As if on cue, the pallbearers followed him down the aisle and the casket rolled ahead as if it were gliding "on eagle's wings."

Atmantle Health and Casualty paid their portion of the family doctor's appointment, but dragged their feet in paying for the MRI. By then, Carrie was through the blood tests, an ultrasound and had referrals for chemotherapy in Ann Arbor. I certainly wasn't going to let the squabbles with an insurance company hinder me from being a supportive husband. At the time I figured that eventually the hospital and the company would hash everything out.

When we drove home from the doctor's office and sorted through the mail, the piles were loaded with medical bills from everybody. The hospital had sent multiple bills too, with plenty of itemized charges, for everything between registration fees to a checkout charge. Before I knew it, the medical bills added up to over a hundred thousand dollars. I never let on to Carrie that things weren't right with our health insurance claim. She was fading too fast to complicate her battle. At the end of her first round of chemo, her skin cancer had spread to her liver, lymph nodes, ovaries, and lungs. Her oncologist wanted to try radiation but she refused. She saw the writing on the wall.

Ray Charles could have seen it coming.

She wanted to come home and face the inevitable with dignity and class. Just her style.

Curtis stood at the lectern and read a passage from the gospel of John, chapter eleven; the story of Lazarus and Jesus; how Lazarus died, and Jesus brought him back to life. *"Jesus called out in a loud voice, 'Lazarus, come out!' The dead man came out, his hands and feet wrapped with strips of linen, and a cloth around his face. Jesus said to them, 'Take off the grave clothes and let him go.'"* *Lazarus had come back to life. He lived.*

Three weeks after her final chemo treatment, when I returned home from the pharmacy, Carrie's car was gone and so was Carrie. She was at the stage in her battle when the bad days outnumbered the good and when the good days were barely tolerable. I couldn't imagine where she might have gone, or how she got behind the wheel. Toby didn't have any answers.

There was no note. I picked up the phone and tried her cell phone, but only got her voice mail.

Halfway through Reverend Robinette's eulogy I looked around the sanctuary, and recognized more faces—from the office, the neighborhood, and even the gas station where I walked to buy a coffee every day. A glance to the balcony revealed Telpher Beaman—one of my patients—nervously working a tuft of hair under his lip. As always, he wore a tweed sport coat, matching vest, and a silk ascot, subtly printed but very distinguished, around his neck. He nodded in my direction, as was his style. In the back of the sanctuary I spotted Dr. Mary Cornwall and Shelly Peacock, both coworkers of mine at the St. Jean Centre in Mt. Pleasant, Michigan. Mary is the psychiatrist, the doctor who prescribes the drugs to our committed patients and our clients. Miss Peacock does the scheduling, handles most of the billing, and a ton of paperwork.

Wherever Carrie went in her Grand Prix, I figured she wouldn't go far. We talked about getting some ice cream, and in my mind I pictured her in line at the ice cream parlor—a slush for herself and a frozen turtle for me. If the line wasn't too long, she could have done it. I imagined her sipping her slush—raspberry, no doubt—and driving back to our rented house on the grounds of the St. Jean Centre. I rolled up my sleeves and got busy washing lettuce for dinner. She'd be along any moment, and put our treats in the freezer so we could enjoy them for dessert.

But Carrie never made it home. When it was well past time for dinner, a couple of deputies from Isabella County Sheriff's Office appeared on my doorstep. I knew by their posture that something horrible had happened. Their hats were in their hands, covering their belt buckles. They said they were sorry, but there had been a horrible accident west of Mt. Pleasant, where the country takes on a rolling terrain, a less populated dimension. Carrie apparently had missed the turn in the road and plowed her Grand Prix into a massive white pine. The impact killed her instantly. They told me that her body was at the hospital, and our vehicle had been impounded. I'd have to identify Carrie's body right away, but wait until the police finished their investigation before our auto insurance carrier could haul away the wreckage.

In spite of Reverend Robinette's efforts, the remainder of the service was just as sad as the beginning. All we could do was cry, and miss our Carrie. It was a sad day, after all. The saddest.

My brother gave me a hug—a wimpy, half-hearted one. Mom's wasn't much better. Mary Cornwall, Miss Peacock, the folks from church, and all the other people acted sincere in their grief, but seemed hesitant or unable to express it. They cried; they hugged. They acted sad, and said they were sorry. It was awkward. It was unsettling. I knew they were sad; I knew they were sorry, but nothing made me feel better. Nothing really could.

Before they loaded the casket into the hearse, I went to the men's room and splashed cold water on my face. I embraced the sensation. I was alive, with all the pains and pleasure that goes along with it. Telpher Beaman opened the stall door behind me, took several steps, and turned on a faucet of his own. "Nothing like a little cold water on the face to stir the soul, right, Jim?" He oozed a dollop of soap on his hand, and worked it into lather.

I nodded and smiled, politely.

"You'll get through this," he said, not looking my way, barely acknowledging that I was there.

I nodded again.

"Time has a way of making things better. You'll see."

I looked at him and said, "Now you're the one that sounds like a shrink."

He smiled, rinsed his hands, then slapped his own face with watery hands. "I had a good teacher." We both reached for a paper towel. "You know, Jim," he lowered his voice, and glanced in my direction. "There's more to this than meets the eye. You know it and I know it."

I didn't know it. "Tell me, Telpher, what do you mean?"

"Carrie's death, that's what."

"I don't follow you, Telpher," I asked him. "She got sick… she died in a car accident…what else could there be?"

"There's more to it, Jim. You know it, and I know it."

"Tell me, Telpher."

He didn't say a word; he didn't flinch.

Just then the funeral director opened the bathroom door and said that everyone was waiting. His eyes panned right, then left, as if he was looking for somebody else.

I followed him outside, into the fresh, spring air.

After Carrie's burial, we all met back at the church for coffee, miniature ham salad sandwiches, and a giant tray of fresh vegetables that the church women's group prepared. I heard more laughter than I had before. The tone of the funeral attendees had changed. Carrie wasn't the center of attention any longer, as old friends chatted with one another.

The people gradually slid by, filtering out the side door of the church and back to their busy lives. It was nice of them to come; it was nice of them to stay.

"What a nice service," they'd say.

"What a nice gal she was," they'd wax.

"What a shame," they'd all agree.

I sent some people home with fresh daffodil arrangements, sandwiches, or carrot spears.

Later that evening, Virginia and my mother threw together a pan of lasagna and a bowl of Caesar's salad for everyone in the immediate family. I turned on a little music, and laid out some cheese and crackers. We had soft drinks, beer, and wine. Toby sat between my niece and nephew's chairs at the kitchen table with a tendril of drool hanging from his jowls. He picked off the bits of Cheerios and pasta that were headed toward the floor. When my sister-in-law hauled her children to the sink, Toby raised his head, turned it slightly, and slurped the rest of their food, right off the plate.

Everyone got along. Everybody tried to put a positive spin on the situation. It was just what a wake should be.

When they all left for their rented motel rooms, and the place was quiet again, I took Toby for a walk. We tiptoed through his favorite dumping grounds, then crept past the Centre's lush shrubbery. He stopped two or three times to leave his calling cards.

Eventually, we made our way to the mailbox, where I grabbed a handful of envelopes. One piece caught my attention. I recognized the handwriting right away—graceful and neat—just like Carrie's.

She always had huge indentions in her handwritten paragraphs, and used ellipses for emphasis. With shaking hands I held the letter up to the street lights.

It was her.

Dear Jim,

By the time you read this I will be far, far from here... I wish there was some way you could join me; I wish there was some way we could be together. You were all I ever wanted in a man; all I ever wanted in a husband. I love you with all my heart, and I know that you love me with all of yours. It seems so unfair that it should end this way; we should have been the ones to celebrate fifty years of marriage, instead of sixteen incredible months. I don't regret our time together for a minute; I wouldn't trade it for anything, for all the money in the world. I have no qualms, no regrets…

    I knew from the second I met you that we were destined to be together… I never told you that my knees were knocking the first time I saw you. I never told you that my heart was racing on that first date. I remember telling my mom the day after that date that I met the man of my dreams. She was just as happy as I was. We both cried at the thought of finding true happiness.

    Please don't be sad. It's okay to cry, but I wish you wouldn't sulk. Everybody—including me—wants you to keep your chin up and get on with your life. It's okay to look at my picture and remember all the good times we had. But Jim, I want you to move on. You'll find someone new, someone that will make you happy. Someone is waiting for you, and I want you to find her. All I ever tried to do was make you happy, and since I can't do that now, I want you to find someone else who can. Life is too short to spend it wishing about what might have been. You'll make me happy if you get on with your life.

    I'm sorry it had to end this way. I'm sorry that things couldn't have been different. I love you Jim, I always will…

Carrie.

I could hardly believe my tear-filled eyes. She took the time to send me a letter. She had the foresight to ease my grief. What a beautiful thing. What a wonderful way to say goodbye. Somehow I pictured her with a big smile on her face, looking down on Toby and me. I smiled, and wanted to hug her all over again.

I re-read it.

Twice.

I folded it, gently, placed it back in the envelope, and let her fragrance linger. It smelled just like her.

I placed the envelope on the kitchen counter and admired her handwriting on the linen-like paper. I would keep it forever; cherish it for the rest of my life.

Strange, though. When I turned my attention to the postmark, it was dated two days after her fatal car accident. She died on a Wednesday, the postmark was Friday, and the funeral was Saturday.

How could that happen?

If she mailed the envelope on her way out of town Wednesday, why did the post office not postmark it until Friday?

Or did somebody mail it for her?

Maybe there was something more to Tepher's words: "There's more to this, Jim."

I had to find out.

Two

S OMEONE AT THE FUNERAL suggested that I should dive into my work. "It will clear your head and get your mind off things," they said. I always wondered about the wisdom of such statements. After all, we don't work for the fun of it, or to occupy our idle time. We work to get ahead, and support our families. Money helps us achieve our goals and helps realize happiness. Now that my wife was gone I had no urgency to succeed. I should have crawled into a ball and pumped gas for a living instead of being the therapist that I was.

I thought about getting some help. I thought about getting a shrink for myself, or at the very least telling somebody what I was thinking. Everyone said that they'd be there for me, "Whenever you want. All you need to do is call." They were nice gestures. Nice people.

I never did see a shrink of my own, or talk to anyone about what was going on in my head. I simply internalized everything. I let the grief curdle. I hoped that day-by-day, things would get better.

My mother-in-law stayed on for a few days—cleaning up

the house, organizing Carrie's wardrobe into little piles according to their value for Goodwill. Her suits garnered the most attention, and were placed in piles to be dry-cleaned. "That way, Jim," she said "you'll get the biggest bang for your buck next April during tax season." The stacks of jeans and sweaters passed her inspection without a trip to the dry cleaners, as did the long coats she wore to work in the winter.

I took some time away from work to tie up her loose ends. I applied for Social Security benefits, wrapped up things with the funeral home and the florist. I plied through Carrie's magazines and cancelled her subscriptions. I found the nearest monument company and made an appointment to look at headstones. Carrie and I never talked about that—it seemed to be something that could wait until we were old and gray. I remember once when we were dating, we took her niece to the zoo and on the way we passed a cemetery. Her niece pointed to the largest, gaudiest tombstone and proclaimed, "That must be where Jesus is buried." We laughed and laughed, half thinking that those funny stories would be standard fare once we had our own children. She wanted three kids; I wanted four, "so that we could cover the infield on the baseball diamond."

"That's not even *true*," she used to say. "You hate baseball. You want a big family because that way you'll never run out of hunting partners."

She did have a point. She always made good points. I did have big plans for my clan when it came to hunting. Her family maintained a small cabin across the Straits of Mackinaw, then west three hours to Marquette County. It wasn't much of a cabin, but it didn't have to be. All the men in the family met there on the eve of the opening day of deer hunting season to play cards, eat bowls of chili, crack jokes in their union suits, and maybe shoot a buck if one happened to stray too close. I was always welcome at deer camp, but since I wasn't a deer hunter, I never went. They told me over and over again that I could use the cabin during bird season, which I did on more than one occasion. I liked it there, not so much because of its proximity to some of North America's best grouse hunting, but because of the way I felt while I was there.

It's fun to step away from the rigors of daily living and into a place where modern conveniences aren't allowed. The cabin had running water and electricity, but there was no microwave oven, telephone, or furnace. We heated the cabin with a wood-stove and bundled under electric blankets when it's chilly. The floors were uneven, the window sills strewn with dead flies, but the view outside was spectacular. The Escanaba River gurgled and poured over boulders the size of kitchen tables on its way to northern Lake Michigan. In the spring runoff, the river's roar is exactly that. In the fall when the water level is low, the roar isn't as awesome but soothing nonetheless. At the end of the day, I used to watch the river and picture my kids nearby.

Anyway, I had no idea what kind of tombstone to get her or what her death would mean during tax season or if I was still welcome at the cabin. All I knew was that there'd be no kids with Carrie, no more joy, no dreams to come true. Maybe everybody was right about my situation—I should dive into my work to get my mind off things.

So that's exactly what I did.

Three

PSYCHOLOGISTS HAVE A BUNCH of nicknames, and none of them particularly flattering: therapists, shrinks, quacks, and counselors. We're trained to help people sort out the trouble in their lives. We do a lot of listening, a lot of analyzing, and a bit of advice giving. We don't prescribe medication, but we refer patients to doctors who can. A combination of medication and therapy can enrich our clients' lives and help make them feel better about themselves and their outlook on life.

Some people have heavy stuff to deal with: abusive parents, alcoholism, drugs, you name it. The committed patients are even more of a treat; we've got really sick weirdos who play with their own feces, eat rocks, and are in the Centre because they were deemed "temporarily insane" during their criminal trial.

After finishing my Ph.D., I wasn't sure about where to settle down, or what I should do with the rest of my life. I could have gone to work for a large company as a consultant, or even for a large city to do psychological analysis of potential job candidates. Those are always fun—discovering what kind of a police chief a guy will be by the way he answers the inkblot test. That's a sure way to make enemies; if the guy doesn't get the job he blames you, if he does get the job and screws up, then the city managers think you're incompetent. Either way you lose. Occasionally you win, but by then you've put ten years into your job and have been pigeon-holed into a career you might not like.

I have a friend from college who works in the attorney general's office and she told me she could pull some strings within Michigan's Health Department, but that didn't sound like an avenue I wanted to pursue. Employees within the Health Department have to deal with the red tape of the bureaucracy, a career constantly threatened by the latest round of budget cuts, or the philosophy of a newly-elected administration.

Then along came the St. Jean Centre, which offered me a position I couldn't refuse. I'd combine the best parts of private practice with the stability of a never-ending supply of sociopaths that the Centre housed. The Centre was once a Canadian-owned operation, and in Canada, they spell "center" in two different ways. The "center" of a golf ball, for example, is spelled "center," but a physical location is spelled "centre." I don't know why they still call it "the Centre" today—the Canadians have long since been replaced with a company who has a contract with the Michigan Department of Health. The bosses said they retained the name for nostalgic purposes—as if people will feel safer or better treated if they're affiliated with an outfit that has a foreign-sounding name. Frankly, I didn't care what they called it; I was impressed with the perks of the job and the long-term stability. I could use my office in the facility to schedule appointments in the private sector, just as long as the Centre reaped twenty-five hours a week for the privilege. I didn't have to mess around with billing or accounting; their staff took care of those functions.

Carrie and I would have excellent benefits after six months on the job. We'd get the standard major medical, dental and vision package given to state employees. They let us stay at the old house—for one hundred and fifty a month—for as long as we wanted. The kicker was that I'd get a two-to-one payoff toward my seventy-five thousand dollars in student loans. For every two dollars I paid toward my loan, they would pay one.

The St. Jean Centre turned out to be its own enclave with quirky employees, unique inhabitants, and its own little boundaries.

The committed patients were always a treat. We had two distinct classes who were on the wrong side of the law: Chapter As and Bs. The As were the really violent types: the rapists, the murderers, the guys who were deemed criminally insane. The Bs were slightly less violent, but still a handful. They were charged or convicted of lesser crimes such as assault and were at the Centre at their defense attorney's behest. Both the As and Bs had a variety of mental illnesses and personality disorders: schizophrenia, neurosis, split personalities, and paranoia. They were the ones who really tried my patience, my training, and my professional ability. We had to teach them to brush their teeth without ramming the toothbrush through the back of their throat. We had to keep them from bashing their heads into walls until they could taste their own blood as it trickled down their faces. Some of them swallowed rocks when we took them outside; others needed to wear muzzles so they wouldn't spit in people's faces.

The committed patients paid the bills, but I always looked forward to dealing with more "normal" clients from the private sector. Not that I didn't think that committed patients needed my expertise; I just appreciated the gratification from the clients on the outside. One of the most rewarding parts of my career was helping people, and those with the mental capacity to say "thanks" made me feel like my work was worthwhile. Like anybody's job, mine had good parts and bad.

Joe was one of my committed patients and my first appointment after Carrie's funeral. Aged fifty-one, he was committed six weeks after his wife's suicide. After he found her body, Joe fell into a deep state of catatonia. All he did was stare at the walls. The blank, hardened walls of the Centre. I tried to be optimistic; I tried to be upbeat as I asked him how he was doing. All he did was sit, chained into his wheelchair, and stare.

That's the Centre's protocol: all patients must be buckled in, whatever their condition, regardless of their perceived inability for violence or escape. "Come on, Joe, let's go for a walk," I said, pushing him down the long hallway of rooms just like his. I glanced at his chart, and noticed that he had a few visitors since the last time I had seen him two weeks earlier: a coworker, his son and daughter-in-law, and a neighbor. The son stayed the longest—forty-five minutes; the neighbor the shortest—only fifteen. Mary Cornwall had prescribed Zyprexa and lots of it, but nothing seemed to work.

Joe and I made it down the hallway, outside, and onto the cement sidewalk lined by dwarf fruit trees. They were in full bloom, and cast a fragrant shadow over everything. "Can you smell those, Joe?" I asked. "Those are crabapple trees planted thirty years ago. Apparently they redesigned the north wing of the complex then and had extra money in the budget for trivial things like trees. Can you smell those, Joe?" I patted him on the shoulder, but he didn't flinch. "It's important that we learn to communicate, Joe. You know, when two people communicate, one person talks and the other one listens. Then they switch. For over a month now, I've done all the talking, and you've done all the listening. I want to thank you for being such a compassionate listener, but I really want to do some of the listening. It's your turn to talk, and it's my turn to listen. How does that sound?"

We stopped at a park bench only a hundred yards from my house. The orderly assigned to watch Joe waited thirty yards behind. "Besides, Joe, the Centre is paying me five dollars an hour to help you, and if you don't snap out of this soon, my bosses will think that I'm not a very good doctor." We sat there for quite some time, enjoying the morning, smelling the flowers. Toby must have known it was me outside. He was barking and jumping straight up and down behind the front door. Then he switched tactics and moved to the front window where he smeared slobber and nose prints all over it. All I could do was shake my head and wonder why God tortured me with such a crazy dog for a companion. I should have listened to Carrie and gotten a house cat.

"You must have had bosses that you had to impress, didn't you, Joe? I understand you're in the window sales business, and that you were responsible for a rather large territory? Is that correct?" I stopped making eye contact, and looked at my house, with the spit and slobber on the front window, the front door. "What could you do for this place, Joe?" I spun him around, so that our knees nearly touched, pointing to the house with the maniac in the front. "Looks like the poor guy who lives there needs double pane windows, don't you think? To do that whole place, what do you think, two or three grand?" More stares. More blank, cold stares.

"You're not going to believe this, Joe. But I know exactly how you feel…" I crossed one leg over the other, flicked a dog hair from my cuff, and stared at the house. "I know what it feels like to lose a spouse, someone you love." I shook my head, and felt a tear well up inside me. It felt good to stare. It felt good to sit and think about her, and what she might be doing right now if things had been different. Minutes passed. Lots of them. The orderly was getting anxious, and nervous, sitting amongst the flowers, with all the bees flitting about. "Remind me to tell you about it sometime. When you're up to it."

Joe and I made it back to his room, where he continued his silent vigil.

I returned to my office to see what I had missed. Miss Peacock gave me a hug in the hallway, and Mary Cornwall popped
her head in to say sorry all over again. I gave her the update on
Joe's condition, or lack of it. She said that perhaps she'd adjust
his meds. They were such nice people, and wonderful coworkers. Besides the billing and scheduling, Miss Peacock was the
liaison between me and the bosses down the hall. I pulled up
the computer and looked at the day's schedule, which was relatively light.

Warren and Irene needed help. Married a dozen years, they
seemed on the verge of divorce. Neither of them wanted to
split, citing their children and finances as the primary reason,
but they didn't want to continue living the way they were, either. Irene called me months ago, and said that she needed help
with her depression. Her health insurance paid for therapy, except for a small co-pay. She wanted to know if I would bill her
insurance for her depression, but counsel the two of them in
their marriage. It seemed like a reasonable idea, and one that I
could slide through her health insurance carrier.

A marriage is worth working for, even fighting for, and
that's where I fit into the equation.

Warren was a nice enough guy, and was rather handsome
in a feminine way. He took pride in his wardrobe, I could tell,
and his fingers were long, thin, and well manicured. Any time
his wife rambled on about his faults, he stroked his short, trim
goatee like it was a pet hamster. Warren worked hard at his job,
didn't fool around on his wife, and was home every night for
dinner. He cooked most of the meals, did a fair amount of the
laundry, and took his kids to school every morning. On the
weekends he liked to play golf, drink beer, and spend at least
one day with his family.

Irene was also nice, somewhat heavyset, and on the outside
seemed compatible with her husband. She worked hard during

the week too, at her job and around the house. She handled the finances, made sure the kids made it to their extra-curricular events and kept the house running smoothly. She was busy; he was busy. They both were busy. So busy it seemed that they wouldn't make time for each other.

Their lives seemed so compartmentalized. They each had little tasks and chores, and then they went to work. Their responsibilities were formidable and there wasn't much time for them to spend with each other. What's worse, the relationship was souring. Warren was bored with Irene, and Irene was bored with Warren. They had become roommates instead of lovers. Their relationship was that of coworkers instead of husband and wife. Little by little, day by day, they kept their kids in diapers and nursery rhymes, while their relationship simmered in regrets and resentment.

When they first came to my office several months before, Irene leveled both barrels at Warren. She carried on for twenty-five minutes straight without so much as taking a breath. She could talk too, a verbal heavyweight. She would hardly finish one topic before moving on to the next. "Warren has an anger management problem," "Warren never makes time for his family." Warren this, Warren that.

Most couples get into trouble when their expectations for marriage and each other fall short. Disappointment breeds resentment. They throw harpoons at each other. Next thing you know one of them starts thinking about how green the grass is on the other side of the fence. Affairs aren't necessarily planned, but they're allowed to flourish because of resentment at home.

Anyway, Warren sat across from me, at the end of the couch, arms crossed—just like he always did. Irene sat next to him; tugging at her earrings, barely sitting close enough to give the impression that she cared about her husband. I noticed Warren's neck brace immediately, but Irene brought it to my attention anyway. Only twenty-four hours before our appointment, Warren got broadsided by a guy that blew a stop sign. His car bore most of the collision, but he did have whiplash, among other ailments.

Of course, the accident served to only complicate Irene's life. Now they only had one vehicle when they really needed three or four for all the activities she and the kids had planned. "What do you mean, Irene, 'it's a major inconvenience'?" I asked her.

"He doesn't have a car now, and can't get a ride to work. I have a doctor's appointment tomorrow morning, and there's the kids' baseball practice tomorrow afternoon. The timing couldn't have been worse."

"Unfortunately, you don't always have a choice when accidents happen," I reminded her. Warren sneered slightly, but Irene kept going.

"Oh, I know that. It's the first accident we've had in a hundred years, almost. He's really a good driver, and this couldn't have been helped. Sure. It was an accident, but it just goes to complicate my life." She rattled on for several more minutes before Warren raised an index finger and demanded the floor.

I extended an open palm his way but she kept rambling. "I don't know…it's just so complicated! Maybe my mom could help us out?" Her best friend was her mom, and according to Warren, her only friend. Privately, he complained that the mother-in-law was at the house too much. When I met with Irene alone, she told me that her mother was the most important person in her life. When I asked her where Warren figured into the hierarchy of her priorities, she couldn't say for sure. I got the feeling Warren was somewhere beneath her three kids, the baseball games, and the scores of other commitments in her frenetic schedule.

I must admit that I really didn't know much about Warren. When we met privately, he said nothing about his family, his pals, or his job. All he ever talked about was how miserable his marriage was, and what a horrible mistake he had made in choosing Irene for a wife. And he knew it right away, shortly after they were wed. I felt sorry for him, and encouraged him to make the most of the situation. We discussed ways that he could turn the tide in the relationship. Romantic ways. Thoughtful things. He tried them, but they were either rebuffed or refused. Either way, I was beginning to worry about him. He was trapped in an awful situation, and he was beginning to shut me out. Our appointments alone became shorter and shorter, the discussions more shallow. I suggested that he meet with Dr. Cornwall to discuss medication, but he refused. I wouldn't have been surprised with anything that came out of their situation.

And there'd be lots to come.

The last of my clients was gone by 7 P.M. I closed the door that led to the outside world, and melted into my leather chair in front of my desk. It felt good to sit there, all alone, without having to listen to a patient or a client and their personal problems. It felt good that I had nobody to counsel, no one to help sort out the problems in their life. I don't know how long I sat there, but it was quite a while. Miss Peacock left me a few messages, from the funeral home, and some medical billing facility in Raleigh that was looking for me to make payment arrangements. There was even a client or two that needed a phone call and a little handholding. I picked up the stack of mail and sifted through the assorted bills and invitations from credit card companies. Nonsense. Two of my clients sent sympathy cards—one from a depressed woman, the other from an older man with a cocaine addiction.

I picked up a picture of Carrie and set it on my lap. All I could do was stare at her, and pretend to brush her wavy brown bangs away from her forehead. She had those pleasing round eyes, and a devilishly cute smile. We were so happy then, so complete. I took that picture of her on the day I asked her to marry me, only two summers ago on the banks of the Muskegon River. I'll never forget how nervous I was. How scared I was that she'd turn me down, or that something would go wrong.

All Carrie knew was that we were going canoeing. All I had to do was make sure I had the ring, and a few extra perks to woo her over. So early one Saturday in the summer I picked her up and drove west to the Muskegon River. She was in her third year of law school then, and was up to her eyeballs in mock trials, case law reading, and advanced classes. I figured that she'd be ripe for some west Michigan air. A little recreation is good for the soul—to clear your head and refresh the senses.

She always laughed at me for saying things like that. She said that I made outdoor activities sound like a Buddhist experience. "Give me a break, will you? If canoeing was so great they'd sell in on the streets in plastic baggies for fifty dollars!" She always told it like it is, without being nasty. Then again, I never faced her in the courtroom or in negotiations over a product liability case.

By the time we reached the canoe livery, we'd had enough of morning coffee and croissants. The man who helped me lift the canoe off the luggage rack looked a little perplexed at the amount of gear I had. "How many weeks are you going to be gone?"

"Very funny," I said, handing him the keys to my truck and twenty dollars. "Just make sure my truck is downstream at the park in Newaygo later this afternoon." Carrie didn't think that one backpack, fishing rods and a picnic basket was out of the ordinary, after all, she had nothing to compare it to. Canoeing was new to her, although she had tried it a couple of times at the cabin up north. "All set?" I asked her.

"Are you sure you brought enough provisions? We're going to be gone two weeks aren't we?"

She jumped inside, gracefully and sure-footed, then pushed us away from the gravelly landing with the end of her paddle.

All at once we were adrift—slaves to the silent current beneath the aluminum craft. At first there were a lot of cabins along the shore, but gradually they thinned out as the river carved its way through the giant hills.

For the first ten minutes she paddled like mad, as if we were in a race. "What's the rush, Carrie? We have two weeks to get these furs back to the tannery before freeze-up!" She laughed, knowing that I had ways to push her buttons too. She wanted to try fishing instead of paddling, so in short order I got her set up with a little spinning outfit just right for probing the log jams along the edge of the river. Carrie wasn't a bad little fisherman either. She dropped her little spinner into the midst of the logs and pulled it out of danger—teasing any trout to give it a smack. She caught several trout before lunch, which was when I had planned my big event.

When we neared a stretch of river called "The Mafia's Lookout," I pulled the canoe to the bank. It's a popular spot with the fishing guides because it has a fire pit and a sandy, weed-free area. Better yet, it's on the inside of a curve, where the current is slow and deliberate. In no time I had the red tartan blanket spread on the sandy bank and a couple of wine glasses filled with chardonnay. She lay down on the blanket and took baby sips of wine with one hand while she propped her head up with the other. It was great fun just to watch her there, with her thick hair wrapped around the back of her neck like a silk scarf. I admired her round hips poured into a pair of faded jeans. I fed her havarti cheese on round, crispy crackers, and dipped small cubes of ripened honeydew melon into her full, curvy lips. We sat there on a beautiful summer afternoon, enjoying each other's company, kissing, giggling, drinking wine and tickling each other in places that made us yelp with joy.

After about an hour, I told her that I needed some help stringing up my fly rod. "I want to be ready for the afternoon hatch," I told her, even though it was part of my grand scheme.

She agreed to give me a hand, just as long as she didn't have to leave the comfort of the blanket. I was hoping she'd say that. I handed her the fly rod, grabbed my backpack, and began walking downstream with the end of the fly line. "Just hold on," I yelled. "I'll tell you when it's time to reel it in, okay?"

"If you're not back in half an hour I'm going to call the Coast Guard," she yelled back.

Minutes passed. I changed my clothes, then asked her to reel in the line "nice and slow." I hid her jewelry box in the webbing of a landing net, then crept through the woods so I was now upstream.

"Jim," she yelled. "Jim! I need some help over here. I caught something!" I let her stew for a few minutes. She was frantic, tearing at the netting, the fishing line—seeing the prize inside—like a kid with a prize from a cereal box. "Jim!"

"What is it?"

"I caught something," she said, without even looking at me. "What is it?" She asked. Finally the line gave way, the netting parted, and the little felt box was free. "Oh my God, Jim, what is this? And what are you wearing?" She asked as she looked down at me kneeling beside her.

"You like it?" I asked, pulling at the lapels of my tuxedo, "I hid it in the backpack."

"Oh my god, Jim. It's beautiful." She pulled the ring out of the box, slipped it on her finger, and smiled the prettiest smile I've ever seen. It was the most incredible moment of my life and by the joy in her eyes, I could tell it was for Carrie, too.

My voice quivered. "Carrie Nunnelly…will you marry me?"

She was crying. "Of course I'll marry you."

She knelt in front of me and we kissed for ten, fifteen seconds. I threw her to the blanket and we kissed for minutes more. We smiled, we kissed, we laughed, and cried all at the same time. "I love you, Jim."

It was incredible.

I didn't want that moment to end.

I didn't want the feeling to slip away.

She laughed hysterically when I pulled a couple of small banners from my backpack that read, "She said yes." She rolled her eyes when I duct-taped them to the edges of the canoe.

For the rest of our trip downstream I wore my tuxedo, and we were serenaded with applause from fishermen, fellow canoeists, and people sipping gin and tonics from their cabins' front porches.

While she paddled in the front of the canoe, I pulled out a camera and asked her to say cheese. It was one of those over-the-shoulder shots, the kind of pose you think of when you look back one last time.

Now I was looking at her, looking back at me, on my lap in the office.

And that's when I heard the knock at my office door.

"Telpher! What are you doing here? You don't have an appointment!"

"I know, but what the hell, this will only take a few minutes. Bill me for an hour, I don't care."

"What is it?"

"Sit down," I rolled my eyes and obliged. "I saw you at the funeral," he said.

"Telpher, of course you saw me at the funeral. It was my wife who died… remember?"

"What's wrong with saying that?"

"I should be the one who said 'I saw you at the funeral,'" I told him.

"Go ahead then, tell me," he scratched his beard, and pointed in my direction.

"I don't have time to deal with you tonight. You don't have an appointment, and I've had a long day. Can we please do this another time?"

"You don't like it that I showed up at the funeral?" He asked.

"No…I don't mean to sound ungrateful. It was very nice that you attended. It meant a lot to me. Thank you."

"You're welcome. Tell me about the couple in the back row."

"Christ, Telpher, there were a lot of people there."

"They were close to forty, he was short and balding, she had a round face, with little slits for eyes."

"You're weird."

"That's no way to treat a client. I might develop a complex and need even more counseling," he said.

"Lord forbid."

"What was that?"

"Never mind," I sighed.

"Aren't you going to tell me who the couple was?"

"No. You know I can't give you names."

"What's their story?"

"I can't tell you that, either."

"Let me guess, he's got a drinking problem and she's got depression. And they're ready to murder each other, except they raise prize cocker spaniels and one of them is going to the Westminster dog show this winter."

"That was a run-on sentence. Are you finished?" Telpher was an inconsistent person. One minute he was serious, the next he was humorous. I never really knew what to expect from him, but I always understood what he was trying to say.

"What about your family?" He was rambling. I said nothing. "Don't you want to dance, Jimmy?"

"I hate it when you call me that, and wish you wouldn't do it anymore."

"Didn't your mother used to call you that?"

"Yes, Telpher, and she's the only person that *can*."

"Why didn't she cry a lot at the funeral?"

"I wasn't watching her, and frankly it's none of your business," I said.

"Oh?"

"Are you done yet?"

"Don't you like to talk about your family?" He looked at me as if I were on trial.

"Not with a client."

"Why not, Jim…me want to."

"Very funny. You're testing my patience."

"First I'm a client, then a friend, and now you call me a patient…I'm having an identity crisis."

I stood up and crossed my arms. "Tell me what you meant about the 'more to it' business?"

"About your wife?"

"Yes."

"I can't. Not now. Not here."

He was going to make me work for it, just like I knew he would. All I could do was smile, open the door to the outside world, and let him out. Telpher, what a card. He was half patient, half client, half stranger or friend, and always showed up at the most bizarre times. We never did talk much about his issues, but beat around the bushes of mine. He never could be serious, or chose not to. But his mustache and goatee were just as neat and crisp as his outfit—brown herringbone, with a silk ascot stuffed behind a starched oxford.

He was okay in small doses, just like our dog Toby.

Four

BY SEVEN THIRTY that evening I was home. At last. Toby greeted me at the door—tail wagging like mad. As was routine, he nearly bowled me over on his way outside. He was always happy to see me, but not necessarily so when there were more urgent matters to attend—like hosing down the shrubbery or patrolling the yard for squirrels. Anyway, while Toby was busy, I went inside, loosened my tie, poured a glass of whiskey, and looked through the stack of mail. More medical bills…lots of them, from facilities and places I didn't even recognize. I put them on the counter with the others, like a loaf of sliced bread. A big, long loaf of bread. The line of envelopes was longer than a yardstick. The money I owed would take me ten years to earn at my current salary, if in fact Atmantle denied our claims.

A flash of white distracted my attention—Toby, racing from tree to tree, sniffing for squirrels, tail swishing merrily. I watched him carry on effortlessly, carefree. Just for a day I'd like to be a dog and have that tremendous sense of smell, the insatiable desire to find game, and no worries whatsoever. That would be the best part. Just then Toby had his nose to the ground like he was looking for something. He spun around in a circle, then spun the opposite direction. It was his pre-poop shuffle.

The strangest thing about Toby, after he "drops a loaf" he turns around and barks at it like it's some sort of demon, or a potential playmate. It wouldn't be so bad if he only did it while we're at home. But no. Toby barks at his poop in public places, on walks, when we go hunting, at parks, on picnics. It's embarrassing, but I still love him.

What's even more bizarre about him is since Carrie died, Toby has begun to urinate in his empty food bowl. I don't understand it. I've heard of separation anxiety in dogs, but it usually takes the form of chewing on furniture, barking for hours on end, or tearing up things in the house. Maybe the poor chap needs a shrink of his own. I've heard of doggie shrinks before, but I'm not sure how they communicate with their clients, or how they bill their clients' owners. He'll snap out if it, I kept reminding myself.

I raised the glass, swished the cubes of ice, and took a nice little sip. I thought about dinner, about the dog, and Carrie. Just then I noticed a letter, handwritten, on the sill above the sink:

> *Jim, There's a meatloaf in the fridge, ready to be cooked (an hour at 375°). The mail is on the counter, and the dry cleaning is in the front closet. I forgot the claim ticket from the other day at the cleaners so the little Chinaman behind the counter asked for your "phone numbers" so he could find your order... I gave him all seven of your phone numbers.*
>
> *I let your dog outside before I left. He seemed to be okay until I saw him barking at his own pooh! I think he needs some serious counseling.*
>
> *Don't worry about all the bills...somehow they'll get paid and you'll get back on track. Carrie's dad said that he wants you to have half of the life insurance we started on her when she went off to college.*
>
> *I'll call you soon.*
>
> *Love,*
>
> *Mom.*

Sure enough, in the refrigerator was a beautiful meatloaf complete with a fresh sprig of parsley on the top. I drizzled a bit of barbecue sauce on it, popped it in the oven, and skipped upstairs to check my e-mail.

One of my best friends from college sent me a note. In her typical fashion, she didn't use any more words than was absolutely necessary.

> *Dear Jim,*
>
> *Just wanted to say that I heard the news about Carrie. I am so sorry; it must be devastating. I know that she meant the world to you, and you must be going through some hard times. If there's anything I can do for you, please give me a call. In fact, it's been a while since we've talked; I think it would be a good idea to get together for lunch. God bless you Jim, and take care.*
>
> *Taren*

Taren Lisk made good on her education and was now an upstart lawyer at the attorney general's office in Lansing. We used to hang out, study together, and go out for ice cream on Sunday evenings. Toward the end of our undergrad programs, we'd escort each other to dinners, seminars, and graduation parties for fellow students. People suspected that we were dating, but we really never did much of anything. There was no spark between us, no thoughts of romance. We used to talk about our careers more than we talked about our dreams for a family. I was happy to hear from her now, because she was fun-loving, bubbly, and extremely competitive. Taren was driven to succeed—marriage, kids and a family of her own would have to wait. I really liked Taren, and had many pleasant memories of her.

Before dinner I took Toby for a walk around the grounds, through the big woods on the backside of the property, and home to where the crazy people live.

Five

I KNEW RIGHT AWAY that Warren was a changed man. He smiled and sat erect in his chair. The neck brace was gone, and he laughed about nearly everything. Work was going fine and the jerk he had for a boss wasn't an issue anymore. When the topic of his wife came up, he brushed it off as if he was completely happy. It felt like an old-fashioned game of twenty questions. Mary Cornwall's happy pills? A new car? I gave up, smiling.

"You know it's the strangest thing," he was laughing too. "Whatever I tell you stays here, right?"

"Sure, unless you're going to hurt someone or yourself," I reminded him.

"So I got in this car accident a few weeks ago, and I'm all bummed out about it. You heard Irene—my gosh—what a bitch. It's like I purposely got in this accident or something. Anyway, the doctor says that I need physical therapy, so I set up an appointment. And believe me, Jim, I don't like the idea of anyone touching me, you know what I mean?"

"Sure I do." The guy was rambling, and I didn't want to slow him down.

"But I walk in and take a seat in this little room with one of those draw-tight sheets hanging from the ceiling…and in walks this woman carrying a clipboard. She reaches out and shakes my hand, and it's like I got butterflies in my stomach. My gosh, she was beautiful! I hate to say it, being married and all."

"Keep going."

"Okay. Okay. She wore a pair of those small, oval-shaped glasses, and had this wonderful brown hair. And her eyes… they were blue, bright blue. I shouldn't say anything. Her eyes went right through me. She couldn't stop looking at me, and I couldn't take my eyes off her. But I was there for a reason, and she was working, you know. So we go over all the questions—about my insurance, about the accident, and the pain in my neck and arms. She asked me if I used my arms a lot in my work and stuff."

"I'm listening."

"The next thing I know she has me face down on the examination table, and is working my neck with her fingers. It felt incredible. She touched my ears and bent my head down and from side to side." Warren was still smiling, moving his head from right to left. It was odd to see him carrying on the way he did; the most I ever could get out of him were one-sentence answers. "I have to tell you, Jim, things haven't been right between me and the missus. Know what I mean?" I nodded. "In twenty minutes with the physical therapist, I had more affection than I've had in six months with Irene."

"Is that right?"

"Yes."

"Did you tell Irene about her?"

"Why would I?"

"I don't know…it would be something that you could discuss. She always says that you never talk to her."

"You know what she's like though, Jim. She'd say that I was cheating on her…that somehow I enjoyed it."

"You did, didn't you?"

"Sure I did. Anybody would have." He laughed.

"Do you think you were cheating on her?"

Warren paused, put his hand to his brow, then started again, "No. No. How could it be? I had an appointment to see a physical therapist for God's sake. What was she supposed to do, make my neck better from across the room? That wouldn't work!"

"What did you talk about?"

"That's the thing. I don't remember. We talked. She talked. I listened. I talked. She listened. And we laughed. Boy, did we laugh. It was great to start a sentence and not have Irene finish it. It was great to have her hands on my neck and shoulders. It was wonderful. What do you think?"

"I think that it would be great, too," I said. "Who wouldn't enjoy it?"

"Sure. We're both men." He snickered, affirmatively.

"Yes, sir," I paused, smiling along with him. "Why did you end up with Irene anyway?"

"Oh Christ, that was so long ago. She was so nice back then, and I suppose that she'd say that I was different too. She'd tell you that I listened more then, or had time to spend with her, or that I treated her like a goddess…"

"Warren, just tell me, why did you end up with her?"

"I don't remember, other than we just fell in love. All our friends were falling in love and getting married, it just felt right to do the same. I figured that I could have done a lot worse. I mean, she was cute and I liked being around her. Plus she liked to be with me. She *liked to be with me*—if you know what I mean."

"What happened?"

"You know, we've already gone over this, a hundred times. The kids came along, and our roles changed. Instead of being husband and wife, we turned into drones…coworkers. We fell in love quickly, but falling out of it took a while. She doesn't have the energy to devote to me anymore, and I'm just a lazy oaf that works his fingers to the bone so she can afford her hundred-dollar Nikes and gas in her new ride."

"You sound bitter, Warren."

"I wasn't until we got on this topic."

"Sorry. What else do you want to talk about?"

He paused, looked at the clock that showed ten minutes left in our appointment, "Do you like NASCAR?"

I laughed. "Why don't we call it a day? See you next time."

"Fair enough. So long."

Car racing is one of those sports that I really have never understood. I don't know why they even call it a sport. It seems all they do is push down on the accelerator with their foot, and make a continuous left turn. But, what the heck, diversity is what makes the world go 'round.

Darvin Wonch was a new client and had his share of unique interests. No matter who the client is, or what their hobbies are, it's always a good idea for the psychologist to act interested. It helps create a bond and an atmosphere of compassion. The only thing Miss Peacock told me about Darvin was that he wanted to get in to see me right away. She said that his only other statement was that he had "good insurance that would take care of charges."

"So why are we here, Darvin?" I asked him right out of the gate.

"I really don't want to be here, but I told my wife that I would come to keep her happy."

"Okay."

"She thinks that I have a gambling problem."

"Why's that?"

"I don't know. I've never been in bankruptcy. I'd never do that."

"What does she say?"

"She says that I spend too much time at the track or going to casinos or betting on football games."

"What do you think?" I asked him.

"I like to gamble, plain and simple. It's what I do."

"How's that?"

"You know, some guys like to golf or go fishing, I like to gamble. She knew I liked to gamble before we got married so I don't understand what's the big yank about it now."

Darvin looked to be in his early fifties, well dressed, with a clean-shaven face and several pieces of jewelry dangling from his neck. He had large, thick fingernails, the size and color of horses' teeth, and a tuft of graying hair that bristled over the top button of his oxford. "I mean she and the kids get some of the goodies when my gambling goes well, so I don't understand what's the big deal."

"Like what?"

"I mean she's got rings and tennis bracelets, pearls, diamonds. You name it. She even has a BMW, what's it called? Their SUV? Whatever." He tossed his hands in the air as if he was throwing confetti at a birthday party. "She only works like two days a week, and I get her all this stuff."

"And the kids?"

"I got my boy one of those 'kitty cats.' You know—those baby snowmobiles for tooling around the yard. He loved it. Had the neighbors over to the house too, and they rode it a lot, all through the holidays."

"What do you mean, 'had' the neighbors over...and why only during the holidays?"

He sighed. "We don't have it any more." Darvin's eyes dropped to the floor. He was hiding something. I let it go, in hopes of getting more information from him and establishing some sort of rapport.

I changed the subject again. "I see. Tell me why gambling is fun for you."

"Oh man, I just love it. I love the smell of the casino, the track. It's hard to explain, you can feel the excitement in the air. You see the bright lights and sense the electricity. Somehow you feel lucky, like you're invincible. And when you place the bet, the anticipation is riveting. You know that you're going to win." He was smiling and staring over my shoulder, like he was betting at the casino himself. It was the same look of rapture that Warren had when he told me about his physical therapist and her sultry ways.

"Describe the best day you had."

"Gambling?"

"Yes."

He paused. Then laughed. "We were up north in Traverse City or Manistee, and I like to play the twenty-five-dollar slot machines. I usually play with two grand, and when it's gone, it's gone. Anyway, I sat down and lost the first ten or fifteen pulls, but I had a feeling that this machine was right with me. So I stay there and hit for twenty-five hundred, which made me more anxious to play. I just knew I was going to win." The tone of his voice was quickening, I could tell he was on a roll. I smiled along with him, to keep the conversation moving forward. "The next roll, I hit it big…two hundred and seventy-five thousand dollars! I mean I'm going nuts. It was awesome."

"Holy cow, Darvin."

"Holy cow is right, man."

"What did you do? Quit your job?"

"Hell no. The government took about half of my earnings, so that wouldn't be enough to retire."

"What did you do?"

"I kept playing."

"Did you win again?" I asked him.

"Oh yeah, after I lost a lot of it."

"How much?"

"After taxes, I had a hundred twenty-five grand left, but I lost about seventy-five grand that night, but on the way out that night, I put twenty-five down on another machine as I'm walking out the door, and I hit for thirty-five hundred."

"So you turned two thousand into…more than fifty grand in one night?"

"Something like that."

"That's pretty good, right?"

"Oh yeah, that's good."

"You must be proud of that."

"Sure I am. I have a gift…a special talent." He didn't realize what I was doing. I must confess I'm not the best example of what a good shrink is all about. Some shrinks will hold their clients' hand and tell them "everybody else doesn't understand you, or your problem." They don't offer any solutions, only sympathy. I tell it like it is. I call it like I see it.

Nobody ever believes that they have an addiction. It's always the other person's fault, the other person's problem. I play along with them at first. I try to develop a rapport with them, so they'll open up. I stroke their ego, so they feel important, and expose themselves even more. The things that they tell me might actually be used as evidence when I show them what they are doing is wrong, dangerous, or is wrecking their relationship with their loved ones. It could be wrecking their lives.

I established a relationship with Darvin, stroked his ego, and now he needed a little kick upside the head.

"You must have a special talent in order to pull that off, but you don't win all the time, right, Darvin?"

"I win a lot, that's for sure."

"But you must lose or your wife wouldn't have told you to come talk to me, right?"

"Okay, I'll go along with that."

"Tell me Darvin, why does she think you have a problem with gambling?"

He paused again, leaned back into the leather sofa, flicking his wrist so his gold bracelet spun slightly. He glanced over my shoulder, and took a deep breath. His face reddened. "Do we have to get into this?"

"No, of course not."

"If it's okay with you, I'd rather not."

"We don't have to do anything if you don't want to."

"That's good."

"Keep in mind that whatever you tell me stays between us, and I won't tell your wife what you say. I mean that sincerely. I am bound by the rules of the medical profession, the same ones that apply to you and your doctor, your lawyer, or your pastor."

He nodded, apologetically, and said that his wife only knows half of the trouble he was in. "She thinks I have a problem because of what I did with my son's snowmobile." I didn't say a thing. "I got into a horrible slump. Bad. And I owed some people some money…and needed to get it to them." He wasn't making much sense.

"What happened?"

"I owed some guys some money so I pawned my son's snowmobile, but didn't tell her that." He was blinking profusely, fighting himself. Half of him wanted to clutch the notion that he didn't have a problem, while the other half of him wanted to get something off his chest. "She thought it was stolen, and wanted me to turn in an insurance claim, but I knew that they'd want a police report. Hell, start making false police reports and you've really got yourself some problems." I sat there, watching him squirm. "I yelled at her and said that 'we're not going to make any God-damned insurance claim,' but she must have figured out why because she started crying like a raging idiot."

"Who did you owe the money to?"

"That's what she doesn't know about. These men. They're horrible. They'll spot you all the money you want for some action, you know what I mean? But if you short them they'll make your life miserable."

"How do you know?"

"I hear things…threats…they told me."

"Told you what?"

"They said that they'd kill me if I didn't get them all their money."

"Who said that?"

"I can't tell you, but there's two different guys that I owe money to. One said he was going to blow my head off if I didn't come up with it, and the other said he was going to break both my legs."

"What are you going to do?"

"I don't know what I can do. I owe them so much money that I can't make it fast enough on my job. I gotta keep betting, hoping that I get hot, so that I can pay them off quickly…"

"Darvin, maybe you should call the police."

"Hell no, that would only make things worse."

"What if you run into them…the bad guys, I mean?"

"I have."

"Where?"

"At the track."

"You're kidding?" I asked.

"No…I was playing the simulcast this spring of the Belmont Stakes, you know the third leg of the Triple Crown, and I'm standing in line waiting to place a bet. I look up from the racing guide and here's one of the thugs that threatened to kill me standing behind the counter!"

"What did you do?" I asked him, thinking that his answer would lead to some real progress or a life-changing experience.

"What else could I do? I had to place a bet, so I stepped out of his line and went to the next one over."

Silly me. Here I thought he was going to get on his hands and knees and beg me for help, or guidance on how to come clean with his wife. I could have suggested some credit counselors so he could free up some monthly income. I could have referred him to some financial planners so he could investigate the tax ramifications of accessing his retirement plans. I could have helped him deal with his addiction, or hooked him up with Mary Cornwall, if he would just asked for help.

No, Darvin left my office in a fit, and I had to wonder if I'd ever see him again. In fact, if I were a betting man, I wondered what the odds would be: I'd see Darvin again, or he'd soon be dead. The guy had a hard time controlling his gambling, and just like most other addicts, refused to admit that there was a problem.

Darvin made the appointment with me to appease his wife, but really didn't care about her, about the whole counseling experience, or anybody else for that matter.

Six

WARREN'S NEXT VISIT three weeks later was a continuation of our last session, although it didn't start out that way. He hemmed and hawed about his wife, and how she dropped fifteen-hundred dollars on a go-cart for the kids without talking to him about it first. But after all, if she had brought it up to him, he would have said no, and World War III would have erupted. Irene needed to talk to Warren first about the budget, and Warren needed to be more understanding. They needed to talk more, to negotiate, to compromise like married couples do.

When I showed him a little compassion, he gradually started to talk. I didn't want to pressure him, because that seldom works. He started out by telling me that he was gradually getting the feeling back in his arms, thanks to the physical therapy and the exercises he was doing at home. I agreed that it was a good thing, but wondered how much longer he planned on going to physical therapy.

"I don't know. I guess until I'm better."

"It seems to be helping," I confirmed.

51

"In a lot of ways," he replied, rather matter-of-factly.

"What do you mean?" I asked.

"It's weird. I go there so I'll feel better, and I do—physically, mentally, and emotionally."

"Really."

"Oh yeah, I leave her office and my shoulder and neck are fine, but I feel like I'm on Cloud Nine. This girl makes me feel great…about myself, about my life, my career, and my family."

"How so?"

"She's just full of optimism. I've never seen her bummed out about anything. She wants me to get along with Irene. She says that 'family is the most important thing,' and stuff like that. She gives me romantic ideas that Irene and I can do together."

"Is this other woman married?"

"Yes, but not very well."

"What do you mean?"

"That's the thing, I don't know yet. We can talk, but the spot where they have the examination rooms isn't totally private. It's not like a doctor's office, where you can shut the door and chitchat. There's just this giant sheet that hangs on a rail from the ceiling. We never know who's listening or just walking by us."

"Then how do you know that she's not happy?"

"She's made a couple of references to the fact that she's not happy, and I think that her husband is a real jerk or something. He's beyond jerky. I think she's afraid of him. I think she's scared."

"Why?"

Warren took a breath, thumbed the hair on his chin a few times, then sounded uncertain, "I forget what it was we were talking about…something about her going to one of those overnight eye surgeons. You know, one of those deals when you get your eyes examined one afternoon, then have the laser surgery the next morning. She told me that her husband would never go along with it. And the way she told me I had a hunch that it wasn't because he didn't like anyone messing with his wife's eyes. I got the feeling that his big beef was that he didn't want his wife to be out from under his thumb."

"How does that make you feel?"

"Jim, you sound like a shrink now." He laughed.

"You're right, I'm sorry." We both laughed. "Let me try again. Do you think that you're attracted to her because she might be in danger and you want to help her?"

"Jim, I never said I was attracted to her."

"Okay, sorry." I overstepped. He wasn't quite ready to have me putting words in his mouth. "How about this: I'm attracted to her. The way you described her, she sounds like she's good looking, good with her hands, and pleasant to be around. Am I right?"

"You're right, but I never said I was attracted to her."

"Okay."

"Hey, you're not going to tell Irene about all this are you?"

"No, no. Of course not. This is between you and me." I pointed in his direction, then mine.

"All right then. I suppose whatever Irene tells you is private too, right?"

"That's right."

"So how does all of this private discussion help us?"

"It's like this: what you tell me about Irene might help the two of you get along better. And the better I get to know *you*, the better I might help Irene become a better wife. You'd like that, wouldn't you? Isn't that the reason why you're here—to have a more satisfying marriage?"

"In a lot of ways I think it's too late for that."

"I understand." He had his arms crossed—the classic defensive, blocking body language that meant, "No more talking."

But I reeled him back in with a comment about the NASCAR race over the weekend. Warren carried on for a minute or two, and I could see new life stirring in his eyes. I tried to look alert and interested, even though the best car races really take place on the drive to northern Michigan. "So," I lamented, "Does the woman you're seeing like car racing too?"

"Sharon? My physical therapist?" He asked, "I think she likes it, but our conversations bounce from topic to topic so much that I can't remember a lot of what we talk about." I nodded, and raised my eyebrows. "It's strange," he continued, "I'm nervous when I'm around her. I feel like a school kid again. You know the last time I was there, she stood behind me, while I was seated, and was working my neck the way she always does. Only this time when she pulled my head toward her, I could feel her shirt rub against my head. Granted, it was only for an instant or two, but I have to tell you, Jim, it was rather arousing, especially because of the electricity between us."

"Where on her shirt?"

"You know." He pointed to his breast.

"You make it sound like something happened the next time you went back."

"It did, but I don't think it was intentional. I'm probably over-reacting to the whole thing."

"Go ahead. I'm listening."

"Okay. She had the ultrasound, and was working it into my neck. My chin was on my chest, so that I'd absorb all those electrodes. Round and around she moved the little probe, until she was standing right in front of me. Her dress was long enough—below her knee—and made from denim. I noticed that the bottom button was missing. She said it popped off when she jumped in her vehicle that morning. I thought it was kinda funny, so I chuckled, but then I looked at the button six inches above that, and the button six inches above that, and the button six inches above that." He raised his index finger—flicking it like he was getting the ashes off a cigarette trapped between his thumb and middle finger. Warren paused for a minute, gathered his thoughts, and started in again: "It was odd...here I was concentrating on the buttons, not realizing what was beneath the buttons. I saw her knee, the top of her knee, the middle of her thigh, the top of her thigh..." His head rose, exaggerating what he saw beneath the denim skirt. He smiled, as if he'd seen Dale Earnhardt's ghost. "And then I blinked, and saw the tiniest trace of her underwear...they were pink, or yellow. Kinda pastel, I guess. It all happened so fast, and I didn't want to stare. I mean she was standing right there, but my gosh was it sexy. The whole thing was very...very kinky." He said after a long pause.

"Right," I said. "You don't think she showed you that intentionally?"

"No...right. I think she wanted to show me her missing button, but I don't think she had any idea that I would look so far up the slits in her skirt the way I did."

"What's going to happen the next time you see her?"

"I don't know."

"Is there going to be a next time?"

"Yes. I need more help."

"There are other physical therapists, you know."

"I know, but I like seeing her."

"What would your wife say if she knew what was going on?"

"She's not going to know."

"So what is this leading up to?"

"I don't know, Jim, but I kinda like where it's heading."

"Do you want to have sex with her?"

"The thought has crossed my mind."

"Do you think it will make you happier?"

"No...I think it will be exciting. I wanna see her undress, to see her naked, to hold her close to me. It's been so long since

I've *made love* to anyone. My wife and I just live together. We say we love each other, but there's nothing there. When we're intimate, and it's not very often, there's nothing between us. There's nothing."

"I see. Warren, I think you should think long and hard before seeing Sharon again."

"Why?"

"Because before you know it you'll be in too deep and your life will be a lot more complicated than it is now. You love your kids, don't you?"

"Of course I do."

"If nothing else, stay away from her for your kids' sake."

He nodded approvingly as he stroked his chin, "I hear you, and I appreciate your advice."

"So are you going to find another physical therapist?"

"I'll let you know at our next session."

Seven

RACHEL WAS ONE of my modest success stories. Several months ago she suffered from depression so bad that it was hard for her to get out of bed in the morning. Mary Cornwall prescribed a round of antidepressants, and she followed up with visits to my office once or twice a week.

She was a young woman—nearing the end of her college career—and had recently lost her best friend in a snowmobile incident.

But her life was headed south long before the accident. She admitted that she had made some poor decisions with men. When I asked her to explain that, she said, "College is no different today than when you were in school. The men are only after one thing." She was smart for realizing that and for inferring that somehow I was one of those Neanderthals when I was in college too.

That was Rachel's style: she would insinuate things, instead of telling me exactly what was on her mind. It was a welcome change when compared to the likes of Irene, who not only told me what was on her mind, but what everyone else around her should be thinking too.

Rachel was mysterious. She wasn't one to lay her deepest secrets on the table. I had to pry things out of her, but when she revealed something, it was a journey for me as well as for her. She didn't volunteer stuff; we had to connect the dots inside her head before I could draw a picture of what was on her mind.

She was also a mental challenge. A pre-law major, she asked a lot of questions. In a way, I felt like I was one of her clients in her make-believe office. We did have a symbiotic relationship ripe with irony. Both of us needed help coping with the loss of a loved one, and the treatment she received from me was actually healing for both of us. I looked forward to our sessions because it was as good for me as it was beneficial to her.

"I'm so sorry, Jim," she told me shortly after the funeral.

"Thank you…and I mean that. It was the hardest thing I ever had to deal with."

"How are you dealing with it?" She asked.

"Okay, I guess…as well as can be expected. Rachel, we've spent a lot of time together, how do you think I'm dealing with it?"

"Better than I've dealt with my grief…my depression," she said.

"How are you doing?" I asked, after all, *she* was the patient.

"Better, I think, but then I hear the news of your wife dying, and I start having awful thoughts all over again."

"Like what?"

"I don't know, like what's the point? I mean here you two went through all that schooling; got going in your careers, found the right person, just to have it all taken away from you? My gosh."

"I know, but what's the alternative?" I asked.

"I could drop out of school, bag groceries for a living, and live out of a cardboard box forever."

"That's certainly an option, but that doesn't sound like fun to me."

"If I don't take any chances, I won't get burned again." She slumped in her chair.

"Is that what happened?"

"With what?" She asked me.

"Your friend that died or the men in your life? Did you get burned by them?"

"That's one way to look at it, I guess."

"Rachel, what did you mean by 'I won't get burned again'?"

"Every time I get close to someone, they either turn out to be jerks or they end up dead. How's that?"

"I wanted you to say what was on your mind, and if that's what you're thinking, then that's okay."

"Don't you feel burned by what happened with your wife?" She asked me.

"In a way, I suppose."

"Maybe if you told me what you're thinking with the loss of your wife it would help me with the loss of my friend."

"What is this, reverse psychology?"

"Aw come on, Jim. I need your help. I need you to tell me what's going on inside your head."

"Rachel, this really isn't how it works. I'm the helper, and you're the helpee."

"I know, but you *are helping* me."

"How is my grief supposed to help you?"

"You're older than I am, more mature. You're supposed to handle these situations better."

"Better than whom?" I asked her.

"Better than really young people."

"Are you really young, Rachel?"

She blushed. "Yeah, I'm young. But thirty seems like middle age."

"It'll be here before you know it, and your life will be more complicated than it is now. You watch."

"If I make it that far, it'll be more complicated."

"Rachel, you keep throwing out these veiled threats that you don't want to go on living. Are you trying to tell me something?"

"No…I want you to tell me something, and you won't. If we're going to converse, doctor, it needs to go both ways. You tell me your secrets and I'll tell you mine, okay?"

I hesitated. "I don't like this arrangement, and that's not how counseling works."

"Don't you want to see me get better?"

"Of course I do, but not at the risk of losing my license, or compromising my professional integrity."

She waved her finger toward me and calmly stated, "Don't get all high and mighty all of a sudden. We're just a couple of friends having a little chat. The more you tell me the more I'll tell you. Can't we do this, doctor?" She looked over my shoulder and asked, "Can you tell me how long it'll be before I feel good enough to date again? Or what it's like to find someone you're really attracted to?"

I sighed. "Rachel, you're a nice girl, a nice person with a bright future ahead of you. I'm not really comfortable discussing my personal life with a client." There was no other way to say it. "You understand, don't you?"

"I'm only trying to help."

"I know, but it'll take some time, perhaps a long time. We'll talk again soon."

"Whatever you say."

Rachel's comments lingered with me for days—at least the part about taking the easy way out. It's hard to get out of bed, and work hard, to try to get ahead. Life is full of struggles and confrontations, decisions and regrets. Rachel was letting life get the better of her. She let life's struggles knock her down, and seemed to lack the resiliency of self-confidence.

She would have crumbled if she had to deal with a boss like the one I had. He wasn't a bad person, we simply didn't see eye to eye on much of anything. Steve Calisto and I got together once a month or so to review my caseload. I couldn't discuss the particulars of the private clients, but the committed patients were fair game.

He showed a peculiar interest in my cases, I thought. Instead of rubber-stamping my strategy for treatment, he wanted to know about all the tidbits of each patient. The plain, white-bread cases never interested him; he wanted particulars on the bizarre, the demented, and the fetishes. I learned to toy with Steve, to give him the details slowly, to make the stories last longer. He was like a kid—on the edge of his seat—eagerly anticipating every sordid detail.

Steve was an administrator for the Centre and bound by the pressures of budgets, personnel decisions, billing, everything. He was a little insecure about his position. It seems that administrators are always the first to get cut when the economy heads south. To combat that notion, he went overboard in trying to justify his employment. When I started at the clinic, for example, he had graphs and charts showing the number of hours the Centre billed the state, and what the Centre received in payments from private individuals. He had goals to increase the number of hours that we billed the state, as well as increasing the hourly rates of private individuals. "After all," he said, "most of that stuff is covered by their health insurance."

He implied that I should treat people more often—to put more dollars in the Centre's coffers—in spite of what they really needed. I didn't acknowledge his wishes, but didn't want to get off on the wrong foot with him, either. Sometimes you've got to pick your battles.

Everyone in the office had suspicions that Steve was flanking the system to pad the bottom line of the Centre. It seemed that the patients on Medicaid were always discharged when their benefits ran out, not when the effectiveness of their treatment was finished. There were whispers among the orderlies that some patients on Medicaid were held against their will, just so Steve could meet his financial projections.

I couldn't blame Steve for wanting to get ahead, to look good for his bosses, to justify his position when the going got tough. It's natural for a guy to want to succeed. But he went about it all the wrong way. Steve abused his authority. He and Mary Cornwall used to get in nasty disagreements over the medications she prescribed for the committed patients. Every time she did that, it cost the Centre money, and was a bone of contention with Steve. She questioned his medical credentials. He almost accused her of over-treating them for fear that they might have to face reality. Back and forth they went—sometimes heatedly—until one of them stormed off.

They had a bizarre relationship, almost like some of the couples I was counseling. They'd get into knock-down, drag-out fights, then kiss and make up—or at least I think that's what Steve wanted to have happen. I'm sure he had romantic ideas where Mary was concerned. He sure seemed to spend a lot of time in her office, for no apparent reason. I think he liked to watch her; perhaps it threw fuel on the fire of his fantasies.

Mary Cornwall wanted nothing to do with him. She hated the way he dressed (usually in tropical-looking shirts unless his bosses were scheduled to visit), his dandruff, his phony personality, and especially the way he questioned the way she prescribed medication. I told her that she should document everything, just in case things got ugly down the road. She never dreamed that her license to practice would be in jeopardy because of what he wanted. "It wouldn't hurt to send him a memo, 'confirming our conversation,'" I used to tell her. "You never know, Mary."

"The only thing that would do is make him madder at me."

"Mary, it might make him realize that he's out of line," I told her.

"Come on, Jim, can't we talk about something else?"

"Just send him an e-mail, and for Christ's sake, keep copies of those e-mails that he sent you while he was on vacation in the Keys."

"Which ones?"

"Come on, Mary. You know."

"Where he said 'how much I miss you' and 'wish you were here' and stuff like that?"

"Sure. You never know what will happen."

"Are you always this skeptical of people?" She asked me.

"Mary, I just think you should cover your backside."

"Are you always this skeptical of people?" She asked me again.

"Just the ones I don't trust."

"Need some medication?"

"Thank you, no, Mary." I smiled. "Besides, that cuts into the Centre's bottom line, and that wouldn't make Calypso Steve look good."

Eight

CARRIE'S OLD LAW PARTNER, Glen Morrison, took up our cause against Atmantle Health and Casualty, but wasn't making very much progress. It appeared as though Atmantle had dug in their heels and weren't going to budge from their premise that Carrie's skin cancer was a preexisting condition. They didn't want to talk to us, or even consider that they were the slightest bit responsible for her death.

Glen thought that they had to deny our auto claim to be consistent with the denial of our health claim. If they gave an inch on the auto, it might open the door on the health, and vice versa.

Glen wasn't a bad guy, or a poor lawyer. He just lacked the motivation to succeed. He wanted the big cases to fall in his lap, with a nice red bow on top.

Only a few big cases ever did end up on his lap. Instead, he filled his days preparing two-hundred-dollar wills and trusts for friends and people he knew. He struggled to put them together, so people questioned his ability to do more complicated stuff like filing a lawsuit for a personal injury case. Carrie used to tell me that he wasn't lazy; he just didn't work very hard. He failed to see the big picture, the potential, of his clients' cases. If he handled a will with professionalism and speed, the more lucrative cases would have come his way. If he worked the lucrative cases with imagination and pride, he wouldn't have to worry about doing wills for two hundred dollars apiece.

After Carrie died I was still loyal to Glen and the firm. After all, he gave Carrie her start, and was extremely fair with her during the short time they worked together. Glen couldn't afford to buy her health insurance, but then again, she wasn't an employee. Their working arrangement was a simple one. She paid him two-fifty a month for rent, and had access to the firm's software, which was fairly elaborate. It had all the law books on file as well as all preprinted documents needed to perform day-to-day operations. Carrie installed her own phone system, and had a couple of paralegals turned stay-at-home-moms to help her several afternoons a week. Carrie and Glen worded their contract so that if Carrie ever landed a contingency fee of more than fifty thousand dollars, Glen would recoup fifteen percent. Plus, when Glen decided to retire, Carrie had the first chance to buy his customer list, the furniture, the building, and the name. The two of them weren't really partners, but merely professional colleagues working out of the same office.

Anyway, I directed Glen to do a little research about "preexisting conditions" as it pertains to health insurance. "You know, Glen, do a little digging, see what the laws are. What's Atmantle's reputation? Do they have any complaints against them? You know…if they don't want to deal with us, we'll go to the next step." Glen hemmed and hawed, something about going on vacation, and having a full dance card. I guess he didn't "know" what I was talking about after all.

That was his style: avoid confrontation, postpone the inevitable, procrastinate, and pray that everything would work itself out.

He was maddening professionally, but I liked him personally. I wished he had a bit more ambition, more gumption. Carrie said he was a persuasive orator, until his research ran thin, then he turned into a bumbling layperson, grabbing at straws. What's worse, when that happened, he doubted his ability. Round and round he went: successes followed by failures, doubts followed by insecurities.

If I was to have him handle our case against Atmantle, it seemed that I'd have to do most of the legwork and research. I needed some help, and immediately thought of Taren Lisk at the attorney general's office.

That night I sent her an e-mail:

> *Taren,*
> *Thanks for your kind words about Carrie. You're right, it has been a difficult time. I'd love to do lunch sometime, but in the meantime, I could use some help from you. What can you find out about Atmantle Health and Casualty? They're the company that denied Carrie's health benefits because of a preexisting condition. They're wrong, I just know it.*
> *Jim.*

It really wasn't much of an e-mail, I admit. But really, I wasn't ready mentally for much of anything. Carrie's death still weighed heavily on my mind. I missed her so much it was hard to deal with things. I kept waiting for her to come strolling through our front door, and say "Hi, honey," the way she always did.

I was still a wreck.

Even though it had been months since Carrie died, Glen and our case against Atmantle would have to wait until I was better prepared to get into the boxing ring and battle it out.

Nine

B Y THEN IT WAS the beginning of October, and my mind turned to grouse hunting with Toby.

Reports from the north woods suggested that there were lots of birds. That was always a good feeling—to know we would have ample opportunities to kill a few birds. But really, even if there were hardly any birds to be had, I'd still go—to watch Toby. He is a beautiful animal, with all that hair flowing as one, and his purpose—to find game. He's just fun to watch, a joy to behold.

Grouse hunting with a dog is the way it's supposed to be done. There's no finer sport in all the land.

On a drizzly Friday afternoon, I skipped out of the office and dashed home. There was a staff meeting planned for 4 P.M. that day but I told Calypso Steve that I had to look up a patient's relative in Cheboygan. Since it was a two-hour drive from mid-Michigan to the "tip of the mitt," I had to leave the office a little early.

Per our routine, I let Toby outside to do his duty while I threw together some of the provisions we'd need for the weekend. I tried to keep the list simple: clothes, food, hunting gear, and dog supplies. All I needed for clothes were flannel shirts, plenty of socks, a pair of jeans, and a jacket or two. Food could wait until I got on the road. I'd have plenty of time to make up a list of provisions we'd need for the weekend.

Hunting gear was fairly simple. I packed my bush pants, gun and boots, then turned my attention to my blaze orange vest, which is the carrying case for everything while I hunt. There were plenty of shells in the vest: twenty-gauge, to match my over and under shotgun. The old compass hung by a thread on the left lapel, just like it had been for the last dozen years. My old buck knife was in the side pocket along with a pill bottle full of wooden matchsticks, a small square of eighty-grain sandpaper glued to the top. The inside pocket held a length of toilet paper and my shooting glasses, littered with the forest duff from a season since passed.

I had grand plans for a long walk through the quiet woods of the Upper Peninsula.

Toby's gear was easy. All he needed was a bag of dog food, a brush to comb the nettles, and perhaps a dozen dog bones to sweeten his teeth. He did require a dog bowl or two and his plastic crate for safe transportation. Almost as an afterthought, I tossed a couple of milk bones into my vest.

An hour later we were underway—dog in the back, my gun and gear tucked away and a feeling of relief on my mind. There would be no urgent patients, no suicidal clients, prying bosses, or incompetent lawyers to complicate the situation. A relaxing weekend in Marquette County awaited us; all I had to do was negotiate the five-hour drive north.

When the terrain had changed from farmland to woods just north of Clare, I pulled a pen from the overhead visor and put together a haphazard menu for the next few days. Saturday morning would be perfect for bacon—to chase away the dank odor of the musty cabin, and to sock away the drippings for

German potato salad later that night. We'd need a dozen eggs, a loaf of bread, and a can of hash for Sunday morning. Lunch would be a smorgasbord of snacks: granola bars, a bag of Fuji apples, a pound of sharp cheddar cheese, and a box of fancy crackers. One of the best parts about being up north is the tailgate lunches, when all you do is nibble and snack on a variety of foodstuffs that neither fill you up nor weigh you down. Dinner was an interesting prospect. Potatoes were a certainty, so were onions. Steak sounded good, and the fat around the edges would do wonders for Toby's stamina—or so I thought. I'd need butter and rolls, a twelve-pack of beer and water, a half pint of whipping cream for coffee, and maybe a pastee or two just in case I decided to stay until Monday morning instead of coming home Sunday night.

By the time I reached Grayling, my list was complete. At Gaylord, I was hungry and ready for dinner. Forty-five minutes later I had a full belly and all the provisions I'd need for a fun-filled weekend.

Three hours after that, I topped off the tank at a gas station south of Marquette, which had an unusual display between the pumps. I was used to seeing bags of mulch, antifreeze, or windshield washer fluid stacked near the gas pumps. Instead, the gas station had stacks and stacks of green-colored gallon pails. After washing the windshield, I looked at their labels: "fancy emerald icing." It wasn't until I read the sign above the display that I realized why they'd be selling tubs of the sweet stuff, "Bear bait $4.99."

Make no mistake, the central Upper Peninsula is bear country.

I didn't buy any icing, but I did pick up a bag of "Trenary toast" and a pound of "cudighi." The toast is made near the town of Trenary in the U.P., and cudighi is a sweet Italian sausage, whose roots come from Northern Italy. Both are delicious, and unique to the Upper Peninsula.

On the outskirts of town, we turned off the straight, paved roads and onto the crumbly paths that knife their way through the bush. With each twist and turn, my headlights panned into the rock escarpments, where balsam and hazel bush scratched out a living in thin soil and long winters. The roads were slippery from the day's rain coupled with the coating of leaves that fell like flakes from an upturned cereal box. Finally—the rusty bridge—and the little trail beyond that led to home for the weekend.

I noticed the intensity of the river as soon as I opened the truck door. It was a quiet roar. The sound of the cabin.

Toby made the rounds in the yard, sprinkling his calling cards on everything. I found the key under the three-sided wood shed and brought in an armload of supplies. The box of blue-tip matches was on the overhead shelf adjacent to the stove. That's part of the ritual at the cabin. You always leave ice in the freezer, kindling in the bin, and a fire ready to be lit inside the woodstove. In no time the newspaper caught fire, the kindling started to crackle, and the cabin was awash in the fragrant odors of the north woods.

An hour later Toby was fed and was resting on the couch next to me, thumping the cushions with his tail, sending plumes of dust into the air. He was happy, and for the first time in a very long time, I was happy too. We were happy together.

I poured a nice glass of whiskey over a stack of ice cubes. It felt good to be alone, to have the place all to myself. I thought about the hunt for tomorrow, and what course I'd take. The lower river made sense, but not till afternoon, when the birds would be in stands of hawthorn, filling their crops with tasty red fruit the size of maraschino cherries. It didn't make sense to get up early, but it wouldn't hurt to spend an hour splitting cedar logs for kindling, either.

I turned on the eleven o'clock news broadcast and noticed unusual faces on the screen. The reports were thin that night in our little slice of the Upper Peninsula, in places with unusual names: Ralph, Felch, and New Swanzy. All I cared about was the weather for Saturday: mostly cloudy, calm northeast winds, and mid fifties. I couldn't have cooked up a better forecast if I had tried.

Toby and I would have an adventure tomorrow.

For some reason I had a hard time falling asleep that night. It must have been the long drive that had me tossing and turning. Of course, it never helps that the next day I'd be hunting, and I simply couldn't wait. Anticipation has a powerful effect on a man.

So does a conscience. I kept thinking about work, the people I was treating, and what I could have done differently to promote their recovery. I had lots of patients, with lots of needs. Joe, I'm sure, would eventually come out of his trance. Rachel needed someone to trust. Warren and Irene? They were almost hopeless.

Maybe I should have been more direct when I warned Warren not to pursue Sharon.

In a way though, I thought about Warren and his miserable marriage. It must have been torture for him to be trapped in that situation. I admired his tenacity for staying with her. He loved his kids so much that he endured a horrific existence. Sharon brought him happiness, hope, and meaning to his life.

There are honorable ways to end a marriage: try to work things out, pour your heart into it, bend over backwards, and yes, keep things simple. Too often couples try to solve the world's problems instead of working day by day on the little things of life, like doing the dishes, bathing the children, and paying the bills. If they'd keep it simple and conquer the small hurdles, they'd gain confidence in each other when the bigger problems came along.

In a way, I could sympathize with Warren and the temptation of Sharon. She seemed to be everything that Irene wasn't. I could almost picture them together, laughing, carrying on.

She'd stroke his ego without even trying. Men like it when women laugh at our jokes. Men like to talk about our accomplishments, our conquests. Sharon must have taken an interest in Warren's career, in his life. Men are simple: we want sex, food, and to feel appreciated, but not necessarily in that order. Clearly Warren wasn't getting two of the three at home. Sharon was a viable surrogate for what he lacked, or so he thought.

There was also the allure of a secret relationship, with all its pitfalls and rewards. It seemed that Warren liked the challenge of carrying on something that wasn't quite right. It wasn't that seeing Sharon was all that bad, it was where they were heading that was so wrong. Sex with Sharon would have been exciting I'm sure, the fact that it was forbidden must have made it all the more intoxicating. It wasn't my job to talk him out of it; he had free will just like the rest of us.

Warren would have some tough choices to make.

So did I: should I split the cedar kindling before or after breakfast?

Ten

The next morning was just like the weatherman said it would be—cloudy. I let Toby outside while I rekindled the fire in the woodstove. A few minutes later he was at the front door, pawing and wagging his tail. I let him in but waited until the bacon was finished frying before I gave him his food. He likes a little bacon grease stirred into the kernels. I figured the extra fat would give him extra energy for the long day of hunting ahead.

He didn't have the chance to lift his leg and whiz in his bowl.

I choked down breakfast, and spent an hour splitting foot-long cedar logs into kindling. They made a nice smell on my buckskin gloves and flannel shirt. When I was sure the dew had evaporated, I led Toby to the drive shed where Uncle Jim keeps the old hunting truck. It's a 1975 International Scout, complete with AM radio and worn-out calipers. Every time you step on the brakes, the old beast lunges to the right. There were other ailments too, but driving that old bugger is part of the allure of the cabin.

Toby and I loaded up our gear and drove south to where the stands of aspen grow as thick as thieves. By the beginning of October the leaves on the aspens were burned yellow and twinkled like gold medallions as they fell from the branches. Toby was dying to hunt, but needed his beeper collar on first. Electronics have made it easy to find the dog in heavy cover. It beeps every six seconds while he's moving, then changes tone when he points. Traditionalists relish the silver-sounding twang of a Swiss bell, but when the dog goes on point, they can't find him. A beeper collar may not be the most pleasant sound in the woods, but it does make us better hunters.

Anyway, Toby and I spent an hour or two in the high country aspens. He pointed five woodcock and three grouse. I killed one of each. When we made it back to the truck, I put the birds in the cooler and we shared a bottle of water. Toby got a milk bone for his effort, and I had a candy bar.

It was a beautiful day. Sweet fern cast a fragrant shadow over everything. I noticed a band of geese in the heavens, in perfect formation, winging someplace south on an easy tailwind. My beautiful dog was at my feet, panting slightly, then rolling on his back, feet peddling an imaginary treadmill. I had a couple of birds in the bag and headed for the honey hole that consistently produces scores of flushes.

Together, we went back to the cabin—dodging potholes and avoiding rocks. Uncle Jim's Scout handled like a beast, but it was fun. The Michigan Wolverines were playing football on the radio, but I didn't care about the score; all I knew was that the sound of the announcers reminded me that it was autumn. I ate a tart Fuji apple while I kept a vigil for birds scratching for grit along the edge of the road. It was like a dream; it was so pretty.

Back at the cabin, I stuffed a candy bar in my vest, along with an extra handful of shot shells. The lower river is one of those places where it's possible to whistle though a box of shells in a few hours. There's always a few grouse, and more often than not, there's a lot of grouse.

At almost three, Toby and I headed out. We took the path that leads to an old deer-hunting blind on the brow of the river hill. Uncle Jim must have mowed the path three or four times throughout the summer, because the grass was barely ankle high. Toby knew the way, dashing across the path, tail wagging, beeper collar beeping. After a short walk he paused on the rock escarpment, looking down on the twisty river and the lush stands of hawthorn bushes beyond.

Together, we limped our way down the rock crevices, amidst the fallen leaves, twigs, and clutter. Below the rapids, the river calmed and became a smooth, flowing sheet. We were in the bottomlands now, where the earth was rich and black, and the beavers keep the aspens trimmed shin high.

Toby was hunting hard—dashing this way and that, moving from one likely hideout to the next, tasting the wind with that wonderful nose. He is so much fun to watch and take hunting.

Hunting grouse with an English setter is like dancing with a beautiful woman: you never tire of the vision; you never want it to grow old.

My mind was racing again, the way it always does when I'm hunting. I had to keep one eye on the dog, the other on my footing, and if I had a third eye, on the cover around me. Grouse are known to keep thick cover between themselves and approaching danger.

It's no wonder that grouse have a reputation for being hard to kill. They flush when you least expect it. There is always a tree between the gun and the bird. Grouse hunters have an old expression about the prey they hunt: The first time you hunt grouse it's for fun, the next time it's for revenge.

Just then Toby's electronic collar changed tones. He was on point, just ten yards off the river's edge, and thirty yards ahead of me. I swung wide, around the dog, telling him "Whoa" in the process. I figured that the bird had run ahead of Toby, keeping a large cedar between it and the dog. Lucky guess. Before I could get to the tree, a grouse rocketed out of the dying ferns and headed across the water, presenting a relatively easy going-away opportunity. I missed the first shot somehow, but at the second report the grouse collapsed in midair, sailing into the cover on the opposite side of the river. Toby dashed ahead just in time to see the bird's fall, but was reluctant to take the plunge across the waterway. "Fetch, Toby," I encouraged him, but all he did was sit there and whine like a puppy. I found a baton-sized stick and told him to sit. When he did, I showed him the stick and threw it across. "Fetch!"

Toby dove in, made the short swim, and found the bird on the other side. Trouble was, he wasn't so sure about bringing it back to me. Back and forth he paced, with the bird drooping lifeless in his massive jowls. So I pulled the oldest trick in the dog trainer's book: I walked away. Toby couldn't stand the thought of losing me, so eventually he made the return voyage, cargo still intact.

We were off to a great start, but still had some territory to cover. I hunt the river bottom as long as the cover is good. As long as there are hawthorn bushes, with that ripe, red fruit, there's grouse to be had. An hour later we were about as far as I had ever gone. Landmarks became less familiar. Toby and I passed the beaver dam, the osprey nest, and the bear's den. I thought about heading for home and making the turn toward the high ground, but Toby had other ideas. He seemed to be after another grouse; his body language said it all: the wagging tail, the coiled intensity, and measured gait. His nose was close to the ground. *Unusual*, I thought. The ferns were thick in that stretch, and at times all I could see was the tip of his tail as he made steady progress. He seemed to be tracking something but for all I knew it could have been a covey of birds, which is always fun. I stayed with him, flanking his side, waiting for the mayhem of whirling wings. Nothing happened.

A hundred yards later we were away from the river and climbing the hill. Toby ran ahead like a shot. I chased. It was all I could do to keep up with him. He was onto something, and now I was convinced that it didn't have wings. "Toby, no!" I yelled, but he kept racing. "Toby, here!" I screamed, leaping over fallen logs, dodging overhead limbs. He ignored me, just like I knew he would. The ferns ahead of him parted as if they were cut by a sickle. I saw a glimmer of black in all the madness.

God damn, a bear.

"Toby, no!" He was gaining on it. "Toby, no!" He was nearly to it. "Here!" I tried every command I could think of, but he wouldn't stop. When the black glimmer melted into Toby's white coat, two cubs the size of basketballs climbed the nearest white pine. I was still running, chasing the chase, closing the gap. When I was forty yards from them I saw the sow: back to the tree, ears pinned against the back of her wide skull. "Toby, no," I cried, but all he did was bark like he needed an exorcist. I approached slowly, and the sow diverted her attention from the bird-dog-turned-bear-hound Toby. She looked in my direction for an instant, which gave Toby his opening. He lunged toward her, which was one of the dumbest moves he ever made. The sow let out a muffled "woof" and spun wildly, catching Toby with a right cross that sent him barreling down the hill toward me. I seized the opportunity and tackled him, clutching his collar in my hands. He wanted to get up but I wouldn't let him.

The sow faced us and curled her upper lip. "Easy, momma," I warned her. She stood her ground, and so did I. I didn't want to shoot her, for a variety of reasons—first and foremost that I might miss and then we'd really have our hands full. And for a few pensive seconds, it appeared as though I wouldn't need to. While holding the dog, I unbuckled my belt, pulled it through the loops on my hunting pants, and then wrapped it through his collar. Next, I unscrewed the cap on his beeper collar, which separated the nine-volt battery from its terminals.

All at once the woods was quiet.

Deathly quiet.

Toby was panting heavily, and so was I. Momma bear stood under the white pine, nose glistening ahead of cinnamon muzzle. Her cubs watched the action from ten feet above, sending shards of pitch-covered bark sifting down the trunk. I wrapped the belt around my fist three or four times and slowly backed away. I let Toby up too…slowly… but he didn't understand the urgency. He wanted to try a second assault for some reason. We made it five yards without harm. Then ten. When we were fifteen yards, I turned and ran, looking over my shoulder. The big sow charged, but it was only a feint. No matter, I kept running, Toby's leash in one hand, my little shotgun in the other.

We ran, and ran, which direction, I didn't know. I didn't care. Toby and I were safe, that's all I cared about. *Wait till Carrie hears about this one*, I thought. I always used to tell her about my adventures up north, but I'm not sure she thought it was as neat as I did. She was results-oriented. "How many birds did you kill? How many birds did Toby find? Did he behave himself?" Stuff like that.

Of course, there was nobody waiting for me at home. Nobody would believe me, other than Uncle Jim. But what a story. In all the years of hunting grouse, I've never seen a bear, let alone have one up close and personal.

And Toby. The dumb ass. I was talking to him as we went. Scolding him. "What's wrong with you? What were you thinking?" He trotted along next to me, glancing upwards periodically with his droopy eyes. "Didn't you hear me yelling at you?" He yawned, then shook his head, jowls flapping.

When I was sure that we weren't being followed, I leaned my gun against a tree, and gave Toby a hug. I love that dog. He had a couple of deep scratch marks on his upper shoulder and neck, leaving a smear of blood on my buckskin gloves. I gave him a pat on the head, "It's okay, boy. Let's go home and have some dinner." He wagged his tail and licked my ear.

I put my belt back on, picked up my gun, and regrouped mentally. In all the confusion I forgot where I was headed, or where I had been. The woods around me were still and getting dark. Not a breath of air stirred, not a shadow could be found.

I looked down at the compass and couldn't believe my eyes.

It was gone.

Eleven

WE WEREN'T OUT of the woods yet, so to speak. Toby didn't know the difference, but I sure did. We were lost, plain and simple.

I looked around me. Everything looked the same. The endless expanse of forest. The cursed mixture of aspen, balsam, birch, and pine. I watched the falling leaves. They floated straight down without the trace of wind. Tree trunks had moss on all sides, instead of just the north.

I could have backtracked, but I'm sure momma bear wouldn't have appreciated a second go round. I had a hunch which way was home—call it an internal compass—but that wouldn't be all I'd need. I needed a lucky break, a familiar landmark or a flock of geese to fly overhead. *Carrie, if you're up there, anything to help me out would be appreciated*, I thought.

If I could get out of this one, I made a promise to help Glen Morrison get after Atmantle. I shouldn't let him flounder in his ineptitude. I let him procrastinate instead of take charge. He was supposed to be working for us—Carrie and me—but he really wasn't doing much at all. If I could get out of this jam he'd have my undivided attention, my all.

And so, Toby and I took a heading for what I thought was home. If we came to a feeder creek, we'd follow it to where it dumped into the river. Once we found the river it would lead us back to the cabin.

Trouble was, it was getting late. I had a half hour tops before darkness would envelope the woods, and make walking nearly impossible. I was tired and sore and didn't want to endanger Toby or myself by falling over a log or off a rocky bank when it was dark. My calves ached from negotiating the rugged terrain. The deal with the bear didn't help either. My gun felt like it weighed thirty pounds instead of a few ounces over six. Toby was starting to fade too. He didn't have the jump in his step that he had earlier in the day.

All at once I noticed that Toby had stopped with his front leg cocked slightly. While I was wondering how we were going to make it home, Toby never let go of the notion that we were still on a massive hunting expedition. Almost on cue, two grouse squirted out, without the usual urgency. They didn't go far, but lit in an aspen about ten feet off the ground. They were so intent on avoiding the dog; they never thought to look in my direction.

True sportsmen never shoot grouse out of a tree; it's not considered sporting. It's not a fair chase. True sportsmen flush the bird again, and take it on the wing. It's more of a challenge that way. But sometimes I hunt more for food than for sport. This was one of those occasions when sustenance ruled over sport.

I shot, and got both birds, lickety split. For the time being I decided to suspend my sporting ways. After all, it appeared as though a night in the woods was a distinct possibility, and one waterlogged grouse between the two of us was hardly enough for dinner.

Sometimes you get lucky, and a pair of birds almost lands in your lap. It felt like a gift from the heavens. "Thank you, Carrie," I said to myself, You always said you'd look out for me."

The more I assessed the situation, the more I realized that if we were going to spend the night in the woods, the little daylight remaining was my biggest ally. And so, I looked around at my surroundings and figured that this would be as good a place as any to make an overnight camp. An enormous balsam had lost its grip on a small rise not far away and the resulting root wad pulled the earth away from the hill. It made a saucer-shaped indention in the earth, with the root wad and the hill for sides. I set my gun down, took off my vest, and began pulling limbs off the cedar. They'd make a nice lean-to, and a mediocre bed.

Next, I yanked as much wood off the balsam as I could, and broke it into yardstick lengths. Before long I had a tidy sum of brittle but suitable firewood. In the twilight of that early October day, I cleaned my three birds. Toby ate the hearts raw, but the entrails, feathers and wings went into a small indention I made with the heel of my boot. No sense in luring more trouble to our camp with the smell of fresh carrion. Toby sniffed at the soil where I buried the remains, but quickly lost interest. He was as hungry as I was.

At first I thought I had lost the little medicine bottle full of wooden matchsticks, but I found it in the bottom of my vest amid the scores of little twigs that had found their way inside. I made a fire pit by scuffing the leaves and forest duff away from the threshold of my shelter. Birchbark from a nearby tree and a small wad of toilet paper from my vest would make some decent kindling. I placed the bark and paper in the center of the bowl and made a small pyramid out of the balsam sticks. The first match took a couple strikes, but caught. So did the birchbark and tissue. A minute later the balsam was ablaze and crackling, sending golden sparks rising into the darkened heavens. Under a pool of a campfire light we sat there, Toby and me, roasting our birds like a lonely caveman and his very best friend.

It took a steady supply of balsam to keep the fire burning,

but I kept it going. I tried not to cook the birds too fast, for fear that I'd singe the outside, and the inside would still be raw. About twenty minutes later, we ate. I can't say it tasted very good, or was very couth, but together we gobbled down the strips of meat I pulled off the bones. We huddled around the fire—keeping warm, a pair of would-be rugged individuals in the heart of the rugged Upper Peninsula. For dessert I had a candy bar, and Toby had the last milk bone. A few minutes later he curled up on the boughs, pulled a burr from the hair under his leg, and fell asleep.

I wasn't so anxious for bed. I knew I would have trouble drifting off, so decided to stay up and watch the fire. I unlaced my boots and pulled up my socks, which were wet from either sweat or swamp water. No matter. What a day it had been.

The entire world seemed at peace. It was so quiet it almost hurt to listen. I had no idea where I was, other than I was a long way from the cabin. The thought of spending the night in the woods had me scared. I was afraid, plain and simple.

I wish I could say that I slept like a baby that night, but the truth of the matter is that it was one of the longest nights of my life. When the fire died, the cool of the night turned unpleasantly cold. I buttoned the top button on my flannel shirt and curled up next to Toby. Together we lay on the boughs of balsam, with my grungy orange vest as a half-hearted blanket.

A loon wailed its haunting call from somewhere in the distance. A bobcat's screech woke me up more than once. Both made terrifying sounds that made the hair stand up on the back of my neck. Although we had no more encounters with bears that day, I couldn't help but replay our close call over and over again. I couldn't believe my dog and the way he took a lunge at something so huge and powerful.

I was tired. Satisfyingly tired. The dog and me both. I curled up next to Toby, put my hat over my head, and closed my eyes…

That's when I heard the footsteps. They were heavy, and sure, too noisy for a bear, too clumsy for a deer. I froze. The steps came closer, and closer, little by little.

"Pardon me," I recognized the voice. He cleared his throat, and in his finest English accent plied, "Do you have any Grey Poupon?"

"Telpher...what the hell are you doing here?"

"I was going to ask you the same thing!" He said. And he just stood there for a second or two, then looked for a spot to set his shotgun. It looked like one of those expensive side-by-sides I've seen advertised in the back of the upscale shooting magazines. I invited him inside our little shelter, but he turned me down. Toby was oblivious to the intrusion. *Sure*, I thought, *go after the big bad bear, but let a stranger into our camp.*

"Is South Beach this way...or that way?" He was smiling profusely, in a taunting way. Our little fire came back to life, and bathed both of our faces in a warm glow.

"Very funny...Toby and I decided to spend the night in the woods, and get an early start on the birds first thing in the morning."

"Sure you did. You can't fool me, you son of a gun. You're lost! How is the dog anyway?"

"He's tired."

"He looks tired. Come here boy." He whistled through his front teeth, but Toby didn't flinch.

"Doesn't the law say you have to wear something blaze orange when you're hunting grouse?" I asked him.

"What makes you think I'm not wearing orange boxers? Or socks?" Telpher didn't like to be the one getting questioned. He liked to do the questioning. "How do you know that I'm hunting grouse? It's crow season too, or snipe. Have you got any toothpaste and a paper bag?" He smiled again.

"Can you help us find our way home?" I asked.

"I thought you wanted to get an early start on the birds?"

"I was lying."

"I didn't think shrinks had a license to lie," he said, smiling.

"Would you please help us?"

"I am...aren't I?"

"Why do you have to answer every question I ask you with a question of your own?"

"I do?"

"See?"

"See what?" He asked.

"You just did it!"

"Did what?" He asked again.

"Answer every question with one of your own."

"I did?"

"Just forget it."

"Suit yourself." He patted his herringbone shooting jacket and vest like he was looking for something. "Want a drink?"

"Yes...that would be fine. Got some?"

"Somewhere...oh, yes." He handed me a concave pewter flask, engraved on the side were the letters T.E.B.

"What is it?" I asked.

"Why don't you take a snort and tell me?"

I shook my head...he answered my question with one of his own. "Well, it's not blackberry brandy."

"Not even close, Jim."

I smacked my lips, and took another pull. "Drambuie?"

"Very good...all the way from Edinburgh, Scotland."

"Why Drambuie?"

"Jim, you're not going to analyze what I drink too, are you?"

"Telpher," I said, "You're in the middle of the Upper Peninsula, you don't have to get defensive."

He shook his head, "Are you scared, Jim?"

"Of what?" I asked him.

"Of the wild creatures that live in these parts? Of being alone? Of facing your future without your wife? Of finding out the rest of Carrie's story?"

"Why does it matter?"

"I'm just trying to help you," he snorted.

"I'm not afraid of being alone, and I don't worry about the future."

"Then what is it, Jim?"

"I don't know...I can't seem to snap out of this blasted grief." Telpher nodded, tossing bits of twigs into the simmering fire, watching it, watching me. "At first I couldn't believe that she was gone, but then I got angry. Now I make deals with the thought of her. I keep thinking that if I barter...if I do certain things...that she'll come back."

"I see. What's the latest barter?"

"If I get out of this pickle," I replied, "That I would help her former partner handle our case against...but why am I telling you all this?"

In typical Telpher fashion, he dodged my question and created one of his own: "Is this what you call this, Jim...a pickle?"

He was making me mad. He was getting inside my head. "Never mind," I said. "Just leave it alone."

"Why can't you face the fact that she's gone?"

"Mr. Beaman, I suggest you find another camp to visit."

He looked at me like I was being rude. "Are you sure you want me to leave? Two guns are better than one, especially when you're up against bears and wolves and an uncertain future."

"I like our odds," I said, patting Toby on the head. He didn't flinch, but continued slumbering. "We'll get through this. The whole thing."

"Suit yourself," he crowed, helping himself off the ground. "Before I go, I'm going to give you and your dog a little advice: when taking on a problem the size of a black bear, you'd better have a plan."

I waved him off, as if it was in slow motion, as if it was a dream. Maybe it was. He put his fancy pewter flask away and mumbled something from my childhood: "Matthew, Mark, Luke and John, bless this bed that I lay on." A prayer seemed out of character for Telpher, but he was prone to bouts of unpredictable utterances. I watched him stand, find his shotgun parked next to mine, and saunter off into the complete darkness.

I don't need him, I thought, *and his 'Grey Poupon,' either. We'll get out of this mess on our own.*

Twelve

When it was barely light the following morning Toby and I began to walk. I knew that if we walked north or west, we'd eventually hit a road, and if we went south we'd stumble into the river sooner or later. Anything but east. The next nearest road east was ten miles away, and the exact opposite direction from the cabin. *Three out of four ain't bad*, I thought.

After almost an hour of hiking we caught a break: a two-track cut through the woods. At last, a sign of civilization. We stayed on the trail for fifteen minutes, until it forked, which was bad. Trails split as they lead away from major roads. I figured we were going the wrong way. We backtracked. Sure enough, the trail we were on had another one leading into it. And another. And another. In no time the two-track was a well-worn dirt road used by bear and deer hunters in the fall, trout fishermen in the spring, and snowmobilers all winter long. A half-hour later we were on pavement, or at least southern Marquette County's version of it. It never looked so good.

By then the morning was getting a little long in the tooth. I didn't recognize the stretch of road we were on, but had a hunch

91

we were north of the cabin. Shortly thereafter, a pickup truck bumped along on large, wide-looking tires, the fittings for a snow plow obscuring its grill. I flagged it down. "Jump in," the driver said. "Your dog will be fine in the back." I unloaded my shotgun, set it on the seat, and helped Toby on board amidst the empty beer cans, spent shotshells and a spare tire in the back. I noticed a bumper sticker on a toolbox the size of a suitcase: *"You can't borrow these tools unless you payed for them!"*

"Where are you headed?" The driver asked, in an accent resonating with Finnish ancestry.

When I described where the cabin was, the truck slowed, then turned into another two-track. A chain was across the trail, and a sign affixed to the center: *Trespassers will be violated.* He threw the truck in reverse, and backed up. I think he felt sorry for us, but he'd probably tell all his pals about the guy from "down below" (the Mackinac Bridge) who he helped rescue. They'd be laughing about that one all winter long when the snow piled up and there was nothing else to do but chuckle about the foreigners. The humiliation was a small price to pay for a ride to safety.

When I made it back to the cabin, I fried up some cudighi with sliced onions, placed it on a sliced hoagie bun, and wolfed it down. Three hours later I woke up to the Green Bay Packers playing football on the little black and white television.

What a night it had been, what a grand adventure we endured.

Thirteen

I NEVER TOLD ANYONE about my night in the woods. I was too ashamed, too embarrassed. I tucked that memory away in the deep, dark places in my mind. It was the kind of secret that people tell their shrink about, and hope that they can make things better.

I told everyone at the office that I had a great weekend up north. They wouldn't have cared about the bear or the grouse hunting necessarily, but the real important things—like the color of the leaves. Folks in Northern Michigan routinely drive around ogling at the red, yellow, and amber leaves of autumn.

It was relatively easy to assuage my fears when the incident was already in my rearview mirror.

Monday morning, I turned on my computer and looked at my e-mail before my first appointment. Taren sent me a short message:

> Jim,
> Thanks for the note. We'll have to hook up soon.
> There doesn't seem to be much with that Atmantle
> outfit. They seem legit according to my sources.
> Take care, Taren.

She made me mad. *Don't blow me off, Taren*, I thought. I sat up in my chair and rolled up my sleeves. I was going to send her a reply that would make her head spin:

Taren, For Christ's sake, don't be so… Miss Peacock rapped on the door. *Damn.*

"Yes."

"Your ten o'clock is waiting. It's a double-session. Here are the orders from the court…District Fifty-four-A."

"Double session? District Fifty-four-A?"

"Yup. Darvin Wonch, fifty-three, bankruptcy, court ordered forty hours of counseling. The guy was supposed to start last week but we didn't have anyone here to counsel him."

"District what?"

"Fifty-four in Lansing."

"And why are we getting him and not someone down there?"

Miss Peacock crossed her arms, raised her eyebrows and gave me the look that all secretaries give their bosses when the bosses have crossed the line of common sense. "I'm just doing my job, Jim. The guy has been here before, and the judge sent him up here because of that."

"How long ago was he here?"

"Couple months. Here's his chart, not much to it. Paid cash. You hardly wrote down anything about his session, other than he had some incident at the horse track." She kept flipping through the folder, raising and lowering the papers inside.

She put his file on my outstretched hand and said, "Good luck."

"Thanks. I'm sorry for being so grouchy. You do a wonderful job here…"

"Shucks, Jim. That was nice of you. You're not being grouchy; you're just a shrink and you get paid to analyze every detail. I know lunch is still two hours away but we're ordering a pizza from Pisanello's…want some?"

"When did they start opening for lunch?"

She gave me the look again.

"Oh, sorry…that would be great."

"Good luck."

I'm not so sure "good luck" is the best thing to say in that scenario, but I wasn't about to criticize her for that either. It would just lead to another apology. Perhaps "have fun" or "keep smiling" would have been more appropriate. Anyway, Darvin Wonch didn't have much in his file. The orders from the court-house made up the bulk of the file. My notes were vague: *Stolen snowmobile, nearly killed at the track.* It seemed strange that I could barely remember him.

I hoped that his face would ring a bell.

And it did.

"Morning, Darvin. Come on in."

I recognized him right away—the gold chain, the gaudy watch, and the bizarre-looking fingernails. He was the guy that gave his son a mini-snowmobile, then had to pawn it to pay off some gambling debt. It was the same guy who said his wife sent him to us, and that she thought he had a gambling problem. Darvin denied he had a problem even after two guys wanted him dead. I remembered all about him.

"Well, it looks like we're going to be spending some time together," I asked him.

He nodded, and rolled his eyes at me.

I showed him the court order, and explained that I would be the one to fill out the documents. After his forty hours were completed, I'd send my report to the judge, and he would rule on the bankruptcy hearing.

He nodded.

"How did this happen?"

"What?"

"The bankruptcy?"

"My accountant said it was the only way out."

"Only way out of what?"

"The trouble I'm in."

"What trouble is that?" I asked.

"Let's not play games right now, okay?"

I was getting under his skin. He was pissed already. "The only reason I'm here is because the judge told me to. My lawyer said I should come here just to keep him happy."

"That's good advice…you don't want judges mad at you."

"Do you think this is funny?" His face reddened. "Do you think this is a joke?"

I raised my eyebrows, Miss Peacock style. "Mr. Wonch, the only thing I want from you this morning is for you to explain the trouble you're in, and apparently you can't explain it, or you don't want to acknowledge…"

"Isn't it all right there in front of you?" He interrupted, "The papers…the court order?"

"Sure, they show that you've filed for bankruptcy, but you said you were in trouble. Now I want you to tell me what the trouble is."

"It's financial trouble." He looked away.

I let him simmer for a minute. He took several deep breaths, and threw in a few sighs. All dramatics.

"Can you explain it for me?"

"I don't make enough money to keep up with my bills. How's that?"

I nodded. "How did it happen?"

"Do we have to get into all of that?"

I nodded again. "That's why you're here. What did you think we were going to talk about for the next thirty-nine and a half hours?"

"It's not rocket surgery," he said impatiently. "I earn 'x' amount of money but I owe 'y' and the difference between the two is the reason I've had to declare bankruptcy."

"Okay, that's fair, but what happened…did you take a pay cut, or get demoted, or lose your job?"

"No."

"Have a medical emergency?"

"No."

"Mr. Wonch," I said, "Why don't you tell me what happened?"

For the next hour and twenty minutes Darvin rambled on about a variety of topics; some were related to gambling and others weren't. He was animated, and enjoyed the spotlight, where he could tell me all about himself and his accomplishments. Some guys like to beat their chests and tell the world about their success.

I let him ramble, and when he came to a topic that was somewhat sensitive, I really didn't push him, but rather polished him up with praise. It worked. He opened up to me, about his childhood, his education, and his climb up the corporate ladder.

When Darvin was a boy he and his pals bet on everything from the number of times they could skip a rock across the surface of Walloon Lake, to the number of times their math teacher would clear his throat in an hour. When that got boring, they'd bet on the scores on their math tests. He loved math in grade school, high school and college. He majored in statistics at the University of Michigan and "loved the odds of probability."

After graduation he got a job in the actuarial department for an insurance company. He set the rates in workman's compensation, autos and homeowners policies, but also predicted the probability of losses among certain demographics, agencies, and locations of the state. His predictions were dead right. The company was so impressed; they had him turn his attention to claims where he devised a formula for settling liability claims quickly, fairly, and before the claimant could hire a lawyer. He called it "a severity index" that took into account every claim that had ever been settled by the company. If a claimant broke his leg in a car accident, Darvin came up with a "settlement cheater" based on the claimant's age, occupation, and a host of other variables. The "cheater' was actually a computer program he devised that allowed clerks to fill in the variables, come up with the correct amount of the claim, and send off the check to the claimant. Three days after the company was informed of a liability loss, the claimant had a check in his hands, and an easy-to-read release that Darvin had created himself. The bosses embraced his ingenuity, and were able to lower their overhead by laying off almost all their claims adjusters.

By the time Darvin was in his mid-forties he had gained quite a reputation within the ranks of the company's regional headquarters. They liked his cost-cutting schemes and his connections with the state's lawmakers and lobbying firms. Darvin's next move was a logical one: to the company's home office in Southern California.

His new wife would hear nothing of it. "She was just a Midwestern girl who liked the idea of raising their kids close to home. Michigan was home for her, and me too. We'd be like a fish without a bicycle." Darvin may have been quick with a calculator, but he had problems with commonly-used phrases.

"What did you and your wife have in common?" I asked.

He paused for a minute or so.

"She liked to gamble…to go gaming. Here's a case in point: we'd travel to different casinos across the state and Canada, and go to Vegas a couple times a year. She'd sit there at the nickel slot machines for hours at a time, and had a knack for when to stay with a machine or move on."

"No kidding?"

"Oh yeah, she was good, but then again, so was I." He laughed. "We used to kid ourselves that we had the genetics to make children that were good gamblers too." More laughter.

"What happened?"

"We had children, a boy and a girl, and who knows if they're going to be good gamblers. If I had to bet, I think my son will be better at poker than…"

"No…I meant with your wife."

"She moved out last week." He shook his head and played with a nuggety-looking ring on his right hand. More sighs. "She folded her cards, cashed in her chips, and bailed on me. Took the kids and moved in with her parents. Some wife, huh? She just doesn't understand me. She quit going to the casinos with me years ago. I should have seen the writing on the wall."

"What writing?"

"That she wasn't into gambling the way she used to be…"

He only had ten minutes left in his two-hour marathon, and I still wasn't clear on how he got in over his head. I smelled pizza. And blood.

"I would like to know more about the way you handle your money. Be honest, I would like to know about credit cards, your mortgage, second mortgage, all that."

"Sure I got credit cards. I play the game."

I scratched my head. "What game?"

"With introductory rates and low interest payments…the credit cards offer you 4.9% interest for the first sixty days of your card, but by the time the higher interest rate kicks in, you move it to somebody else."

"How many cards do you have?"

"Eight or ten…like most Americans"

"How much credit card debt do you have?"

"About a hundred and ten thousand," he said, quietly. "It's a lot, I know."

What a dumb ass, I thought. "That's not a lot, that's a ton!"

"I know, but if I had better luck it would be nothing."

"What do you mean?"

"Me and the wife agreed that it was stupid to carry that much debt, so we took out a second mortgage on the house… you know…an interest-only loan on your house's equity?"

"Sure, I'm with you."

"The bank loaned us an extra ninety-three thousand, which was cool."

The dumb ass. "Don't tell me," I said.

"I had a really bad string of luck though. Bad casinos. Bad dealers. You probably don't understand."

"You're wrong. I do understand, Darvin."

He lightened up. "You like to gamble?" He half smiled.

"No, that's not what I meant. I understand your situation perfectly. You have a gambling problem, plain and simple. You need some help."

He shook his head no, and shrugged his shoulders. "No, it's just been a string of bad luck."

"Okay, fine. Is there anybody that you would believe if they told you that you had a gambling problem?"

"No."

"Well, if you're not going to believe me, how about your wife?"

"No."

"Your kids?"

He shook his head.

"The judge? The bank? Your lawyer?"

"No...they all..."

"How about the two thugs that want to kill you?"

"I don't play at their track anymore."

"Darvin...you got a problem, man."

"Do not."

"What about your employer?"

He looked at me plain and simple. "I'm the top dog at the company. They can't fire me."

"And your gambling problem hasn't affected your performance at work, right?"

"That's right."

I should have guessed.

"What do you do, anyway?" I asked.

"I'm the president of a company. The top dog. The grand poobah."

"Of what?"

"It's a small, regional-type company with headquarters not far from here. I started it myself a dozen years ago, with nothing more than my two hands, and the money from my old employer's 401k. Gotta lot of blood, sweat, and tears into it. We only have a hundred and twenty employees or so, based in Lansing. You've probably never heard of them, like I said we're a small company. I don't know why the name is relevant."

"I'm curious. Most people are proud of the company they work for, especially men. They gain a sense of worth from the company…"

He looked at me as if he was giving me the time of day. It was simple for him to say, but the four little words poured from his lips as easily as a breakfast order at a diner. "Atmantle Health and Casualty."

What did you just say? I couldn't believe what I just heard. "I'm sorry, Darvin, what was that?"

He repeated himself, very slowly, "Atmantle Health and Casualty."

You son of a bitch.

My heart sank in my chest. I couldn't believe my ears. I thought it was a joke, or a set-up. "Have you ever heard of it?" He asked, matter-of-factly.

"Um, yeah…"

"Are you okay?"

"Sure. Sure."

"You look like you've just seen a ghost."

"Sorry. I apologize. Really, I don't want to offend you." I was stammering. "I'm a diabetic, and my sugar is low. And high…it's time that we wrapped this thing up. Your two hours are finished and I'd better get something to eat. I'll see you soon."

"Whatever. Just sign my paper, will you?"

"Sure. Sure, I will."

Good old Darvin Wonch put on his leather jacket, cinched the belt across his midriff, and sauntered outside.

I sat in my chair for several minutes in disbelief. The man partly responsible for my wife's death was now in my care. The guy who denied our claim for health benefits was sitting across the room from me. The guy with all the accomplishments wrecked my life, and was also my new client. It made me sick to my stomach.

I stayed in my seat. Thinking, thinking, talking to myself. "What are you going to do, Jim?"

You really should tell him that you couldn't handle his case anymore. The conflict of interest is clear. You could lose your license.

Just then, Miss Peacock poked her head inside and said that the pizza was getting cold. I told her that I lost my appetite and that maybe I'd have some later. She asked me who I was talking to but I shrugged her off.

On the other hand, You really should see where this thing could go.

Stay with it.

Get even.

Carrie would approve.

In one session you could get more ammunition against Atmantle than Glen Morrison could in a week's worth of depositions.

As I sat there weighing my options, I thought about my life and all the crazy things that happened since Carrie's death. I am a scatter-brained, reckless nitwit. I can't stay focused. I'm alone, and lonely. I've been searching for something or someone to give me a reason to live. I have no wife, no kids, a distant family, and a psychotic dog that pisses in his food bowl and barks at his turds. If I keep counseling the guy and somebody finds out, my career is over. My license isn't worth much either. Nobody will hire me.

Nobody cares.

I thought being lost in the woods and how similar it was to my predicament now. I *had* no compass when I was lost. I *have* no moral compass when it comes to Carrie. I am lost in the woods, without a clue to which way to turn.

Was it fate that brought Darvin to me? Was it fate that made those two grouse appear at dusk when I was lost and hungry up north? If I didn't get that lucky break up in the woods I wouldn't have had much to eat. If I don't pursue Darvin now, I'll be giving up a golden opportunity, a pair of grouse in hand.

It was a lucky break; it was fate. Darvin Wonch was in my lap, and I wasn't going to let him free. And if I played my cards right, I just might be able to pull it off without getting into trouble with Calypso Steve.

I turned to the computer, swished the mouse, and the screen came to life. The curser was where I left it, to the right of Taren's name. I hit the backspace key until everything but her name was gone. The words erupted from my soul; they bled the icy, cold fury of revenge.

> *Stand by, Taren,* I typed.
> *This is going to get really ugly.*

Fourteen

A T ALMOST ONE that afternoon we all got together at the conference room to celebrate Mary Cornwall's birthday. We usually make a big deal out of birthdays, if nothing else than to get together for a fifteen-minute break. Our head nurse was making small talk with the recipient rights advocate near the coffee pot. The human resources manager was standing there, arms crossed uncomfortably, wishing he was somewhere else, I ventured. He was a curious fellow—uncomfortable in social settings, but surely considered himself a "people person" during the hiring process. I couldn't see him making the decision to fire someone—anyone—because it might make waves. He seemed to be the type to avoid conflict. He'd rather be liked by a handful of people because he was a nice guy, than be admired by everyone because he had the guts to do what was right.

Miss Peacock brought in a chocolate cake that she proclaimed, "Took her four hours to bake." We all laughed half-heartedly, knowing full well that her statement was far from the truth. All she did was go to the bakery at the south end of town and had them doll up one of their German chocolate cakes with a little inscription on the top. Mary was all smiles when she opened the box and read, "Happy Twenty-Ninth Doc!" She gave Miss Peacock a modest hug and thanked her very much for the gesture.

Mary was in her mid-thirties, just entering the prime of her life. Never married; she seemed to rule out the possibility.

There was something or someone that prevented her from even thinking of the notion. I could read Mary like a book: she had a troubled past, and a skeleton in her closet. There are certain things that you leave alone, and Mary's past, as well as her personal life, were two of them.

One of the orderlies popped his head in the break room and wished her a happy birthday. "Hey, don't mind if I do," he said, scooping a wedge-shaped piece of cake on a paper plate. We watched him as he poured a cup of coffee and stirred in a spoonful of creamer. Calypso Steve asked him if everyone's meds had been dispersed. The orderly nodded, almost apologetically, shoveling cake into his mouth while gripping his plastic fork like a screwdriver. In less than a minute the cake was gone and he disappeared into the hallway.

"Gee whiz, Steve," Mary said. "Have you lost your tact? All the guy wanted was a piece of cake."

"What?" Steve asked, as if he had no idea what she was talking about. "He took the first piece, before the birthday girl."

"Never mind." She looked at me, and rolled her eyes, as if I was supposed to back her up. I let it go, figuring that I'd have nothing to gain if I came to her rescue on such a trivial thing as Steve's little escapade with the orderly. Instead, I pulled out a greeting card from the breast pocket of my sport coat and handed it to her. "Oh, thanks," she smiled.

For a moment or two we watched her fumble with the thick paper envelope. Someone asked her the usual birthday question: "Feel any older?" She laughed again. "Let's see here… *When I found out how old you are…I almost croaked.*" More laughter. "Thank you everyone, that was so nice…I think." We all signed the card that had a picture of a frog on the front, along with *Happy Birthday* inside. "That's really nice."

"Oh Mary, we're just getting started," Steve cried. "Behind door number two we have this grand prize." He had a small, rectangular box in his hands, wrapped in fine, shiny paper.

"Why thank you, Steve. You didn't have to do that." She pulled at the pretty red bow and asked if it was the two-week sabbatical to St. Thomas that she always wanted.

"I wish…"

"Oh, my." She crinkled the paper in her hand, but had a confused look on her face. "A bottle of Red perfume. I don't know what to say. Thank you." Her cheeks were as red as the bottle in her hands.

"You're welcome. Read the card."

We couldn't believe that he gave her *that* for a present. It seemed to be a little much for a coworker. After all, Red is an expensive brand of perfume, known more for its sexually charged advertising than its actual use. We watched her find the tiny card around the neck of the bottle. Her reaction was less than enthusiastic. "Oh my, look what time it is," she said. "I've got some work to do."

Calypso Steve told her to wait, but she marched right by him, stomping her heels on the ancient tile more forcefully than usual. The HR director wandered back to his office, and so did everyone else. Miss Peacock wrapped the cake in clear plastic wrap and placed it on the top shelf in the refrigerator. Nobody wanted to be nosey. Nobody really had the guts to ask Steve what the card said. Except me.

He tossed his little paper plate in the garbage can under the sink. I was waiting for him with the coffee grounds in one hand and a small bottle of dish soap in the other. "Do you want to wash or dry?"

"Oh…sure. I'll dry."

Steve was notorious for leaving certain communal jobs for everyone else. By judging his reaction, I was certain that he'd planned on pitching his coffee cup in the sink with the others and going back to his miserable little office. After discussing the results of the Wolverine's football game, I brought up the business with the perfume.

"What?"

"Steve, you don't give a coworker stuff like perfume."

"Why not?" He asked. "I like her, and since she doesn't have anyone in her life to get her things like that, I figured that she'd appreciate it."

"She doesn't have anyone in her life because that's her choice."

"Well she didn't give it back to me."

"That's not the point."

"Why don't you tell me exactly what is your point, Mr. Counselor?" He was getting angry, but I didn't care. The dumb ass.

"Don't get defensive; it's just a matter of professionalism." I replied in my best shrink voice. "You've got to maintain a certain amount of distance between yourself and your coworkers. I can't believe you don't know that. You could be hung out to dry if she decides to sue for sexual harassment."

"Are you finished, Mr. Professionalism?"

"As a matter of fact, I'm not."

"I don't have to listen to this."

He crossed his arms, but I kept on going. "Does your wife know what you bought Mary?" I asked more strongly.

He tossed his dish towel on the cupboard, and jabbed his index finger in my chest. "Don't forget who you're talking to, Mr. Subordinate. I'm the one that hands out the job performance reports around here. You won't get a raise around here until you're sixty-five, and nobody in their right mind will hire a quack with a lousy record."

I think he was waiting for me to move his hand, or punch him in the stomach, but I didn't do either. I couldn't believe that he'd stoop that low in the gutter. What a creep. What a tool. "Mr. Personality" seemed to be building a case against me, even though he was the one that was wrong.

From now on, I'd have to watch my back where he was concerned.

Fifteen

LORD ONLY KNOWS THAT I needed the money from the Centre. I was just starting to make a dent in my student loans, thanks to the one-for-two payoff that they were providing. But still, my balance was a huge number. It seemed that it would take me a lifetime to get it paid.

Carrie came out of her undergrad work with relatively little in debt—fifteen thousand dollars. Law school was a different matter, where she racked up another thirty thousand. I didn't have any life insurance on her, for a variety of reasons, and none of them very good. Still, even now, somebody had to pay off the loans, and between my in-laws and myself we would do our best.

Her medical bills were staggering. I owed the hospital, the clinics, and the labs $123,000. They each accepted my monthly checks of a hundred dollars each but at the rate I was going, I would need two lifetimes to get it paid.

And that's what was so depressing about my situation. I lost my wife, which was bad enough, but then I had to pay for it too. When I went to school and envisioned my career, I never thought that things would be this bad. After all, you go to school to further your education, so that you're more market-able in your chosen field. I could have dropped out of school, bagged groceries for a living, and would have been further ahead. Now, though, I was in financial ruin.

Toby didn't know the difference. After our adventure to Marquette County, Toby didn't greet me at the door, which was unusual. He was sprawled out on his fleece-padded floor mat, like an unsuspecting speed bump. Oh sure, he acknowledged my presence with a few thumps of his tail, but there wasn't much more to his greeting. In a way I felt sorry for him. He poured so much into the weekend's hunting adventure that he was stiff and sore. When I bent down and patted his belly, he was covered from his ears to his genitals in scrapes and scratch-es. And his jowls; they needed a serious coating of balm.

But Toby didn't miss an opportunity to whiz in his food bowl. Crazy dog. After cleaning up that mess, I pried him off the floor and lead him outside. He was stiff-legged and sore. All he did was taste the air and sneeze, seemingly ridding himself of the Upper Peninsula's odor. Maybe that wasn't all he was try-ing to get rid of; the memory of the bear certainly was worthy of expulsion.

I left the old hound to his bliss and went upstairs, where I turned on the computer, took off my trousers and checked the answering machine. My mother-in-law had called to say hello and make plans for dinner in Ann Arbor. By the time I changed into a sweatshirt and blue jeans the computer was busy down-loading a document of considerable size. I peeked through the slats in the Venetian blinds and watched Toby stand in the yard as the leaves whistled around his legs. He was barking at his poop again.

What a dog.

I reached for the photo of Carrie and me on our wedding day. She was so beautiful when she floated up the aisle, the stained glass dappling shades of pastel on her white gown. She looked like an angel. The church was hot that day, and I remember the little bead of sweat on her upper lip. I'm sure I had a bead there as well. We were nervous, excited, and thrilled to be there. We had our whole lives ahead of us. We had a wonderful future.

The computer screen brought me out of my trance. My mother-in-law was the first message. I always looked forward to her calls and e-mails because she was direct and to the point. She didn't mince words or dance around with silly questions like "How are you?" That's not to say that she didn't care about me, she had more subtle ways to open the dialog.

> *Jim,*
>
> *I left a message on your machine, but figured I might as well e-mail you. Carrie's father and I have resolved matters with the life insurance company, and we want you to have half of the benefits. We know that you have taken on a lot of her medical bills, her loans, and who knows what all. It's just our way of helping out. You're family, and we take care of ours. It's probably not enough to retire all her debt, but we want you to have it. Your share is $75,000 and I'll send it out this week, or maybe we could get together for a bite to eat.*
>
> *By the way, Uncle Jim wants to know about your visit to the cabin, and told me to say hello.*
>
> *We'd like to visit you soon, to catch up on things. Hope all is well with you and that animal. Love.*
>
> *Mom*

I nearly fell out of my chair…seventy-five thousand was a lot of money. She was right, however, it still wouldn't be enough to retire Carrie's loans and medical bills, but I certainly wouldn't refuse it either. At least I'd be on the plus side of things, and not living hand-to-mouth. Her comment about "Hope all is well" was her way of saying, "let me know if you want to talk." I always liked her. She is still family to me, too.

The last e-mail, which took so long to load, was from the monument company. They had photos of several headstones for Carrie with the inscription I gave them several weeks prior. The stones were of diverse sizes and shapes, and the fonts varied from fancy to ornate. At the bottom of each image were the dimensions, the type of granite, along with the price, "installed." Thank goodness they cleared that up. I couldn't imagine "installing" it myself.

I answered both e-mails and got on with things. I seemed to be on a roller coaster of life—the highs kept getting higher, the lows not so low. Carrie *did* mean the world to me, but with every day that passed I was clawing my way free of the grief.

Sixteen

RACHEL WAS MY FIRST appointment Tuesday morning. She was the one with the self-diagnosed depression, the low self-esteem, and the tremendously inquisitive nature.

She was also the one with all the perfume. I don't know what brand she wore, but she definitely used a lot of it. It permeated the office, the couch, even the wastebasket, where she threw out the tissues she used to dab her nose. I've always been a perfume-liking kind of guy. If a woman wants to wear it, I'd be happy to smell it. Call me a weirdo, but that's just me.

Lord knows that I never asked Rachel why she wears the perfume she does. That would be unprofessional. Gradually though I noticed that the scent of her had been getting stronger, as she made more and more strides towards happiness. There were other signs that suggested she was on the road to recovery. In the heat of summer she wore dreadfully large sweatshirts that were so long that they covered her hands. When most women her age would be wearing as little as possible, she bundled up for some odd reason. She had a pretty face and hair, but chose to hide her appearance behind long, unkempt bangs.

Lately though, she was different. Even though it was autumn, when daily temperatures averaged in the upper fifties—so a sweatshirt was appropriate—she seemed to wear less clothing. She wore half-hearted cardigan sweaters that barely covered her sleeveless tee shirts. She got a haircut and kept her hair in a ponytail or in a bunch on the top of her head. And her face—no longer was it making eye contact with the floor. Her chin was up, to match her confidence. She wasn't exactly smiling a lot, but she was hardly the depressed young lady who first came to see me.

And in a strange way I noticed things about her that I probably shouldn't. She was cute, plain and simple, and she stirred a part of me that was dormant for quite some time. Even though it is taboo to engage in sexual relations with a client, I was still a man, and prone to fleeting thoughts of lust, or a fantasy here or there.

I had forgotten what it was like to share my life with anyone other than Carrie. I missed Carrie's stories about a bitter client, an impossible judge, or a jerk for an opponent that she had faced in the courtroom. I missed the hand holding and the easy conversation over a glass of wine at the end of a long day. I had forgotten what it was like to lie down with a woman—and watch her sleep. I liked to watch her bosom rise and fall with each breath, to watch her get dressed in the morning, and to unfasten her bra in the dim of candlelight. But those intimate images were more distant now, and harder to remember.

Carrie liked to undress herself in front of me. She'd take her time, and peel her clothes off, item by item. She'd wriggle her hips and let her skirts fall, inch by inch. I never was any good at unfastening her bra. It was more fun to watch her do it anyway. Ah, the joys of being young and happily married.

I would have never said anything about Rachel's physical attributes. Her hot button was trust. If I said anything, what little trust she seemed to have in me would have been ruined.

I say "little" because our sessions were hardly engaging. They were light-hearted, whimsical, and almost non-productive. We covered serious topics such as her hair, her taste in music, and what her class schedule was for this semester. I wanted to ask her what made her turn herself around, but figured that as long as she was headed in the right direction and keeping the channels of communication open, I figured that it was a good thing.

I thought about Rachel a lot. I felt like she was getting better and no longer needed my help. I was also starting to feel like she was missing out on what I could offer outside the confines of a patient/doctor relationship. I thought about her when I cooked dinner for Toby and me. I thought about her before I went to sleep. I wished there was more I could do for her.

Behind that pretty face, nice figure and fruity scent was a deeper story waiting to be told.

Seventeen

I CERTAINLY EARNED SOME brownie points where Mary
Cornwall was concerned. Word got back to Mary that I had
confronted the jerk down the hall. She had just about had it
with Calypso Steve, his suggestive comments, and the lousy
perfume he gave her. All she wanted was to come to work and
do her job. Most employers would be happy to have such an effective, efficient, and steady worker. Most organizations would
take a hundred employees just like Mary Cornwall. She was a
great colleague and a really good person.

At mid morning I poked my head into her office to say
hello. "What's up in the loony bin?"

"Good morning to you too, Jim," she smiled, gesturing for
me to close the door.

"So how was the rest of your birthday?"

"You mean after the incident with the dope down the
hall?"

"Something like that."

"It was good. We went out to eat and stuff."

"That's good. You only turn twenty-nine once, right?"

"What brings you by, anyway?" She asked, laughing.

"Nothing. I just wanted to tell you what happened after you left the party yesterday afternoon."

"I heard the news," she said. "Now give me the Paul Harvey."

I told her about Calypso Steve's diatribe, and him calling me all those derogatory "Misters." She rolled her eyes and shook her head. "What's his deal anyway?"

"You mean with the 'mister this' and 'mister that'?"

"Yes."

"I'm not sure," I said. "I think we could have some fun with him, though."

"How so?"

"My couch, your drugs, and an hour or two of intense therapy."

She picked up her prescription pad and waved her index finger back and forth. "You're horrible. Besides, he's too white bread, too boring."

"Right."

"He wouldn't need any drugs to tell us why he calls everybody mister."

"I know," I said, now waving my finger. "His second grade teacher probably called him that, and anytime he gets in a bind he reverts to his childhood."

"Maybe she made him pee his pants, then called him Mr. Puddle."

"Oh stop, Mary. You're cruel."

"Jim, come on, you've heard weird stuff before…besides, he's a jerk."

"I know it and you know it, but you don't have to be that mean about it."

"That's easy for you to say, Jim. You're not the one he's pursuing."

"True." I watched her put the prescription pad back in her

top drawer, without locking it. "Don't put that away just yet," I said. "I need a favor."

"Why...do you need some happy pills?"

"It's not for me," I said.

"Are you sure?"

"Yes...it's for Joe, remember?"

"The catatonic widower?" She asked.

"Right," I nodded.

"Is he still a mess?"

"Is the Pope Catholic?"

"Jim!"

"Oh yeah, he's a mess. Hasn't had communion in months."

"You're horrible," she said. "Besides, that's not funny."

"I just want a little help."

"Just a minute." She pulled up Joe's chart electronically. I watched her and the way she crossed one knee over the other. "You know Jim, he really should be out of his stupor by now. Does he act dopey or anything?"

"I don't know..."

"Does he act like he's been drugged?" She plied again.

"You just asked me that in another form."

"I know, doc, remember, I'm a shrink, too. Just answer the question."

I laughed. She had me there. Joe and I get together and don't do much of anything. Our appointments were as good for me as they were for him. I just talked at him, stream-of-consciousness style. Whatever I thought, I blurted out. My aim was to get him to talk. It didn't work. Nothing did. All he did was stare. "I don't think so, Mary. Nothing seems to help him."

"That's fair," she nodded.

"What do you suggest?"

"Why don't we turn the tables on Soundless Joe?" She nodded again.

"How so?"

"Do you think there's anyway he could be faking his condition?" She asked, uncrossing her legs.

"Joe?" I asked. "I don't know. What did you have in mind?"

"How about giving him some gel-caps?"

"What's that?"

"A placebo," she said, matter-of-factly.

"Really?"

"Yup. What have we got to lose?"

"Right. He hasn't gotten any better on the other stuff."

"Exactly…and I think there's more to Joe's story," she suggested.

"How so?"

"How did his wife die? And don't say suicide."

"She did."

"Yoo-hoo, I know."

"Boy you're testy…she overdosed on sleeping pills, had a blood alcohol rate of 2.5, then asphyxiated herself."

"Hat trick, huh?"

"I beg your pardon?" I asked.

"What did the police say?" She asked, impatiently tapping her nails.

Mary had a way of making me feel silly, the way she mumbled one-liners. "They thought it was legit. What do you think?"

"Let me get this straight. Joe can sit up and eat his food, take showers, go to the bathroom by himself, but doesn't say boo? Is that right?"

"Pretty much."

"I thought I smelled a rat," she said emphatically. She looked at her watch, then her calendar. It was time for me to leave. "Why don't you keep an extra sharp eye on him? He's got something to hide, something to tell. I just know it."

Eighteen

SEVERAL DAYS LATER I RECEIVED a packet of material from the Office of Consumer Affairs in Lansing, Michigan. Inside was a copy of the letter I sent them, stamped "Received," and a typed note, *Enclosed please find the names and addresses of the complainants against Atmantle Health and Casualty. Please be advised that we do not have the capability to disclose the nature of their complaints; the cost and energy required would make it prohibitively expensive.*

That was fine. If they had to make a copy of every complaint it would have taken them all day. I had what I was after, and that was the list. At first glance, I noticed that the complainants were from all over the state. There was one from up near the cabin, and plenty from the most populated areas of the state. I noticed a name from Bad Axe, a small town at the top of Michigan's thumb that Uncle Jim used to call "nasty hatchet."

The Office of Consumer Affairs regulated my profession too. They were the people that issued the licenses, and who sent me friendly reminders that my continuing education credits needed to be completed. They were the people that investigated complaints against psychologists, physical therapists, dentists, and all sorts of health professionals. Fortunately, I didn't have any complaints against me, which was a good thing. The word on the street was that once the regulators received a complaint, they poked and prodded in areas that had nothing to do with the original case. In an effort to justify their existence, they had to find misgivings. The fines they levied helped pay their salaries.

Atmantle Health and Casualty seemed to be immune from inquiry, resistant to recourse. Almost all the complaints were dismissed.

Toby and I had fallen into a routine that wasn't especially admirable. I was losing my interest in cooking. The pride I once took in preparing meals for Carrie and me was gone. Instead of filling the crock-pot with the ingredients for Italian round steak like I used to do a couple of times a month, I was relying on a frozen package of chicken patties for dinner. I watched television non-stop. I needed something to fill my evenings, something more to live for.

And so, I tried cooking spaghetti. Toby watched me intently as I fried a hamburger patty for the sauce. He should have been more tired, as we squeezed in an hour of grouse hunting east of Mt. Pleasant after work. He just sat there; drool sliding from each jowl, eyes glued to the ceremony. I asked him what was wrong, but all he did was lick his chops and sit more urgently on his haunches the way dogs do. When the patty was browned and crumbled, I poured some of the grease over his food. He dove right in, choking down the kibbles as if it were his last supper.

By the time he was finished, the pasta was nearly cooked. I plunged a fork into the boiling pot and pulled out a single noodle, but before I could blow on it, the darn thing slithered off the fork and onto Toby's back. He didn't think anything of it until his meal was finished, and he smelled something delicious. He reached for the smell, but couldn't quite get to it. And so, around and around he spun, chasing after the aroma that was so hard to reach.

A moment later I had the noodles draining in a colander. I decided to torture Toby by putting more of the warm, sticky pieces of spaghetti on his coat. But Toby wasn't stupid; he tried to snare the pieces out of midair, and did a pretty fair job of it. Any time he missed, however, I had an opening to lay one across his tail or ears. After five minutes of fun, I decided to leave the old boy alone. Besides, he looked like he was wearing dreadlocks. I had to laugh. He made me smile.

For the first time in months I ate at the kitchen table. No television blaring. No computer screen to stare at. I read the paper, front to back, and looked up the stock reports. It always amazes me how the so-called "experts" have built-in alibis for why or why not the market performs. "Investors were concerned about the drop in manufactured orders, so stocks took a nosedive." How do they know that? How does a drop in manufactured goods affect the stock price of a telecommunications company based out of Singapore?

"Initial public offerings" are another source of intrigue for me. "IPOs" as they are known, involve the sale of a private company to the general public in the form of "shares." Typically, the privately-held company goes public to infuse the company with cash. Even though I didn't have any money to invest, it seemed that everyone else was making boat loads of cash by investing on IPOs. I promised myself that someday I would play the market and make some easy money, just like everyone else.

After dinner I did the dishes, then went to the garage to clean the pair of grouse we killed earlier in the day. Toby, now free of his edible ornaments, watched me with one eye as I brought the birds inside for rinsing. He jumped off his little quilted pillow and followed me to the sink. I give him the grouse hearts, that's part of our routine.

The other part of the routine is when we comb the burrs out of his coat. He always complains and makes a fuss, but I think he's glad when it's finished. I keep a two-sided hairbrush in the end table next to Carrie's favorite chair. It's the same chair that Toby used to sulk in after Carrie died. Anyway, I pull him up on my lap, and draw his hair through the teeth of the brush, placing hair, burrs and seeds into a round, glass ashtray. It's amazing how much hair you can pull out of a dog. You'd think that he'd have horrific clumps missing from his coat with the wads of hair missing. Last, but not least, I check the corners of his eyes for tiny seeds that might irritate a tear duct.

It was nearly eight o'clock when I went upstairs to the computer with the list from the Office of Consumer Affairs. Toby went along with me, his nails clicking the hardwood stairs. Before I had my e-mail on the screen, he had curled up into a ball. His nose was tucked under his spotted thigh; he looked like a newborn fawn in a May hayfield.

I looked at the names and addresses of all the complainants. They each had a story to tell, a tragedy hidden behind the broken promises of a shady insurance company. I wondered how many of them were just like me—making payments on medical bills that they never thought they'd have to pay, dealing with the grief of losing a loved one, then having the government deny their grievance. Oh sure, some of the medical bills must have been for relatively minor claims—like broken bones—but maybe Atmantle paid those because they were so small. There had to be something I could do. A complaint of my own seemed silly; they'd just deny mine too, if it was anything like the other complaints in my hand. I had to find out more about their claims, more about their stories.

And so, I finished up a couple of e-mails, and then wrote a letter on my laptop that was less than honest.

Dear...

My name is Jim Nunnelly, at the law firm of Morrison & Nunnelly. Our office is conducting an investigation into the Atmantle Health & Casualty Company and the way they pay or don't pay their claims. We understand that you have filed a complaint against Atmantle with the Office of Consumer Affairs in Lansing.

We also understand that your complaint was deemed "unjustified" by those officials.

At this time we would like to ask for your help in our investigation. We want to hear about your situation...what happened with Atmantle Health & Casualty, what they did with your claim, and what happened to the people who were denied. Please contact our offices at the number listed above, and tell us what happened.

> *Sincerely,*
> *James Nunnelly*

I looked at the computer screen and was quite proud of myself. It looked like a letter a lawyer would write. It sounded like a letter a lawyer would write too. I never said I was a *lawyer* with Morrison & Nunnelly, but anyone reading it must have thought that I was. Trouble was, *Nunnelly* was my wife's last name, not mine. She kept her maiden name when we got married, and I kept the boxes of letterhead and envelopes after she died. Glen had too much invested in the awnings, letterhead, websites and printing to change the name of the firm again. Four months after Carrie died, they still called it Morrison & Nunnelly. It was one of those things that Glen was going to get around to changing, but never did.

In no time I had the printer humming. I entered the people's names and addresses into a database, then linked them to the envelopes. Toby occasionally lifted his head to hear what all the commotion was about, yawned, and went back to sleep. At midnight I had a stack of envelopes eighteen inches high, each with my little letter inside. At midnight I dialed onto the Internet and sent Kathy an e-mail telling her what was going on. She's the legal assistant who works at the firm.

Just take down the people's names and phone numbers, and tell them that somebody will be contacting them soon. Please don't tell Glen, I reminded her. *He'll be happy about it later, trust me.*

And the best part of all? I had the names and addresses of complainants from three more states on the way, due to arrive any day.

It felt good to take out my frustrations on Atmantle. It felt good to finally be taking action against the company I felt was at least partly responsible for Carrie's death. I wasn't going to be a doormat for them, but a thorn in their side, and a very big thorn, indeed.

Nineteen

WARREN ARRIVED AT HIS APPOINTMENT obviously upset. He sat on the edge of his chair and buried his face in his hands. He pulled a tissue from the box, and blew his nose until it was a red cherub. All I could do was watch him writhe in his despair. I didn't say a thing.

Finally he started talking. Quietly. Very quietly, like he thought my office was bugged or something, and if he spoke quietly, the microphone wouldn't be able to record what he was saying. "I can't believe this. This whole thing. What a mess." I didn't need to ask. I knew what had happened, and could almost see it coming. "I just have to tell somebody what's going on."

"Warren," I started. "You sound upset."

"I am."

"Why don't you tell me?" I said, thinking that this was going to be a relatively easy session, where there's not much counseling going on, but a whole lot of listening.

"It's Sharon *and me*," he sobbed. He made the "*me*" sound like he wasn't there, like his naughty twin was the participant in their first tryst, and not the upstanding, repentant man that was seated on the couch across the room from me. I nodded my head, and he continued. "We've…" I wanted to hear him say it. I wanted to hear him say that he cheated on his wife. I got a version of it, "We've begun seeing each other…romantically…and I can't help myself."

What a bunch of baloney, 'can't help myself,' I thought. What I said was far different than what I thought. "What do you mean?"

"You know, I've told you a lot about her, and what she does for me. My ego. My stupid pride. I like to be near her. She is so much fun to be around." He wasn't crying any more, but kept a tissue in his hands.

"Sure, Warren. I remember."

"Well, the last appointment we had…things got out of hand."

"I thought you were going to see another physical therapist?"

"No. That's what you suggested."

"Okay. I remember now. You're right. How did it get out of hand?"

"Everything started out fine, I mean we were having fun and talking." He was smiling. "She made her innuendos, and I made mine. And that's the thing about flirting—you go back and forth. You try to one-up the other guy…I mean, the woman." I listened attentively. "And honestly, I wasn't doing much flirting…maybe a little, but nothing obvious. We finished our session, and I put my shirt on. When I went up front to schedule another appointment, she met me in the lobby and asked if I could give her a ride to the shop where her car was getting repaired. It sounded harmless enough, and the garage was on my way home."

On and on he went. I nodded.

"So a minute later she jumps in the front seat of my vehicle. You're not going to tell Irene about this, are you?"

"Warren, of course not, remember?"

"I know what you told me, but if she ever found out…my ass is grass."

"Right."

"You won't tell her?"

"No. I can't. It's one of the sacred principles of being a doctor. But why don't you tell her?"

"What? Are you nuts?"

"Some people think I am."

He laughed. "It's true…shrinks aren't the tightest wound ball in the bag, right?"

I gestured toward my temple with an index finger and made the universally accepted sign for the mentally disturbed. Now we both were laughing. It was one of those laughs that had a tail on it. It lingered there in the room for a moment, like Rachel's perfume. "What happened in the car?"

"I drive a Monte Carlo, with bucket seats, you know, and a console in between?"

"I'm with you."

"She said several times how grateful she was to get a ride. How she couldn't ask her husband because he's a workaholic. But then she did this about face, a U-turn in pit row if you know what I mean. 'Let's just forget about him,' she said. So I say 'Okay, let's forget about what's bugging us all together.' So it's about dinnertime, and she suggests that we stop for a bite to eat."

"How does that sit with you? I mean, would you like the thought of your wife having dinner with another man?"

"I know, I know…but this thing feels so right."

"Help me understand," I ordered him.

"We've already gone over this."

"True, but how does Sharon differ from Irene, when you met her?"

"It's just different, that's all I can tell you."

"That's fine, but why don't you tell me what has you so upset?"

"All right…I'm okay now. I dropped her off at the garage, and then we met at a restaurant around the corner. It felt weird. I was embarrassed that someone would recognize us but it was a weeknight and the place was almost empty. It felt weird that on every other occasion she had her hands all over me, but over dinner there wasn't any of that. You know what I mean?"

I nodded.

"So we order a couple drinks and some appetizers. I ask her if she's feeling weird too. She says 'I'm excited. This is exciting. It's part of the allure. I'm having fun with a friend who happens to be married.' I asked her what she meant by 'the allure,' and she told me straight up. She said 'Let's quit beating around the bush, and be open and honest. I think you are an amazing man. You're good looking, a good listener, caring, and considerate. You pay more attention to me in a half-hour appointment than I get in a week at home. I'm attracted to you, and I believe that you are to me. I want to see you more often, and the fact that this is so naughty makes it so much more fun.'

"Jim, I gotta tell you, her words shot through me. After so many years of neglect at home, her words were all I ever wanted to hear. And she's not some homely girl either. She's beautiful, and she really, really likes me. That's a thrill in itself…to have someone that adores you. You remember those days, don't you, Jim?"

"Kinda." I rolled my eyes. "But I can appreciate a guy in your position…" He laughed. "What happened after dinner?"

"During dinner!"

"Oh?"

"Oh yeah. She ran her toes up my pant leg, which was wild. I've never had that happen to me. While she toyed with the pasta on her plate, she batted her blue eyes at me. She licked her lips as if she wanted to kiss me. I wanted to kiss her right there. I mean her lips were like firm pasta…*al dente.*"

"Keep going," I said, appreciating the metaphor.

"I found myself falling for her. I wanted to run away with her, right there and forget all about my responsibilities. It feels so right. It has to be right."

"Did you kiss her?"

"Yes, but not until after dinner in the parking lot."

"Why there?"

"Because it was either that or follow her to a motel…"

"Really? Whose idea was that?"

"Hers."

"What stopped you?"

"I guess I wasn't quite ready for that."

"What do you mean?"

He paused. "I'm struggling with…" He paused again. "Keeping my vows to Irene."

"Is that what's got you so upset?"

"Yeah…" He reached for a tissue. "I've never really been tempted until now. I mean I've had a few women make advances toward me, but I was never attracted to them. I mean it's one thing to be tempted; it's a whole other thing to be tempted by *something tempting*. Know what I mean?" I nodded, and then he asked, "What should I do?"

"Warren, I understand what you mean, and I can't tell you what to do. You have to decide that for yourself."

"Okay, but what should I do?"

He didn't hear what I said. "What are your options?"

He blew his nose, tossed the tissue into the wastebasket, and continued "I could completely leave Irene, and Sharon for that matter, and start over without either of them. I could leave Irene and start over with Sharon, or leave Sharon and start over with Irene."

"Each option has its own set of consequences, right?" I asked.

"Right."

"So this isn't a matter of what I think you should do," I said, "but it's a matter of what you believe is your best option."

He nodded his head like he understood, but then asked a silly question, "So what do you think I should do?"

"Warren...I can't tell you. You have to decide for yourself."

"What would you do, if you were me?"

"Warren, if it were me, I would think long and hard about things before I went any further." He seemed to be a little insecure, a little unsure of himself. On one hand he was tied to his marriage to Irene, to his family and a well-rutted lifestyle. On the other hand he was drawn to a new and engaging woman who made him feel special.

In the weeks and months to come, Warren's life would get awfully, awfully complicated.

Twenty

I T WAS THE END OF OCTOBER when the state of Indiana mailed me the complaints against Atmantle Health & Casualty. The complaints were remarkably like those from Michigan. Atmantle refused to pay claims, the Insurance Commissioner's office refused to entertain their complaints, and that was the end of the story. It took me three hours to send them all a letter like the one I sent to the folks in Michigan, but I figured it was worth it. If there were a hundred people filing complaints, there must have been a thousand who were mistreated, I just knew it. Blood was in the water. I could smell it.

On the eve of Halloween, I walked to work amid the falling oak, beech, and maple leaves. Per routine, I made a small detour to the local gas station for a cup of caramelized coffee and a peanut butter cookie. Jane, behind the counter, was always happy to see me. She called me "Doc," and charged me the cheaper price for coffee instead of the more expensive amount for cappuccino. Whatever the case, I was always friendly to her, and even brought her little goodies like jam and small gifts that some clients brought me. That always amazed me—why would anyone think that they could curry favor with me, just because they brought me a ten-dollar wind chime or a jar of homemade jam?

On the way to the office I noticed a sign in the intersection of Main Street: "Haunted Forest, Thursday, Friday, and Saturday." Everyone I worked with thought it was as customary in late October as a homecoming football game. Miss Peacock informed me that the Haunted Forest was nothing more than a fundraiser for the Greeks on the campus of Central Michigan University. They had hayrides, ghosts and goblins in a setting aglow with strobe lights and black lights, college students dressed in ghastly costumes, and spooky music.

Throughout the day, I heard ads on the radio for "hayrides through the haunted forest" and dismissed it as just another part of life in mid-Michigan. It seemed like an odd practice, a peculiar tradition. In a way though, the forest down the street from the Centre was a terrific place for such an outing. The forest was old, too old really for any diverse ecosystem. In the summer, the canopy of leaves a hundred feet above the forest floor kept all but the most ardent plants from thriving in it. Squirrels, both fox and red, had plenty to eat, with all the acorns and beechnuts on the forest floor. Now that it was Halloween and the leaves had fallen, the squirrel nests stood out against the gray sky like flak during a bombing mission.

And then there was Memorial Cemetery, which made the whole "haunted forest" thing creepier yet. Carrie was buried there, several feet away from some man named Viktor Linfors, a Swede, I presumed. Toby and I planted some fake daffodils on Carrie's grave on one of our walks earlier in the week. It was chilly when we planted them, and I told Toby that they "were good and sturdy. Even the frost couldn't kill them." Toby couldn't have cared less, but I was proud of Carrie's grave, proud of the work that we did to make it so presentable.

Memorial Cemetery was on one end of the property, while the festivities would be held at the other end. The only thing between the two was a quarter-mile stretch of overgrown forest.

When I made it to the office I checked my e-mail. Miss

Peacock had sent me my appointment schedule for the day, and a note about clients who had outstanding balances on their accounts. Calypso Steve sent me the agenda for an upcoming meeting—something about compliance with a governmental agency. I skimmed through most of the e-mails until I saw Rachel's, which read:

Sorry, but I just couldn't resist. I laughed and laughed, thinking of you trapped in that dreadful sanitarium!

Here's an actual greeting from an answering machine from a down-state Mental Hospital.

'Hello, and welcome to the mental health hospital: if you are obsessive compulsive, press 1 repeatedly.

If you are co-dependent, please ask someone to press 2 for you.

If you have multiple personalities, press 3, 4, 5 and 6.

If you are paranoid, we know who you are and what you want. Stay on the line so we can trace your call.

If you are delusional, press 7 and your call will be forwarded to the mothership.

If you are manic-depressive, it doesn't matter which number you press, nobody will answer.

If you are dyslexic, press 96969696969696.

If you have a nervous disorder, please fidget with the pound key until a representative comes on the line.

If you are bi-polar, please leave a message after the beep or before or after the beep, or just wait for the beep.

If you have short-term memory loss, press 9. If you have short-term memory loss, press 9. If you have short-term memory loss, press 9.

> *If you have low self esteem, please hang up. Our*
> *operators are too busy to talk to you.*
> *If you are menopausal, hang up, turn on the fan,*
> *lie down and cry. You won't be crazy forever.*

I laughed out loud, and I wanted to share it with half the
people I worked with. Then again, maybe that wasn't a good
idea. Nobody would appreciate it as much as I did, and besides,
I'm sure Calypso Steve wouldn't approve of me getting amusing
e-mails from my patients. He'd think it was inappropriate, or at
the very least, a "billable" event. It was his job to make money
for the Centre. There were no excuses, no gray areas, unless he
was the one that could benefit.

I sent her a response.

> *Thanks, Rachel. I laughed myself silly. Really. I*
> *especially like the part about the short-term memory.*
> *Oh, and keep in mind that the only reason why I'm*
> *trapped inside the sanitarium is because I'm one of*
> *the patients! Keep in mind that the only reason why*
> *I'm trapped inside the sanitarium is because I'm one*
> *of the patients!*

It felt good to see Rachel in such an upbeat mood. She
was reaching out, taking chances, like most healthy people. I
was proud of her; proud of the way she was taking control of
her life. Oh sure, she might have some hard times ahead—like
we all do—but with every day that passed she seemed to be
gaining confidence and poise. And the strange thing about her
recovery…I didn't know what I did that helped in it. She was
doing it on her own.

Joe was hardly making the same strides. He was on a steady
diet of placebos for several weeks, and yet he kept his silent vigil. For the first time in several days the weather was nice, at least
nice enough to see the sights and smells outside the dank monotony of the walls inside the Centre. Indian summer seemed

to have a grip on mid-Michigan. I asked Joe if he wanted to go outside. He didn't answer. I asked him if he would rather sit inside, the way he had been for the last several months. Nothing seemed to faze him. Nothing seemed to matter.

So I packed him up into a wheelchair and threw a woolen blanket over his white jumpsuit imprinted with the letters SJC (St. Jean Centre.) When we made it outside, I mentioned the smell of the woods, the smell of fall. I pointed out the balsam needles on the sidewalk, and how they made wheelchair's ride less than smooth. I picked up a yellow aspen leaf, dipped it in a puddle, and raised it to my nose. It was fragrantly delightful, and reminded me of the cabin many miles away.

When we made it to the last park bench along the walkway, I stopped. After turning Joe toward me and setting the parking brake on the wheelchair, I sat down on the bench. It felt good to be outside in the fall of the year, even if I didn't have a shotgun in my hands, or a bird dog at my beck and call.

All I could do was talk. "See those, Joe? Everything is moving." I gestured toward the sky. "Those robins there...they flock together in the fall and eat fruit on their way south. They must like the fruit after the first frost of the year. The frost must make the fruit taste better. Must be sweeter." He stared right past me. "You don't see these big groups of robins in the spring. They come back with their mates—in pairs—and that's it." More stares. "You know, Joe, I lost my mate, too."

I looked over Joe's shoulder, and saw the orderly gesture that she wanted to have a smoke. I knew her name was Esposito, and she was a darn good orderly, too. I raised my chin—the nod for "go ahead." She gave me a little thumbs-up sign, and disappeared around the corner.

It was just Joe and me. "I know what you're going through," I told him. "I know what it's like." For a moment or two the silence lingered. The robins chirped their little warning call, then dashed away like the Sunday choir leaving the pulpit. Joe broke his silence with a question that sounded somewhat bitter.

"Is that why you coddle that god-damned dog of yours?"

I couldn't believe it; Joe was out of his stupor.

I hesitated. "What makes you say that?" I asked him, almost incredulously. The guy had been a vegetable for months, and his first words were less than friendly.

"Don't you coddle your dog?"

"Not really, I mean I like taking care of him, but I don't think I coddle him."

"Whatever…is that why you always take me by your house and check in on him?"

"Does that mean that I coddle my dog?"

"No, but if you go on and on about that stupid dog, and then come to work with dog hair all over your pant legs, it might look like you coddle your dog." I looked at my pant legs and there were a few white dog hairs on the cuffs. Maybe there were more than a few hairs. I brushed them off and looked back at Joe. His facial expression didn't change.

"Is that it? You're not going to take your vow of silence again are you?"

He was staring again. "What difference does it make?"

"Joe, I'm only trying to help you out…and frankly, I look forward to our time together. You help me out too, you know." I was trying my hardest to warm up to him, so that he'd warm up to me.

"You don't say?" He was staring.

"Well, sure. We have some things in common, you know… our spouses."

Joe sat there, and took a deep breath as if he had to get something off his chest. "You know…" he said, "I killed her…"

"Who?"

"My wife." A tear dribbled down his cheek.

I tried not to look surprised. "You did?"

"Yup. I killed her."

"Why?"

"I just had to."

"Why did you do it?" He didn't answer me, so I waited several seconds. "It's okay Joe, if you don't want to tell me you don't have to." I leaned back on the bench and flicked a few more hairs off my trousers. It was getting late in the day; the robins made their way into the big balsams in my yard to roost. A carload full of college students ripped around the corner, their stereo blasting Michael Jackson's "Thriller." The coeds in the back seat were screaming mock cries of terror.

"Would you mind if I met your dog?" He asked me.

I looked back his way and he seemed sincere enough. Dogs have a way of making people feel happy. Many pets do. Joe seemed to be reaching out to me, and I didn't want to discourage him. I looked his way one last time, and saw a man that appeared to be genuine in his interest to meet Toby. Once Joe met Toby, and his wagging tail, I'm sure he would tell me the rest of his story. Joe might even get a few dog hairs on his pant legs too. Who knows, maybe I could use the dog hair to forge a bond between us.

"No, no," I said. "I don't mind. In fact that's a good idea. He's probably ready for a potty break."

I had a twinge of second thoughts, a momentary sense of regret. *Was it a set up? A ruse?* I couldn't back off now; I couldn't chain him to the wheelchair after he had just broken the ice.

We were on the park bench forty yards from my entryway. I released the parking brake, and rolled Joe toward my front door. When we neared the door, I set the brake again, and told Joe "I'll be right back." He stayed right there. He didn't flinch when I turned to the front door of my house.

Toby must not have expected me. When I poked my nose in the door he wasn't waiting for me as usual. I had to whistle several times before he came to the threshold, tail wagging like mad. "Okay, okay," I cautioned him. "There's somebody here

I'd like you to meet." I held both the screen door and the storm door open. The old boy made it outside; seemingly shaking the cobwebs from his skull the way dogs do sometimes.

In as long as it took to do all that, I turned to the wheelchair and couldn't believe my eyes. It was empty. He was gone!

"Toby, come!" I yelled. He trotted my way, confused. I slammed the door and cried out for the orderly. My head spun right and left, my eyes glued to the surroundings. I felt my heart pounding in my chest, the impending feeling of doom. Here the guy was in my care, and I let him get away. "Help! Help! Help!" I screamed. The orderly appeared, out of breath, out of aces. "Find him…now!" I yelled. She ran, toward the door of the Centre where not only more help could be obtained, but where more blame could be distributed when the shit hit the fan.

I spun, wildly, and raced around the backside of my house. My eyes scanned the shrubbery, the trees, and the surroundings. Nothing. A second later I was right back where I started, only now it was getting dark. The alarms sounded inside the Centre, which added to my panic. *Great, now this has become a big deal,* I thought. For some reason I ran towards one of the outbuildings, but halfway there I discovered that the manhole cover was pushed away from one of the underground tunnels. Quickly, I dove down the steps to where the alarm was louder, and the emergency lights in metal cages were blinking spastically. I didn't know where the tunnel went, or why they were there, other than they'd make a hell of a bomb shelter. All I cared about is that it seemed like a logical place for a fugitive to hide.

I ran furiously, bypassing the spider webs and custodial closets. The doors that lead up to the administration building were locked, so I continued east, where I thought I heard someone running. I turned a corner and saw Joe racing a couple hundred yards ahead of me. "Joe, wait!" I yelled, but he kept running.

Next thing I know he's climbing another ladder and shoving another heavy manhole cover out of the way. I followed him as fast as I could, but it appeared that he had a several-second lead on me. "Joe, wait!" I yelled, in vain. He was free again, out there, in the center of the mature woods, in the bowels of "The Haunted Forest."

My mind was racing. I wanted to call for help, but I was afraid of the consequences. It was my fault that he was on the loose, my fault that Joe was getting away. I had a fleeting thought that I could resolve the situation without further incident, but I was afraid of what might happen if he wasn't soon corralled. I heard police sirens wailing and getting louder.

When I poked my head out of the tunnel, all I could see was a bag of an old lady in a pointy black hat stooped over a giant metal pot. A dry ice haze oozed from the pot as she stirred it with a large wooden spoon. Black and strobe lights cast a ghastly pool of light on the setting. She uttered Shakespeare in a crackled voice: *Double, double, toil and trouble; Fire, burn; and cauldron, bubble.*

Of course it wasn't an old lady after all, but a college student dressed up like a witch. And she was convincing too, with her cleft chin, green makeup and a pointed, wide-brimmed hat. I barely noticed the people sitting on bales of hay behind the clopping hooves of draft horses.

Mannequins hung from ropes wrapped around their necks.

Just then I saw Joe standing with his back to me. I charged by the witch, the hay wagon, and the extension cords laid to and fro. "Joe, wait!" I cried, but he didn't move. "Joe, don't!" I hollered, but he hardly flinched. I ran, headlong into the white jumpsuit with the letters "SJC" emblazoned on the back. My shoulder struck him under the ribs, and I heard the air gasp from his lungs. We hit the ground together, and I felt like a linebacker in a football game the way they blind-side quarterbacks. But this was no football game; he squirmed like mad, crying out "my shoulder!" At once a gang of fraternity brothers pulled me off. They all wore white jumpsuits identical to Joe's. "What's wrong with you, man?" They yelled.

A woman on a passing hay wagon screamed, "Oh look, kids, the patients are staging a revolt…." She thought the incident was part of the show.

"Joe" rolled over, and to my amazement it wasn't him. He got up, right arm dangling unnaturally. The fraternity brothers had me by the armpits and looked at me in disbelief. One of them cocked his right arm and caught me under the ribs, then belted me again under my right eye.

"Wait, there's been a horrible mistake," I cried.

One of them laughed. "Ya think?" He yelled, hitting me again and again.

They were wearing the same jumpsuits that we use in the Centre for our patients. "We have a patient on the loose and he's dangerous! Please help me find him!" They looked at me in disbelief. "I swear to you, it's true. His name is Joseph Del-Banco, and he's gone! Gone! Look at my name badge…I work here. You've got to help me!"

The woman on the hay wagon applauded. "Come on, kids, isn't this something. These guys are good! They want us to believe that there's a real kook on the loose!"

I shook myself free of the arm holds, and they stood there for a few seconds.

Double, double, toil and trouble; Fire, burn; and cauldron, bubble.

Time stood still in the dizzying madness. The fraternity guys let me go and I raced toward the forest's parking lot. Nothing. Out of breath, I reeled in a state trooper and told him to help me out. He wanted to know all the details. Too many. I told him to follow me, and I'd explain on the way. We ran back to the witch and her boiling pot.

The frat boys identified me. One of their own was writhing in pain on a hay bale. Suddenly the trooper changed his tune.

"Look, can we sort this out later," I screamed. "One of the Centre's patients is gone. Escaped."

The trooper reached for his microphone, clipped to his lapel. He called for backup and an ambulance.

Oh shit.

I couldn't really run from the trooper, but I knew that I had to find Joe.

The setting was surreal. The strobe lights and black lights. The spooky music and sea shanties. The mechanized bats spiraling on nylon string. The mannequins dangling lifelessly.

Joe's lead was only a few seconds when this whole thing started, but now he could have been anywhere. I pictured him throwing a woman out of her minivan and driving off with the kids still in the backseat. I imagined him running across the street, into neighborhoods, where he'd accost one of the citizens. It was horrible. I yelled at the cop, but he kept telling me to wait.

Then I heard children crying in terror. The fraternity brothers ran to the commotion, shining their flashlights in the heavens. Another trooper was there too, shooing parents away, shielding the eyes of their little ones.

"What is it?" I asked one of the state troopers. They asked who I was and why I should know. "What is it?" I demanded.

Just then one of the troopers raised his flashlight skyward, and I saw another body dangling from an orange extension cord. Only this time it wasn't a mannequin. I recognized the white jumpsuit, the broad forehead. It was Joe, dripping the drops of the recently deceased. The son of a gun was dead. Hung himself, just as he confessed to his wife's murder.

Calypso Steve was going to have a fit.

Before long, more troopers joined the two who were guarding Joe's resting spot. One of them had a yellow roll of plastic tape that had the words "POLICE LINE DO NOT CROSS" printed on it. In no time he had the crime scene secured, and was taking snapshots with a digital camera. The other trooper pulled a pocket-sized pad of paper out of his breast pocket, and was quickly scribbling notes with a fidgety left hand. He sauntered my way and asked me what happened.

I started to answer, but was interrupted by his police radio attached to his lapel. He reached for the knob on his belt, and the dispatcher's voice was less irritating.

"His name is Joseph DelBanco, and he's a patient here."

"But what happened?"

"He was in my care and he got away from me."

"Where?"

The interrogation went on for ten minutes and I told him almost everything about Joe and Joe's condition. I say 'almost' because I failed to tell the trooper about Joe's epiphany. The trooper didn't need to know that.

The entourage waited until the state police captain showed up before they cut down the body with the help of a front-end loader on the face of a John Deere tractor. I recognized the man driving the tractor from the maintenance department. Calypso Steve showed up just in time to see the body taken off by the local funeral director, "Who's responsible for charges?" The funeral director inquired. Everyone looked in Steve's direction.

Steve was hot, and seemed to take Joe's incident personally. He fired questions at me as if they were arrows fired from a crossbow.

"What the hell happened here?"

"I can explain."

"Well that's a very good idea."

"Excuse me, sir," the trooper was back in front of me again, looking in Steve's direction. "What's your name?"

Steve was seething, and stated his first name quickly, then spelled his last name. "Chief Administrator, St. Jean Centre." The trooper didn't write very fast, and it seemed to make Steve even more irate. He clenched his jaw and stared at me with his laser eyes.

"Is this necessary?" He demanded.

The trooper didn't flinch but continued to write very s-l-o-w-l-y. "Was the subject suicidal before tonight?" Asked the trooper.

"Noooo," Steve stated it slowly on purpose, to insult the trooper. It worked. The trooper was insulted. He reached into his breast pocket and pulled out a card, handing it to me. "Please stop by the police post tomorrow morning and give me your statement. Mr. Calisto and I are going to be a while here tonight."

"Okay…" I said, raising my eyebrows in surprise.

"He'll be at the post right after he gets shit-canned from his job," Steve snarled my way. "You be at my office first thing in the morning, and bring boxes to carry out your stuff."

What a jerk, I thought.

I wandered off, looking back to see the trooper firing a pointed index finger Steve's way. "Okay, okay." Steve was heeding his warning. "I get it."

He wasn't the only one who was going to get it. I was in the crosshairs for some trouble of my own. The last thing I needed was to get fired, but it seemed like Steve had it in for me. I knew I bent the Centre's procedures about patient handling, but I never thought that Joe would end his life that way.

I couldn't believe that Joe had snookered me the way he had. He was looking for a way to distract me, and I fell for his ploy—hook, line, and sinker. I was mad at Joe, mad at myself, and mad at Steve for his outburst. It seemed that I had to come up with some sort of angle to shift the blame from me to Joe.

In no time I was back at my house. Toby saw me coming

through the slobber-stained window, his tail wagging like mad. He charged outside while I took off my necktie and jacket. I poured a little drink and listened to the messages on the answering machine. Only an hour after the incident a reporter from the local paper wanted me to give her a call and provide a few comments. A television crew from Cadillac was on their way to Mt. Pleasant, and wondered if I'd be available for an on-camera interview. I wasn't going to do either. All I wanted to do was hide from the world. All I wanted to do was hide in my own little house.

The house smelled of tomatoes, garlic, meat, oregano, and Worcestershire sauce: Italian round steak I put in the crock-pot earlier that morning. I love that stuff.

Toby scratched at the door and I let him in. I poured a scoop of food in his bowl and he was in hog heaven. Boy, the simple life of a dog. Eat, sleep, mind your manners, and please your master just by being yourself. What a great life. What a wonderful, uncluttered existence.

I put a pot of water on to boil and found the last of the egg noodles in the pantry. From there we moved into the den where I closed the shades and opened the flue on the chimney. I built a small teepee of cherry wood in the fireplace, lit a match, and had it crackling under the mantle. Toby laid his paw on the arm of my old recliner, begging for attention the way he often does. We sat there and enjoyed the smells of cherry wood smoke mixed with the pungent odor of dinner.

The next morning I made it to Steve's office for a little meeting with him and the personnel manager. They wanted to know everything that happened. They wanted to know why I didn't make sure Joe wasn't strapped into his chair the way procedure calls for. "That's the orderly's job," I reminded him.

"The patient is your responsibility, so you should have made sure of that. Besides, Esposito told us that you're the one that secured Joe."

They wanted to know why I told the orderly she could leave.

"I didn't. She wanted to go have a smoke so I nodded for her to leave."

They told me that she was terminated.

"It wasn't her fault, really."

They wanted to know why I went to my house.

"The patient expressed an interest in seeing my dog, and I didn't want to rebuff his first request in months."

They reminded me that animals represent a liability hazard, and prior approval should have been obtained.

"Like I said, I didn't want to thwart his first request."

They wanted to know why I cold-cocked the fraternity brother in the white jumpsuit.

"I had no idea that they had jumpsuits just like the ones we use."

They told me that a lawyer called the Centre regarding the injured fraternity brother.

There was nothing I could say.

They wanted to know why I didn't take more caution where Joe was concerned, considering that I knew his medications had been altered.

"I have nothing else to say other than I regret what transpired." I think they thought I was going to beg for my job, but it never crossed my mind. They wanted to know more about the conversation Joe and I had, but I didn't volunteer a thing.

The personnel manager shuffled through my file, flipping the pages up and down quickly; as if he did it fast enough this whole sticky situation would blow away in the breeze. "Jim, even though you have only been here a short while, we have taken notice of your excellent work here. You have been a fine employee, an asset to the Centre. Unfortunately, I'm afraid…" his eyes dropped from the papers to his socks, or his shoes. It was an awkward situation for him, even though it was his job.

"We're going to have to suspend you for a week, with…"

"Without," Steve interjected.

"*With* pay," he finished.

I looked at the manager, and at Steve. It was over. I could live with a commuted death sentence. A little time off didn't sound that bad.

But the real questions were still brewing inside me. Why did Joe kill his wife, and why did it send him into a catatonic state?

Twenty-One

LATER THAT MORNING I spent an hour or so at the police post, sipping coffee and patiently giving my account of the previous night's disaster. I hoped I'd never see the trooper again. He was a nice enough fellow, even though he did write extremely slowly. There was something about the *smell* of the police station that gave me the creeps. It reminded me of gun cleaning oil and the cologne you'd buy in quart jugs. I hated the crinkling sound of his leather holster and the way his bulletproof vest made him look like he had a chiseled chest of muscles. I walked out of there with the whole day ahead of me. I had nothing to do for the rest of the week.

And it bothered me.

I'm a man of routine, of measured gambles and habitual nuances. I like the regimented customs of getting ready for work, following a well organized schedule and meeting clients every hour on the hour.

Idle time seemed strange. If I was at the cabin—where time was irrelevant—I still followed a schedule of hunting the highlands midmorning, then the lower river in the swansong of afternoon. I liked planning a menu where I could use the bacon drippings from breakfast for German potato salad that night. I enjoyed the satisfaction of "warming myself twice" when cutting wood. It was relaxing to listen to polka music on the radio after dinner, then watch the strangers broadcast the eleven o'clock weather report.

I made it home close to noon and put a leash on Toby. We walked to the gas station where Jane asked what was up, but I didn't volunteer any information. She didn't ask why I was wearing blue jeans or had Toby tied to the cement pillar in front of the station. In a way I felt like taking Toby up to the cabin, or to some state-owned land east of Mt. Pleasant for a little grouse hunt. On the other hand, with a week off I felt like I had a gift of free time, and I wanted to make the most out of it.

Miss Peacock had already heard the news of my suspension and left a message on my cell phone. She assured me that she'd call my clients to reschedule their appointments for the week. "Jim, this isn't your fault. I'm on your side." When I returned her call she was even more sympathetic. "I can't believe that creep of an orderly bailed out on you like that."

"Thank you, really, but there's a lot more to it than what you've heard."

"Is there anything you want me to tell your clients?"

"Whatever they told you to say. Don't be foolish. It's only a week, you know. I'll be back in the saddle soon enough."

"Take care then, and we'll see you soon."

I hung up the phone and crossed her name off the list of things to do, thankful that I had one advocate at the office. She'd put a positive spin on the party line that Calypso Steve would want her to spout. She'd tell people that I was ill, or had another family emergency or something innocuous.

Later that afternoon, I put on a couple of Carrie's Christmas presents—a sweater and leather jacket—and walked downtown to the law offices of Morrison & Nunnelly.

Kathy seemed happy to see me when I arrived. I noticed a copy of the local paper on the edge of her desk, the lead story *"Patient escapes, took his own life before authorities arrived."* She took off her headset and had to ask me if I had anything to do with the guy's escape. I nodded, and she pouted, disappointed with the bad news. Kathy seemed genuinely concerned with what was going on in my life, even though our case against Atmantle added extra work to her already hectic schedule. She wanted to know more about the letters I sent out to Atmantle's complainants, and when I was going to tell Glen about it.

"Have you had any responses?" I asked her.

She laughed. "Does Raggedy Ann have cotton eyelashes? My gosh, Jim, we've been overwhelmed."

"That's great!"

"Maybe for you," she reminded me. "I have to sit on the phone and listen to these poor people and their miserable stories."

"Isn't that in your job description…to be the compassionate assistant?"

"Jim, I am compassionate, but you're not the one signing my checks, are you?" Kathy was a hard person to read. She was loyal to Glen and the firm, and I knew that she really had liked Carrie too. It seemed that I had better come clean and tell her what was going on, or I'd lose her loyalty.

"Why don't I tell you what we're doing?" I said.

"I'm listening," she said, somewhat relieved.

We sat there for a few pregnant seconds, as I grappled with where to start. I felt like going *way* back, to the time that Carrie's first health claim was denied…but that was too much information for her. She only wanted to hear why it was relevant to the firm and her well being. I should have practiced what I was going to say, but then again, I've made a living by thinking fast on my feet. So I started, "Bottom line, Kathy, I believe that the insurance people that denied Carrie's benefits are crooks.

When they first denied her benefits, I thought it was just the way big business operates, but then I started poking around and found out that there might be more to it. I don't have anything yet. It's just a hunch…"

She raised her finger for me to "pause" put her headset back on, and stated "Morrison & Nunnelly." I sat there for a moment listening to the idle silence on the end of the line. "One moment please," she said. "Jim, it's for you. It's one of your people. They called twice already and are tired of waiting for you to call them back. Pick it up in the conference room, line two." I raised an eyebrow in disbelief, encouraged not only with the fact that one person called back three times, but also that Kathy seemed to think that there were many, many more waiting in the wings.

"Jim speaking, can I help you?"

"This is Margaret Denton from Bad Axe, Michigan. I've been trying to get ahold of you about your letter, and this Atmantle outfit. When are we going to sue the bastards?"

"Mrs. Denton, I think we're getting the cart a little ahead of the horse, aren't we? Why don't you tell me what happened?"

"Over the phone?" She asked.

"Can you come in and see me?"

"You're in Mt. Pleasant, right? I'll come over. When?"

"How about ten o'clock tomorrow morning?"

"I'll be there. Just give me directions."

I hung up the phone and realized there was no turning back. Mrs. Denton was on her way to see me, and she thought I was a lawyer. I didn't have long to think about my predicament; Kathy charged into the conference room with a fresh pot of coffee. "Still chasing a hunch, Jim, or do you want to talk to more people?"

"How many are there?"

"Take a guess?"

"I don't know…ten…fifteen?"

She shook her head, no. "A bunch…seventy-four!"

"You're kidding!"

"No!"

"Holy cow. What do we do?"

"*We*," she laughed, sarcastically.

"Where's Glen? Maybe I should talk to him about this."

"He's in court, but should be back soon."

"Why don't I call some of these people back in the meantime?"

"Don't you have to get back to the office?" She asked.

"No, I have all kinds of time."

"Suit yourself. The conference room is open the rest of the day, the rest of the week."

I flipped through the messages, and called someone from Clare, just a few miles north of Mt. Pleasant. They were hesitant to discuss the matter over the phone, so I set up an appointment for eight o'clock the next morning. A couple from Houghton Lake took the noon appointment, and folks from Big Rapids, Cadillac, and Midland filled up the rest of the day. I felt pretty good about myself. I had a schedule again, a routine.

Glen wasn't that impressed. I tried to break the news to him gently, subtly, but he was skeptical. "These people don't think you're a lawyer, do they?" He asked, reaching into a cavernous credenza. He grunted slightly from the strain. "Have a drink, Jim?"

"No, no thanks, Glen." I watched him pull out a fifth of Jack Daniels and pour several fingers worth into an imprinted crystal glass. The scene reminded me of the stories Carrie used to tell me about Glen, and his tradition of tapping into the whiskey bottle just before quitting time. It seemed that it was his little way of getting a head start on happy hour, the way he liked to unwind.

"Glen, I haven't told them that I *am* a lawyer, but I didn't say I wasn't a lawyer, either. Law firms hire investigators all the time, and that's what I'm doing."

He rose from his chair and wandered across his office, shutting the door dramatically. "Jim, I really have to admire your tenacity." He was pacing in front of the wall cluttered with photographs in frames of varying colors, shapes and sizes. A grandfather clock ticked in the corner. "It appears as though you've already put in quite a lot of effort into this case, and that's remarkable, but I've got to tell you that this really isn't the kind of litigation we like to handle." He swished the whiskey in his glass. "We do mom and pop stuff, here…you know, wills, trusts, estate planning, and real estate. Even if you developed the foundation for a suit, there's still a lot more legwork that has to be done, and I'm not in the position to take on that kind of commitment." I didn't say a thing, but looked at him in a decade-old photograph taken at the Isabella County Fairgrounds. Unlike now, he still had a wisp of hair that hadn't turned a brilliant shade of silver. He had his arm around a youngster who was wearing a yellow registration badge safety-pinned to his shirt. A massive hog was in the foreground, oblivious to the ceremony, or the grim circumstances that would follow. Glen was verbalizing his fears the way my clients do at times.

"What are you afraid of, Glen?"

"It's not what I'm afraid of, Jim. It's what I don't want to happen…I don't want to get into something deeper than I can handle. I'm nearly sixty years old, and I don't have the energy to take on a class action lawsuit. Do you know how much effort something like that takes?" He looked my way and held out his palm; pinky cocked the way orators do sometimes.

"I know, Glen."

"No, I don't think you do." He shook his head. "There are depositions, statements, scheduling, pre-trial motions, and a suit that's bound to linger for years. My God…it'll be overwhelming. And the expenses involved! Do you have that kind of dough lying around?" He raised his voice, for emphasis, and loosened his necktie hidden behind his wavering brisket. "Jim," he sighed, taking a sip of whiskey, "I really miss having Carrie here, you know that. She was a wonderful person, and a darn good lawyer too. I can't imagine what you must be going through. My gosh…" He slumped into his leather, high-backed chair and ran his fingers through his eyebrows, which were thick enough to hide a small flight of woodcock. "Why don't you let this go…this Atmantle stuff? Even if there's something to prove it won't bring Carrie back, you know that."

I looked at him and nodded. I understood what he was saying, and I wanted him to be sure that his message was coming through loud and clear. It seemed that all Glen wanted was to be heard. Lots of people are that way. They see a psychologist so they have somebody to talk to. They want someone to care, someone to listen to their worries, someone to give them advice without passing judgment. Glen was no different.

"Glen, I hear you loud and clear. You make some very good points." I was poking him gently with my hickory cane, like the hog in the show ring. He didn't know where I was leading him, but the little jabs must have done the trick. Flattery lets down the defenses; praise makes a man more open to compromise. "Carrie had so much respect for you and your judgment. She loved working here with you, with Kathy. Carrie saw the value in preparing a case, in doing research." I was jabbing him, leading him around the show ring. "You have nothing to lose with this investigation. I'll do all the legwork, and then I'll come back to you with my findings. Believe me, I'll have more ammo on these clowns than you've ever seen. I'll even put a bow on it when I'm finished. If you still don't think there's a case, I'll take it to another firm…promise."

"Jim!" He scowled at me.

"Glen, I need to do this…for Carrie, for Carrie's memory. For Christ's sake, Glen, if there's something to the case, we could expose these people at Atmantle for what they are. If we don't stand up to them how many more lives will be ruined…or lost?" He swiveled in his chair, staring out the window, sipping his drink. "This case could define your legacy, Glen, and I want to help you. Let me do this."

He sighed again, and weighed his options. He deliberated. His grandfather clock in the corner ticked a stately tick. His phone blinked, and the whiskey swished in his crystal glass. "All right, all right. But don't mislead anyone. You're no damned lawyer! Got it? I'm going to keep you on a short leash."

"You won't regret it. I promise." I stormed out of his office with a smile. "Talk to you soon, Glen."

He waved.

At last, a vote of confidence. At last, some sort of validation of a grudge that had been stirring in me for quite some time. Glen said that he'd run with my investigation, and that was all I needed. It felt great to be alive; it felt great to have the time on my hands away from the Centre. At almost five o'clock that afternoon, I said goodbye to Kathy and told her I'd see her first thing in the morning. She laughed, "Very good counselor… maybe you should call me something like 'Miss Poindexter' just to make the whole thing more…more…clandestine."

"Nah." She laughed again.

"I'll see you in the morning."

"Okay, Jim. See you then, and good job in there."

"Thanks." I smiled. I couldn't help but smile.

Half an hour later I was home, after stopping at the local butcher shop for a thick ribeye steak. No messages on the answering machine, no mail to speak of. I put a giant potato in the oven to bake and checked my e-mail. My mind was already on tomorrow's interviews. It seemed reasonable to have a list of issues to discuss with the complainants, so I sat down at one of the barstools at the kitchen's island, pen and legal pad in hand. About then the doorbell rang.

I peered through the little peephole and recognized the red hair amassed on the top of her pretty head. It was Rachel. "Hello Jim." Just like every other time I heard her say my name, she stretched out the "J-i-i-i-i-m." She said my name like a lonesome hen turkey calling to a willing tom in the springtime.

I loved the sound of it.

I gobbled back, if only in my head.

"Come in, come in." I held the door open, and she walked inside, carrying a massive pot that smelled absolutely wonderful. "Can I take your coat?"

"Sure, that would be great." Toby was just as happy to see strange company in the house. He wagged his tail like mad and sniffed at her thighs. "Oh my, who's this, the welcoming committee?"

"Toby, please!"

"He's okay," she said. "Let me put this down." She set the pot down in the kitchen, and stooped like a catcher in a baseball game. "Come here boy." She was patting him all over—his ears, his muzzle, his rump. He was lapping it up, wagging his tail, almost smiling...*eat your heart out, Master.*

"Toby likes company," I said.

That kind of company, I thought to myself, *would be great indeed.*

"What a nice dog. What a soft coat he has. No wonder you always come in with dog hair all over your pant legs."

"I do?"

This hair thing was getting old.

"Don't worry about it, Jim. I don't think any less of you. You're still a good shrink."

"Thanks...I think." I watched her stand, turn to the sink and wash her hands. It was nice to have a woman in my house again, even if she stopped by unannounced. It was nice to steal a glance, admire her curves, and notice the pair of rivets hammered to the back of her blue jeans.

They smiled at me like the dimpled cheeks on the Mona Lisa.

"Do you like my pot?" She asked, twirling it around.

I was still in dreamland. "It's…it's….marvelous. Yes."

"I made it in art class, as an undergrad."

"Smells wonderful too," I confessed.

"Thanks, it's chicken & dumplings."

"Homemade?"

"Of course it is," she smiled gracefully. "I heard you weren't feeling well."

"Who told you that?"

"I got a call from your assistant…Miss Parakeet or something, and she said that you would be out for a week or so. I figured that you must have been pretty sick."

"Miss Peacock…and thank you. It smells delicious, but I feel fine."

"You're welcome. Don't tell her I said that…" We stood there for a few seconds, and I had the feeling there was more to her visit. "That's good…nice place you have here," she gestured. "It's old, but it has tons of character. Look at that, the tall ceilings, hardwood floors."

"Glad you like it."

"I do. I do. But you know, Jim, I came here to tell you that I won't be coming in to see you anymore."

"Oh?"

"Yes…I'm doing much better. I feel like I've really made strides. I have a lot more confidence, and I've learned to deal with my problems."

"That's great, Rachel! I'm so happy for you, and I've noticed how much better you've been doing. You know, it doesn't have to be forever. If something comes up down the road you can always look me up."

"Well that's the thing, I'll miss you. I've shared so much with you, I feel like you know me better than anyone else."

"Those are normal feelings to have, Rachel."

"Here I go again…spilling my guts." She reached for a paper napkin, and dabbed her nose with it.

"It's okay to do that."

"I know but I told myself I wasn't going to get all misty." She drew a deep breath and exhaled slowly.

"It's okay to cry too."

"Give it a rest, Jim. I came here to ask you out on a date, and I figured I couldn't do that as long as you were my shrink…I mean…my counselor." She couldn't look at me, and her cheeks were reddening.

So were mine. All of a sudden.

"You're right about that. We're supposed to wait two years." We both looked at Toby, because we were embarrassed about being caught in an embarrassing situation.

"I'm sorry, I shouldn't have asked." Her comment made things worse. "It was a wild idea…I'm sorry."

"No…it's fine, really."

"Well I should go; I'll just take my coat and be on my way." She was blabbering. "Nice to meet you, Toby." She passed by me and I smelled her perfume, as fragrant as a June morning after an overnight rain. "Just leave my pot on your back porch and I'll pick it up in a few days." She had the back door open, and one foot across the threshold.

"What did you have in mind?" I asked.

She stopped without turning around, confused. "Pardon?"

"For a date?"

She slowly turned and smiled, looking me squarely in the eyes. "I thought we could see a play this weekend at the university…do you like musicals?"

"Sure, but it's been a while. What's playing?"

"*Oklahoma!*"

"Really? I love that show," I lied; I liked it, but love was an exaggeration.

She hummed a little tune. "You know, *'Gonna give you barley, carrots and pertaters.'*"

I picked up an imaginary conductor's baton between my

thumb and forefinger and swished it like an old pro: "'*pasture fer the cattle, spinach and termaters!*'"

We laughed for a minute on the doorstep, and together added '*Where the wind comes sweeping cross the plain.*'"

"What time is the show?"

"Eight."

"Should we have dinner before?

"Love to."

"Do you want to meet me here, or should I pick you up?" I asked.

"Why don't you pick me up," she said confidently.

"Great, at six then...Friday."

"Sounds like fun."

"Sounds like fun."

I shut the door and stood there for a minute, taking an inventory of the butterflies in my stomach. It had been so long since I had those feelings, so long since I had a date. I looked down at Toby, with his long snout and sleepy eyes. He just looked back and wagged his tail. I don't know if he could read my mind, but for the first time in months I had a really good day.

A really good day.

Twenty-Two

MS. DENTON HAD THE farthest drive to Mt. Pleasant, and yet she was a half hour early for her appointment. The losses she had against Atmantle weren't the most costly, but her case was one of the most blatant. It involved her four-year-old Chevrolet Impala, which was totaled in a car accident.

She bought the car new, and signed a sixty-month note to pay for it. Her credit wasn't the best, so she ended up paying a pretty steep interest rate. When her car was in the wreck, her adjuster told her that they wouldn't be able to pay off the loan.

Mrs. Denton said that she wasn't concerned with the amount of the loan, but rather the value of the car. The insurance company said that the value of the car was thirty-two hundred. The blue-book value was more than double that amount, she said, plus, she had bids from different car dealers for nothing less than eight thousand. The online dealers advertised cars of like kind and quality for eighty-two to eighty-five hundred dollars.

When I asked her what the adjuster told her, she said, "'Atmantle was justified in offering what we did.'"

"Did they offer you any explanation of how they came up with the offer they did?"

"No, other than 'we've done our homework.'"

"Have you settled the case?" I asked.

"No, but now they're throwing a fifteen-dollar a day storage fee at me."

"Where?"

"At the salvage yard."

"What's the guy's name...your adjuster?"

"Kevin Schultz, at extension 548. His office is in Lansing somewhere."

"When did you file a complaint with the insurance commissioner?"

"About three weeks ago, when I started getting the run-around."

"Did it help?"

"No. They rubbed my nose in it...saying that 'no matter how much I complain to the insurance commissioner, it wasn't going to help my case.'" She began to cry, and said that she couldn't afford to take that kind of financial beating.

"Bear with me here, Mrs. Denton. I'll call this Mr. Schultz and get to the bottom of it." I called Atmantle's claims office in Lansing, and was promptly placed into Schultz's voice mail. When I went to leave a message, his recorder said that there was no more room in his mailbox. I pushed the pound key and was eventually routed to the operator. Once there, I asked for Schultz's supervisor, who didn't seem overly pleased to handle my call. I introduced myself and the reason for my call.

"What can I do for you?" He asked.

"Please explain to me how Mrs. Denton, whose car was valued at eight thousand dollars, is being asked to settle for only thirty-two hundred?"

"That's easy," he replied. "She probably didn't tell you that she has a five- hundred-dollar deductible. Our price was really thirty-seven hundred before her deductible."

"Keep going."

"The prices she itemized were dealers' prices, not retail. In other words, what the dealer asks and what they'll take are two completely different numbers."

"I'm listening."

"That's it. We feel that our offer is fair."

"If it was your car, would it be fair?"

"That's irrelevant."

"It is not. Mrs. Denton has proof that her car was worth much more than what you've offered her."

"This conversation is over I'm afraid."

"Hello…hello?" The guy hung up on me. I looked back at Mrs. Denton and she smiled, knowing that the company was just as rude to me as they were to her. "What happened after you filed the complaint with the insurance commissioner?"

"They said that my complaint was 'unjustified.'"

"Why?"

"They never said, other than to say that I didn't prove my case."

"What did you do about it?"

"What else could I do? I called my state representative."

"Really?"

"Well, sure I did." She was a stand-up kind of woman.

"And what did he do?"

"*She* said that she'd get back to me, but they haven't yet and it's been two weeks now."

I scratched my head in disbelief. "What are you going to do?"

"That's why I'm here. Let's sue the bastards!"

"Mrs. Denton," I laughed. "You've certainly have been given the short end of the stick, but I don't know if suing them is your best option right now. Let's see what the state representative has to say about it first."

"What about the storage charge from the salvage yard?"

"Don't worry about them just yet. Tell them that you have a law office working on your case, and if they were smart they'd figure out a way to freeze the storage charges until your legislator calls you back."

"Do you have a business card?"

"Mrs. Denton, you don't need my business card. You need a tiger in your corner, an army of battleaxes on your side… someone who cares. Give me a call as soon as you hear from your congress person." I opened the conference room door and sent her on her way. There were several more people waiting, each with similar stories in varying degrees of tragedy.

The couple from Cadillac had a son covered under their health policy, but when he came down with lymphoma, the company denied his benefits because it was a "preexisting condition." When I asked how a blood cancer could be construed as preexisting, they said he had been tested for anemia several years previous and somehow the company considered that a reason to deny his claim. When I asked them what happened with the Commissioner's Office, all they said was that "we find that you haven't proven your case."

The man from Midland was just as bad. His wife allegedly failed to disclose "any other medical condition or symptoms" on her health application. Several weeks later she fell asleep at the wheel of her car, crossed the center line, hit another car, and wound up in a coma. Atmantle denied her health benefits because she failed to disclose her sleep apnea, which—they contended—was the proximate cause of the crash. To be consistent, they denied her auto benefits too—the value of the vehicle, the towing, everything. In Lansing, the Office of Consumer Affairs said that Atmantle was justified in denying the claims, even though the application didn't specifically ask about apnea.

I thought it was simply awful. Every person cried when they told their story. They were honest people, good-natured folks, with trusting characters. Atmantle denied their claims, for all sorts of reasons—none of them very good. What was even more disturbing, as far as I could see, was the reaction of the government to their claims. The Office of Consumer Affairs didn't even bother to listen to what these people said. It's like they didn't want to know that a problem existed; they ignored it altogether. There had to be more to it. I smelled something foul in the wind, a skunk in the woodshed.

It was just about then that I closed the conference room door and headed toward the lobby. My mind was already at home, and the thought of tonight's ribeye steak added to yesterday's potatoes fried with bits of onion. Rachel's chicken & dumplings were delicious the night before, and I made a mental note to ask her for the recipe on our date. I liked the sound of "date," I was amused with the notion of having somebody interested in me. Rachel and I have a date. *I am dating Rachel*, I thought. *We are going out on a date.* I'm really a weirdo after all.

"Jim?"

I looked up from my smiling rumination and saw Warren standing three feet from me. "Yes…hello, Warren."

"Funny running into you like this…"

"Yes, I imagine it is."

"What are you doing here?" He looked puzzled.

"Come on in," I said, gesturing toward the conference room, "so we can talk." Kathy looked up from her computer screen, diligently finishing her work for the day. I opened the door, and he sat down in one of the leather-bound chairs. "I'm doing a little consulting work for my wife's old firm…you know, jury stuff. There's a big trial coming up and he wants me to give him a psychological analysis of the potential jurors," I lied.

Warren nodded, but not necessarily in agreement.

"I suppose I can tell you why I'm here, can't I?" He looked my way and raised his eyebrows. "You're still my shrink whether we meet here or at the Centre, right?"

"Well sure, Warren, but we don't have to get into it here if you don't want to."

"No, I want to tell you, I want to get this off my chest."

"What's up?"

"I came in here to talk to Glen about becoming 'legally separated' from my wife."

"Really?"

"Yup. The checkered flag is flying. Our marriage is over."

"What brought this on?"

"It's been brewing for quite some time, you know that."

"Right, but what pushed you over the edge?"

"Sharon. I think I'm falling in love with her, with the promise of what will be."

"What happened?"

"I don't know...I just love being around her." He stroked his chin hair the way he always does, and got this big grin on his face. "I had my regular appointment with her and right off the bat I told her that I felt like Little Red Riding Hood, and she says, 'Why's that?' And I say 'my, what long nails you have, Granny.' And I'm telling you her nails are wonderful: long, and healthy, just like the rest of her. And she says 'All the better to scratch you with my dear.' And I say, 'My, what nice eyes you have, Granny.' And she says 'all the better to see you with my sweetie.'" His grin kept getting wider, "Back and forth we went, you know, her arms, 'all the better to hold you with.' Her long legs, 'all the better to ride you with my pretty.' Her lips, 'all the better to kiss you with, my lovely.' My gosh, it was so exciting because we had to whisper it so nobody would hear us."

"What happened next?"

"We met after my appointment at Bennigan's Restaurant, you know, the one connected to the hotel at the south end of town?"

"Sure, I know."

"We ordered some finger food and a round of drinks. Then another round. I was getting a little buzzed I guess, when all of a sudden she gets up to go to the bathroom. I didn't think anything of it until she was gone for twenty minutes. I start looking around, and think that she's no longer in the restaurant. So, I pull out my pager, and realize that I have a message. It was her! She had to see me, more of me, in room 217, at the top of the stairs." Warren shook his head. "It was horrible, it was like I had the devil on one shoulder saying 'go man go!' while my guardian angel said 'leave, leave, leave!' Well, I listened to the devil. I just had to. I stood at the door forever, weighing the gravity of it all. Finally I knocked."

"What happened next?"

"She threw open the door and said 'Oh, I just knew you'd come up here.' And it was weird too, she still was wearing her topcoat, you know like a raincoat?"

"I'm with you."

"She gives me a huge, wet kiss at the door, then spins me around, inside the room. I'm ready to rip her coat off when she sets me down on the chair in front of the mirror. 'You're late for your appointment,' she says. 'Now sit down and let me take care of you. We have many new exercises to review.' I'm holding my breath, and she tells me to be quiet, just like at the office. 'And if you don't do it right the first time, we'll have to do it over and over again until you get it right.' I'm thinking that this girl is a wild woman. She undoes my shirt, button by button, saying naughty little things like 'let's get rid of that nasty shirt so I can see that nice chest of yours. Let Granny take good care of you, Red Riding Hood.' I just sat there in the high-backed chair, with her straddling me. When I reached for the tie on her raincoat she warned me, 'Now, now, let's not forget, I'm the professional and you're the patient. You keep your hands to yourself.' I put my arms down and was a good patient. When my shirt was off she stood behind me, rubbing my shoulders the way she always does at our appointments. 'Now lift your arms,' she says, and I feel her nails on my sides...on my chest... all over. Better yet, I can watch her in the mirror. She stooped so that our cheeks were touching, her tongue in my ear. It was incredible. I lowered my arms to the rest, and she wrapped her belt around me so I couldn't move. I say 'whoa there' but she ties the other arm up without batting an eye."

"Warren, it's okay if you don't want to tell me all the details."

"No, I want to tell you so maybe you'll understand."

He didn't miss a beat.

"So without a belt on, I can see what's underneath her raincoat…a matching set of red underwear. Man, she was beautiful…behind me, with my head between her. And her hands, she was all over me…pushing my head back so I'm looking up at her. I wanted to reach behind me and scoop her up, but I couldn't because I was tied to the chair. Next thing I know she takes off her topcoat and is in front of the chair, pushing my face into her chest. She hopped on top of me, grinding her hips—panting, moaning—and I just sat there. I couldn't do anything. I felt like a toy, like a prize in the bottom of a Cracker Jack box. Slowly, she unzipped my fly and pulled me out…never taking her eyes off mine, never doubting what she had in mind. My god the party we had. I've never had a thrill like that—the newness of her… the taste of her… her smell. I've heard of guys screwing their brains out but never thought I'd get to do it. She's an animal!

"In a way," he continued, "I think she liked the idea of being in control. She didn't want to hook up and go for a joyride, you know what I mean? She wanted to be in charge, and liked me being tied up and helpless. She wanted to see me squirm, to beg for her to let me go, to hold my toolbox in her hands when I was completely vulnerable. In a way I think she was acting out a fantasy she had of me and her workplace."

"I think that's exactly what was going on," I said.

"That's okay, right? Everybody has fantasies?"

"Yes," I said. "But what you do with those fantasies can get you in trouble."

"I'm not going to get in trouble. This is what I want."

"Did you like being tied up and all that?"

"Oh god, yes. It was awesome. This girl is really, really kinky."

"Would you want that every time?"

"I never thought about that, but this thing is so new and exciting I can't imagine it ever getting boring, or ever being a problem."

"Did you ever think that married life with Irene would ever get boring?"

"No, but it sure has. Everything has, especially in the bedroom. All she does is lay there. I feel like I'm making love to a bowl of soup. She doesn't want to try new things, even old things, or experiment with role-playing like Sharon does. And that's if and when she's in the mood. She gives more attention to our kids, our pets—hell, the garden—than she does to me. I've fallen so far down her totem pole of priorities that I can't even see the top. And really, when it comes right down to it, for me, sex is about being close…intimate. I like the feeling and thought of being totally vulnerable, so intimate, and close to her."

"Now what?" I asked.

"Sharon and I are going to hook up next week in the same hotel room, only this time she said she wants to be my pit crew chief. She promised me she'd wear her underwear made from a checkered flag, and give a whole new meaning to the phrase 'power tools.'"

"Wow! Sounds painful."

"Come on, Doc, don't be silly. It'll be fun. I can't wait!"

Twenty-Three

IT WAS SHORTLY BEFORE SIX when Virginia and I were seated in the back of Metzger's restaurant west of Ann Arbor. The chairs were high-backed, oak, and trimmed in padded red velour. Eighteen inches beneath the ceiling, a wooden railing held dozens and dozens of authentic beer steins of all shapes and sizes, each with their own thumb petal. Somewhere behind the rows of porcelain treasures were the speakers that yodeled the sounds of "Edelweiss" and "My Father Was a Wanderer."

Metzger's was a German restaurant, and one of my favorite places to eat since the days I took Carrie to the University of Michigan hospital.

"This is nice," she said, pleasantly.

"Yes…it's one of my favorites." I looked across the table and marveled at the woman seated there, all upright and proud. "You look well, Virginia." I wasn't lying either. She looked too young to be in her early fifties, with her graying flits of hair coiling off her trim shoulders, eyes a sparkling crystalline shade of blue. The last time I saw her was at Carrie's funeral, when her eyes were puffy and red from all the crying. Months later her eyes were as pretty as I remember her daughter's. Even the subtlest crow's feet at the corners couldn't diffuse the beauty they possessed.

"Thank you," she said. "I'm feeling okay."

"That's good, right?" I smiled her way.

"Sure it is…" She picked up the menu, leather bound and embossed with the Metzger's coat of arms. "Say, what's good here?"

"I guess it depends on what you're in the mood for. Do you like German food?"

"I guess I've never really gone out of my way to try it," she said. "We took the kids to Epcot's version of Germany many years ago but I suppose that doesn't count."

"This is about as close as you can get to Munich without passing through customs. Lots of meat and potatoes, ginger and vinegar."

"I see…" Her head was buried in the menu, sifting through the litany of items, eyes following her finger. I could hear her read, with the silver charms dangling cleverly off her wrist. "*Rouladen* looks interesting, but I'm not sure if I should order it."

"Why don't you have a bite of mine?" I asked her.

"All right," she said, without looking at me. "I'll get the *sauerbraten* just for kicks."

"*Auf Wiedersehen!*"

A moment later our waitress parked in front of our table, pulling a pencil and a pad of paper from her laced apron. "Your dish comes with two sides."

"Oh dear, I never thought about that…what do you suggest?" Virginia asked the waitress.

"*Spatzen* is good, it's like a thick noodle, or we have German potato salad. We also have pickled beet salad, red cabbage…"

"No, no. That's okay. I'll have the *spatzen* and potato salad."

We ordered a bottle of Beck's and a glass of Liebfraumilch, just to make our dinner more authentic. The waitress nodded, jotting cryptic acronyms before gathering the menus and marching away. "How's work, anyway?" Virginia asked.

"Oh, I don't know. At the moment I'm on administrative leave."

She looked surprised, and wanted to know everything about it. I took my time and explained every detail because I knew that as long as I was talking about a harmless topic like work, it would reduce the time we may have talked about something uncomfortable, like Carrie. I didn't want to tell her that I had a date on the docket, or that I was gradually getting over Carrie's death. By the time I finished my story, I was halfway through the plate of *rouladen* and my bottle of beer. And honestly, it felt good to tell her about my problems. Hey, even shrinks need to vent. "So how's your dinner?"

"Delicious. *Sauerbraten is goot, yeah?*"

"I'm glad you like it."

Our conversation lingered for a minute, until I asked about Uncle Jim, her second husband, and the plans she had for remodeling her kitchen. "We're also putting in some workout equipment in the basement," she added.

"For who?" I asked.

"Me. That's who. I've always worked out. You knew that, didn't you?"

"Yes, I remember."

"Now I don't have to go the gym anymore, with those young, gawking personal trainers," she said, patting her tummy. "I'm full. And tomorrow I'll regret it when I'm burning the fat from my thighs on the stair-master."

"Tell me something," I asked. "Why do you work out?"

"You're not going to analyze my answer, are you?" She smiled.

"No, no. I'm just curious."

"Well, I guess I like being healthy. I'm not a health nut or anything, but I like taking care of myself."

"Do you like how you look?"

"Sure. I'm happy with my looks."

"Do you think that being healthy is a by-product of looking good, or is it the other way around?"

"You mean can you look good but be unhealthy?"

"Something like that," I said.

"I think that being healthy is good looking, whether you're in your forties like me," she winked, "or in your twenties like Carrie." There it was, what I really wanted to avoid. Apparently she wanted to avoid it too, because her eyes turned away from mine. I peeled at the label on the beer bottle, then picked up the little liqueur menu stuffed behind the salt and pepper shakers shaped like mini beer steins.

"Yes…I suppose so."

"I'm sorry, Jim. Why did you ask me about working out, anyway?"

"Because you look so fit, so healthy, I just wonder if you're doing it for yourself, or somebody else. You look great."

"My husband doesn't pay much attention to me, period."

"Now I'm the one who's sorry. I didn't mean to pry…have you ever tried *Rumpleminze*?"

"Not that I remember. What is it?"

"I can tell you that it's not pickled beets or red cabbage. It's glorified peppermint schnapps."

"You go ahead. I'll watch your nose turn red."

"No, that's all right," I said. "I've got to get home and take care of Toby, and I'd hate to get in a wreck."

"How is *that animal*, anyway?" She snubbed her nose.

"He's fine. We had some good times up north hunting birds."

"Does he still bark at his poop?"

I laughed.

"Does Raggedy Ann have cotton…"

"Booties?"

More laughter.

"Listen, Virginia," I said. "I didn't mean to make you feel uncomfortable, and I'm sorry."

"I am too…sorry. If you're still grieving over Carrie, I understand."

"I miss her." I said.

"I wish there was some way to bring her back."

"I know." The waitress brought the check and laid it on my side of the table. "I can tell you that I'm working on something to make sure nobody ever gets burned by that company again." We were back on safe footing again, and I told her all about the business with Atmantle Health and Casualty. She was shocked to hear that the insurance company had scores of complaints against them, and that the authorities in three states didn't do anything to stop them. Virginia snickered when I told her that I was working at Carrie's old law firm under the name of Jim Nunnelly.

"That's so sneaky." She whispered. "Is it legal?"

"I'm not impersonating a lawyer or giving legal advice, I'm merely investigating the situation."

"That's great, Jim. I'm proud of you for taking on something like that. Those people are crooks for not paying her bills. It's a risk, but I think it's worth taking…" She crossed her arms and fiddled with her watch. "You know I'll never forget the time that Curtis had some bully after him in grade school. I think Curtis was in the fourth grade and Carrie was in sixth. Anyway, this bully kicked Curtis off the top of the slide at recess. He fell backwards and bumped his head. Had a concussion! When I picked him up at the principal's office he kept crying, 'I want my mommy! I want my mommy!' He was so messed up that he didn't know it was me." Virginia was upset recalling the story. She kneaded a clenched fist into the palm of her other hand. "One day Carrie found the bully and that was the end of that. She beat the snot out of him. Curtis never had to worry about someone throwing their weight around. Maybe I should have realized that Carrie was destined to become a lawyer, a good lawyer." She paused for a moment. "You know, Jim, Carrie would have approved of this. She'd want you to beat the snot out of those Atmantle folks."

"Really," I said. "This investigation…it's just a wild goose chase at this point. It may fizzle out into nothing, but at least I'm doing something about it."

I didn't have the heart to tell her that I had the head of the company in my care.

"Who knows what will happen," Virginia said. "But like you said, at least you're doing something about it. Carrie would be proud of you. She was always caught up in making things right. I'll never forget the guy who took her to the senior prom. He had a sporty little convertible and turned out to be a real jerk. You know, I tried to tell her that…but anyway, they went to the prom together and then things went bad." She was snickering, "This guy took off with another girl from the dance and left Carrie high and dry. By the time she got home she was crying, and almost admitted that we were right. I saw the pain in her face, but she was smart about it too. When she saw him a few days later she told him 'it's no big deal,' and I think he believed her. Well, time went by—a week or two—and she found her opening. She poured five pounds of sugar in his precious little car's gas tank. Wrecked the engine of his convertible." She laughed and laughed. We both did. "Revenge is a wonderful thing, a powerful emotion, Jim, you know that."

"I know. I see it in my work all the time."

"You mean people come in with an axe to grind?"

"Some people are consumed with revenge. Others are looking for someone to blame for the speed bumps in life, or a person to help them support their addiction…"

"Don't they call those people 'enablers'?"

"Right."

"See…I remember some things from my college psychology courses."

"That's good." We were smiling again, and had a very good visit. I put my Visa card in the leather check holder and picked at the crumbs on the white linen tablecloth. It seemed that we had run out of things to say.

"Listen, Jim, thanks for driving down here like this. It really has been nice to see you again, to catch up with what's going on. I was always so proud of you as a son-in- law." She was getting choked up, again.

"Virginia…"

She held her finger up for me to wait while she took a drink of water. "I have to say this. I just have to. I am so pleased to see that you're moving on with your life. I know that you loved her, and you tried your hardest to make her happy. In fact, I know that you made her happy while she was here." She reached for her handbag and pulled out a withered tissue and a check. "I want you to take this…" Her hand reached across the table, tissue exposed. "I'm sorry. You don't want that!" She sniffled and laughed at the same time. "Here, take this check. It's half the money from the policy we took out on Carrie when she was a teenager."

"Virginia…really, I'm okay."

"No. No. That's for you. Her father and I discussed it, and that money is yours. We bought it because we knew that she'd rack up substantial student loans in college and law school, and she could use the life insurance as a hedge against the loans she'd need for her first house. We never thought that we'd collect on it, not in a million years. Now that you're paying for her medical bills, final expenses, not to mention her student loans…"

"I know, but this feels a little funny."

"Jim, you're family." She gulped a sophisticated gulp, choking back the tears. "Do something nice with it…something to remember her. Consider this money as a gift of love…Carrie's love. Don't fritter it away. Pay off the medical bills if you want. Save it for a down payment on your first house if that suits you. I don't care…but think of it as something tangible you can do with her memory. Okay?"

"Sure, sure. I'll do what's right, I promise."

"You don't have to tell me, either. You don't have to call for my approval."

"That's fine, but I'll still call you."

"That would be great. I should go, Jim."

"Say hello to Curtis, and thank you very much."

"I will and you're welcome."

We hugged for what seemed like a minute or two outside the restaurant in a spitting rain. She was still grieving, but like me, gradually learning to accept the fact that Carrie was gone. Little by little we were getting on with life. We were moving ahead, while not forgetting the past. I opened the door to her Lexus and she slid inside. "Oh, and there's one other thing…"

She reached behind the front seat and pulled out a shoebox. "This is for you." It was heavy, and the sides felt like they would pull away from each other. "It's photos of Carrie…her scrapbook and things." Her car came to life and I watched her buckle her seatbelt. "We found it in the rafters of the basement when we were making room for the exercise equipment." Slowly she backed out of the parking spot, looking both ways before waving a little wave like she was leaving her second grader for the school bus.

I walked to my truck, started the engine, and reached into the breast pocket of my sport coat. Virginia's gift of love was a hefty one: seventy-five thousand dollars.

It was a ton of money, I must admit, and more than I was used to handling. It would take me over a year to make that kind of dough on the Centre's wages, and there were no with-holdings either. It was all mine to use as I liked. It was all mine to save, to invest, to have in my back pocket in case things took a turn for the worse with my employment. I had every intent on using it wisely, to be smart. I wanted to do something special with it, to honor Carrie's memory, to turn the money into something good. Most of all, I wanted to keep it a secret from the people around me.

A foolish man would have frittered it away on a new shot-gun, or a classic double-barrel like the one Telpher Beaman toted around the woods of the Upper Peninsula. I didn't need that, or want it either. My trusty over and under twenty-gauge suited me just fine.

I was in dreamland as I drove home. Between Lansing and St. Johns I thought about paying some bills. Medical bills. Doctor bills. Oncologists, anesthesiologists, laboratories, and technicians. Student loans. The funeral home. Hell, I was still making payments on the car that had been in a junkyard since a week after the accident, six months ago. Any of the choices would have been honorable. Any of the options would have served Carrie's memory. They all seemed logical and prudent, but hardly endearing.

No, I would treat Carrie's money like an organ transplant. She retuned the financial blood back into me, and I was bound and determined to move mountains with it. I was going to hold on to it until the right thing came along. If it ever did.

The following morning I opened an online account with one of the brokerage houses, and parked the whole seventy-five thousand. My plan was to let it sit there and let the marvels of compounding interest add to my balance. It would be safe in an online money market, yet ready to jump off the bench at a moment's notice.

Poor Virginia. Her second husband turned out to be a jerk and she seemed to regret marrying him. She lost her daughter, her closest friend. I think she was vicariously living a happy married life through Carrie and me. For some reason Virginia's words kept coming back to me, even though they were hardly insightful: "Revenge is a wonderful thing, a powerful emotion." Carrie and Virginia were going to help me get even with the schoolyard bully, with the crumb for a prom date, with the people at Atmantle Health & Casualty.

Twenty-Four

THE FOLLOWING DAY dawned bright and sunny, not especially abnormal for early November in mid-Michigan. When I let Toby outside first thing in the morning, I figured that I hadn't been grouse hunting in almost a month. I stood at the kitchen sink, sipping coffee, and watched my dog make his rounds. He sprinkled each tree, hoping optimistically that some hot female would find his scent irresistible and they'd run off together, making puppies and living in eternal bliss. Strange dog. Deprived dog. I missed grouse hunting with Toby. In the heat of summer I'd die for a few spare hours in the chilly grouse woods. In the dead of winter, I'd do anything for a morning of hunting with Toby when it was thirty-five degrees instead of just plain five.

So with little more than a second thought, I decided that a few hours in the grouse woods was just what the doctor ordered. I called Toby inside, gave him a scoop of food, and went back upstairs to get ready for the day. Donned in a half turtleneck and my favorite flannel shirt, I was confident that I'd stay warm without getting hot. A thin pair of silk long underwear would keep my legs nice and comfy under my brush pants of heavy canvas. Toby made it upstairs and immediately recognized the wardrobe. "Yippee!" He seemed to say. "Yahoo!" He barked.

"I know…you wanna get some birds, don't you?" More barking and tail swishing.

"Birds" is a word you don't use lightly around an English setter. They're programmed from birth to hunt birds and the mention of the word sends them into a ravenous frenzy. Toby watched me pull my twenty-gauge from under the bed along with a change of clothes for later. He never left my side. My plan of a leisurely morning followed by a couple of appointments in the afternoon turned into a quick little adventure. And I liked it.

Driving east of Mt. Pleasant, I figured that the grouse would be out looking for food after the last day and a half of wet weather. Grouse are really fair-weather birds. They don't venture outside of their conifer lairs when it's wet or nasty. Not coincidentally, the best hunting takes place when the weather is decent.

A half hour later we turned off the blacktop east of Mt. Pleasant and were bouncing our way along a well rutted two-track. A good-sized porcupine waddled across the trail in front of me, tail scuffing November's hoard-frosted leaves. Soon after, I parked the truck, loaded my gun, and let Toby out of his kennel. We were away. At first he was all wound up, dashing far ahead, then returning with a bumptious grin. It was fun to watch him blow off steam, to release a month's worth of pent-up energy. We were still a few hundred yards from the good hunting area and I didn't mind him running willy-nilly through the woods.

When we made it to the creek, Toby got down to business. He recognized the cover, smelled intrigue in the air. No more careless sprints, no more rabid compulsion. He combed the woods in front of me, dashing from one pocket of cover to the next with that wonderful nose and his beautiful coat of ermine white and black. Just then, he struck gold—or more like it—a brick wall. He didn't move; he didn't flinch. Toby was paralyzed by the scent of a grouse, a slave to the call of his ancestry. I moved toward him, toward a fallen aspen top that a beaver had discarded. Bang! A grouse boiled out of the top, then another out the side. I threw the gun to my shoulder, and nailed the first, then set my sights on the second, but missed.

"Good boy, Toby!" He was all over the first bird, mauling it gently for a second, then scooping it up in his massive jowls. "Here, boy!"

It would be the start of an outing that would see us flush almost a dozen grouse in the next two hours. I managed to kill two more birds before we made it back to the truck without running into the porcupine or consulting my compass. Since the time we got lost in the Upper Peninsula I bought two compasses; tied one to my vest with a leather strap, and put the other one in the inside breast pocket. I learned a valuable lesson about having the right tools for the job, and always being prepared.

I also packed a spanking new lint brush to take care of those pesky dog hairs that stuck to my pant legs like nettles. After putting Toby in his portable kennel, I changed into a gray wool suit, white dress shirt, and black penny loafers. A few licks of the lint brush removed the dog hairs. As I tied my necktie in the reflection of the passenger's side window, I kidded myself that I looked pretty sharp. Maybe even a bit lawyerly.

And really, I should have looked my best for what I had in store for the rest of the day. My first stop was at the DeWitt Free Methodist Church on the west side of DeWitt, Michigan just north of Lansing. Joseph Francis DelBanco was going to be buried that day. I knew him as Joe. Catatonic Joe. Joe, who faked me out so he could complete his *danse macabre*. Most importantly, Joe, the guy with the grim confession.

By the time I made it to the church, most of the attendees were already there. The crowd was sparse—only three-dozen or so—which wasn't unusual considering the recluse that Joe was. Most attendees were looking at the strange surroundings, just like me. The church was old, just a decade shy of its one hundredth anniversary, with plaster walls, a steep roofline, and a dozen steps leading to a vast foyer. It was the kind of church that you'd imagine your grandparents getting married in, then climbing into a Desoto, or a fin-tailed Cadillac amidst a shower of thrown rice. It was a church of beautiful stained glass, hymnals loaded with the classics, and a layer of foyers that had been added to it over the years.

I sat in the rear of the sanctuary, alone, and didn't take off my topcoat. The casket was at the oak altar, dressed in an American flag. Of those seated in front of me, nobody seemed to know each other. There was no apparent family unit. It was just a clutter of people gathered in a place of worship with nothing better to do before a funeral luncheon.

At once the organ pipes came to life, filling the sanctuary with a funeral dirge. I stood with the rest of the congregation but lowered my head to read the bulletin. Joe's son Jerry was scheduled to read the scripture, and that's exactly who I needed to talk to. The preacher lifted his hands, then lowered them slightly. We all sat down.

After a few kind words the pastor asked Jerry to approach the pulpit. Jerry was slightly shorter than his dad, and walked with an unusual gait. I wondered if Joe had the same gait when he walked, or if Jerry picked it up on his own. He had Joe's broad forehead and thinning brown hair. They shared a lot of the same characteristics, but one of them wasn't speech. Jerry had a lisp, or "wisp" I should say. When he approached the podium everyone watched. And listened.

"This is a reading from Isaiah," he said, as he looked toward the rear of the sanctuary. *"Fear not, for I have redeemed you. I have called you by name."* Jerry wiped his brow with a hanky. *"You are mine."* It was difficult for him to read. It was tough for him to say the words. We all bit our tongues when he slurred his speech.

When the ushers and funeral director loaded Joe into the

hearse, everyone headed for their vehicles. Joe's car was the first in line. It was just the opening I was looking for. "Jerry?"

"Yes."

"My name is Dr. James Ong, from the St. Jean Centre. Your dad was a patient of mine…"

"Yes."

"I'm very sorry about what happened…you must be devastated." He nodded, but looked slightly impatient. "I'd like to talk to you about your father, but not right now. Here's my business card, along with my cell phone number on the back. Please give me a call when you're ready to chat."

He took the card from my hand, then asked "Did you have anything to do with my dad's death?"

"Listen, please give me a call and I'll tell you everything."

He nodded.

"Again, I'm very sorry." I backed away, and half-heartedly waved. Jerry stuffed my card in his breast pocket and buckled his seat belt. They were on their way to the cemetery for a graveside service.

Poor guy.

I hoped he would call me.

With an hour or two of spare time, I decided to go downtown and pick up the police report regarding the suicide of Lucille DelBanco. The desk sergeant—I think his name was Barnard—looked at me a little strange, like I shouldn't be looking into things that were that old. "Is there a problem, Officer?"

"No, I just don't know why you've got to go poking around a case that has been closed for months." I frankly wasn't in the mood to dance with him so I let his invitation go. He seemed to be disappointed that I didn't put up more of an argument. I just stood there, listening to voice of central dispatch give instructions and relay information. "That'll be five dollars." I handed him my money, then skipped to the bottom of the page where the investigating officer signed his name.

"Does Officer Gutierrez still work here?"

"Yes, midnights."

"Thank you, Sergeant."

From the police station I drove downtown to one of the municipal parks that lies in the valley of a nearby river. I parked my truck toward the back of the park, near one of the footbridges.

Lucille died from three things: an overdose of sleeping pills, alcohol poisoning, and asphyxiation. Nothing suspicious. Nothing unusual. It was just a run-of-the-mill suicide.

Toby had been stuck in his kennel for several hours so I let him out to stretch his legs. He was stiff and sore, but thankful for the respite, tasting the air with quick little breaths. A couple in their seventies approached from the footbridge, the man patting his thigh the same way I do. Toby acknowledged his invitation, wagging his tail half-heartedly. "Beautiful dog you have here," he said, slapping Toby on the head.

"Thank you. He's a little sore today."

"You've been hunting, haven't you?"

"Yes sir…ruffed grouse."

"Any joy?" He asked, wiping a drop from the tip of his nose with a red polka dotted handkerchief.

"This morning we did. Got three." It felt good to thump my chest a little, because I quite often don't get any grouse at all.

"Well done! He's gorgeous. Did he point the birds?"

"Yup."

"That's great. When I was younger I had a setter too…" His wife picked a couple Toby hairs off his sleeve and sent them adrift. "We used to hunt the U.P. a lot. Boy, there were birds! They were so thick you'd almost have to shoo them off the front porch. Got lost too, and spent the night in the woods a time or two. My gosh." I just nodded, approvingly, as his wife pulled him away. "Good luck." He waved and smiled at the same time, looking back at Toby one more time.

It seemed that Toby had rekindled some memories of the man's youth, when he could walk half a day and not get tired, when the birds were so plentiful he could whistle through a box of shells in a weekend. Even though our conversation only lasted a few seconds, I believe the man thought of me as himself. In a strange way, the old man reminded me to enjoy my youth, my good health, and my good dog.

From there, I visited Sparrow Hospital in Lansing and made my way to the records department on the third floor. I forged Lucille's signature on one of the Centre's medical releases, and slid it across the counter. The lady behind the counter was suspicious, but I think my nice gray suit may have tempered her doubts. She tapped the computer's mouse, and stared at the computer screen. A few seconds later her printer hummed, and the paper slid forward like an enormous tongue. "Did you want *all* her records, or just the discharge papers?"

"Just the discharge."

"That will be seven-fifty then. It's ten pages long."

I handed her the money, and wandered back to the truck. Lucille had leukemia, the worst variety. It appeared as if the hospital ran a variety of tests and treatments, but nothing seemed to work. The prospects for recovery were slim. The diagnosis bleak. They gave her a referral to Mayo Clinic, but nothing ever came of it.

I read between the lines.

Her time had come.

She wanted to go home to die.

What a way to go.

Taren Lisk and I agreed to meet for a cocktail at an establishment a block or two from the Capitol. It was one of those bars with a tall brick interior, under an inscribed, tin ceiling. I was early for Taren, but none too early for a rush of interns, aides, and journalists from a host of outlets across the state.

They huddled around the bar, under a television blaring the senseless monotony of C-Span, "Lansing style."

My eyes dashed from television to television, then back to the bartender, who was up to her eyeballs in banana daiquiris, Absolute martinis, and bottles of Heineken. She seemed to be the model college student: upstanding, hard-working, and quietly financing her education with dreams of a more rewarding career years down the road. Finally she approached, pointing a finger hurriedly. "Sir?"

"Gray goose, ice cubes and a twist."

"Lime or lemon?"

"Lemon."

She dashed away, amidst the gathering din of laughter, back-slapping and idle chatter.

"Mind if I join you?"

It was Taren, smiling like a long lost friend. I stood, spread my arms wide and gathered her in. We hugged. Then kissed. "Of course you can. How are you?"

"Wonderful," I replied, happily. She was smiling, and decked out in a sharp navy pantsuit and a string of pearls looped around her throat like a loose necktie.

"How long has it been, anyway?"

"The wedding, I think."

"Yes, that was such a beauty…full day, wasn't it?" She was blushing.

"Yes it was, Taren. Can I buy you a drink?"

"Yes, chardonnay…Miss, if you have it…Joseph Drouchin." The waitress nodded, and asked me if I wanted to start a tab. Taren wriggled out of her winter coat, and I lent a hand.

"So…you're finally coming out of the closet…" I winked in her direction.

"I can drink whatever brand of wine I want, and let me remind you that I can still drink you under the table. Besides, something tells me that you're not drinking Mohawk vodka like you did in college."

"I'm a professional now. I can afford better booze." I reminded her.

"Well here's to our budding careers and cirrhosis of the liver." Our glasses chinked and we both took a satisfying pull.

"So tell me, Taren, what's up?" I asked her.

"With what?"

"With you, silly."

"You're not going to analyze me, are you?"

"Of course I will. You're my longest-standing client. You were my patient before I had a license to practice." I smiled.

"Good," she said, laughing. "Then this means that nobody else will know about it."

"That's right."

"What do you want to know?" She said, with a certain amount of terseness in her voice.

"Taren, gee whiz," I said. "I was just trying to catch up with an old friend, if you'd rather talk about the weather or the football games last weekend we can do that too."

"Sorry. I guess I've learned to keep up a facade, a pretense around the office, and it takes a while to download after a long day."

"How does that make you feel?" I asked in my best shrink voice.

"Shut up with the psycho-babble stuff will you?" We both were laughing, and were just as loud as rest of the crowd. She raised her glass, and swallowed, making the knot of beads rise ever so slightly around her neck. I noticed she was slightly larger than she was the last time I saw her, a bit more full in the face, but she was still mildly attractive. Even though she had the money to spend on a decent wardrobe, hairstyle and makeup, she hardly paid any attention to the latter. She was one of those women that could have been a knockout if she wanted, but for some reason didn't have the gumption to make it happen. "Got any smokes?" She asked.

"Fresh out," I said, shaking my head. "You haven't changed a bit have you?"

"Because I like to smoke when I go to the bar?"

"Yes."

"You used to smoke with me!"

"I know. I know. We used to have a lot in common."

"We still do, don't we, Jim?"

"I suppose so."

"We've made the change from Mohawk and Boone's Farm to Gray Goose and Joseph Drouchin. Here's to French imports." She mocked another toast.

"We wear real business suits, made of real wool." I nodded her way, complimenting her taste in clothes.

"We're on the road to riches, great success, and fame."

"Fame? As a shrink?" I asked her.

"Sure. Dr. Laura, Dr. Phil…What's his name, Leo Buscaglia?"

"Ha! I doubt I'll ever be that famous. Do you have any doubts that you'll be famous?"

"No," she said, confidently.

"How are you going to get there?"

"I'll get there," she said boldly. "I'm still paying my dues, and my student loans."

"Do you have a plan?"

"No, but I'm still learning the ropes, too."

"What do you do, anyway?" I asked.

"I work for the attorney general, in the transportation department."

"I know that, but what do you do?"

"The attorney general is the chief law enforcement officer of the state, and head of the Department of the Attorney General, whose duties are prescribed by constitution, statute, court…"

"Yeah, yeah, that's all very well and good, but what do you do?"

She took a quick sip. "I kick ass."

I chuckled. "I'm sure you do."

"Seriously…I look into all sorts of things within the transportation field—audits, bid rigging, federal guideline compliance in highway safety. Stuff like that."

"What do you mean by 'bid rigging'?"

"It's quite common in the road construction industry. I cracked a good case here last winter. Got an employee who was steering business to one specific construction company instead of the lowest bidder. You may remember the case, the construction company was named Don Bendini, and the guy who we nailed in the department was Ian Jorke." I shook my head, no. "It all started last fall during deer hunting season, which in Michigan is sacred."

"Really?" I said.

"Yup." She snapped her finger and gestured to the bartender. "Everybody in Michigan deer hunts." Before I could cut her off and say something clever about deer and deer hunting she continued. "It's human nature to cheat, but I cleaned house… another round, please!"

"Thank you." I said; she didn't miss a beat.

"Jorke shuffled government contracts to his buddies in exchange for a slice of the pie. Kickbacks, perks, the old boy network. But we fried his ass. It was great. Our office had a couple of undercover state troopers follow Jorke up to some hunt club near Mio, know where that is?"

"No."

"It's about here." She held out her hand like a mitten, a representative of Michigan's Lower Peninsula. "It's about…oh, rats." Her mitten was facing the wrong way; the "thumb" should always be on the right.

"It's about right here." She pointed to the middle knuckle of her index finger. "Anyway, the hunt club is in the boonies…down dirt roads, around hills, creeks, I mean way out in the middle of nowhere. The troopers had to leave their vehicle at a locked gate, and follow a homing device we put under the bumper of Jorke's vehicle. It led them to this massive log cabin lodge next to a huge lake the color of Tidy bowl." She paused for a quick sip. "The troopers snuck in there, and watched the members playing cards, drinking scotch, and having a grand old time."

"What else?" I asked.

"I think they have trout fishing and turkey hunting in the springtime."

"No, I mean was it legal?"

"We had a court order."

"I guess that's legal enough."

"Yeah but this is where things really got interesting. The troopers cut the chains on the gate, and drove their van right in there on the morning of opening day. The lodge was empty; even the cook was out hunting. They snuck in there and installed cameras and transmitting devices over the card table, the bar, and even in our guy's bunkhouse."

"They didn't get caught?"

"Almost…one of the members forgot their boots, or license, I don't know, and caught the troopers in the act of installing an antenna off the balcony…"

"What happened?"

"They played it off, like they were an exterminator or the health inspector."

"Wow," I said, not so much at the content of her story, but the way she was telling it.

She was beaming, nostrils flaring with testosterone.

"Oh yeah, but this is where it gets interesting."

I interrupted her. "Do you want to get a table and have some dinner?"

"Sure…I can eat." She stood, grabbed her coat, and followed me to the front of the bar, where we were led to a table draped in a red-checkered cover and matching cloth napkins. "We got

Jorke telling Bendini's people that they'll get the hundred million contract to widen I-75, but he wants a two hundred and fifty thousand dollar piece of the pie. Can you believe that?"

"Why did he do it?"

"Greed…that's all. I mean after thirty years on the job, the guy probably had a pension worth three or four hundred grand. If he closes a couple of deals like that under the table he could double what he's got to spend in his golden years."

"Now what's he got to look forward to?" I asked.

"Eight to ten."

"Did Jorke come right out and say that he wanted the money?"

"No, no. He was a little more subtle," she said. "When the state of Michigan posts road work to be done, everyone in the transportation department knows the specifics of each job. There are ways to cut corners, especially if you know that the engineer made mistakes. Jorke knew that the engineering firm over-estimated the plan quantities and was giving Bendini a heads-up on those inconsistencies." She shook her head again. "Jorke was steering business to Bendini, that's all there was to it."

I shook my head. "What's good here?"

"Burgers, ribs, chicken fingers…the usual suspects." She winked. Then drank. "Our surveillance system helped put Jorke away, but it also stirred up more than we bargained for. A lot more. We got a judge talking to a developer…whose case was on his honor's docket. The judge was to decide if the developer's golf course was a threat to wetlands near Leland. Know where that is?" She paused, and I thought we were up for another geography lesson on her mitten. "Ah, it doesn't matter if you know where it is. After a weekend with the boys and all the perks that go with it, the judge decided that another golf course wouldn't be that bad."

"You couldn't use the tape of him, could you?"

"Since it was obtained accidentally?" She prompted.

"Right."

"Not really, but the judge didn't know that when I played the tape to him in his chambers…"

"Taren! That's just plain mean, if not wrong."

"Jim, like I said I'm learning the ropes. How else were we going to get a crooked judge? It would have taken weeks, tons of man-hours. I was doing a little freestyle, that's all. That son of a bitch had it coming."

"Holy Christmas! I can't believe you did that!"

"What?" She shrugged her shoulders like it was no big deal. Her dinner order was just as nonchalant: a fish sandwich, house salad with raspberry vinaigrette on the side. I placed my order: half rack of spare ribs, Caesar's, and a tall glass of water. Taren excused herself from the table and made her way to the bathrooms at the opposite end of the bar. She was amazing.

While she was gone, I checked my messages on my cell phone and pretended to be one of the preppy professionals that were gradually parading out of the bar. The pretense Taren talked about was real; they seemed to have an air about them, a facade. No wonder so many people need shrinks to make sense of the madness.

Taren returned to the table clutching a cigarette in her fist. I laughed.

"Do you always get what you want, Taren?"

"Naturally…why do you ask? Because I bummed a cigarette from one of the clerks at the courthouse?"

"I'm sorry. I was just thinking that your case with the judge didn't have much to do with transportation, but you made sure that justice was done."

"So I did a little freestyle, what's your point?"

"Taren, why don't we talk about something else?"

"No, I want to know what you're getting at."

"Okay, fine." I thought for a second or two about how to break the ice. "You have always been a go-getter," I began, "someone that knows how to get things done. I want you to help me out with a situation that's been festering for quite some time."

"With what?"

I started in with everything about the time our meals were served: Atmantle, Carrie's illness, Morrison & Nunnelly, the Insurance Commissioner's office, and the complainants who were listed on a sheet of paper in my breast pocket. Now that it was my turn to have the floor, Taren listened intently, making notes, and asking few questions. I think she was impressed with my organization, the volume of names of the list, and my commitment to investigating the whole situation. Before I knew it we had finished dinner and I had a promise that she'd look into the case again. She laughed approvingly at the thought of me being a lawyer, too, or at least working at a law firm. "I can't make you any promises, but let me do a little more free nc n o my own and see what turns up."

It was getting late, and we had a lot to drink. I thought about driving home but it seemed foolish, after all, Mt. Pleasant was an hour's drive from Lansing.

Taren ordered coffee and when the bill came, we went Dutch, like old times.

"Why don't you crash at my place?" She suggested.

It was exactly the invite I had hoped for. "Are you sure?"

"Hell yes, I'm sure. Come on, it'll be fun. My apartment is only a few blocks away. I usually walk to work if it's not too snowy. There's a pullout couch and fresh sheets in the closet."

"What about my truck?"

"It'll be fine on the curb, and if you get a ticket our office will take care of it."

"Great, but did I mention that there's two of us?"

"You're pregnant?" She laughed.

"No, no. It's hardly that." I said, rubbing my belly. "No really. It's my dog. Can he sleep on the floor?"

"Um…what kind of dog is it?"

"English setter. We went hunting today on the way down to Lansing. He's really a sweet animal, and I promise to clean up the piles of dog pooh. Did I mention he has a spastic colon and a catheter?"

"Very funny. What the heck. Let's go get…him? Her?"

"Him…Toby."

We pushed away from the table, and I helped her with her coat. She smelled a bit smoky. The air outside was a welcome change, refreshing even though it was charged with the smells of passing motorists. "I'm parked down the street."

"Good, it's on the way to my apartment." She put her arm in mine, and mentioned how nice it was to see me again. I nodded, and smiled. When we made it to my truck and popped the hatch, she mentioned how cute my vehicle was. "It's big, and safe I bet. I like it." Toby was sprawled out in his little travel kennel, tail thumping the gate as he looked over his shoulder, like a model. "Man, he's gorgeous," she said. "English setters are one of my favorites. What kind of birds were you hunting?"

"Ruffed grouse."

"Neat. Don't they call 'em 'pats' too?"

"Some people," I said, handing her my cased shotgun. "Here, hold on to this for a second."

"Jim! Is this thing loaded?"

"No…just a bit tipsy."

"Shut up, will you?" She whispered. "But I'm serious. Are there bullets inside it?" Her head was on a swivel; she must have thought it was illegal to carry an unloaded shotgun in the city, even though she was in charge of upholding the laws.

I retrieved my gun from Taren, and explained that I couldn't really leave my gun in the truck overnight. "Someone might steal it."

"I feel like Bonnie and Clyde or something."

"Actually, I do need to stop at a store. Is there a place that sells dog food on the way to your apartment?"

"A party store, yes."

"Good."

"Don't forget to get a bowl."

"Okay. Okay." I stopped and gave Toby a few pats on the head. "It seems my old friend Taren here will take a little time before she warms up to you." Taren just rolled her eyes.

"Is Toby the new love of your life?" She asked.

"You mean since Carrie died?"

"Yes."

"Boy, you don't mince any words, do you, Taren?"

"Have I ever?" She rebutted.

"No, you haven't, and no, Toby was in my life before Carrie and after. He's just a pet, that's all. He's replaceable."

She nodded in agreement and then changed the topic. "Do you remember when you asked Carrie to marry you, and she said yes, but she wouldn't take your name?"

"Yes…and apparently you do too."

Her gloved hand was still on my arm, which was clutching Toby's taut leash. He was ahead of us by a step or two, pausing to sniff the metal poles that kept the parking meters chest high. "I've got to tell you, Jim, that was one of the funniest stories I've ever heard. 'How can I be a lawyer with a name like Carrie Ong! It sounds like a command: Carrie Ong!'" She said. "Oh Jim, I still laugh about that one." She was laughing so hard and loud that strangers were glancing at us as we passed.

And what the heck, I was laughing too. It was one of those happy moments we had—Carrie and me—when we could chuckle at each other and the twist of fate that led a "Carrie" to fall in love with an "Ong."

"You two had a lot of fun together, didn't you?"

"Oh boy…we sure did," I said.

"I'm really sorry, Jim."

"I know you are. A lot of people are. It was such a sad ordeal to go through. Horrible. But you know, I'm gradually moving on with life, but I haven't forgotten what happened. We were taken to the cleaners by that insurance company, I know it. We were seriously wronged, and I really need your help, your expertise, and your connections. If you would look into the mess at the Insurance Commissioner's office I would really appreciate it. There's got to be something there. I just know it."

"I know Jim. I'll check it out."

"If you could just see the look on some of their faces, you'd never forget it. Their lives were destroyed by that company. The company is crooked and they're getting away with it. They're getting away…with murder."

"Jim, you have my word on it. I'll check it out." We stopped in front of a party store, under the radiant dim of Budweiser's logo. "I'll stay here with Toby and keep the getaway car warm. Toby will ride shotgun."

I made my way inside the store and found the dog food and a medium-sized dog bowl. Taren looked absolutely ridiculous—with her cashmere coat, a shotgun in one hand, an English setter on the other. She was hardly dressed for hunting and the middle of downtown Lansing wasn't exactly a good place to try. Five minutes later we were at the entrance to her downtown complex. Taren warned me about the doormen and their fierce practice of enforcing the rules. "Most of the doormen are nice, but they really need to get a life." We made it inside, past the leather couches, potted plants and front desk to the elevator. Ten floors later we were inside her apartment—a bit Spartan in its appearance, but functional in its proximity to downtown. Together we watched Toby gulp his vittles as if he hadn't eaten in months.

The second he finished his meal I picked up the bowl before he had a chance to raise a leg to urinate. Taren looked confused. "Trust me," I said. "My dog is certifiably insane."

Taren shrugged her shoulders, then marched down the hall to a closet where she pulled out a set of linens the color of surgeons' scrubs. "Would you like me to help you make the bed?" I shook my head, no. "Suit yourself...sleep well, Jim." She placed the bedding in my lap, gave me a kiss on the forehead, then stopped at the threshold, "It was really nice to see you again." I watched her take off her little heeled shoes one at a time, then wave goodbye. "I'll be gone by the time you wake up."

It *was* nice to see her again. She was an old friend, and we seemed to have more in common now that Carrie was gone. Still, there was something I didn't trust about her. She had changed since our days in college. She had always been aggressive, but now she was compulsive-aggressive. I couldn't put my finger on it, but there was something about Taren that wasn't quite right. She seemed to have a swagger about her—call it an invincibility—that belied my confidence. Regardless, I had to trust her to look into the mess with Atmantle. And who knows, maybe the Tasmanian devil would stir up something good.

As I lay there, listening to the sirens wailing toward some distant emergency, I noticed Toby sitting next to me. He was staring, like some psychotic killer. He brought to mind the Menendez brothers. He wedged his muzzle under my hand, and I realized I forgot all about his dessert. My suit was hung on the coat rack next to the bed. I reached up and found the breast pocket with the wadded up napkin inside. Toby's tail thumped the edge of the mattress quietly. I gave him another pat on the head, and a rib bone, still showing the traces of sauce from the restaurant. "Good boy, Toby," I said quietly. "I was only joking."

Twenty-Five

I REALLY DIDN'T HAVE much to do Friday, but it was one of those days that when it was over I figured that I got a lot accomplished. It all started when I got up at seven and got dressed. Taren left me a note on the kitchen table. *There's milk in the fridge if you're thirsty, and eggs, but I doubt if either are edible. I usually stop by the bakery on the way to work (it's across the street from the dog food store). Talk to you soon. Taren.*

It was just like Taren, too: wake up early; eat on the run; go, man go.

I made a pot of coffee and turned on the television. The only thing that interested me was the previous night's broadcast of "Evening Business Report." They do a fine job of summarizing everything that happened on Wall Street. The format is quick-hitting, factual, with just enough commentary to make something like the stock market palatable.

I am always amazed by the way stock prices plummet at just the hint of bad news.

At noon we were back in Mt. Pleasant. It felt like we were gone much longer than twenty-four hours. I checked the answering machine and waded through the mail…I had one call from a collection agency and a bill from a lab that performed Carrie's toxicology report almost a year ago. They finally got around to realizing that nobody but me was going to pay the bill. Toby lapped up a bowl of water without stopping, and couldn't care less about my little problems.

I made it upstairs to brush my teeth and change into a pair of jeans and a sweatshirt. There was a lot to do before my date with Rachel. I found a colander and my shears, the ones with the chewed-up plastic handle, compliments of Toby. Together we made it outside to the picnic table, where I usually clean my birds. Toby has the curiosity of a child when it comes to bird cleaning. He sits upright and watches the procedure with great interest, occasionally dripping a drop of drool. Ever since his days as a puppy, I've given him the hearts of the grouse we've killed. He loves 'em.

It took about a half hour to clean the birds, but it's one of the things I don't rush. There's nothing worse than biting into a bb from a shotgun shell, or finding a feather in an otherwise beautiful meal. Besides, it was such a nice day, and I felt like taking my time.

I like to look through the birds' crops after snipping off their heads to see what they've been eating. Buds? Leaves? Twigs or catkins? Fruit? Some guys make a journal of the birds they kill and what was in their crop. Me, I usually count on seeing lots of green leaves inside during the early part of the season, fruit in the middle, and buds at the end. Over the years I've come to realize that there are certain places that are better for grouse during certain times of the season. I'm either lucky or good when it comes to grouse hunting. Maybe both. By the end of the ceremony, I had my birds rinsing in the colander under freezing cold water. From there, I put them into their own little Ziploc bags and tucked them into the freezer with the others from earlier in the year. Someday—maybe this winter—they'd make a fine meal.

I was flying after lunch. I pulled Toby's kennel from my truck and almost tossed it down the basement stairs. My gun was placed in its usual spot—upstairs under the bed. My hunting pants, vest and boots were hung by the back door, on the hooks shaped like little shot shells. The back of my truck was a mess: feathers, dog hair, leaves, and bits of carpet from Toby's kennel had it looking rather shabby. Even the front of my truck was a mess, with almost a full season's worth of mud caked to the floor mats, and a layer of dust on the dash so thick I could have inscribed my initials on it. Yes, there was more dog hair—in the creases between the seats, around the console, and near the seatbelts. Lots of it.

A filthy vehicle is no way to impress a lady, I thought. I gave Toby a milk bone and headed toward town—to the car wash. *Maybe it's okay to have a dirty car after you've been married for a year or two,* I thought again. *I'm just like all the other jerks in the world.*

"No, I'm not a jerk," I told myself out loud.

"I am a good guy," I said, louder still. "Let me hear you say it, Jim."

"Okay…Okay". I said to myself. "I am a good guy."

Very good. I said, silently this time. *Now, let's go clean up your hunting vehicle so we can impress your girl.*

An instant later I heard the car next to me honk its horn. I looked over and saw Mary Cornwall waving from behind the wheel of her black Thunderbird. She gestured for me to roll down the window. "Having a little counseling session, Jim."

"Me?"

"Yeah, you! I saw your lips moving. Don't tell me you were talking to yourself?"

"No…I was having a little sing-along on the radio."

"Oh bull, everybody knows you listen to talk radio." The traffic light turned green and traffic lurched ahead. "We'll see you next week. Have fun talking to yourself this weekend."

I waved at her and she sped away. She would remind me of that little episode next week, I was sure of it. It's not the first time I've been accused of talking to myself out loud. Nor was it the first time that somebody thought I was talking to a person that wasn't there. I hoped there would be plenty of talking with Rachel.

Toby's hairs were everywhere. That wonderful coat was nice to look at, but not very practical when it comes to combing out the burrs or keeping it from showing up in a million different places. Those coin-operated vacuums that are kept outside the car washes are hardly adequate with their giant hoses. I did my best to get the inside clutter free, and then turned my sights on the dashboards, windows, and the outside.

Cleaning a car is hardly an exciting activity, or mentally challenging, but that allowed me more time to think. I was already hours ahead of myself, on to my date with Rachel. I pictured her seated across the table from me, with her mild red hair dancing off her shoulders, eyes pulling in the scene. We'd have good conversation. We'd have a fun time, I was sure of it.

An hour later my truck was looking fine. I dashed inside, gave Toby a scoop of food, then jumped in the shower. With only an hour to spare, I still hadn't decided what I should wear. Jeans seemed a bit too casual. A pair of khakis seemed stuffy. Oxford? Sweater? Since I was older than Rachel, I tried to look a little more hip. I decided on the widest legged pant I could muster, a plain red sweater, and ankle-high suede shoes. Bah! I didn't want to be older or smarter, or look like anything that I wasn't. I needed to be myself. I needed to be a nice guy, a thirty-something widower with a mediocre sense of humor and average looks.

"Okay, fine, I have an average sense of humor, mediocre looks and plenty of confidence," I said out loud. If Toby heard me, he really didn't seem to care.

Twenty-Six

AT 6:15 P.M. I FOUND Rachel's house, a two-story brick and vinyl-sided duplex several blocks west of campus. I was early—too early, really—so I drove around the block and ran into a party store for a pack of gum and a container of mints. It may sound immature for a guy in his early thirties to stock up on stuff like that, but that's what I did. Maybe I am immature, to go along with my other insecurities. As the gal at the cash register rang everything up, I tossed a pine-tree-shaped air freshener on the counter.

"Got a date tonight, huh?"

"How'd you guess?" I asked her.

"The gum, the air freshener, and shaving nicks on your neck."

"What?"

"Yeah, you got a couple whoppers, mister." I raised my chin and tried to see my reflection on the back of the register. "Here's the key to the men's room," she said. "You'd better clean yourself up or she'll think you're a klutz."

I plunked a ten-dollar bill on the counter, and made my

way to the restroom. She was right; my neck looked like I got into a fight with a weed whacker. I grabbed a handful of paper towel and ran it under cold water. After a minute or two of self-basting, I checked my watch. Now I was late. The gal handed me a paper sack and said, "Good luck…your change is in the bag. You'll be fine. Don't be so nervous."

I was nervous. Even though there was nothing to be nervous about, I was still nervous. It was just a date, just an evening out. It would be fun. It would be a change of pace, a welcome change of pace. *I am confident. I am a good man*, I thought.

I knocked on the door, waited several seconds, and was invited inside by Rachel's roommate. She was the one who was chronically late paying her bills, a bit of a slob, and was prone to weekend drinking binges. She asked me if I wanted a beer or a glass of wine while I waited for Rachel. "No, thank you," I said. She shrugged her shoulders, and took several steps toward the stairs.

I scanned the kitchen, which was a little unkempt with stacks of papers, glassware and empty beverage containers. Rachel's description of the roommate was right on the money.

"Rachel!" The roommate yelled. "Company!" I nodded approvingly, and the roommate added, "She's always late, it seems. You know how women are, they want to look their best." I nodded, and thought, *and smell their best, too*. I looked at my watch, and heard footsteps patter the stairs. She appeared, gloriously, like the sunshine after a spring rain. I nearly lost my breath.

"Hello, Jim. Sorry you had to wait." She was smiling. "Are you ready?"

"Yes—you look great. Got the tickets?" I helped her into her black leather jacket, then opened the front door. My stomach was tied in knots, my heart a snare drum.

"Right here," she tapped her purse—a dainty little number that clung to her hip on a strand of thin leather. Together, we made it to my truck, still showroom clean from the bath I gave it earlier in the day. I opened the passenger side door, and she hopped inside. "Nice truck…I mean SUV."

"Thank you."

"I don't suppose a lot of shrinks drive SUVs," she said.

"Why's that?"

"I don't know…in a way, I think some guys make up for their insecurities by driving a great big vehicle."

I grunted.

"I'm sure you're not one of those types," she said, smiling.

I laughed.

"What?" She asked.

"Maybe I do have insecurities."

"You?" She asked.

"Why can't I have them?"

"You don't act like it…and where are we eating, anyway?"

The conversation was off to a quick start, a rapid pace. "I thought we could try the Doherty Hotel."

"In Clare, right?"

"Right. It's really, really old but it's kinda nice in there. They call it a 'motor lodge,' but the bar food isn't typical bar food. It's good."

"Great."

I was already through most of Mt. Pleasant, and was headed north to Clare, which is the break between the farm fields of Southern Michigan and the woods farther north. Soft music played on the stereo. It was nearly dusk, and I spotted several pickup trucks parked near leafless woodlots in the fifteen minutes it took to get there. Bow hunters. We talked about safe topics like the weather and her college courses, before she piped up and said, "You know, Jim, I hardly know you."

I agreed, laughing. "There's really not much to me."

"What do you mean?" She crossed one corduroy leg over another.

"What you see is what you get. I'm a simple man." I looked her way and noticed the strawberry red hair, gathered neatly at the crown of her head, a pair of opal earrings, dancing. I didn't need the air freshener after all, my truck smelled like Rachel. And it was good.

"I want to know all about you…after all, you know my story, and all the sordid details." She glanced in my direction. A fair request.

"That's different," I said. "I know those secrets so I could help you. There's a lot more I want to know about you, too."

"Like what?"

"Like what we might have in common."

"How will I know what we have in common if you won't tell me more about yourself?" She glanced in my direction and raised her eyebrows, chin puckered. "Why don't I throw you a few softballs, call it twenty questions."

"Okay, shoot," I said.

"What do you like to eat?"

"Meat and potatoes," I affirmed.

"Ever have sushi?"

"Once in college, but I didn't inhale."

She giggled. "Calamari?"

"Yup, but they told me it was rubber bands."

"Ew. Ever been to Europe?"

"Nope, but I've been to Paris…Michigan."

"Very funny. Ever been out of the country?"

"Mexico…spring break in college."

She smiled again. "Why meat and potatoes?"

"That's what we ate. That's what Mom cooked us."

"What part of Mexico?" She asked, quickly.

"Cancun."

"Did you like the chicken & dumplings I cooked you?"

"It was really good. I'm serious, thank you. Your pot is in the back of my truck."

More smiles, and a second or two of music. "How many brothers?"

"One, an electrical engineer in Austin."

"Sisters?"

"None."

"See him often?"

"Never."

"Why not."

"I don't know. We're busy," I answered, reluctantly.

"With what?"

"Our careers. Our families. He's got a couple of kids and an obnoxious wife."

"Poor guy."

"I know," I replied.

We were soon in Clare, in the rear parking lot of the Doherty Hotel. Even though our date was only a few minutes old, we were able to communicate like we were old friends. It was nice to have a conversation with someone and not have it in the context of a counseling session. I had to remind myself that it was okay to be talkative. It was okay to be charming. There was no hour-long appointment to observe, no professional protocol that had to be obliged. On the other hand it felt weird; it had been so long since I had been on a date.

It seemed that lately all my conversations were purpose-driven. I spoke to Taren Lisk so she'd look into the mess with Atmantle. Glen Morrison needed to see things my way, after chatting with all those disgruntled claimants. Jerry DelBanco had a story to tell about his father. The only reason I communicated with my coworkers was because it was part of my job. If the Centre closed tomorrow I'd probably never contact those people again, outside of Mary Cornwall. That's just a fact of my life.

"Cute," she said. "This place is cute, in an old-fashioned kind of way."

I parked the truck and turned down the stereo. Rachel un-buckled her seatbelt and climbed out. She made mention of how nice my truck looked, but I shrugged off her compliment modestly. "It's as nice as I've ever seen it."

"Why do you know what my truck looks like?"

"I've kept track of you for some time now," she said.

"Really? You're not a stalker are you?"

"Don't be silly. When I dropped off chicken and dumplings I saw your truck parked in the driveway. I figured it had to be yours because your dog kennel was in the back. It was a lot dirtier then than it is now. A lot dirtier." It was a chilly evening, and I could see her breath pass through her painted lips. It was fun to watch. It was great to hear her speak. "Have you ever been stalked?" She asked.

"No…why would I?"

"If you gave bad advice to someone. There are a lot of losers out there, that want to blame somebody else for what's wrong in their life."

"No, thank goodness." We were inside the Doherty, but instead of eating in the 'motor lodge' section, I decided that we should get a cozy table close to the bar. After all, we did have a show to catch in a little more than an hour. "That would be scary."

"What would you do?"

Before I could answer her question the hostess directed us to our table. I helped Rachel out of her coat and ordered a couple of drinks. She commented on how nice it was to get out of the house and away from the rigors of school. When she opened the menu, I watched her for a second and the way she crossed things off her mental checklist. I told her that I've never had the fish, but the frog legs were good. Our waitress said that the lamb chops were on special. Rachel never did revisit the stalker question, but that was okay. I didn't have a clue how to answer it because I never thought it would happen to me.

Through the rest of dinner, I tired to keep our conversation light and lighthearted. I avoided sensitive topics like politics, religion, and her counseling. She didn't pry into my affairs, and I didn't meddle in hers. The whole idea was to have fun, to giggle a little, and to enjoy each other's company. Mission accomplished.

When our meal of frog legs and perch was served I asked if she liked to people watch. "Doesn't everyone?" She suggested.

"Sure they do, but I like to do much more than that."

"Like what?" I suspected she thought I was weird.

"I don't know; let's just say that I like to fill in the blanks."

"Come on, tell me more." She was curious.

"Look at the couple in the corner. The older couple under the television…the man has the green sport coat on…"

"I see them." She pressed a lemon wedge against the edge of her spoon and the juice drizzled onto her fish. "What about them? They look like a nice couple out for dinner."

"Why are they out for dinner? What's the occasion?"

"They're hungry?" She snickered sarcastically.

"Come on Rachel, where's your imagination?"

"You mean there's more to it than meets the eye? You mean more than just a couple in their late sixties out for their anniversary dinner?"

"Yes."

"Like what?" She took a bite of fish, dabbed her lips with a cloth napkin, then sipped her wine.

"I think the two of them are eating here because it's halfway to their cabin on Higgins Lake."

Rachel nodded. "I get it. They live in Jackson…where he's the warden at the prison…"

"You're catching on. What's her story?"

Rachel hesitated, eyes sparkling in the candlelight. "She's on her third husband. The first one was killed in a train wreck, and her second she divorced after she found out he was cheating on her with the milkman."

"Nice," I said "*He* was cheating on her with the milkman! Why the green sport coat?"

"He's a realtor…no…an usher at the Catholic church in Jackson. All the ushers wear green sport coats, and they stuff those little inserts with the embroidered crosses into their lapel pockets."

"Nice image. Keep going," I said. "What's the secret he's keeping from her?"

"He has an illegitimate son—a ten-year-old from an affair he had with one of the prison guards. He pays for her apartment, and sees the boy about once a month."

"What does he tell his wife about the missing money?"

"He doesn't tell her anything, because there is no missing money. He pays her rent in cash. He pays for everything in cash. She still thinks that he's one of the rank and file instead of the warden. He keeps bringing home the same amount of money that he always did so she never thinks anything of it."

"How can they afford the cabin up north on a warden's wages?"

"They don't," she said, with a sheepish little grin. "It's her cabin, not his…she took the money from her first husband's train wreck settlement to buy the cabin and the lot next door. When things got rough after the divorce from her second husband, she sold the lot next door for five hundred dollars a foot," she said with a cute grin.

"She walked away from the real estate sale with over a half a million dollars, and she's not afraid to rub the warden's nose in it every chance she can." Rachel was creative. She was fun. And I liked her.

I took a small bite of food, pointed a frog bone across the table and asked her if they had any regrets.

"Who…the man or the woman?"

"Either or."

"Let's see." She paused, and played with the pretty watch

by the sleeve of her snug, v-neck sweater. "The man goes to Confession every Monday and tells the priest all about his exploits with his subordinate. He likes telling somebody about it because he can't deal with the guilt. He likes rehashing his sexual conquests, even if it's in the context of a Confessional. For portraying himself as a righteous man, his life is a rueful paradox. He regrets the relationship he has with the other woman, but he loves the benefits."

I nodded.

Rachel had been around the block, and I wanted to ask her about her regrets, but thought the better of it. We'd get around to regrets, both hers and mine, in due time. I wished we had more time to people watch, and chitchat, but we had a schedule to keep. We did manage a cup of coffee after dinner, and had a few more laughs at the expense of other diners. Our waitress was nice and attentive, and seemed like she was having fun too. She gave us great service and our food was excellent; that's all you can ask for when you go out to eat. Our date was off on the right foot and I was having a great time.

When we made it to my truck I asked her about *Oklahoma* and why she knew the words to one of the songs. Just like me, she had a part of her high school's production. She was in the play; I was one of the guys in the pit, "the thankless job."

Rachel didn't miss her opening. "How does that make you feel?" She asked.

I laughed. "You sound like a shrink now."

"I know…that's why I asked you. Didn't you feel love as a member of the band?"

"Sure I did, but it's not as glamorous as the people on stage."

"So to make up for it you bought this big SUV? That way you'll get noticed…you'll stand out from the crowd?"

"Doctor…" I sighed. "You must have skipped that part in college about being subtle. You've got to lead your clients to their own conclusions, not tell them what's wrong with them."

"Ahhh! You're right," she chuckled. "I guess that wasn't very subtle. I'm going to have to work on that."

"They'll go over that when you work on your Ph.D. too."

"I'll never get a Ph.D., thank you."

"How'd we ever get on this topic, anyway?" I asked her.

"I forget. It doesn't matter."

More music. More silence. More conversation and gum chewing. Just north of Rosebush a red fox trotted across US-27, bushy tail flowing behind it. We both saw it at the same time, and remarked about what a pretty animal it was.

When we made it to the theatre on campus, a crowd of two hundred gathered in the lobby. People were standing single file, eventually making their way to the box office where their tickets were being held or sold. Rachel said hello to a friend or two, and introduced me to one of her professors. I never like those situations, where I might run into a client. Technically, we're not supposed to acknowledge a client in a social setting unless the client acknowledges us first. You've got to respect the tenets of doctor-patient confidentiality even in public settings, especially in a small town like mine.

Rachel's head was on a swivel. She relished those social settings, where she might run into more friends or have the opportunity to introduce them to her date. I felt a little awkward, like maybe she was showing me off instead of paying attention to me. In a way, I was showing the classic symptoms of social anxiety disorder. I was nervous. I was uneasy, antsy. I wanted to wait outside until the show started, where nobody would see me, and I wouldn't recognize any of my patients.

I didn't have long to worry about it. A pair of ushers swung open the double-hung doors, kicked the little kickstand at the bottom, and began passing out programs. The crowd's volume rose and began a slow march toward the theater entrance. Several men toward the back of the line let out a cattle call. We were jammed together, only inches apart. Rachel was in front of me, and I put my hand on her elbow. I didn't want to lose her in the hoard of people, and yet I didn't want to put my hand anywhere else. I could have put my hand on her shoulder, but that was what we did in grade school when it was time for recess. I could have put my hand on her hip but that seemed a bit too forward for our first date. Heck, I could have kept my hands in my pockets, but I wanted to express the first sign of affection towards her. The cramped quarters gave me the opening, and I took advantage of it, however small.

She didn't pull away from me; she didn't squirm. I was relieved, then heard a strangely familiar voice. "Good evening, Doctor." I looked to my right and saw one of my former patients.

"Hello…Maury," I said, recalling that he was one of my first patients when I went to the Centre months ago. I only saw him a time or two but I remember his situation like it was yesterday. Guys with foot fetishes leave a lasting impression on you…especially when they're in the business of selling shoes. He was just plain weird. He liked the smell of feet, "the stinkier the better" he used to say. He liked to watch his customers giggle when he inadvertently tickled their undersoles.

After work things became even more bizarre; he once told me that he'd suck on his wife's toes until she begged him to stop. And she liked it too. "She'd feed me with her toes…carrots, Jell-O, rice, everything. If we were at a restaurant or a public place it was even more of a turn on."

That was the first thing I thought of when I looked in his direction. I tried to be cordial when he asked, "Having a nice time?"

"Yes, thank you," I said.

"This is my wife, Janice."

I smiled politely and nodded. "Nice to meet you, Janice."

He turned to her and said, "This is the nice doctor I was telling you about."

She nodded politely too, and I think she was waiting for an introduction to Rachel. It didn't happen. "Enjoy the show. Nice to meet you, Janice."

They both nodded again, and found their seats in the back of the theatre. I looked down at Janice's feet. On a blustery, cold November night she had on a pair of open-toed sandals.

Just dandy.

A few seconds later, Rachel found our seats in the middle of the auditorium—a dozen rows from the stage. I helped her out of her coat and noticed a diamond-shaped pendant dangling hypnotically around her neck in the valley of her breasts. The pendant swung ever so slightly. I could have stared at it all night.

"Who was that?" She asked.

"An old acquaintance."

All at once we were only a shoulder-width apart. It felt a little odd, sitting so close to someone. Maybe it was the insecurities in me. "Oh?" She glanced in my direction, eyebrows cocked again. I was growing accustomed to the way she asked questions. She was fishing for information about Maury.

"Yup. I'll have to tell you about him sometime."

"Okay," she said. Her eyes turned from mine to the program on her lap.

I looked at her program, then the pendulum. Program-pendulum. Program-pendulum. My mind flashed to those Abbott & Costello reruns when a vampire hypnotizes Costello: *You're getting very sleepy.* I laughed to myself. "What's so funny?" She asked.

"Oh, I was just thinking to myself."

"About what?"

"The old days…when I played in the band…when the band played in the orchestra pit."

"What instrument did you play?"

"Trombone," I said.

"Really?"

"No fooling."

I nodded in her direction and our eyes met for a second or two. They twinkled green. "How about you? What was your part?"

"I played Aunt Eller," she said.

"That's cool."

"I had a lot of fun, too."

"Was it hard to memorize all those lines?"

"Sure, but we used to practice a lot too."

I nodded. *So did we.* "Did you ever want to get into acting as a career?"

"Nah. I only got into doing plays because my advisor said I should. It was just another activity that would look good on my transcripts for college."

The lights dimmed and the audience simmered to a whisper. Several people coughed or cleared their throats the way they always do when it's really quiet. Just like fifteen years ago, the curtains opened and Curly entered, singing *"Oh what a beautiful morning."* It brought back old memories. It made me think of simpler times, when I had fewer responsibilities. In a way, I wish I had grown up in the 1950s like they did in *Oklahoma.* Call me nostalgic, but it seemed to be a lot easier to grow up then than when I was a kid. Heck, they didn't even have marijuana way back then, or did they?

We both really liked the show. At intermission we stood in front of our seats and made small talk about the actors and the band, and how much better they were than what we were in high school. We watched the people, and giggled when we recognized the man with the green sport coat from the restaurant. "I guess they're not going to Higgins Lake after all," I said.

I thought about Maury and Janice looking for a secluded place to do a little toe sucking.

Rachel waved to another one of her pals, who came over

to say hello. I forgot her friend's name, but she seemed like a busybody. The two of them talked and talked. Neither listened to the other. Through the banter and blab, I heard the friend whisper "my gosh, Rachel, he is really cute." It was slightly embarrassing, but it made me feel good.

When the play ended, and the obligatory standing ovation finished, we made our way to the truck. "That was fun," she said.

"Thank you, it *was* fun."

"Now what?" She asked.

"What do you want to do?"

"Let's go have a coffee or something, okay?"

"Where to?" I asked.

"Downtown. The coffee shop."

"Good idea."

We drove downtown, parked the truck, and made our way to the coffee shop—a quaint little place that also served fresh pecan rolls, Danishes, and chocolate chip cookies the size of saucers. On the weekends it was a popular destination for folks that didn't want to go to a bar, and didn't want to go home.

Over the course of the next two hours Rachel and I talked about a lot of different things. I asked about her roommate and how the two of them were getting along. Apparently they had reached a truce when it came to the dishes, the light bill, and taking out the garbage. They agreed to split up the jobs around the house, and the roommate said she'd try to pay her bills on time. Difficult roommates affect people in different ways. Some people can shrug off slobs or delinquents and think nothing of it. Rachel hated conflict.

I told her that sometimes I liked conflict. I liked the little challenges life throws my way. You win some, you lose some. Hopefully I win more than I lose. If I lose, I lose, and hopefully I learn something from the ordeal. I told her about my love of hunting grouse with a dog.

She wanted to know more. I told her about Carrie. About Atmantle. And the case I was building.

She wanted to know more about me, and what made me tick. I told her that I'm just a normal guy, an average man. I take pride in earning a living, in fixing things around the house, in working with my hands. I like my job. I like helping people. I like being a shrink. I love it when I get inside someone's head.

"But you know what, Rachel, I don't really like to talk about myself. I hide my feelings. I don't tell anyone what I'm thinking. I repress a lot. If I'm sad, you'll never guess it. If I'm happy you'll barely be able to tell. And I'm really, really sorry about it. I wish I could be more open…more honest with myself. With you."

"That sounded like you really are honest with yourself."

"Maybe you're right."

"When will you come to grips with…was it…Atmantle?"

"I don't know…I'm just beginning to look into this whole mess. I've got to find out if Atmantle was either right or wrong about the way they handled our case. And now that I've talked to all these other people in situations just like mine, I know that the company is wrong. I know there's something there. I can smell it. I can taste it."

"Can I help?"

"Sure. I can keep you informed. I'd like to have you to listen to me, and tell me if what I'm doing is right, wrong, or indifferent. Okay?"

"I'm not going to get in trouble am I?"

"No…no," I said. "I need someone to talk to."

"Are you doing anything illegal?"

"No."

"Okay. I'll do my best. I'll listen."

"Thank you. I really appreciate that. It's been a long time since I had someone to talk to, someone to listen. I really miss my wife. We did a lot of talking. A lot of listening."

"I'm sorry, Jim," she said sadly.

"I'm sorry too. I shouldn't have thrown that at you, especially on a first date."

"It's okay. I think it's fine. It shows what kind of man you are, and what a great person your wife was."

"Are you leading up to a compliment?"

She laughed. "I'll give you a compliment: I think you are a great guy, and I admire the way you're handling your grief. A lesser man would crumble under the strain, or develop a drinking problem. I admired your cool head when I threw all that stuff at you during our appointments…"

"Keep going."

She laughed. "Don't get your head all swollen now."

"Reel me in…I'm floating away."

"Earth to Jim, come in, Jim."

"Sorry. I have latent 'typical man' tendencies…and I like compliments."

"You sound like a shrink when you say 'typical man'."

"It's true. Men are predictable…they crave four things."

"Oh? Are you going to tell me about it, or do I have to guess?"

"I'll tell you…food, sexual fulfillment, respect, and the need to feel needed."

Rachel nodded. "In that order?"

I laughed. "It depends on how long it's been since they've had a good meal."

"I get it. The perfect day for a man is to come home from work, be appreciated by his wife, fed a good meal, then jump in the sack."

"In its simplest form…yes."

"And you are the 'typical man'?"

"No, no. I've evolved beyond that. I've left those caveman days behind me. There's more to life than just those four things. Don't get me wrong, I like a good meal; I like to be appreciated, but I also like to communicate. Maybe that's why I became a shrink in the first place. I like to listen to what people have to say, and I'm compassionate about their needs."

"So what is your idea of a perfect day?" She asked.

"Oh that's a toughie…outside of winning the lottery, and having an unlimited budget." I scratched my head, and swished the remains of the coffee in my cup. "I can't forget my dog in the perfect day, so maybe I'll start off by having a little grouse hunt at the cabin. It would be the second week of October, when all the leaves are in full color. After lunch I'd work for a few hours and I'd have an appointment where the client really makes some strides. It's not every day that the light bulbs pop in their head, and they see the truth of their ways…"

"Is that it?"

"No…I'd save the best for last."

"Oh?"

"When I'd get home from work I'd kiss my wife at the door, and ask her about her day. I'd build a little fire in the fireplace and have seven or eight martinis." She giggled, scuffing one index finger over the other. "Seriously…we'd have a fire and maybe a drink. We'd fix Caesar's salad and ruffed grouse for dinner, and eat it by candlelight, with a little Ray Charles, or something jazzy on the stereo. I'd tell her about my adventures up north, and she'd tell me about whatever was on her mind. We'd plan a vacation, refine our dreams, and remember the good times we've had. I'd look into her eyes a lot and we'd hold hands even more…"

Rachel blinked and blinked, like she couldn't believe what I was saying.

Heck, I couldn't believe what I was saying either.

"Sounds like a romance novel," she said, wryly.

"I know. It's a fantasy. It's fun to think about. In a perfect world, ruffed grouse are always easy to shoot, my patients always listen to my advice, and my home life is a bed of roses."

"Isn't that the reason why a lot of people get in trouble?"

"Emotionally? Sure. They have a distorted view of reality. Couples get married and think that it's going to be the *Good Ship Lollipop*. Men start their careers thinking that they're going to be the CEO of the company, but when that doesn't happen they get depressed. Even in my perfect day, room service clears the table and does the dishes, instead of the reality of doing them myself. The trouble is that expectations and reality seldom coincide. Marriage is hard work, just like the working world, like life…"

"Just like college," she interrupted.

"You're right. College is tough…that's why so many people drop out or don't pursue it in the first place." Rachel nodded, like she needed a little affirmation that her 'job' was important too. "College is tough."

"You know, Jim, when I asked you out, I really wanted to get to know you, and until now, I didn't think I was making strides." She toyed with her watch again. "Now that you've opened up, I want to get to know even more. We'll have to do this again sometime. I've had a lot of fun tonight."

"I'm blushing."

"Come on…take me home."

She pushed the spoons and silverware into a pile on the table and reached for her jacket. It was getting late; it was time to go. Rachel had to get up early in the morning and I was tired from a fitful rest at Taren's apartment. Toby was probably getting antsy at home too.

When we made it outside, a needle-fine rain covered the sidewalks in a slippery glaze. Rachel reached for my arm and I held on to it tightly. She remarked again what a nice time she had, and how much she'd like to do it again.

I parked my truck in her driveway then ran to the back to retrieve her pot.

"Thank you for the dumplings, they were excellent," I told her.

"You're welcome, Jim. I'd invite you inside, but my room-mate's probably passed out on the couch."

"No thanks, that image might soil my impression of her."

"Besides, she grinds her teeth at night, especially if she's been drinking heavily."

"Nice."

"I had a really great time tonight." She fiddled with the pot.

"Me too." It seemed that neither of us wanted to open the door, the date to end. "I'll give you a call soon."

"That would be great." Finally, she looked at me, leaned across the console and gave me a kiss. On the lips. It wasn't a mad, passionate kiss, but the kind of kiss that someone would give someone else if they were really good friends. She didn't smash her lips into mine, and it wasn't too sloppy. She didn't run her fingers through my hair while she kissed me, or close her eyes. It was just a really nice goodnight kiss, which was perfect for the occasion because we were, after all, saying good-night.

On second thought, it was just a kiss, plain and simple.

I guess I do analyze things too much, but at least there was something to analyze.

I waited a long time to go on a date, to have reason for hope. Now that I actually went on the date, I liked it. I had a really good time with Rachel and I hoped that the feeling was mutual. She lit a spark inside me that had been dormant since the days when Carrie and I were falling head over heels in love. She energized the embers; she fanned the flames. I loved the potion that coursed through my veins. And I wanted more. Much more.

Twenty-Seven

THE FOLLOWING MORNING I woke up early and took care of my dog. He was eighteen hours overdue for a grooming. After that, I put him on a leash as we walked through the grounds, but took it off when we entered the woods on the outskirts of the asylum. When we passed by the former "Haunted Forest" I got mad at Joe all over again. That was a horrible situation, a ghastly event.

We made it to the gas station a block away from the Centre, and Toby took his post—tied to a post—just outside the front door. Jane said that she missed me the day before. I told her "I bet you say that to all the boys." She winked and put my peanut butter cookie in the paper bag, just as I like it.

"Always nice to see me," she said somewhat concededly as I walked toward the door.

"Until tomorrow, sweetheart," I waved.

Toby wagged his tail as usual when I came out to get him. "Nice boy, now let's go home." He barked, and we were on our way again.

November isn't one of my favorite months. In my business,

it kicks off the unofficial start to the "depression season." People become depressed when they look outside and see nothing but the lifeless trees, and the prospect of four months of cold weather ahead. Add in a possibly volatile family reunion at the holidays, and you've got the start of a busy time of year in the counseling business. My mind was already ahead to Monday and the regimen of appointments as I reached into the mailbox for Friday's mail.

As usual, I got a couple medical bills, but I also got a rather innocuous-looking plain envelope with no return address. The handwriting looked familiar, extremely familiar. I set my coffee cup on the opened door of the mailbox and held the envelope to the sky. It was fairly heavy, and whoever sent it put a second ounce stamp on it just in case it required one. Slowly, I tore off one side of the envelope and pulled out the contents. There was a letter, and literature—flyers with pictures of white sandy beaches, starfish, and smiling couples hand in hand. I looked at the handwritten letter…the elegant style; the exaggerated indention of each paragraph, and the way she'd use ellipses to embellish sentences that had a deep meaning. It was Carrie!

I dropped everything, the leash, the bills, and my jaw.

> *Dear Jim,*
>
> *I hope this letter finds you in good health and fine spirits. Knowing you, you've probably been up to the cabin several times this fall… chasing birds and living the rustic lifestyle. Although I never let you know it, I thought it was really cool that you enjoyed bird hunting as much as you did. It seemed like a "gentlemanly" thing to do, and you were always the perfect gentleman.*

Tears rolled down my cheeks. I couldn't believe it. I called Toby's name, not knowing where he was, not caring about anything but the letter in my hand.

Don't be alarmed, I have not come back to haunt you; I merely wanted to give you something that we didn't make happen while we were together. It has been more than eight months since we've been apart, and I wanted to let you know that I still love you. I still care...

The worst part of writing this letter is acknowledging what I'll miss. By now we would have talked about starting a family. Who knows, maybe we would be expecting... It would have been fun to repaint the spare bedroom together, and buy all the stuff that our little girl would need. I imagined rocking her to sleep at bedtime, and nudging you out of bed when she wanted a midnight snack. Wouldn't it be fun to have birthday parties and sleepovers? Wouldn't it be great to show her how to ride a horse, or drive a car? You'd be a great dad, you were a great husband. I couldn't have asked for anything else, for anything more from a man. You were my dream come true.

I'm so sorry it had to end this way; I regret that we never had a vacation. Please Jim, take the honeymoon we never had. Take the trip I always wished we could. There's no cost involved, nothing to pay for. Go to the Bahamas and lie on the beach. Have some rum punch and think of me and my Grandpa. Look for seashells, ride horseback through the surf, read a good book and don't worry about the money. I paid for everything. You're booked the middle of February. Have fun, and happy anniversary.

With love, Carrie.

I laughed and cried at the same time. It was just her style. She was always full of surprises, unpredictable. Toby was near me again, and sniffing at the envelopes piled at my feet. I lowered Carrie's note to his level, and he wagged his tail. We both smelled her perfume.

There was one more line:

> *P.S.—Don't ask everybody who helped me send this to you...there's a company in Mt. Pleasant that specializes in the last wishes of sick people. I saw their advertisement on the hospital cafeteria's placemats.*

I laughed aloud and picked up the mail scattered all over the grass. Toby and I flew up the hill to our old house. I whooped and hollered. It was amazing...Carrie set me up for a trip to the Bahamas! A real vacation. I couldn't believe it, and neither did Virginia when I called to tell her the news.

I made my way inside, sat down at the kitchen table, and laid all the paperwork out in front of me. She thought of everything. The airline tickets were from Northwest—Flint, Michigan to the international hub in Memphis, Tennessee. From there, I'd fly directly to Nassau, Bahamas, and stay at a cushy looking place—the Half Moon Resort. If the Half Moon was half as nice as the brochure, I was going to have a ball. There were pictures of croquet courses, sandy white beaches, Olympic-sized swimming pools, and elegant dining. The brochure emphasized the resort's black and white motif complete with tiles in the concourse and fluffy black and white towels hanging in the bathrooms. It looked posh beyond words, nicer than any hotel I had ever visited.

Carrie didn't leave any detail forgotten: a parking pass and bus ride from the parking lot to the terminal in Flint, and more importantly, a ride from the airport at Nassau to the resort. Once there, I had passes for the breakfast buffet every morning, and the grand Bahamian feast at the end of my stay. It was going to be fantastic.

Toby wasn't impressed. He sat on his padded floor mat in the kitchen and sulked—turning his head away from mine and making the sighs of a spoiled child.

I gave him a pat on the head and went upstairs to my bedroom closet where I found the shoebox from Virginia.

There wasn't any rhyme or reason to the shoebox. Slides in their plastic containers had hen scratching written on their faces: "summer camp 1983," or "Vail vacation 1990." There were dozens of prints too, in various shapes and sizes, mostly black and white, with a few in color. I tried to organize everything chronologically beginning with her baby photos. She was a cute kid; with the dash of freckles dabbled across her cheeks, and her trusting, innocent smile. It was easy to smile back at her.

I found the pictures from the Bahamas. They were small pictures, perhaps only three by four inches, but they showed in detail what a marvelous time they had. There were sand castles, bareback horse rides, steel drums, and seashells. Grandpa, with his horn-rimmed glasses and his wide-brimmed hat, looked silly. Carrie used to laugh about that, and his dark socks and white legs. Now that I saw the pictures, I was laughing too. She must have cried at the photos of the two of them together, at the breakfast buffet, on the lounge chairs by the edge of the pool, or in the plane that took them there and back. The Bahamas was one of the first trips we'd planned to take. We vowed to have a drink in Grandpa's memory, if we ever made it there.

The cement lion in Carrie's box of photos looked familiar. In fact, it was the same lion draped in a screen of palmetto that I recognized from the brochures. I was going to the same resort where she went many years ago.

There were other photos too. There were plenty of Carrie and me—from the early days when we were dating to the time we were engaged. She hated getting her photo taken, and closed her eyes as a sign of protest. I remember asking her about it, but she just replied that she closed her eyes to avoid the flash.

Her family took me in. The photos of Carrie and me emphasized what a big part of her life, and the life of her family, I had become. I saw the jerk for a prom date, and dozens of pictures of Carrie and her brother, Curtis. Just the two of them. They seemed like they were happy. They seemed like the typical brother and sister. So young, so right. So naïve. They were oblivious to the fate that belied them, unaware of the perils that sullied their future.

I had to wonder if Carrie had any regrets. After all, if she knew she had only thirty years to live, would she have lived her life any differently? Would she have gone to college, studied as hard as she did? In these pictures, she had no idea her life would be cut so short. No concept.

All I could do was look at the photos and realize the gravity of the situation. Oh sure, the world still spun on its axis, and the sun still rose and set the way it always had. The jerk for a prom date dealt with the sugar in his gas tank, and the bully on the playground is probably all grown up and is raising a new generation of bullies. But there would be no replacing Carrie. She was one of a kind, one in a million. Of all the girls I met, of all the girls I dated, I chose her…or more likely, she chose me.

Those were the greatest times of my life. I never could wait to see her. I couldn't wait to hold her hand, to listen to her talk and hear all about her life. She was interesting. She was fun.

She was gone.

I still had a hard time believing that I was going on a wonderful vacation. It had been a long time since I'd last entertained such an idea. Maybe I was too conservative or prudish to think about it. For being a young man I was a bit set in my ways even when Carrie swept into my life. I had no problem giving her all that I could, but finances were a problem until our careers got on track. We had student loans and no jobs. We wanted to get married but we couldn't justify taking our honeymoon. The last thing Carrie wanted to do was ask her parents for money for a wedding trip. The strings attached to a gift weren't worth the aggravation. Besides, she wanted to find her way in life.

And then there was always the part about the Bar exam.

We were married between the time she finished law school and took the Bar. She said it would be hard to have fun "while that damn albatross still hung around my neck." So we waited until she passed the exam. We waited until she found a job in Mt. Pleasant. Then we waited until my year at the Centre was up, and I was eligible for two-weeks' paid vacation. When she got sick she never felt up to it, and besides there were always doctors' appointments and treatments to endure. The reasons to wait always outweighed the reasons to go.

I felt guilty all of a sudden. Really guilty. We should have gone to the Bahamas. I should have whisked her away right after the wedding. I should have run up my charge cards and had a wonderful time. I was too damn stubborn. Too set in my ways. Guilt is a horrible feeling. I hated it. I wanted to blame something or somebody for what had happened, but there was no denying it: it was my decision not to take her on a honeymoon, and I alone was at fault.

So, as I looked over a lifetime of her memorabilia, I decided right then and there to change my ways. I wasn't going to let the little things in life stand in the way of my new dreams. I wanted to become more spontaneous, more footloose, less stodgy. I was going to the Bahamas to realize a dream, my dream and Carrie's. I had about two months to get ready for it—emotionally—and today marked the beginning of it all.

Twenty-Eight

S UNDAY EVENING I GRABBED a gym bag and walked across the courtyard to my office. The place was nearly barren on Sundays—the result of the latest round of contract negotiations between the nurses union and the administration. The nurses wanted to get paid double-time on Sundays. They got it, but the administration cut the number of nurses in half so the net result was financially the same.

I chose Sunday evening to go to the office because none of the bosses would be there. Even though I appeared to be doing a little casual overtime, my intentions were anything but sincere.

It's strange what you think about when you're doing something wrong. Maybe that's why God created us with a conscience. I looked around my office and saw nothing unusual: the chairs, the couch, and the coffee table between the two. The painting hanging on the wall looked the same, as did the cherry bookshelves with their rows and rows of books. I was going to do something illegal in a doctor's most sacred environment, and it was beginning to gnaw at me.

But first I pulled up the Internet. My online brokerage account was still there, making money. I like how interest works, how you can make money just by having money.

Next, I passed along a little e-mail to Rachel:

Here's a little number to tickle your funny bone:

Canine Quotes For Dog Enthusiasts Everywhere:

The reason why a dog has so many friends is that he wags his tail instead of his tongue.

The average dog is nicer than the average person.

If you think dogs can't count, try putting three dog biscuits in your pocket and then giving Fido only two of them.

My goal in life is to be as good a person as my dog already thinks I am.

My dog is worried about the economy because Alpo is up to three dollars a can. That's almost twenty-one dollars in dog money.

Ever consider what our dogs must think of us? We come back from the grocery store with the most amazing haul—beef, pork, and chicken. They must think we're the greatest hunters on the planet!

Have a good week. I hope to see you soon. Oh, and Toby sends his best too.

Jim

Sometimes I think I'm funny, but it's only to fend off the bitterness that wells up inside of me. I had tons of things to think about: Rachel, Darvin Wonch, Atmantle, my clients, my job, the dog…everything. I had to wonder if Rachel had as much fun as I did on our date. I had to wonder if she laughed at my funnies just to be polite, or if she was really sincere. I really liked being with her. I really liked the way she made me feel, and I hoped that the feeling was mutual.

I found the picture of Carrie on the bookshelf above my desk. I smiled at her, and she smiled back. I gave her a hug, a long one, and brushed the hair from her face. It had been long enough to mourn her. It was time to move on with my life. I opened my briefcase and tucked her into one of the pockets, behind the pencils and calculators and bank statements from months ago.

"There now," I said out loud. "I don't want you to be ashamed of what I'm about to do."

On the bottom half of my briefcase was a plumber's snake, electrical tape, and my package of goodies from the online detective resource. I made sure all three doors were locked. I was alone and had a plan, although not much prowess when it came to seeing it through.

My listening device came with forty-five feet of cord to connect the microphone to the digital recorder. Since my office had three doors, I couldn't really take the risk of running the cord along the edge of the floorboard. Somebody would trip over it, or it would get caught in a vacuum. It was equally risky if I ran the cord up the back of the bookshelf.

The only logical way to install it was to run the cord under the carpet. I'd cut a tiny hole in the carpet near the leg of the coffee table, and another behind my desk. Nobody would notice the cord behind my desk because there was so many others just like it. After all, I had a fax machine, a computer, telephone line, and a calculator. The only thing I had to negotiate was how to get the cord from the back of the desk to the hole near the coffee table. The snake had to poke its nose between the carpet and the padding, which looked like it had been there since Roosevelt was president. Teddy Roosevelt.

After twenty minutes of trial and error—mostly error—everything was in place. Just to be on the safe side, I locked my office door and ventured to the maintenance garage where I borrowed a power drill and a drill bit that was almost a foot long. The idea was to drill a hole through the wooden leg of the coffee table so it would better hide the microphone's wire. It seemed like a lot of extra work, but getting caught was not an option. The stakes were too high.

At almost midnight, I vacuumed up the shavings with a dustbuster and tried out my little contraption. It worked. It even worked when I hooked it up to the computer. My "testing: one, two, three" came in loud and clear over the speakers next to the monitor. On the way home, I returned the drill and bit. In a few hours Darvin Wonch would be sitting across the room from me in a double session, singing like a canary.

I would be recording every word.

I found it hard to sleep that night, but it seemed like business as usual back at the Centre Monday morning. When I arrived at a little past seven, the orderlies that worked the night shift were giving instructions to the day shift about medications, dietary needs, and physical ailments of some of the patients. I recognized the booming voice of the shift supervisor and the way she barked out orders: "Dee Wilson in 235A is having a birthday today. We'll have cake and ice cream at 2 P.M. in the parlor. Let's try to make her happy…smiles please. It's a biggie for her. You only turn fifty once!" As I passed them, the discussion simmered. Then they whispered.

"Good morning, everyone," I said, without hesitation.

A few of them responded but the majority of them bit their tongues, which was fine. I was convinced to put the incident with Joe behind me, but for a handful of them it would take a little longer. Some people are like that, especially in groups. They like to see an outsider squirm. They resent the people in administration, the guys with multiple college degrees and an extra digit in every paycheck. Some of them would probably hold the incident with Joe over my head for as long as we worked at the same place.

Their attitude didn't bother me. It was their decision to snicker behind my back; it was their choice to delight in another man's disappointment. Whatever.

It felt good to be in my office, my little world. I liked the stacks of books on the shelves, and the painting of a gazebo, flowers, and children holding hands. Even the leather-studded couch on the opposite side of the room looked inviting and comfortable. I couldn't wait to dive back into my work, to get on with things, to help people with their troubles. *Who was I kidding*, I thought. *I was going to make some trouble of my own.*

First things first—there was paperwork to do. Mary Cornwall left a note on top of a stack of files a foot high:

> *Jim, welcome back, we missed you! Please review the changes we made to these patients' meds...many of them had their dosage reduced. It was also decided that we will look into buying our medications from a group plan out of New York. I'll have to explain the logic (?) to you soon. Give me a bump when you catch your breath. Per procedure, I had to sign the acknowledgement forms of each patient, just to make sure that I understood what was going on.*

The personnel manager left a letter of reprimand for me to sign:

> *I hereby accept the consequences of an incident involving Joseph DelBanco and I regret the unfortunate outcome. Furthermore, I accept sole responsibility for the situation and believe that the St. Jean Centre was in no way a contributor to his death. I realize that if I have any more lapses in my performance as a psychologist, my employment with the St. Jean Centre will be immediately terminated.*

It seemed blunt and harsh, but fair. I signed the letter, and put a sticky note on top: *I hope this isn't a bad time to ask, but I need about a week off for a vacation in mid-February.* It probably wasn't good timing, but I couldn't help that. A minute later I sealed the envelope, dropped it in interoffice mail, and sent it on its way.

Calypso Steve wasn't about memos and written reprimands. As much as he loved to backstab and betray his subordinates, he enjoyed the process of watching them squirm while he held them under his thumb. And as it turns out I didn't have to wait long for the verbal assault.

"Good morning, Jim."

"Morning." I watched him.

"Ready to get back to work?"

"Oh yes," I said.

He stood blocking the doorway—the one that leads to the hallway, Miss Peacock, and the offices down the hall. There were two other doors as well, one to the waiting room and one to the outside. My clients came in through the waiting room door and left via the outside door.

Steve fumbled with the coins in the pockets of his worn-out khakis. "We've got a full schedule planned for you this week since you were on administrative leave last week."

The dumb ass, why don't you state the obvious? "That's good… I like to be busy. You know the old saying about 'idle hands'?" He had a blank expression on his face as if he had never heard the expression before in his life. "You know, 'idle hands are the devil's workshop.'"

"I knew that." He crossed his arms.

"I know you did."

"Why did you say it then?"

"Steve, you don't have to get defensive. I just finished the sentence. What else is going on…anything?"

He uncrossed his arms and his hands went back to his pockets. "We've got trouble. Big trouble."

"Oh?"

"It's the kid you white-washed at the Haunted Forest," he said. "He's got a separated shoulder and a broken *clavicle*… um…collarbone. Had to have surgery with pins and plates. What the hell did you do to him?"

"Come on, Steve. Do we have to get into this all over again?"

"Yes, we do. The kid's hired a lawyer…I got a copy of the retention letter at my office. You had better tell me what happened so I know how to defend us. Do you know what this incident is going to do to our reputation? We're lucky to get any new patients here! We're lucky that Joe's family doesn't come after us too. He was in our care and custody."

"I'm sorry, Steve. There's really nothing I can do about that now other than continue to do a good job here. I plan on working twice as…"

"Just tell me what the hell happened."

Steve liked to say 'hell' a lot. "When?" I asked.

"With the kid."

"It was an accident. I was chasing Joe down the east tunnel…he climbed the stairs and popped out in the middle of that Halloween deal. There were people everywhere, music, strobe lights, and horses and hayrides. And then I saw him standing there, with his back to me, wearing the Centre's jumpsuit. I swear I thought it was him, so I charged."

"Didn't it occur to you that the other guys standing there were wearing the same jumpsuits?"

"No."

"Didn't you read the memo we passed out at the last staff meeting?"

"What staff meeting?"

"The one you missed."

"When?"

"In late September or October; remember, you had to go to Cheboygan or something?"

"Oh that one…" I said.

"While you were having fun up there, we were taking care of business. We passed out a memo about the upcoming fundraiser, and how we would once again be providing the volunteers with jumpsuits."

"I'm sorry…I guessed I overlooked that."

"I guess you did. Your carelessness could cost us our license, or yours. It could cost us a bundle of money we don't have."

"I'm sorry."

He stood there, looking down at me, shaking his head. Guilt by the slice. "Did you sign the letter of reprimand?"

"Yes."

"That's good. You could make this whole thing easier if you'd polish up your resume and start looking for another job."

I shook my head. "Is that what you'd like, Steve?"

"It would certainly make my life a hell of a lot easier."

"Yeah, but if that happens I turn into a hostile witness if the kid's lawyer sues us."

"What the hell does that mean?" He retorted.

Behind him I heard the phone ring and Miss Peacock's voice.

I stood up, eye to eye with him. "It means that if I lose my job here, I'll tell the kid's lawyer all about you and your cocka-mamie scheme to cut people's meds. I'll tell the government that they should look into the way the Centre bills Medicaid for the services they aren't receiving." My voice was growing louder. "If we kept Joe on the meds he needed, he wouldn't have run away. He wouldn't have strung himself up by a cord, and I wouldn't have tackled the frat boy."

"Oh, so it's my fault!" He was yelling.

"Never said that!" I yelled back.

Miss Peacock slid under his outstretched arm, "Gentlemen, please…" She said.

We both took a breath. "Is there a better place to discuss this?" She asked. I rolled my eyes at her.

"Jim, your eight o'clock appointment is waiting for you, and I don't think you want to give her the wrong impression. And what is this?" She asked, "a place of business or the next episode of Jerry Springer?" Steve spun and stormed off in a huff, steam billowing from his ears.

"I'm sorry you had to hear that, Miss Peacock," I said. The day was only a few minutes old and it felt like I had apologized a hundred times.

"Don't worry about it. I'm glad somebody has the guts to stand up to him."

"Right. Who's my eight o'clock, anyway?"

"Jill Cordell, fifty-five…widow…depression."

"That's it?"

"That's all she put on her questionnaire."

"Anything else?"

"She paid nine hundred in cash, for the next six Monday morning appointments."

"Wow, she must have a lot of depression. Okay then. Is that coffee ready yet?"

She smiled. "Give me your cup; just this once I'll fill it up." Miss Peacock was right; Jill Cordell's questionnaire was completed, but she didn't volunteer a lot of information. The only thing she offered was that her nickname was "Jill," her real name was "Margaret."

Miss Peacock put my cup on the desk, in between the stacks and stacks of patient files, but I'm not sure if she heard me say "thank you." That was okay; I'd have to apologize for that too.

Jill was an anomaly of sorts. She was fifty-five, but she thought of herself as much younger. "Margaret is an old lady's name," she said, "and I don't think of myself as old. I always wanted to be called Jill." She wore her hair behind a headband that she tucked behind a small tress of pearl earrings. Her eyes were coated in an aqua shade of shadow, to match her monogrammed sweater.

"It says here on your form that you're depressed."

"I think I am."

"How do you know?"

"I watch television and see those commercials about 'not feeling yourself' and all that."

"What else?"

She reached for a tissue, and dabbed her eye. "God…I just want to feel better. I hate myself, and what my life has become." She cried. "I need some help." She cried like a baby. I just listened. "My husband died a year ago, and I've been a wreck ever since. We had no kids. We had no friends. I'm miserable."

I backed her up for a few minutes and wanted to hear about her husband. She started out by telling me that he was a great man: easy-going, fun, considerate, great sense of humor, the whole ball of wax. It was easy for Jill to remember his business pursuits too. He started out in the oil business back in the seventies, when the oil embargo made gasoline prices skyrocket. The federal government subsidized exploration, and investors paid thousands of dollars for shares in drilling projects throughout Michigan. Her husband arranged the leases with the landowners, and took on a partner with the wherewithal in seismic telemetry. Together, they bought some drilling equipment and began boring holes all over the North Country. With the subsidies in place, they'd break even. If they found oil, they stood to make a killing.

And find oil they did.

He took the money from the oil business and invested it in real estate: hotels, strip malls, and property in Michigan, Chicago, and Las Vegas.

And then he tried horses. "The ponies," she said. "He boarded a couple of horses at the same stable where I was doing my internship for my biology-management major. My God, I knew from the second I met him that I was going to marry him. He was so handsome, and so were his horses. They were beautiful. Well…needless to say, I dropped out of school and we got married three months after I met him."

She wasn't crying anymore.

"He was older than I was, but that never bothered me. I liked the thought of an older man. My dad was much older than my mom so it felt natural to me. We tried having kids for several years, but we never could. It was horrible, the anguish, the stigma. The doctors said that I was normal, but he was the one with the problem."

"What happened?"

She dabbed the end of her nose with a tissue. "Low sperm count."

"No, I mean *what happened* with the rest of the story?"

"Oh…since we didn't have kids we had little in common with a lot of other people. And there was one other thing that kept us from mingling with our peers: we were rich. We had so much money that we could go anywhere, do anything without having to worry about a budget. My husband left me with twenty-three million, and I don't know what to do with it."

"Wow, that's a lot of money."

"I know. But it can't buy happiness. I am miserable. I have no friends. None." She was crying again, and the mascara smudged her tissue.

"Why don't you join some social clubs? Travel? Join a riding stable? Get outside and do fun things."

"Like a grieving support group?" She asked.

"That's not what I had in mind, but it isn't a bad idea."

"Already tried that. All the people in there were miserable…and they don't understand my situation."

"What do you mean?"

"My situation?" She asked.

"Yes."

"My husband meant everything to me. He was the most wonderful man; he treated me like a queen."

"That's what grieving support groups do, Jill, you talk about the dearly departed and what you have in common."

"But it all boils down to the money. They're not like me. I've got money…tons of it…but they don't."

"You make it sound like your money is a curse."

"It is, but I'd give it all away for just one more day with him."

"I don't know what else to tell you, Jill. It's going to take some time, but I think you will get over your loss. You should never forget about your husband, but you really need to move on with your life. Go for a horse ride. Go see some old movies. Pull out your photo albums and lounge around in your pajamas for a weekend. Heck, get a massage, or go to a spa."

She sat there for a moment or two, thinking about what I just told her. Without batting an eye she proclaimed, "I should go." I watched her pick up her riding jacket and stuff a wad of tissue into the pocket.

"Did I say something wrong?"

She shook her head. "No, I'm sorry to have burdened you. I thought you might understand my situation, but I guess I was wrong."

"Jill. I'll see you next week, and we can discuss that. Okay?"

She stormed off, through the door that leads into that big, cruel world filled with complete strangers and folks that didn't understand. I never did see Jill again, and I don't know what happened to the money she advanced us. When she didn't show up the following Monday, Miss Peacock sent her one of the approved letters regarding the Centre's protocol on missed appointments. She was odd. Sad and odd. But compared to my next appointment, Jill was a bit of a bore.

Warren was beaming with pride and excitement. I knew there was something outrageous going on in his life just by the look in his eyes. It didn't take long before he was telling me all about his latest conquest. He just had to tell somebody.

For a married man, he seemed awfully proud of his infidelities.

"Jim I just gotta tell you about what happened with Sharon. She is absolutely amazing."

Here we go again, I thought.

"It's Friday afternoon and I'm wrapping up a few things at the office...paperwork, reports...stuff like that." Warren was almost whispering, like someone would hear him otherwise. "And I get this page. It says, *'The work day's done...let's have some fun...toast a drink with the Captain's rum?'* And I think to myself that I have no idea what she's getting at. So I page her back: *'I'm in.'* A few minutes later she leaves another message. *'Pickard and Main...ask for Jane...she'll give you a bottle for pleasure or pain.'*"

Warren was really getting into this, and frankly so was I. What a novel idea: an erotic treasure hunt. This girl Sharon was uninhibited to say the least.

Jane was my pal who worked at the party store at the corner of Pickard and Main, I thought to myself. *I wonder if she's going to play along with this.*

"Heck, I thought we were going to go out for a drink somewhere, you know. There are lots of places to drink in Mt. Pleasant. I put on my coat, and said goodbye to everyone at the office, but the whole time I'm trying to place a bar on the corner of Pickard and Main. I'm in my car, and I'm zooming through traffic..." Warren was waving his arms, and getting louder. "Then I get there and realize that there's no bar at Pickard and Main, but just this little party store connected to a gas station. They sell magazines, bread and eggs..."

"Coffee and cookies, too...right?"

"Oh yeah, you've probably been there...it's close by." I nodded. "Anyway, half of me was thinking that I'd meet Sharon there, and the three of us would have a drink, but that wouldn't make sense." Warren often pitted his wants and desires versus his responsibilities; a vocalized version of "id" versus "ego." His head dashed right then left, "Sharon wasn't there, but I go up to the girl behind the counter, and I see her name tag is Jane. She's kinda heavyset, and I say to her 'Hi, Jane. I understand that you have a bottle of Captain Morgan for me?' She looks across the counter and laughs hysterically. The people standing in line stare at us. Anyway, I laugh along with her, pay her for the bottle and get out to my car."

"Keep going."

"So I page Sharon again *'all set.'* She pages me back: *'pretend it's spring...and you're having a fling...she wants a picnic...now what to bring?'* She's got me stumped, so I page her: *'flowers,'* and she writes back, *'very good.'* So I whip around the corner and buy half dozen red roses from the florist. The guy behind the counter looks at me like I'm a tightwad or something, so before I know it he gives me a good deal on the second half dozen. I write back to her: *'your wish is my command.'*" Warren was laughing and smiling at the same time. "She writes me back. *'You got the booze...you got the flowers...see Terrie at Golden Showers.'*" Warren scratched his head and mimicked a confused look on his face. "I'm sitting there looking at my beeper wondering what the heck she means by 'Golden Showers?' I have no idea what she's getting at...not a clue. But I gotta tell you I really didn't want to radio the crew chief again. You know what I mean?"

"Sure I do, you didn't want to tell her that you've never been to an adult bookstore."

"Right, right, even though I haven't." We laughed. "So finally I see the light and realize where the hell I'm going...

"I gotta tell you Jim, I felt a little weird going into that place. I felt a little awkward even parking in the parking lot. I'm thinking that I'm liable to run into my sixth grade teacher or something. And what would I say? 'Hi, aren't you proud of me?' Of course, I could say the same thing to them, 'strange running into you like this?' But this whole thing with Sharon has got me revved up. I've taken it this far; I can keep going. This is fun. This is every man's dream. I walk inside and the place is almost empty, I think..."

"Why do you *think* it is almost empty?" I asked him.

"Because I wore sunglasses inside and the damn things fogged up on me. I felt like I was half blind. I'm looking over the tops of the lenses and under a baseball cap so nobody will recognize me. If I had a fake mustache I would have worn that in there too. It was horrible. I'm walking towards the counter and I trip over one of those metal display racks, you know the ones that spin?"

"I'm with you...you see them in restaurants...they sell postcards and stuff."

"Only these weren't postcards."

"How did I know that?"

"They were penises, Jim, and I knocked over the whole display. There were long ones, rubber ones, plastic ones, two-headed monster penises." I was laughing. So was Warren. "This woman comes over to me and says 'sorry sir, this happens all the time.' I'm lying on the ground covered in genitals...purple ones, Neapolitan; some of them looked like they were rolled in toasted coconut. I felt like the Good Humor man. She says 'give me a hand with these.' Next thing I know I'm handling more sausage than Bob Evans. It was sickening..."

"So what happened?" I asked, laughing.

He was laughing too. "I looked at her name tag and I noticed that it's Terrie—the woman I was supposed to meet."

"What happened?"

"She went behind the counter and pulled out a little gift bag full of goodies. There's a card hanging off the handle that reads: *you passed the test of the second best, now make me yell at the Microtel.* I'm thinking 'wow.' I look in the bottom of the envelope and there's a room key inside with the numbers 221 written across its face. She thought of everything, it seems. Terrie says something like 'good luck,' as I head out the door. Isn't it amazing?"

"You know, I've handled a lot of different situations..."

"This is weird," he interrupted.

"Well you could say that it's unusual."

"Come on, just tell me."

"Warren, why does it matter what I think?"

"I need you to tell me that this is unusual."

"Why?"

"Because if I'm going to have a fling I want it to be a wild one."

"Why is that important?"

"Because it is. That's all I want to say."

"Okay. That's fine. It seems that you want to tell me all about Sharon, but you don't want to acknowledge any of the perils that are in front of you…"

Warren stared in my direction as if I betrayed him. "Why do you have to be so pessimistic? Can't a guy talk about his deepest thoughts without getting a wet blanket thrown on him?"

"I'm not being pessimistic. I just hope you realize what risks you're taking. There are hundreds of them."

"Name ten."

"Warren…listen, I'm not here to pick a fight, or be a wet blanket. I'm just being realistic."

"How about five…give me five reasons why I should stop this thing."

"Okay, fine. She could get pregnant. She could give you a disease, a paternity suit. It could cost you your job and the respect of your kids. And what are you going to do when her husband finds out? Or your wife?"

Warren paused. "Don't you understand, it's all worth it. I love Sharon, and I think she loves me too. How can you put a price on that? True love is hard to find."

We both took a breath. It was deathly silent. He wasn't going to listen to me, or anybody else. He may have thought he loved her, but then again, lust had his vision clouded. Very clouded.

"Don't you want to hear about what happened at the Microtel? What was in the bag of goodies? The padded handcuffs, the mink glove, or the massage oil?"

"Oh boy. Let's just leave those images to me and my imagination, okay?"

"Suit yourself. It was awesome."

"I'm sure it was." I looked at my watch and realized that his hour was finished. "I'll see you next week."

He shrugged his shoulders, put on his winter jacket and left. I smiled and shook my head at the same time. The guy was headed for trouble, but he didn't want to listen. Some people are that way.

It felt great to be back at work, back in the saddle. I liked having my day divided into measured blocks of time. I enjoyed the constant barrage of situations and personal issues.

In a devious way, I looked forward to tape recording the next appointment, the man of the hour.

"Morning, Darvin."

"Morning."

He took off his leather jacket, flipped it over the arm of the couch, and took a seat. Just by looking at him, I could tell that he really didn't want to be here. He crossed his arms in front of him and stared at me like I was some kind of idiot. The feeling was mutual.

There's never a good place to start with a client, unless they had an upcoming event like a family reunion, a confrontation with a coworker, or a job interview. I usually allow the client to dictate the agenda. "Did you have anything specific that you'd like to talk about?"

"Like what?"

"Like what's up?"

He stared some more. "Listen, I'm a very busy man, and I wanna get our forty hours over with as quickly and painlessly as possible. Is that all right with you?"

"Wonderful!"

"And don't try to butter me up either. I'm not in the mood for it."

"Great. I'm glad we got that out in the open."

He looked at his watch, a gaudy, heavy thing with dials and buttons protruding from the sides. "Would you mind if I made a phone call?"

"Yup."

"What are you going to do, stop me?"

"No, I'll just tell the judge that you haven't been making an effort to curb your gambling addiction, that's all. Besides, you just sat down."

"Aw, Christ. I knew you wouldn't understand."

"Understand what, Darvin?"

"That I'm a businessman, a wealthy guy. I've got responsibilities…"

"Wow. That's great. I'll tell the judge that too." He was silent. Maybe I leaned on him too much. "I'm sorry, let's not get off on the wrong foot. You like to barter, don't you?"

"Of course I do."

"Okay then, why don't you help me for a while, and then I'll help you, okay?"

"What do you mean?"

"I would like to know more about horse racing, and odds making," I said. "I've got some family down south and they want to take me to the Kentucky Derby this year. They make a big deal out of it. They've got an RV and they spend the whole weekend camping…"

"And you don't want to seem like a newbie in front of your family, when it comes to the ponies, right, Chief?"

"Right."

He seemed to be open to the notion. "But what's in it for me? Where does the 'barter' thing come in to play?"

"You want to make a phone call, don't you? How bad do you want it?"

He glared in my direction. He was sizing me up. "You got a deal, but I get to make it in private."

"My office will be all yours."

For the next forty-five minutes he explained how betting on horses works…odds, odds-making, the best trainers, what makes a good trainer, breeding, the Arab influence on American thoroughbreds, Trifecta, Super-trifecta, lifespan of thoroughbreds. Everything he thought I needed to know. When that was finished he turned to greyhound racing. And then he got into online betting on horse racing. "How does that work?" I asked him.

"It's easy. You want to try it?"

"Sure, but this is the middle of winter, are they racing somewhere?"

"You bet. California, Florida."

"Let's do it." In no time he had my computer up and had dialed into a website offering *the hottest action, the best odds from all over the country!* "Wow! That's impressive."

"Oh, this is nothing. There are a lot of places you can bet on horses. I've had the best luck at this one. The first thing you've got to do is set up an account. Hand me your credit card."

"Maybe I should do it."

"Whatever." He moved his chair over a bit, and I punched in the numbers. "Okay, good. What do you want start out with…five, ten grand?"

"No…no. Let's start out slow. Can we do two hundred fifty?"

He looked at me and rolled his eyes like I was a wimp. "Whatever, but keep in mind that the more you wager, the more money you'll win."

"I'm with you, but two fifty is a lot for me to lose."

"That's your problem, Doc. You can't look at it like it's the money you'll *lose*; it's the money you'll *win*."

"I believe you. What should I bet on?"

"It all depends…are you a risk-taker, or a more conservative gambler?"

"You know, I haven't given that much thought," I said. "I'll take a risk if the rewards are high enough."

"All right, then. Let's check it out; next Sunday in California, Santa Anita is a mile and an eighth. You probably don't know it, but it was Seabiscuit's home track. I've been watching this colt, Hot Tamale." He pointed at the screen to a non-descript animal with long legs and a smudge of white on its forehead. "He's the son of Motel Lady, who finished second at Louisiana Downs five years ago. Not many other horses in Sunday's race, which is good because he tends to get bottled up in traffic. The odds are seven to one. Then again, you could take a chance on Warden's Worry or Roar, and really make some dough, at thirty and forty to one."

"No, let's play it safe. Place the bet. Let's go two hundred to win. And fifty to place."

"Okay. You're the boss."

His fingers banged at the keyboard for several seconds. "Are you sure?" I nodded. "Okay, I'm going to place your bet." He looked at me one more time. I nodded. He hit the enter key, and I had made my first online bet.

"So if the odds are seven to one, and my horse wins, that means that I'll get a check for…"

"Sixteen hundred."

"Wow!"

"Come on, Doc, that's chump change. If you think that's fun, you should try it when you've got twenty grand on the line. Now we're talking excitement!"

"I can't imagine."

He smiled. "Isn't this fun? A week from now you'll be thanking me."

"I hope so."

"Now…what about my phone call?"

"You got it. I'll give you five minutes…"

"Why don't I go outside and you stay in here?"

"It's against the Centre's policy. We had a problem here a

while ago. You're technically in my care, and I'm responsible for you. Sorry."

We both stood up, and I unlocked the door that lead to the hallway and Miss Peacock's desk. Five minutes felt like five hours. I had a fleeting thought that maybe he'd rummage through my desk, and find the recorder with its red "record" button depressed. Or the microphone. Miss Peacock looked at me like I was strange. *I am strange.*

My conscience was working overtime.

It was a horrible thing to do. Shrinks don't gamble with their clients, or use their clients for their own agenda. Shrinks don't barter with them or leave them alone in their offices either. What a mess. I'm breaking all the rules.

But what a way to connect with him. He loves me now. He'll tell me everything I want. He's going to rue the day he ever stepped foot near me.

After four minutes, I knocked on the door and walked inside. Darvin was just finishing up, "I gotta go." He slammed his little phone shut and apologized for the interruption.

"No problem," I told him. "You're an important man, right? You've got a job and responsibilities."

He was eyeing me up, sizing up the situation. "You don't see a lot of executives in your day-to-day operation?"

"Not a lot of executives, so I would like to hear about your operation some time." He shrugged his shoulders nonchalantly. "I see a fair amount of middle managers who are frustrated in their career for whatever reason."

"We've got a few of those at our place."

"Really?"

"Sure. I don't know if they're seeing a quack, but you can tell who the guys are that want to get ahead but can't."

"I think most men that are frustrated have a tough time reconciling their expectations and reality." He nodded his head in agreement. "A lot of guys think they're going to set the world on fire, but that seldom happens. They're too impatient. They don't want to wait until they're fifty-five to take over the reins of the company."

More nodding.

He liked what I had to say, now set the trap.

"Your career seems to be the exception to the rule. You have a special talent to start your own business and see it prosper after all these years."

Instead of saying, "I've been lucky" or something modest, he fell right into my ambush. "It's not by accident that my business has gone well. I've got a great nose for opportunity, a vision of where I want the company to go. Of course, it doesn't hurt to be a bit of a gambler, either…"

"What do you mean…'gambler?'"

He paused for a moment, and traced his chin with the inside of his thumb and forefinger. "There are certain risks you've got to take as a businessman. It's like the old saying 'you gotta grow or you gotta go.' It's hard to grow, to stay ahead of the competition, and the regulators. You gotta take calculated risks; it's like going to the casino or the track. See what the odds are, lay your wager, play to win…not to lose."

"I still don't get it." He looked at me again like I was stupid, which is exactly what I wanted.

"This is going to be hard for you to understand, but I'll explain it anyway." *Perfect.*

"For years I've wanted to take my company to the next level, to make it grow by leaps and bounds, and the only way to do that is by taking on investors. You probably don't know much about investing, but I'll boil it down to its simplest form…" He took a deep breath and I could see the wheels turning in his head.

"In order for our company to grow—I mean really prosper—we needed to spend a substantial amount of money on technology, marketing, all that. I don't have that kind of money, and the only way to raise that kind of dough is if I turned the company into a *publicly*-held company instead of a *privately*-held company," he said in a condescending tone. "But there's a lot to going public…you've got to open up your books, you've got to show that you're solvent."

"When's that going to happen?"

"It did happen…about a month ago."

"Great, right?"

"Oh yeah, but to get where we are today, a lot went into it. And here's where the gambling comes into play."

"Oh?" I tried to act concerned.

"In order to show the SEC that we are solvent, I had to shuffle some of the money around the company, and in order to show as much profit we had to do some things that were less than honorable in the insurance business." He paused for a breath. My canary was getting ready for the next verse. "And in order to get away with it I had to make sure the regulators would look the other way. But the whole point is to keep an eye on the prize…that when my company goes public, I'll make a ton of dough. I mean a ton of dough."

"Good for Darvin, right?"

"That's right. That's why this whole mess with the bank-ruptcy is such bad timing."

"I imagine it would be."

"Of all the times to have a bad string of luck. If I had taken that re-fi money and hit it big, we wouldn't be here now."

"Bad luck," I said, almost sincerely, "nothing you can do about that."

"I know it…you gotta keep your eye on the prize. Keep looking ahead, not behind."

We both sat there for a second or two, until I asked him about the 'shuffling money' business.

"That's easy. It's like a shell game. You take it out of the premium trust accounts, and move it into your general fund.

On paper, the money is still in the trust account, but in reality, it's over here." His hands were on the coffee table, shuffling imaginary shells inches away from the microphone hidden under the coffee table.

"What about the regulators?"

He looked up at me with his intensely grim eyes. "What about them?"

"How do you keep them quiet?"

"I'm not so sure I should tell you. How do I know that you're not going to make a big mess of all this?"

"You're right. That's fine...we can move on to something else if you want. I'm just fascinated with your story, and the amazing things you've accomplished." *Flattery will get you everywhere.*

"I pay them." He chuckled.

"Really."

"People are people. They've got human nature, just like the rest of us."

That was brilliant. "Who do you pay?"

"Everybody."

"What do you mean?"

"Everybody."

"Why won't you tell me?"

"I thought you said you liked to barter?"

"I did?"

"Remember...the phone call I made earlier today?"

"Oh yes," I said.

"I'll tell you whatever you want if you can beat me in one hand of poker."

"What?"

"Seriously. Are you in?"

"This isn't how counseling works, Darvin. I'm not supposed to play cards and make bets with my clients."

"Interesting stakes though, don't you think?"

I laughed, nervously. *Not only are you sick, you're deranged.* "Yes they are."

"We've already been gambling today. Now isn't the time to have cold feet. Are you in?"

I thought about it for a second or two. The guy was convincing without being manipulative. He had information I wanted, and I would do almost anything to get it. "Okay, but I don't have any cards."

"I do, but they're out in my car. I'll be right back."

"No, no, Darvin. Remember what I told you about being in my care? You stay right here, there must be a deck at the nurses' station." He shrugged his shoulders, and I disappeared again. Several minutes later I returned, and he was finishing another phone call. "Everything okay?" I asked him.

He grinned, and stuffed his phone inside his jacket. "Let's play poe-kah!" He took the deck from my hand, opened the box, and shuffled the cards like an old pro. "What'll it be: five-card stud, Texas hold 'em, pass the trash, cold petroleum, tick tack doe?"

"Got me. I've never played poker."

"It's easy, really. You might like it. In its simplest form, you try to get a better hand than your opponent. But if you don't have a good hand, you can either drop out of the game, or bluff your opponent into thinking that you do. It's easy. Watch this." For the next half hour he explained to me the nuances, strategies, and theories of each kind of poker game. "It's a thinking man's game, really, if you're into numbers and odds the way I am." I didn't quite understand what he was getting at, so he explained. "If you play poker with one deck of cards, the odds are four in fifty-two that you'll get an ace, eight in fifty-two that you'll get either an ace or a king, and so on. There are four suits in every deck of cards, and each suit has thirteen ranks." Math was never my strong suit, and he lost me after the part about "half the deck will help you, half will hurt you." He rambled on and on about probability, correlation, and standard deviation and how it relates to the number of players at the table, the number of cards in each hand, and the number of cards that were face up, and the odds of getting a card that would help the hand. He was just amazing.

Finally, he suggested five-card stud. "One card up, one card down, followed by a round of betting. Ready?"

I nodded. *This is idiotic. Lunacy.*

I had a ten showing and a five down. He had a jack showing.

"So what do you want to bet? The low card starts…"

"If I win you have to tell me about your operation."

He laughed, and stretched the palm of his hands my direction. "Yeah, but what's in it for me?"

"I'll sign your paper for the judge."

"That's nothing, man. You gotta do that anyway. Let's say if I win, you gotta sign the paper that we met two hours longer than we actually did."

I laughed. "Sorry, Charlie, maybe this wasn't a good idea. I shouldn't be gambling with a client, anyway. Let's just forget it."

He looked me over for a second. "Suit yourself." He scooped up the cards on the table, and sat back on the couch shuffling the deck with his thick fingers. "I should have bet that you wouldn't go through with it."

I stared at him. "What is it, Darvin?"

"What?"

"Why do you gamble?"

"Not this again. I keep telling you. It's fun."

"What else?"

"It's exciting."

"Keep going."

The hands quit fiddling with the deck. "It's what I do. I told you that. I've always gambled."

"There's more to it, though. You're obsessed with it."

"I am?"

My office got real quiet. I nodded my head. "You are." He set the deck of cards on the coffee table.

"Gambling for me is an escape. Some guys drink, have mistresses, or play golf to get away from their problems or their conscience. I don't have any of those. I just keep moving ahead, keep rolling." He sat back on the couch and stretched an arm along the back. His mind was working, and I didn't want to interrupt him. It seemed that five minutes went by, but it was probably closer to two. "I love to gamble…to get away from the pressures of life."

"Like what?"

"Like the deal with the regulators," he said.

"Tell me."

"I can't."

"Why, Darvin?"

"Because it's illegal."

"You can still tell me, Darvin, I'm your doctor, for Christ's sake. Whatever you tell me stays between us, and it might make things better. That's why we're here, to make things better. Besides, anything you tell me stays with me." He didn't answer. "You already told me about the premium trust account. Is that illegal?"

"Yes," he sighed. "There's more. God, there's more, but they'll never catch me, I got 'em where the hair grows short. Know what I mean?"

I looked at the clock on the little stand next to the couch. We had two minutes left in our appointment.

"Tell me, Darvin. I think it will make you feel better."

He shook his head and pulled at his hair. "You're not going to repeat this, are you?" He asked.

"Darvin," I said, affirmatively, "I can't say anything, to anybody. You'll feel better if you talk to me."

He stared at me for what I thought was a long time. He grappled with himself, it seemed. I didn't say a thing. Finally, he started. "I've got so many people on the books that I can't keep track of it sometimes. But that's the way I do business. I cheat.

I look for ways around things." He shook his head and stared at the set of books on the shelves.

"Like who?"

He paused, and uttered the words almost inaudibly. "I can't tell you," he said. "They're important people."

"Tell me, Darvin."

"I can't."

"Tell me. You'll feel better. You can't keep things bottled up, or it'll tear up your insides."

"They're important people, though."

"It doesn't matter. Your secret stays with me."

"I can't," he whispered.

"You can, Darvin. I won't tell a soul."

He sighed, and reluctantly, but quite arrogantly said, "How about the governor? The attorney general? The insurance commissioner? How's that for a start?" His head turned back to me and he blinked. And blinked. "They all owe me favors. They're all on the payroll. How do you like them apples?"

I nodded. "Why do you have to pay them?"

"So I can keep running my business without getting harassed. They can't prosecute someone who has paid for immunity."

"I don't understand."

"It's probably better off that you…" His watched chimed in with an annoying little beep. His attention, and his strange-looking fingers, turned to his watch, and the beeping stopped. "I guess that's it, Chief. We're done, right?"

"Yes we are, but don't you want to tell me something?"

He couldn't wait to get out of there, to be free of the hot seat. If I had one more minute he would have told me everything, I just knew it. But instead, he put on his jacket as fast as he could and headed for the door. "You keep shrinking and I'll keep gambling, okay, Chief?"

"Hey, sounds good."

"I'll be rooting for you and your Hot Tamale at Santa Anita."

I laughed, and put a little extra effort on it to make it sound sincere. "Bye, Darvin."

The large, metal door slammed shut, and my office was silent. I sighed with relief. Exhausting relief. *What a start. The guy never suspected a thing.*

I was dying to hear the tape, hear his confessions, hear the phone calls. Quickly, I pulled the recorder from my desk drawer, unplugged the cord from the back and sent the tiny tape spinning in reverse. When it was about halfway rewound, I pushed the play button. My voice wasn't as loud or as clear as Darvin's, but it wasn't muffled either: "Come on, Doc, that's chump change…" I pushed the forward button until the gibberish hesitated. "Mr. Brian, please. Darvin Wonch speaking." Silence. "Hello Francis! How are you sir…okay…I know it. That's good. Hey listen, the reason for my call, I'd like to thank you for helping me out on the Rome matter last Friday. That was great. A broken leg, and only forty-five hundred…simply wonderful. You really did a good job." His voice paused again; he laughed, devilishly. "Listen, I've got to be out of town next week and can't use a couple of Red Wings tickets…against Vancouver…blue line…row fifteen." He listened. He waited. He back-peddled. "Okay, then…I'll throw in dinner too. You like seafood? How about Joe Muir's? The Rattlesnake Club? That's fine. I don't care what it takes…an extra grand for you is fine. I owe you big time. I'll have one of my people drop them off. And thanks again, I really appreciate it. I gotta go."

His conversation ended as quickly as it started. I heard my footsteps, the office door shut, and the second half of our appointment begin. As our conversation started, I had to wonder about "Francis Brian," and what he had done to earn a couple hockey tickets, a thousand bucks, and dinner. He could have worked for anybody…a lobbyist, an employee of Atmantle, the governor's office, the attorney general, who knows. It was one of those names I'd have to file in the memory banks.

His second phone call was to the office. "Good morning, Lydia. How's everything?" The silence was interrupted with periodic utterances: "Right...I see...okay." Then all at once he spoke like a dictator. "Here's what we need to do, are you ready? Tell Meyerson that he needs to deny that claim based on the fact that the applicant had a pre-existing condition." Lydia checked his conscience; she must have put up a fuss. "Lydia, *it was pre-existing*, even though it was diagnosed after the policy went into effect. They knew there was something wrong when they took out the policy, and now they want us to pay for it? No way! Meyerson needs to remember the old rule: 'pry and deny.' Didn't he do his homework and find out more about the applicant? Was she a smoker, a social drinker, bad driver...she must have had something in her closet that would make her think that she lied on the application. I don't care. Just tell him to deny it, Christ. I'll see you after a while."

That's how they operated. When a claim was presented, Atmantle Health and Casualty gathered skeletons in the applicant's closet and planted them front and center. The idea was that the skeletons would bluff the applicant from pursuing a claim. Atmantle didn't care about their clients; they were after profits, profits, profits.

That's exactly what they did to Carrie and me. That's precisely what they did to quell our zest for fair treatment, for benefits that should have been paid for. Pry and deny. It was a disgusting practice, a despicable revelation.

Darvin Wonch was an evil man, and somebody had to stop him.

That somebody was me.

Twenty-Nine

LATER THAT AFTERNOON I saw Mary Cornwall at her office down the hall. She was happy to see me, but anxious to hear more about the incident with Joseph DelBanco. After hearing the sordid details, she kept shaking her head in disbelief.

"I can't believe that he did that. I mean, he showed no signs of suicide, made no threats, or even remotely mentioned that he had a plan."

"I know."

"What did he say to you, anyway?"

"He told me that he wanted to see my dog. Can you believe it?"

"Odd…he never had pets, at least that's what his son told me."

"I didn't want to turn him down, you know what I mean?"

"Sure…sure. It must have been a ruse…some sort of feint." We sat there for a few seconds. She rearranged the clutter on her desk. "I don't think there was anything wrong with what we did to his meds…I've been over his situation a hundred times. The guy was just sick. He wanted to kill himself."

"Did Calypso Steve say anything to you about him?"

"No, but he acted like he was in a really bad mood the whole week you were gone. He told me to clean up my desk, my office. You know me; I didn't say a thing; I try to stay out of his way." She crossed her arms, and furled her eyebrows. "Why?"

"Because he told me that the kid I tackled in the Haunted Forest has hired a lawyer, and they're going to sue us."

"Lovely."

"You don't regret the placebo do you?" I asked her.

"Not at all…it wasn't a bad call to make."

"That's right."

"It's a commonly accepted practice. Plain and simple."

For several minutes we discussed the stack of files that were on my desk earlier in the day. In the week I was gone, none of the patients killed themselves or had to be restrained. And just about the time that I got up to leave, Mary asked me something that threw me for a loop.

"Are you okay, Jim?"

I looked at her in disbelief.

"Why?"

"I don't know, you just seem to be acting a little weird lately."

"How so?"

"Friday I saw you talking to yourself when you were driving."

"And? That's nothing unusual…"

"Saturday, one of the maintenance guys told me that they saw you yelling and wailing on the front lawn of your house."

"Oh yeah, I remember that near the mailbox…"

"But that's not all. Miss Peacock said that she heard you talking to someone after one of your appointments today…"

"She did not."

"She told me, Jim, and don't get mad at her. She likes you…we all do."

"It was the Internet. I can explain everything…"

"Are you okay?"

"I've got a lot on my plate, that's for sure."

Silence. She let me stew.

"It's nothing I can't handle," I said.

More silence.

"What did you have in mind?"

"I can refer you to another therapist, or I can prescribe something." She rummaged for a prescription pad...in her desk, on her calendar, under the keyboard. I saw three or four within arm's reach. "It wouldn't be permanent, but a little anti-anxiety script may be just what you need."

"Think so?"

"It wouldn't hurt, Jim. It really can help. A lot of people are on it, you know that."

"Right."

"You're going through a lot right now. Sometimes grief doesn't boil to the surface until months after a loved one is gone."

"If I deny that there's a problem, I'm showing the first signs of trouble, right?"

She drew a deep breath, and crossed her arms. "Jim...we care about you. Now are you going to tell me what's up, or do I have to make waves?"

"Mary, please. I appreciate your concern. Sincerely. There's really nothing here. You're barking up the wrong tree." She frowned, as if I was calling her a dog. "It's an expression, Mary...relax."

"I'm going to be watching you, Jim."

"Okay, but you're going to get awfully bored. There's nothing here."

"See you tomorrow."

"See you then, and don't forget to clean up your office."

She smiled again, and waved.

Mary had a flair for the dramatics. She liked to make waves, get into the middle of things, and spread gossip. Even though she was one of my allies at the Centre, I had a real problem trusting her with anything but the cursory. And now that she had poked her nose into my affairs, she sunk a rung or two on the reliance ladder. Her intentions may have been sincere, but I thought she was a little too premature for an intervention.

Me, on meds?

No way.

Everybody talks to themselves sometimes, especially when the going gets rough. I may have had an odd way of dealing with stress, but it didn't mean that I needed to go on medication, or talk to a shrink. And what was I going to tell him or her…that I was plotting to crush the man responsible for my wife's death? I'd lose my license in the time it takes to brush your teeth.

I'd be on my own. I was on my own. I had to do some research on the man that was in my midst. I had to find out as much as I could without tipping my hand. I had to let him open up to me naturally. I had to control the agenda.

But most of all, I had to have a plan. You've got to have a plan when dealing with a much larger opponent. You've got to exploit a weakness, take advantage of a flaw. You don't just lunge at a bear like Toby did up north; you gotta have a plan. Surely Darvin Wonch was a gambler, but he had smarts, too. He was way out of my league in the intelligence scale, but I always relished the role as an underdog. I had one thing going for me at this stage in the game: surprise. Darvin Wonch didn't know who I was, what my story was, or how profound my motivation.

I knew just enough to be dangerous.

But that was going to change.

An hour after work, I was into the computer to find out as much as I could about Atmantle Health and Casualty. The company's website was remotely familiar, having visited it several months previous. There was no photo gallery of the executive team, as the case with other insurance companies. The only thing I could glean from the organizational structure was that it was a privately-held company with assets in investment grade bonds, real estate, and blue chip stocks. The estimated net worth of the company was slightly less than thirty million, with an impressive return on premiums of thirty-two percent.

Thirty-two percent? On real estate, bonds and blue chip stocks?

Impossible.

Impossible, unless they didn't pay claims, or the premiums weren't recorded accurately, or the money was invested in something other than the most conservative vehicles on the market. It just didn't wash.

And what about their connection with the Bahamas? How did that all work?

Atmantle Holdings Limited was domiciled at a post office box in Nassau, Bahamas and is the management company for Atmantle Health & Casualty. The Bahamian government's website stated that management companies typically get a fifteen percent cut of all premiums. The premiums and cash run through the Bahamas, the costs and expenses through the states. Their subsidiaries were set up in Lansing, then Columbus, Fort Wayne, and Peoria.

The people of Michigan, Ohio, Indiana, and Illinois were grateful to have another carrier offering affordable health care. The legislators in each state were happy too because health care is always a hot button during the election. Atmantle appeared to be a viable alternative to the big blue networks that had rates so high that the constituents screamed bloody murder.

I discovered that the *Atmantle* was a sturdy, iron-hulled

ship built in a Pennsylvania shipyard during the late 1800s. She was one of the first steam-driven ships on the Atlantic Ocean, and was under contract to carry a load of cotton and grain from New Orleans to Baltimore in September 1888. But the *Atmantle* never did make it to Baltimore. A hurricane caught the steamer in heavy seas, cracked her hull, and sent the captain scrambling for cover. He tried to make it to one of the harbors on Bermuda, but ran aground on one of the reefs five miles offshore. Storms since then have strewn her remains on the ocean floor, but the stern section is pretty much intact. She lies in twenty feet of water, with the steam boilers and propeller still visible.

Over the years the reefs in the Bahamas claimed scores of ships—rumrunners, pirates, and treasure hunters—that added to the mystique of the "Bermuda Triangle." It seemed odd to me that Darvin Wonch would name his insurance company after one of a thousand ships that had sunk in such an ordinary way.

But Atmantle Health & Casualty wasn't all what it was cracked up to be. Insurance regulators had a hard time regulating them because it was an offshore company. With the political environment so stressed for affordable health care, Atmantle Health & Casualty took advantage of the situation by bending the rules. The politicians encouraged leniency; after all, they didn't want to chase off a company that might offer their constituents affordable health care.

There were hundreds of complaints against Atmantle that were either deemed justified or unjustified. Atmantle had virtually no justified complaints. I thought that was odd. If anybody had a claim just like mine, most of them should have been justified.

Why did the company claim to be one of the state's most "preferred health carriers" when they had so many complaints against them? The photos on the website instilled confidence, for sure, but they were hardly truthful.

It was just an example of how Darvin stayed one step ahead of the trouble that followed him. He was slick. He was slippery. He was smart, but let his gambling problem get the better of him. That was his weakness, his Achilles' heel.

And that's exactly where I'd level the crosshairs.

About eleven o'clock that night, I sent a little e-mail to Rachel: *If you're not too busy Saturday, maybe we could go up to Caberfae and go skiing on Saturday.*

I must have stared at the note for two minutes, and said out loud: "That looks like I'm an insecure school boy, and redundant too! Why don't you say 'Saturday' a few more times?"

I changed the note again: *Would you like to go skiing with me Saturday up north this weekend? I had fun with you last weekend.*

"Dumb, dumb, dumb!"

Wanna go skiing with me this weekend?

"Can you get any more bland?"

I'm going up north skiing this weekend, would you like to join me?

"Why don't you tell her that you'd like to sleep with her too?"

Finally, I agreed with myself on something generic and mildly cute. *Have you ever been snow skiing? I'm going up north for the day Saturday, and was wondering if you'd like to go with me... It probably won't be as much fun as the play, but you stand a better chance of breaking your leg. Jim.*

My note wasn't the cutest in the world, but it was direct. I hoped she'd say yes.

Thirty

THE FOLLOWING SATURDAY I woke up early and swung by Rachel's apartment. She had her skiing gear outside, leaning against the side of her house, behind the shrubs adjacent to the door. A snow shower the night before had nearly everything coated in a mint fresh blanket of white.

She looked as good as I remembered, and came bounding off the front porch decked in a snappy red turtleneck, sweater, and button-fly jeans. A yellow and black nylon shell draped over her arm like a mink shawl. I could smell her perfume, the hint of hairspray, the lotion she smeared all over her long legs the night before…She was wrapped up in a cute little package.

"I guess you are a skier, aren't you?" I asked her.

She laughed. "I'm not really; these old skis are from high school."

"Better than renting, right?"

"Much better."

"Did you pack a swimsuit?"

"No, I thought you said we were skiing."

"We are, but they have a heated outdoor pool and hot tub in case you're interested."

"No, I didn't pack one, but I'll be right back. I assume you brought one too."

I nodded, approvingly. She disappeared inside her apartment while I loaded her gear in the back of my little Jimmy. In no time we grabbed a couple of flavored coffees from our newfound favorite coffee shop and were on our way north, past Clare and their famous motor lodge. Gradually, farm fields gave way to woodlots that melted into cedar swamps near the broad valley of the Muskegon River.

"Where are we going, anyway?" She asked me.

"Caberfae Peaks, near Cadillac."

"I've never been there."

"It's kinda nice…one of the oldest ski resorts in the state. They've got a couple of steep runs but it's not too tough."

"Have you been there?"

"Yup, once in high school. We organized an outing, chartered a bus, and a whole bunch of us came up here."

She sat there for a moment, watching the December sunshine cast meek shadows across the two-lane highway. "I see that you have an old set of skis too."

"High school. They're so old, they're almost a collector's item." She smiled. "They're so old that I've threatened to take them on the Antiques Road Show and have them appraised."

"How old are you, anyway?"

"Thirty."

She took a sip of coffee and did the math. "That makes you six years older than me."

"Okay," I said, then winked. "I believe you."

"Was there ever any doubt that you wanted to be a shrink?"

"Oh sure, all the time."

"Still?"

"Every once and a while. Everybody has good days and bad days at work."

"I know."

"It sounds like you're not sure about something," I suggested.

"I've been thinking about my career…my life, and where it's headed." She looked at me, and winced nostalgically. "What will I do for work, where will I live and all that." I nodded. "I don't know. There's nothing that I want to do. There's nothing that just stands right out at me. I should be interviewing. I should be getting my resume sharpened up. Moving on with things."

She's just as insecure as I am.

"What's the worst thing that can happen, Rachel?"

"With what?"

"With polishing up your resume? With finding a job? With getting on with things?"

"I know. It's weird. I can't be a student the rest of my life." She was batting her eyes, trying to hide her emotions.

"You know, life goes on after school. You can actually make money. You can get ahead, and do the things you always wanted to do."

"I know…I'm sorry, Jim. I didn't mean for this to turn into a session."

"Me neither."

She pushed me, playfully, and laughed.

"I wanna do something, wild. Something crazy. I had this dream last night I just gotta tell you about." I tried to act like I wanted to hear about her dream, but I had to pay attention to the traffic, too.

For the last three or four miles we had been following an older person's car, which was traveling at a mile or two above the posted limit. Three or four other cars filed in procession, one behind the other and much too close for comfort. It looked like the third turn at Daytona, or Michigan International Speedway.

Warren would have been proud of me for thinking of that.

Rachel's mouth was motoring. "There were three men in a pickup, and one of them had a gun…a long gun."

The guy behind me was breathing down my neck.

On the north side of the Muskegon River, the terrain

changes. Farms and fields reappear. Deer carcasses lay on the shoulder of the road in various stages of decay. It's easy to see their deformed limbs or cracked necks at sixty miles an hour. Some of them had crows perched on their hindquarters, digging for breakfast. I saw crosses, some of them nailed to the trunks of scarred trees. The crosses were adorned with plastic flowers if they didn't have names printed on their faces: "Mom" or "Martha" or "Martin…we'll miss you."

Highway 115 crosses the Lower Peninsula diagonally—from the southeast to the northwest. The roads that run north and south intersect 115 at forty-five-degree angles instead of the usual ninety. Michigan's Department of Transportation installed a third lane in select stretches, for passing slower traffic.

I hate to say it, but Rachel was blabbering, "One of the men pointed his gun at the building above my head…"

The car behind me was really starting to get on my nerves. He was nearly in the back seat. I saw the passing lane ahead. I saw the older man behind the wheel of his Lincoln; he adjusted his rearview mirror, and looked like he just had cataract surgery. An arc welder could have used his glasses.

More blabber. "The gunshot was so loud…I hid…I didn't want them to see me."

The situation was tense, and getting tenser.

I saw the passing lane.

The rearview mirror.

The coffee. *The caffeine.*

The beautiful girl. *The testosterone.*

Gentlemen, start your engines.

The old man in the Lincoln must have felt the adrenaline too. He punched the accelerator as we neared the passing lane. We're doing sixty, sixty-five, then seventy. He eased to my right, I lost my draft. I kept going…faster and faster. The guy was still on my tail…pushing me harder and harder. My little Blazer snorted, pinned back its ears, and dropped a gear. We were in the lead, the pole position. I lost the Lincoln in the sideview mirror; he must have gotten picked off in traffic, or blew a rod.

Poor guy.

When I was sure I had lapped the slower traffic, I moved to the right lane. The guy behind me sailed by with a string of cling-ons in his wake. They barely fell in line before the third lane merged with mine and the oncoming traffic hit them head on.

"What do you think?" She asked me, eyes staring right through me.

I looked at her like I missed something. *She* missed something: my fine piece of driving on one of Michigan's most dangerous thoroughfares.

"I think that was a close one," I said safely.

"Yeah, but why the three men in a pickup, who would they be shooting at, and why was I there?"

I laughed. "It sounds like you have an active imagination."

She smirked. "You're just thinking I need more counseling, aren't you?"

"Don't be silly."

"Don't you think that's a weird dream?"

"Oh yeah, it is."

"What should I do about it?"

"You should follow my instructions." She sat up in her seat, and pulled at the seatbelt, so it was just off her chest. I really think she was waiting for something profound, something helpful. "I want you to go home tonight, and get a good night's sleep. If you have that same dream take two aspirin and call me in the morning."

"You goofball!"

For the rest of the way to the slopes, our conversation was light, and lighthearted. We passed a billboard for a tattoo parlor, and I asked her if she had any.

She said yes.

"Do you regret it?" I asked her.

"No." She looked out the window again, and I knew she was hiding something.

"Are you going to tell me where it is?"

She sighed and batted her eyes. "My bikini line."

I tried to act like it was no big deal, but it rather piqued my interest. It would any man. "Oh…cool." We didn't talk much after that because my mind was working overtime—flip flopping from her bikini line to the tattoo. I imagined Rachel in a bikini, then I imagined her tattoo—a kitten, an angel, a little ski bunny or who knows, Willie Nelson.

My, my, as if it isn't thrilling enough to see what's beneath a bikini, she's got a tattoo as well, I thought. *A tattoo…the ultimate inkblot.*

We parked the car, bought our lift tickets, and got suited up. Caberfae Peaks isn't one of those ritzy resorts with folks decked out in the latest fashions and high-tech gear. It's got a come-as-you-are feel to it, which suited us just fine. There were plenty of younger people, with their headphones, snowboards, and cries of joy. It reminded me of my youth, of our youth, which wasn't that long ago.

There's always a bit of trepidation when you're standing in line for the chairlift. I'm always worried that the chair will send me flipping over the back, or it will knock me headfirst into the snow. It had been so long since I had been skiing, or jumped on a ski lift. Rachel giggled…she was feeling it too. We watched the others' technique: they bent their knees slightly, stuck out their butts and took in the chair gracefully. Before we knew it they were on their way, with the metal handrail snugly resting on their laps. "Are you ready?" I asked her.

"We did come here to ski, didn't we?" She winked.

"Let's go."

As is the case with most of life's little challenges, the chairlift was no big deal. We were on our way up the hill, side by side. I enjoyed having her next to me; sensing the way she swayed in the chair, feeling her arm brush against mine. Despite our heavy clothing, it felt as if we were separated by nothing but more romance, more conversation, more chemistry. The chair could have accommodated four people, but we were side-by-side, cheek-to-cheek so to speak.

The higher we climbed the hill, the more scenery we took in. The Manistee National Forest was at our feet, with its rolling hills, rivers, swamps, and pines: white, red and jack. Before we knew it we were at the summit of the intermediate hill, which didn't look that intermediate. I held my breath and jumped off the chair. Rachel yelled in my direction: "Geronimo!"

We were on our way, slowly at first—finding our legs, tinkering with the combination of muscles, balance and technique that led us down the hill. I let Rachel go ahead of me, as she was a lot less rusty than I was. She was actually a pretty good skier: agile, athletic, and in control. There was no arm flailing or awkward turns. She weaved in and out of traffic, carving up the hill like an old pro. By the time we reached the bottom, I was nearly out of breath, and my legs felt like they were cast from stone.

"That was awesome," she cried. "Come on, let's do the black diamond!"

Who was I to argue? *I can keep up with her.*

After *three* runs down "the bullet," my legs went from stone to jelly to fossilized dust. I suggested a little hot chocolate, and she agreed. One hot chocolate turned into another, which lead to bowls of chili and a side order of pate with wheat crackers. It was easy to sit there in the shadow of the two-story, stone fireplace and watch the traffic in and out of the lodge. We talked about whatever came to mind. She never mentioned her nasty dream again, and that was fine. Our conversation jumped from topic to topic, but by no means became boring, or languished in redundancy. We even had a chance to do a little armchair analyzing—the same way we did at the restaurant in Clare. She came up with some bizarre stories, some unusual situations:

"See that guy in the corner? He's got Obsessive Compulsive Disorder…the worst case I've ever seen. He's a neat freak- washes his hands constantly, won't go to potluck dinners because he's afraid of what other people put in their food. He wears rubber gloves when he flosses his teeth or goes to the bathroom." She had me laughing, chuckling, rolling my eyes and wondering why I didn't spend more time with her. There's nothing quite like a beautiful woman with an engaging personality and a wonderful sense of humor.

By late afternoon the weather took a turn for the worse. An angry northwest wind was howling, and in the process, sucked the moisture off the face of Lake Michigan. Once over the drier, higher climes of the mainland, it dumped that moisture in the form of snow. Lots of it. The skiing was great, even on the steepest of slopes. Fresh powder is a welcome sight even when it was so early in the skiing season.

Before dinner, we agreed that a dip in the heated pool was in order. Caberfae has one of those pools that is half inside, half outside, with a small moat-like passage between the two. By that time it was twilight, and the pool shimmered in a foggy, snow-shrouded haze. I thought about waiting for her, but considering the fact that it was freezing cold, I decided to jump in.

As it turned out, I didn't have long to wait.

She stepped from the locker room door as if it were the stage to a beauty pageant. Beneath the peach cover-up, I liked what I saw: the stride as delicate as a lullaby. Her calves were as round and sweet as a summer fruit basket. It was the most of Rachel I had ever seen, and I wanted more. She waved in my direction, and I waved back.

"Sorry I didn't wait for you."

"I don't blame you. It's chilly out here." She untied the cover-up, flung her plastic flip-flops under our chair, and dipped her toe in the pool. I glanced up at her and reeled in the view. Her nipples were a pair of pearls. "How's the water?"

"Wet...and warm," I said. She tossed her cover-up on the chair near my stuff, and hopped inside. I hardly had a chance to check out the rest of her, but I didn't want to gawk, either.

"It's nice in here," she said. "Much warmer than I thought it would be. I gotta tell you that my legs are really burning after that exercise today."

"Oh?" I tried to sound surprised. "What exercise was that?"

She laughed. "You mean that you don't feel that in your thighs, your calves?" She was swimming mock circles around the shallow area, in water that was only three feet deep. Her strawberry red hair clung to the back of her neck as she made playful laps around me. I could feel the warm water swirling at my thighs. "Don't tell me that you're one of those workout fanatics, that a day on the slope is no big deal." She glanced in my direction and I looked at her over my shoulder. I was making circles now too, however small.

"Tell me, Rachel, how would a macho he-man answer your question?"

"Is that what you are, Jim? A macho man?" Her circles were getting smaller and smaller. She was close to me, and I let my eyes wander to her round, athletic shoulders. The straps of her bikini barely indented her smooth skin on the subtle bend of her collarbone. I pictured the strap sliding over the edge. I looked for a tattoo. There was none.

Not that bikini line, silly.

"No, I'm not, and yes they are."

"You're not a macho man, but your thighs are burning, right?" She asked.

"Right."

"If you're not so macho, what kind of a man are you, Jim?" Her blue eyes darted from the ceiling to my face. She was flirting. She was sizing me up, daring me to kiss her. I was scared. Afraid of rejection. Afraid of making the first move. Her hand brushed my thigh as she passed. It felt like the graceful stride of a ray on a white coral beach. Without the sting.

I turned with her, watching her face. Inching ever closer. She licked her lips. Her eyes batted playfully.

"What kind of man are you, Jim?"

I bit my tongue, because I didn't know how to answer it.

She wants you, Jim.

She's sending signals.

Kiss her.

Tell her that she's beautiful.

Tell her that she's wonderful.

Take her by the hand. Hold her by the wrist. Wrap her in your arms and kiss her like you've never kissed before.

We crouched there—in the shallow end of the pool—only inches apart, a mile away. I should have scooped her up, or whisked her away. Anything but nothing. I waited too long.

We were interrupted. It seemed that the entire high-school field trip entered the pool area at the same time. There were dozens of them. Rachel and I swam under the partition, through the moat, and into the outside pool. The kids followed us.

The moment was lost, the situation gone.

But at least we had that occasion. It was fun. It was erotic. I found myself wanting her, wanting to kiss her, to hold her, to touch her in places that only a lover could. As much as I tried to capture that ambiance over dinner, the ride home, and the goodnight kiss in the driveway, she slipped through my fingers like the flakes during a Michigan snow squall.

Thirty-One

I T WAS NEARLY FIVE THIRTY by the time Toby and I walked downtown to the law offices of Morrison & Nunnelly. Kathy was finishing up her work for the day.

"Why did you bring that thing?" She asked.

"What?"

"This is a law office, not a kennel club!" I sensed a bit of sarcasm in her voice.

"Rats..." I hesitated. "We got a call that you needed an exterminator for your rat problem...and this is my rat-sniffer-outer."

"Pah-leeese!"

"What?"

She laughed. "That dog couldn't find its shadow on a sunny day!"

"Now, now, personal attacks aren't warranted. You don't make fun of a newborn baby's looks and you definitely don't criticize another man's dog. Especially a hunting dog."

"Whatever...you've got a lot of work to do here."

"Like what?"

"Like get back to these people from Indiana, that's what. They keep calling here and telling me their problems. It's driving me nuts. I've got work to do. I don't have time to listen to their sob stories."

"I'm sorry."

"No you're not." She pulled two folders out of her desk drawer, labeled "Michigan" and "Indiana."

"Come on, Kathy, we're almost done with this project."

"What do you mean?"

"I mean, once we wade through this stuff it'll be smooth sailing. Be patient, okay?"

She rolled her eyes and gestured for me to use the conference room. "There's water and soft drinks in the fridge, and here's the key to the office. Glen's out of town until next week, but don't tell him I let you have the key."

"Thanks."

"And for Pete's sake," she said, "don't forget to lock the office."

"I won't."

She waved goodbye, gathered up her purse and winter coat, and paraded by the office window. We had the place to ourselves.

Toby and I didn't waste any time. We moved to the conference room, where I laid both files across the massive cherrywood table. "Michigan's" file had the names and addresses of the complainants listed on a spreadsheet, along with a brief description of their damages. She also stapled an envelope containing a floppy disc to the inside cover of the file.

And there were phone messages, lots of them.

Indiana was worse. A lot worse.

It was painfully clear that if I was really going to pursue the civil matter against Atmantle, I had a lot of work to do. There were lots of people that needed to be contacted. They all needed to have their stories heard, and have their hands held. They needed someone with a little compassion; someone who would take up their cause and give them a sense of hope. Even though I wasn't a lawyer, I could do a lot of the things necessary to build a case. I was the man for the job.

So for the rest of that evening—and the rest of the week— Toby and I walked downtown after work and burned up the phone lines of Morrison & Nunnelly. The stories were all the same. Their outcomes had varying degrees of tragedy; their reactions to the whole ordeal were as diverse as the people themselves. Some folks wanted an explanation and an apology, while others wanted to sue Atmantle for millions of dollars. Either way, they were happy that I called and were content to wait to hear from me.

By the end of the week Toby was on a first-name basis with the pizza deliveryman.

About ten that evening, I called Rachel, just to chitchat. She was in the throes of mid-term exams, but still had time to dye her hair "winter's mistress," she said. "At least that's the color on the box."

"Sounds intriguing," I told her. She giggled. It was nice to hear her voice, and to hear her say that she'd meet me for a coffee and a Danish in the morning at our favorite little shop downtown. Since I met her, she had been a faint blond, a strawberry red and now a mysterious "winter's mistress." It seemed that she had a different color hair for every season.

From there, I jumped on the Internet and did a little investigation regarding Darvin Wonch's claims that he paid off the governor and the attorney general. I discovered that the state of Michigan requires candidates to report every contribution, no matter the dollar amount. It was all right there on the Internet; at the top of the heap for the attorney general was Atmantle Health and Casualty's gracious gift of seventy thousand dollars. The United Auto Workers, the Michigan Education Association, the Trial Lawyers Association, and the law firm of Goos, Slaymaker & Brian donated similar amounts.

It made me wonder, how could elected officials maintain their objectivity when they had donations from groups they were supposed to regulate? How can the attorney general remain fair and unbiased when the trial lawyers have a situation that needs attention?

What's more: Goos, Slaymaker & Brian...was "Brian" the same "Francis Brian" that Darvin Wonch called from my office? It was. It had to be: their website said it all. All three partners touted themselves as "the lawyers that are all business." Elliot S. Goos specialized in "commercial litigation, including environmental, health care and product liability." Gordon F. Slaymaker seemed to be the tax professional of the bunch, with a laundry list of appointments, organizations, and memberships to his credit. J. Francis Brian was a self-proclaimed "expert in executive compensation, arbitration summary, and white-collar crime."

No kidding.

Brian must have arbitrated the "Rome matter" in Atmantle's favor, and that's why he deserved a pair of $150 Red Wings tickets, a stack of currency with Ben Franklin's picture on it, and dinner at one of Detroit's ritziest nightclubs.

I was really getting sickened with the whole situation. The further I looked into the matter, the worse it became. The tip of the iceberg had a much seedier underbelly, fraught with cozy little deals, symbiotic relationships, and collusion. It was just horrible.

So I sent a letter to the insurance commissioner, explaining that I was aware of a substantial number of people who have "considerable differences" with the way Atmantle handled their claims. *Furthermore, we are very disappointed in the manner in which your office has investigated the complaints against the aforementioned insurance carrier. I would hate to suggest that your office's inability to conduct a fair and impartial analysis has anything to do with the fact that you, personally, have received contributions and gifts which may have clouded your judgment.* I signed my name *"Regretfully yours, James P. Nunnelly."* Even though I had no evidence that the commissioner was on the take, I was in the mood to stir the pot.

I was on a roll, and it felt good. I sent another letter to the Securities and Exchange Commission. They needed to know about Atmantle too, even though it served no strategic purpose. I didn't have any proof of what Atmantle was doing wrong. It still felt good to fire off a letter stating *We have reason to believe that the head of the company is absconding funds from the premium trust account to pad its bottom line.* I probably worded my letter a little too harshly, but I also mentioned *The company is domiciled in Nassau, Bahamas, and our sources suggest that the company may be abusing the overseas tax benefits associated with such an arrangement in lieu of their recent Initial Public Offering.* As long as James P. Nunnelly was signing the letters, I figured that I could hide behind the shield of anonymity.

Taren Lisk was next on my list. She had been on my mind since Toby and I spent the night at her apartment. I considered sending her an e-mail, but thought the better of it, after all "James P. Nunnelly" couldn't share an e-mail account with a shrink at the Centre.

Her voice was groggy, sleepy. "Jim…what the hell are you doing calling me at this hour of the night?"

"Sorry, sorry." I pleaded.

"Jim, it's almost one o'clock in the morning. And I seriously doubt if you're sorry."

"Okay fine, I'm not sorry, but I wouldn't have called you if this wasn't important." The line went dead. She was faking me. "Hello?"

"Remind me to choke you later." Our conversation crackled. "Make it quick, will you?"

"Taren, I told you before, and I'll tell you again. There is something going on with Atmantle."

"Jim!" She hesitated, clearing her throat for the next barrage. "You're full of shit. Full of it! I told you that I'd look into it, now goodbye."

"Wait! I know what you told me, Taren, but I know there's more to it."

"Why are you doing this, Jim?"

"What?"

"Why are you torturing yourself like this? It won't bring Carrie back."

Now it was my turn to be silent. I gave her a chance to apologize, but I knew that it would never happen. "Taren. That was mean. I'm being serious, here."

"Send me an e-mail."

"I can't."

"Why not?"

"I just can't. And you can't call me at the office, either."

"Jim…are you losing it? What's wrong with you?"

"I'm telling you, I got stuff you can use."

"Fine. That's fine, but can we talk about it during normal waking hours?"

"When?" I asked her.

"How about the end of the week, Friday, I think." She hesitated. "I've got a meeting in Grayling in the morning…I could call you from the road."

"That's fine, let me give you my cell phone number."

"Whatever."

I asked her not to say anything to anybody…especially at the office. She agreed, but the way she said it wasn't very convincing.

And really, I had a hard time trusting Taren with the whole Atmantle deal. I remember telling her that I was working at the law office, as an investigator. I recall telling her that I thought there was something going on with Atmantle and the collusion with the insurance commissioner's office. But I could never tell her that I was counseling the man responsible for the whole debacle with Carrie's denied benefits. She would have me arrested if I had done anything illegal; I just knew it. If she found out that I was tape recording our sessions, she'd have my license in a New York second.

It was okay for her to secretly tape record conversations, but she worked for the good guys. I was just a workingman, a common citizen, and handcuffs would fit me just fine if I broke the law.

No, I would have to feed Taren Lisk information that could be documented through legal means. Darvin Wonch could tell me about his exploits, but I'd have to prove it through lawful channels before I'd pass it on to Taren.

By the time Taren came to visit me Friday, I had discovered that J. Francis Brian was doing almost all of Atmantle's arbitration work and he was doing it with reckless malice. Wonch and Brian were in bed together and were hosing their clients in the process.

The insurance commissioner was a regular at Atmantle's condo in Nassau, according to a story printed in the *Lansing State Journal* from three years before. The reporter who broke the story no longer worked for the paper, and nobody in Human Resources would tell me where she went.

Taren apologized for not looking into the Atmantle situation sooner. She was extremely busy with her job and gave me the usual song and dance associated with a weak alibi.

After an hour of rehashing the ammunition I had dug up, Taren seemed more convinced that there might have been something to pursue. She didn't slam her fist on the round table Sir Arthur style. She didn't sound the battle cry, or blow the houndsman's bugle in an effort to rally the troops.

In other words, her reaction wasn't a resounding endorsement, but it was a backing nonetheless.

And any endorsement at all would be a welcome addition, indeed.

Thirty-Two

THE FOLLOWING MONDAY Darvin Wonch was all grins. Chuckling grins. I could see the excitement in his eyes; sense the confidence in his face.

There was no hiding the thrill of victory.

I asked him what was going on, and why he had that sheepish look on his face.

"You won!" He cried.

"Won what?"

"The horse race...*Hot Tamale at Santa Anita?*"

"Really? I forgot all about it." He had me smiling too. "Cool! How much?"

"Peanuts, really. About sixteen hundred dollars."

I laughed along with him. "That's not peanuts to me. That's a lot of money."

I'm not sure who was happier, Darvin or me. He pumped his fist as if he had just sunk a putt to win the U.S. Open golf tournament. "Let's go online and check out your account." He stood up from the couch and approached me. I thought for a second about telling him no, but I really didn't want to quell his enthusiasm either. In an instant he was on a knee next to my desk and pulled up the Internet on my computer. My heart skipped a beat. I couldn't remember where I had done all that research on his company's campaign contributions…*was it here, at home, or at the law office downtown?* "Looks like you've been doing a little surfing on the net, huh?" He scrolled down the list of Internet addresses: MSNBC, Yahoo, Morningstar, Schwab, Price Waterhouse. *I was safe.* "Doing a little research, are we?"

"Darvin, can we just get to the website."

"For Christ's sake, you don't have to get all defensive. I'm the one who helped you win all that dough. Now how about a little gratitude?"

"Sorry. I just don't need you poking around my business."

"Got something to hide?" He laughed. I just gave him the look, Miss Peacock style. "Here we go. Punch in your password." He slid the keyboard my way and I typed in the letters as fast as I could. "Look there," he said, pointing at the screen, "you just won sixteen hundred dollars. Isn't that awesome?"

"Yeah, that's great! Incredible. Thanks, Darvin."

He stood up from the edge of the desk and pulled up his trousers, proudly. "I told you I was good at this stuff."

"Yes, you did."

"Doesn't it make you want to bet some more? To win again?" He returned to the couch and sat there, erect and smug, waving his odd fingernails at me.

"Not really."

He laughed and shook his head incredulously. "Why not?"

"I don't like to lose what I've got, I guess."

"How many times…"

"I remember, 'Keep your eye on the prize.'"

"That's right. You can't think about losing. You gotta keep a positive mental attitude. Your next big win is only a play away, know what I mean?"

"Yes I do, but I don't like to lose the little money I do have. Besides, I don't think you're really a good role model for an up-and-comer gambler like me."

His posture turned defensive. "What's that supposed to mean?"

"You still don't think you have a problem even after your marriage is on the rocks, you're bankrupt, and close to losing your house?"

He sat there, silent, eyes burning a hole through me. I didn't say a word. I didn't retract. "You want a sure thing to bet on? Is that what you want?"

"You missed my point."

"I heard what you said. I know things aren't right at home, with my wife and our finances."

"What are you getting at?" I asked him.

"Things are going to get a whole lot better. You'll see."

"How?"

"I own a ton of shares in my company, that's how." He took a deep breath, and exhaled as if he was blowing smoke rings from a hand-rolled Monte Cristo. "I told you at our last session that Atmantle went public. We offered 340,000 shares in our company at twenty dollars each. The idea was that we'd raise over six million to use for advertising, a new information technology system, and to expand into other states. Of course, I got a fifteen percent discount on the shares I bought."

"Wow. That's really great."

"Oh yeah, Chief. It was great. I was there, on Wall Street, got to see the Initial Public Offering. Really incredible. You've heard of that term before, haven't you?"

"Initial Public Offering? Sure."

"Would you mind if we checked to see what it's up to to-day…the market opens in half an hour."

"No, I don't mind. You went to New York on the day your company went public?"

"Hell yes, I did. I've got a lot of blood, sweat, and tears in that company, and it was a little sweet and sour seeing it go."

"What do you mean?"

"Once a company goes public, you give up a lot of the control. I go from president of the company who's accountable to nobody, to one of the bosses with a board of directors breathing down my neck."

"But it's a good thing, isn't it?"

"Oh yeah. I made a ton of dough already. I own seventy thousand shares that are worth over twenty-five dollars a share as of Friday's close. I could pay off my house, and all those creditors if I wanted to sell some of those shares."

"Will you?"

"Hell no. I'm betting the share price will go up to two hundred a share, like it did for Google. Remember that?" I shook my head, no. "Almost overnight it went from twenty a share to two hundred, then six months later three hundred. Unbelievable."

"What does your wife think?"

He paused. "She doesn't think at all." Darvin looked away. "I didn't even tell her what's going on."

"You're kidding."

"Nope. She doesn't need to know. Besides, she's moved out. Took the kids and everything."

"How does that make you feel?"

He tossed his hands in the air and confessed, "It's her loss. I still love her, but if she's not willing to stick with me through thick and thin then what the hell kind of marriage did we have in the first place?"

I nodded. "Do you talk to her?"

"Only about the kids, that's it. She moved into a house on the other side of town, and the kids spend a lot of time with her parents. What a mess. Of all the times to leave me…"

"How do you know that you still love her?"

"I just do. I buy her all kinds of stuff; have given her a great lifestyle. Doesn't that mean something? I mean I'm at the office seventy hours a week, and I don't have time to talk to her about things."

I chewed on his last statement for a second or two. "Maybe she doesn't want all those gifts. Maybe she wants to feel loved in other ways—like affection, like honesty and open communication. Have you ever thought about that?"

"I give her everything she needs."

The guy seemed incapable of listening. "Is she seeing somebody else?"

"No way. She's as strait-laced as they come. She'll be faithful to me for the rest of her life, even though we hardly speak and never have relations. I mean we never have sex or make love, whatever you want to call it. She's a prude. She'd be happy being celibate the rest of her life."

"Has she begged you for attention?" Darvin was starting to get uneasy. He thumbed his watch, and glanced at the clock. My questions were swirling in his head, pinging off the sides. He wasn't sure about much anymore…and that was exactly my plan. It was time to move in for the kill. "Now that I've got a few bucks compliments of Hot Tamale, how do I buy some of your stock?"

His reaction told it all: at last, a life ring. He didn't want to talk about his wife anymore, and I reeled him in. "There are lots of ways, but the two most popular are online accounts or you can do it through a regular stockbroker. Do you want me to help you set up an online account?"

"No, that's okay; I can do that at home."

"That's fine. Our ticker is AHC, short for Atmantle Health and Casualty."

I acted sincere. "That will be easy to remember."

"You're going to thank me someday."

"I'm sure I will." I nodded. "Are there a lot of shares available?"

"Yeah, but they're going fast. A lot of high rollers and mutual fund managers have heard about it, and are scooping them up."

"Really?" *Come on Darvin, bite.*

"Oh sure. The governor, the attorney general…they formed an investment group to handle it all. They didn't buy shares individually. They hide behind the walls of the Limited Liability Corporation they formed. I thought I told you that last week."

"No…you told me that you had paid them for immunity."

"I did?"

Wanna listen to the tape?

"That's what you said…" I nodded, and he shrugged his shoulders. "How does that work? How did you first get involved with the *governor,* for Pete's sake?"

He laughed. "He wasn't the governor when I met him. He was a rising star in the legislature; you could just see it. I helped him get reelected to the House, the Senate, and eventually to the lieutenant governor's post. When he ran for governor six or seven years ago, he wanted his constituents to have access to fairly priced insurance. That was one of the planks in his platform. I promised him that, and came through."

"So your company…what was it again?"

He puffed out his chest "Atmantle Health and Casualty."

"That's right, I forgot already. Your company has fair rates, pays claims, and has the ear of the governor's office too?"

He was gloating now. "Life is good."

"Didn't you say something last week about doing things that were 'less than honorable' in the insurance business?"

"Yeah, what's your point?"

"That just doesn't make sense to me." I scratched the top of my head to make my question even more effective. "You pay the governor for the privilege of doing business in Michigan?"

"There's a lot more to it then that, and I hate to sound condescending, but you probably wouldn't follow the progression."

"What is it, rocket science?"

He shrugged his shoulders. "No it's not rocket surgery, but it is complicated. It's business, and I don't think you'd understand."

"I'd better understand if I'm going to buy some of...At-mantle's stock. I don't want to get stung."

"I see...you're doing some homework?" I nodded. "All right...that's different. Listen up...here we go." Darvin cracked his knuckles and I was expecting something extraordinary. I was disappointed. "In its purest form, we paid the governor a handsome sum and we got him elected. In exchange, the governor waives the three percent premium tax because we're not a domestic company. We also don't pay property taxes as an additional incentive to stay in Michigan."

"Wow. That's cool. But doesn't that give you an unfair advantage over all the other companies that are paying those taxes?"

"Sure it does, but they're not on the same terms as we are with the state's real decision makers."

I shrugged my shoulders and tried to look confused. "Isn't there some sort of insurance referee that would look into that?"

He chuckled the same way he did when he mentioned Hot Tamale. "The commissioner, you mean?" I nodded. "She's appointed by the governor...hand-picked." He laughed, harder. "And guess who had a say in that?" More laughter. "She's just a stooge, a yes man. That's all she is. We send her to the company's condo in the Bahamas for two weeks a year and she thinks we're the greatest."

I laughed along with him. "What an incredible racket you have!"

"I know it." More laughter. "What did you call her, 'the insurance referee?'" He laughed, "That's funny!"

"Why do you have a condo in the Bahamas?"

He was still smiling. "That's where our company is located. We have a post office box for a mailing address and an office or two down the street from our condo, but there's a lot more to it than that."

"Oh?"

"Hell, yes. You have to have a local management company and a resident representative, both of which get a small cut of the premiums."

"What else do they do?"

"They handle the money for us. We have an account set up with the Royal Bank of Scotland and we're constantly wiring funds through the management company."

"Why do you bank there?"

"There are hundreds of banks to choose from…from all over the world: Denmark, Spain, Saudi Arabia, Hong Kong, Brazil. The Bahamian government has unique rules that help businesses like ours. When we started, we enjoyed a fifteen-year 'tax holiday' they call it, for start-ups like us. Our fifteen years is almost up, but now that we're public, it really doesn't matter." He sighed. "We chose the Bank of Scotland because they gave us the most juice on our money. Plus, they're safe and quiet. Much quieter than the Swiss banks."

He seemed to have every angle covered. "How do you sleep at night?"

"What do you mean?"

"You've got a full dance card…a lot on your plate." He was listening intently. "You say some of what you're doing is legal; some of it's not. Your wife left you, but you say that you love her. And then there's the reason why we're here: bankruptcy. Wow!" He was agreeing with me, even though he didn't say a word. "If that wasn't enough, you've got a couple of guys that want to kill you, right? Are they still threatening you?"

He held up his index finger. "I paid one of the guys off, there's only one left."

"That's good." *Pathetic, really.* "Who is he?"

"His name is Jones…and he hangs out at the Turf Club at Great Lakes Downs in Muskegon. He's a jack-of-all-trades there. A track rat. Sometimes he's in the parking lot, passing out flyers, or in the stables shoveling manure. Every Saturday during the winter, he handles the simulcasts and betting from tracks around the country." I was listening intently. "He even fills in for them at the betting counter when they're in a pinch. I think he's on the board there too, but I can't say for sure."

"And how much do you owe him?"

"Sixty grand, more or less."

Unbelievable. "Was he the one who wanted to blow your head off, or break your legs?"

He laughed again. "He was the head hunter." More laughter.

After a minute the office was quiet again. "So are you going to answer my question?"

"Which one? I forgot."

"I asked how you sleep at night."

"Oh that question." Darvin scratched his chin. "Not very well."

"What happens?"

"I think about stuff."

"Like what?"

"Like how I'm going to make more money. Like how can I keep claim costs low, or deny them altogether, or dodge somebody's attorney, or get out of this mess with the courts and my wife."

"What's it like to deny claims that you owe?"

"You make it sound like we don't pay any at all. We pay the little ones."

"Do you ever think about the people who have big claims?"

"Not really. I can't get emotionally involved with them."

He showed no remorse. "Is that all?" I asked.

"Pretty much. I can't think about stuff like that."

I paused for a second or two, then asked him, "Have you ever been on medication?"

"Never, why?"

"Because I'm starting to see a pattern in your behavior that may be helped."

He stared in my direction. "You think I'm nuts, don't you?"

I laughed. "Hardly…here's how I see it." Darvin nodded, approvingly. He was ready for a little analyzing. "You told me that you gamble to get away from things. It's an escape for you." More nodding. "I think you have so much going on in your life, that you suffer from an anxiety disorder. Gambling is how you deal with it." Darvin sucked it in. "It's unhealthy."

"What do you mean by 'anxiety'?"

"This will be easy for you to understand." He nodded, as if to say 'I know, because I'm a smart guy.' "When you're anxious, you can't stop worrying that something horrible will happen to you. What's more, anxiety makes you think that you are powerless to change the things that cause your worry. Doesn't that sound like you?"

"I guess so."

"Don't you sometimes have shortness of breath? Sweating? Nausea, chills or light-headedness?"

"Occasionally."

"Inability to sleep?" He nodded, half-heartedly. "You want to get better, don't you?"

Darvin was awfully quiet. "What are you getting at?"

"I think if you were on a mild medicine you would like yourself a lot more. And if you liked yourself a lot more, you would gamble a lot less."

He was taking it all in. Chewing on it, like his cigar that he was puffing only a moment ago. "What kind of medicine?"

"Xanax."

"What's that?"

"It's a drug that helps people with predisposed urges for impulsivity."

"I don't get it."

"It works like this: when you feel anxious, you take a pill instead of going gambling."

"That doesn't sound like fun," he said.

"But it is. The pill gives you the same kind of satisfaction that a round of blackjack would, without the side effects…like bankruptcy."

He let out a "Hmmph!" He crossed his arms.

I had some selling to do. "What are you afraid of?"

"I don't know…I don't like the thought of being on medicine for anything other than high blood pressure…or cholesterol."

"Or Viagra?"

He laughed. "Exactly! You know…the stuff that means that you're getting old."

"I hear what you're saying, Darvin, but you really have nothing to lose." He only winced. "Besides, you might like it."

"All right. How do I get it? In stores?"

"No, no, you need a prescription."

"So write me one."

"I'm not licensed to write prescriptions, but there is someone down the hall who can. Let me see if she's available." Darvin put up a minor fuss, but I appeased him with a gesture to use my computer. "You'll like her. She's good, too. Let me do most of the talking." In short order, I had Mary on the phone and on her way down the hall.

There really wasn't much to Mary's observation. She glanced at Darvin's chart once or twice, then at me. She repeated the things I told her about him: the anxiety, the shortness of breath, and the reasons for his addiction. She hardly batted an eye before whipping out her prescription pad and jotting down Xanax, one milligram. Her second prescription was Zyprexa, five milligrams.

She turned to Darvin and said, "Mr. Wonch, I want to tell you that Xanax is designed to relieve anxiety and nervousness in the short term, but the Zyprexa may take a week or two before it kicks in. The Xanax will give you almost an immediate high, while the Zyprexa will have a calming effect, unless you take too much of it." He nodded and smiled at the same time. She continued, "If you take too much of it, it'll make you anxious, which is exactly what we're trying to avoid. It can be addictive too, so I really want you to watch it." Darvin flicked his wrist like she was just joshing him, like her warning was a mosquito buzzing close to his ear. "If you forget to take a dose, don't double up the next time, okay? It's a very powerful drug."

Darvin nodded confidently, but dismissed her warning as frivolity, "Nice to meet you."

When Mary left the office, Darvin was drooling all over himself. "Wow, she's quite a little number. How do you keep your hands off her?"

"It's easy...we're coworkers."

"I know, but she's quite attractive. Is she available?"

"I didn't think that you thought about sex."

"I don't think about having it with my wife. She's a prude, remember, Chief?"

I nodded. "Darvin, do you have any questions about the prescription Dr. Cornwall wrote you?"

"Yeah, can I meet with her next time...alone?"

"Maybe this would be a good time to take a break."

"What about my stock?"

"What about it?" I asked him.

"You said we could check it."

We checked it all right. Even though the market was only open for a short while, Atmantle's stock was up fifty-three cents on volume of twenty thousand shares. Darvin grinned. "If I own seventy thousand shares at twenty-six dollars a share, that means I'm worth..." He reached for the calculator on my desk. "A little over $1.8 million."

"That's a ton of dough."

"I know it is, but the trouble is I've got to sell the stock to realize the profits."

"You could pay off your debtors. Get out of trouble, come clean with Jones at the track."

"I could do a lot of things."

"You could take a wonderful trip with just you and your wife—a second honeymoon."

"I could afford two wives...and a handful of mistresses... maybe Dr. Cornwall would be interested," he said, smugly.

"So what about the medicine?"

"What about it?" He asked me.

"Are you going to try it?"

"Maybe."

"Why wouldn't you try it?"

"Because I like to gamble, and I'm afraid that those drugs might keep me from it."

"Darvin, why don't we have a little bet on the drug?"

I knew he would be intrigued with the prospect of another bet. "What's your wager?"

I thought for a second or two. "If you try your medicine, I'll visit you at your office instead of you having to come visit me, okay?"

"And if I don't?"

"We'll be right back here next Monday morning."

"But if I do take the meds, I don't want you to announce yourself at the office as a shrink, got it?"

"No problem. Tell your staff I'm a financial planner or something," I suggested. "I'll even wear a suit."

"All right then. I'll call you tomorrow and leave a message."

"Okay then."

Darvin was a complicated character. The guy loved his business so much that he would do anything legal or illegal to make it succeed. He claimed he loved his wife, but made no effort to make her happy. He enjoyed looking at Mary Cornwall but wore his celibate relationship with his wife like a badge of honor. He seemed like a loose cannon, but possessed all kinds of business moxie. When I asked him difficult questions he hid in his shell, but took every opportunity to get things off his chest.

The next day he left me a message about the wonderful effects of Xanax, and how he couldn't wait show me around his "kingdom."

Thirty-Three

I WASN'T REALLY SURE what to do about Warren. The guy never did listen to my advice, and seemed to be growing more and more comfortable with the fact that he and Sharon would be together. I had a hunch that he would quit coming to see me, which was fine. I like to think that my services are valuable, my advice is important. For the last few sessions Warren ignored my advice and dodged my questions. I really wanted him to come clean with his wife.

It was becoming more and more clear that he was a slave to his libido, a servant to his urges. He would become tired of my intrusion and weary of my interference; he didn't need my advice, didn't want my counsel. Long gone were the days when he cried about stepping out on his wife, he was now more and more comfortable with the notion.

But still, I liked Warren, and considered my hour with him like a little break from the routine. He was easy to deal with, and a quick two hundred bucks in the Centre's coffers.

In a way, I wanted to wrap things up with him in case it was our last appointment together.

I think that he was on the same page.

"So what should we talk about?" He asked me.

I had to laugh. The guy didn't hold anything back. "What did you have in mind, Warren?"

"The weather is always safe, or we could talk politics in case you're in the mood for something a little more risky."

"How about religion?" I conferred.

"Or who's the best stock car driver of all time: Richard Petty, the Unser boys, Dale Earnhardt or Jeff Gordon."

"You got me there."

"I'm a Richard Petty fan myself. He was the most dominating driver in his time."

I nodded.

"You never got into car racing?" He asked.

"Never have."

"You should look into it sometime. It's a lot of fun, a great sport."

"I just might."

"You should see my office; I've got framed posters of all the drivers. A couple of them are autographed."

"What do you do again?"

"I'm a stockbroker."

"That's right. Didn't you have a problem with your boss?"

"I did, but now he's cool."

"What happened?"

He laughed, confidently. "I landed a few nice accounts in a row. Made him look good."

"Strange how that works out."

"I know it." He grinned. "Everybody just wants to make a buck."

I leaned back in my chair and he did too. It seemed we had reached a momentary impasse.

"I have a question for you," I said. "It's about the market, and stocks."

"Sure. Whatever you want."

"Can you tell me about insider trading?"

"Sure. It's not hard to understand, really." He loosened his tie. "In its purest form, it pertains to the buying or selling of a security based on information that is not privy to the general public. Most often officers of a company are guilty of insider trading because they know about the company and the direction it's headed." He took a breath. "That's why officers of the company have to report to the feds when they sell shares of stock in their own company."

"What about options?"

"That's a little more complicated, and speculative. It's like betting. You can buy options in a company's stock that it will either go up or down. If you believe the stock will go up in price, your option is called a 'call'. If you think the price will go down, your option is called a 'put'."

"Okay."

"Did you want to open an account?"

"No. No. I just was curious."

"It's a fascinating business."

"I'm sure it is, but why would someone take out a 'put' instead of selling their shares in the company?"

"You're talking about two different animals. Options are options and stocks are stocks. You can buy an option on whether or not the price of a stock will rise or fall."

"I'm sorry Warren, is there another way you can explain it?"

He laughed. "Sure...sure. Let's say shares of Ford Motor Company are trading at ten dollars a share and you've got some money to invest. You can buy an option on the stock that it will either go up in price or down in price. The guy writing the option might charge you a three dollar premium, and sets the strike price. If your strike price is $9.50, but the stock falls to five dollars a share, they still have to pay you the $9.50 a share."

"So you could really make a killing if you knew the price was going to fall?"

"Oh yeah you could, but the feds would be all over you if you made a big killing. Don't forget the old saying: pigs get fat, hogs get slaughtered."

"How much would I make on my investment in that scenario?"

"That's easy. Every option you buy represents a hundred shares, and in this case you'd net about $6.50 a share...or six hundred and fifty dollars."

"Wow. So I pay the option writer his three-hundred-dollar premium, for the privilege of buying a hundred shares of Ford stock that may go below $9.50, right?"

He nodded his head. "Even if the stock goes in the tank, you still get paid."

"Why don't more people do that?"

"Because you only collect if the price of the stock meets the strike price. If it doesn't hit that number, you lose your premium." Warren knew his stuff. "Plus, options don't last forever. They expire on the third Friday of every month."

I nodded again. "I see."

"Maybe when this whole thing blows over I can do some investing for you."

I nodded again. "Sure. We'll have to talk about it."

"After the smoke clears."

"Sure...but when will that happen?"

He hesitated. "Who knows? Man, this affair I'm having is steam-rolling along. I can't get enough of this girl. I want to be with her every waking moment."

"What's keeping you from it?"

"My wife...my kids...my conscience."

"Those are three good reasons."

"I know it."

"Does your wife think there's anything going on?"

"No, I don't think so. We only live together. We raise kids, and go through the motions of marriage, that's about it."

"So what are you going to do?"

"I don't know for sure." He sighed. "I feel like I should take a break from seeing Sharon, just for the sake of catching my breath."

"I thought you liked to be with her?" I asked him.

"I do…I do. But she does some things that make me wonder where it'll stop."

"Like what?" I asked him.

"It's a little embarrassing."

"That's fine, if you'd rather not…"

"No, that's okay…we're on the Internet." I didn't say a thing. "Sharon and me. She took pictures of the two of us…in bed…engaged…you could say."

"And how did they get to the Internet?"

"She posted them."

"Why?"

"She's into that stuff…porn…and toys…and role playing, I've told you that, haven't I?"

"Yes, but watching dirty movies and getting kinky is one thing, posting intimate photos on the Internet is a whole other matter, don't you think?"

"Oh yeah."

"Why'd she do it?"

"She told me that it was her way to express herself. It was her way to be an amateur porn star. And honestly, she's proud of herself—her body—and the way she makes love. She loves sex, plain and simple…at least with me."

"Are your faces on the Net?"

"Oh yeah."

"What are you going to do if someone recognizes you?"

"I guess I'll worry about that when the time comes. It's an obscure site; something like 'homecookin dot com.' And there are millions of other sites out there."

"Why did she choose that site?"

"It's one of those sites where you post your own images. She says she likes to pull up the pictures of the two of us when she's bored. She has her own gallery, called 'Bare'n Sharon', which is a unique name I thought."

"I suppose so. How many images are there?"

"Eight or ten, I'd guess. I told her that I was mad about it but she kinda blew me off like it was no big deal."

"How does that make you feel?"

"Like I'm really just a toy after all," he said. "Like I'm just good for a romp in the hay."

"And?"

"I don't know. We have great sex…I mean great sex, but it's beginning to get old. I want to feel loved not for what I can do in bed, but for who I am inside. Do you know what I mean?"

"I suppose. But what are you going to do?"

"I don't know." He ran his fingers through his hair, then petted his goatee. "She left her husband. I still live at home. What a mess. I don't know what I should do. What do you think?"

"I think you've got a lot to deal with." I let him simmer.

"You know what, I think I'm going to stop coming here," he said abruptly. For the first time in several months he showed a little backbone. I could see it in his posture. "We just keep hashing and rehashing the same things over and over. You don't tell me what I should do, and I keep floundering between the things bouncing in my head. I need to make a decision between my wife and my family and the other woman. That's all there is to it." He took a breath, and continued, "And at this point I'd rather be admired by my kids than carry on with a woman who is only after one thing."

"Wow," I said, convincingly.

"What do you think?"

"I think that's a great idea. The whole thing."

"Is it okay if I make an appointment down the road?"

"Sure, you're welcome anytime, just talk to Miss Peacock for my schedule."

"Can I bring my wife with me? Just for a refresher if we need it?"

"Absolutely."

"What do you think I should do?"

He was smiling like he had just told me the punch line of a joke.

I laughed. "I think that when this whole thing blows over we should get together and talk about doing a little investing."

"That would be great."

It seemed that Warren was starting to realize that maybe a fling wasn't all that it was cracked up to be. Sharon was using him; he was using her. They had no future together, but were simply two lonely people with selfish needs. I was happy nonetheless that he decided not to see me anymore. It was time for him to move on.

Although I usually let my clients dictate the agenda of most sessions, I was glad that I asked Warren about the stock market. He gave me some information that I'd use in the weeks to come.

And boy, would it pay dividends.

Thirty-Four

IT WAS NEARLY SIX that evening when I finally checked my cell phone's voice messages.

"Jim, I should have listened to you all along. *You were right, damn it.*"

I laughed at first, but then realized Taren had an unfamiliar resonance in her voice. She sounded insecure.

"Don't call me back; I'll be at your house close to six."

I hung up the phone and peered through the bunched madras curtains near the kitchen table. Taren had just pulled up and was rifling through the back seat of her Chevy Colorado. I knew this was coming. I knew she'd find smoke; I knew she'd find fire. She had always been motivated by crisis. She was notorious for procrastinating until whatever it was boiled to the surface and consumed her life. The incident with the attorney general and the corrupt politicians was right up her alley. She had found something all right: her latest crisis.

"You son of a bitch," she yelled before I could say hello. "Do you know what the hell you're getting into? Do you know what you're doing?"

I didn't know what to say. I didn't want to say anything as long as she was venting.

Toby's tail was between his legs. He hadn't heard yelling like that since the time he chewed the heels off seven pairs of Carrie's Nine West shoes. One heel in each pair.

"They are going to hose you, man!" She tossed her coat over the back of the kitchen chair, flailing the curtains in the process. Her heels stomped the hardwood floors. Her fist slammed the countertop over and over again. She had been practicing her opening argument all the way from Lansing.

"Aren't you going to say something?" She was still yelling. "Jim? Hello in there!"

I held up my index finger, like there was something profound. "I told you so."

"That's great. Very funny. I'll be telling everybody that at your funeral. Is that what you want? I'm serious, Jim." Finally she had started to simmer down.

"I'm serious too. Will you please tell me what's going on? Tell me what you found out."

"I found out that there's a lot more to find out, that's what."

"Like what?"

Taren got a hold of herself. She unbuttoned the top button of her starched, stiff blouse. "Got any whiskey?" She asked in a tone that bordered on civil. "I could use a stiff drink."

"Sure. On the rocks?"

"That's fine." She sighed. "After we met on Friday, I went back to the office and did a little investigating of my own. Did you know that this outfit Atmantle donated seventy thousand to the attorney general's campaign? Did you know that they did the same for the governor?" I handed her a drink. She stirred the cubes with an agitated finger.

"That's not bad, right? I mean they all need money to get elected."

"Right, right, but Atmantle's getting special favors in return. They don't pay any premium tax; they don't pay any property tax." She took a drink. A big one. "It seems that all three are in bed together."

"What else?"

"I start doing some checking and realize that Atmantle doesn't pay unemployment tax or payroll tax either. Can you believe it? They've got the best of everything. These guys have got it made, and nobody's doing anything about it." Her mind was racing. "That was all on Friday afternoon. Today, I go visit the insurance commissioner's office to find out about the complaints against them. You know the list you gave me?" I nodded. She drank, heartily. "You should have seen the look on her face. She was flustered, big time. Her face was beet red. I'm serious. She looks at me and says 'Is this all you people have to do over there? I'm doing a hell of a job, and how dare you stomp in here like that and suggest that these complaints are warranted.' Boy was she hot."

"Wow. Was she mad because of what you said, or because she thought you ambushed her?"

"Both, I guess."

"Is that all?"

"No...my boss's boss pays me a little visit late this afternoon. This guy's the deputy AG. The guy that hired me, really. A real tough guy... tough as nails. He starts asking me why I was at the commissioner's office. Grilling me. I didn't know what to say, other than I was looking into the number of complaints against Atmantle Health and Casualty. I didn't tell him about you, but he asked if I knew any lawyers in Mt. Pleasant."

"Oh, no, Taren."

"Yes. He did."

"I tell him 'No, why do you ask?' and he looks back at me and says 'There's some god-damned attorney up there stirring up trouble'." Taren took another drink, swished the cubes and drank again. It was gone. I got a glass for myself. "I ask him 'What's his name?' and he barks at me 'Jim Nunnelly, with some pansy-ass firm up there—Morrison & Nunnelly.' That's you! You're the guy that's stirring up trouble."

"I told you."

"Why didn't you say something?"

"I did, remember?"

"Just forget it. You'd better watch yourself." She stood next to the bar, flailing her arms. Raking her hair. She was pacing, anxiously.

"What else did he say?"

"He basically chewed my ass for about the next ten minutes. I shouldn't be messing around with cases that aren't mine. I should stick to the work that I've got on my plate."

"Was that it?"

"No, his parting shot was that, 'We like team players on the force. There's no room for renegades or rebels.' His real message was that I had better stop messing around with anything that has to do with Atmantle and the commissioner."

"But I could really use your help."

"With what?"

"I don't know yet, but I'm sure a lot of things will come up."

"How is that going to work?" She asked. "You're the blasted lawyer that everyone in Lansing wants to crucify."

"I'm not the bad guy, your bosses are. Whose side are you on, anyway?"

"What a mess. I can't tell anymore." She was upset. Riled.

"There must be something we can do together," I told her. "This thing isn't going to go away. It'll implode on these guys. If you're part of that crowd your career will be tarnished. Somebody somewhere will come in there and clean house."

"I know it."

"You could go to jail if you know there's something going on, right? You're part of the conspiracy?"

"Let's not even go there. I hate that word."

"What's going to happen?"

"They're going to come after you if there's half as much stuff going on as there really is."

"How are they going to come after me?"

"They think they're tracking down a lawyer named Nunnelly, but it won't take them long to realize that it's you who's making all the trouble. I don't know what they'll do to you, Jim, but I know that it won't be pleasant. You can't call me anymore. We can't talk, because they may put someone on your tail, and if you lead them to me then we're both in hot water."

"You can reach me, though."

"I'll call your cell from a pay phone and tell you everything I find out, okay?"

"I think that's all we can do."

Taren and I realized that we were both in over our heads. We ordered a pizza for dinner and quit drinking whiskey shortly after. Our attitude had gone from a state of panic, to a condition of preparedness. We popped some popcorn at 10 P.M., and reviewed our strategy over and over again. She lamented her decision to work for the attorney general, and wondered out loud if she should quit before things really got ugly. Up till then, I had never seen her squirm or thought of her as vulnerable.

In the weeks to come, Taren's world would be turned upside-down.

Thirty-Five

B Y THE TIME I CALLED the offices of Morrison & Nunnelly at almost noon Tuesday, it was too late. Kathy told me that the exterminators were just finishing their work.

Taren was right: they were on to me. They had cut the chains, and had found their way inside my deer camp.

They weren't exterminators after all, but the goons at the state police that got the evidence on Jorke at the transportation department. They told Kathy that they were there to take care of the termite problem. She believed them. They were waiting for me in an unmarked van with their antennas, and their remote microphones, and tape decks rolling from wheel to wheel. They were after me, all right, and I knew it was coming.

But that's not to say that we weren't prepared.

My first appointment of the day was with a terminated orderly from the St. Jean Centre. Darla Esposito looked to be pushing thirty with dark black hair that she pulled into a bushy-looking ponytail. She nervously toyed with her blouse. There was no denying it—she needed help. Legal help.

"What seems to be the problem, Mrs. Esposito?"

"I came here for advice," she said. "Legal advice."

"What seems to be the problem?" I asked her again.

"It's with my former employer…the St. Jean Centre."

"What happened?"

"I want to make sure that I won't get in trouble." She bowed her head, and shed a tear behind her dark sunglasses. "I've got a family at home…kids."

"Mrs. Esposito," I asked her. "Can you tell me what's wrong?"

She reached into her shabby purse and pulled out a ratty-looking tissue. "I think I was fired because I found out my employer was cheating the government. They were billing Medicaid and people's insurance for more than they should have."

"How do you know that?"

"Because I see the patients' records. I know exactly what we did for those patients, and I see what the administrators charged the government."

"Can you name names?"

"Sure. Edwin Drea has been committed for ten years. The guy has schizophrenia but was diagnosed with severe allergies, and they gave him a prescription for Claritin. I knew that he needed Claritin, but they gave him aspirin instead. The bosses billed the insurance for Claritin, even though they were giving him aspirin." She was rambling.

"How do you know all that?"

"The billing is on the computer and his allergies were as bad as ever. Plus, I was giving him his medication, and I sure know the difference between Claritin and aspirin."

"Any more?"

"Plenty." She had a list in her purse. "Dennis Jarmin was treated and billed for a broken wrist when all he had was a sprain. Georgia Niland never did have the colonoscopy that she was scheduled to have, but I know we got paid for it." I nodded. "There were lots of them."

"When were you fired?"

"The day after one of our patients got away from us and killed himself."

"And who is your employer again?"

"The St. Jean Centre. They're crooks, I'm telling you."

I acted confused. "And why do you need legal advice?"

"Because they're breaking the law, and I don't want to be a part of it."

"Mrs. Esposito, it'll be okay. I'm sure that the authorities will exonerate you."

She gathered up her belongings and told me one last time, "I hope you'll help me. I got kids at home, and I can't get in any trouble." I hoped that the guys in the truck would hear Mrs. Esposito's confession. I hoped that they would check out the Centre, specifically Calypso Steve. Sometimes all the cops needed was a little nudge in the right direction.

After lunch, I paid a visit to the post office and my favorite hairdresser. By the time I made it back to the Centre, Calypso Steve had a couple of gruff-looking men wearing tweed sport coats in his office. I wanted to hear what they were saying. Oh, how I wished I were a fly on the wall. If they were cops they wasted no time in taking Mrs. Esposito's testimony to the source. Calypso Steve must have been squirming, sweating bullets, back-peddling like a frightened mallard in a stiff breeze. Maybe Mary Cornwall was right, and "Mr. Puddle was peeing his pants."

It would only be a matter of time before the two detectives with the state police would knock at my office door and want to have a little talk. I just knew it was coming. If they asked about the billing practices of the Centre, I knew that they were acting on Mrs. Esposito's comments. If they wanted to take me to the state police post it had to be that they knew my most egregious secrets.

Fortunately, it was the former, rather than the latter. Calypso Steve was a bumbling idiot when he introduced them to me. "Dr. Ong, these two gentlemen are from the state police, and have a few questions for you about the billing practices of the Centre." He was stammering. "Be sure to tell them everything you know."

All of a sudden I was Calypso Steve's buddy-old-pal.

The two men shut the door to my office and sat in the chairs I usually occupy. I could smell their cologne—Brut, and Old Spice.

"Dr. Ong, my name is Detective Conroy, this is Sergeant Pennelton. We're here to talk to you about a report we received about some over-billing at the Centre."

"Oh?"

Conroy pulled a small notebook from his breast pocket, and flipped the pages with the back of an index finger. I was a little nervous, even though I was relieved they weren't after me for more serious infractions. "We want to talk to you about some accounting improprieties with Medicaid." I stared at the thin wisp of hair Conroy wore over his receding hairline.

"I really can't tell you much because I'm really not involved with it."

"Why don't you tell me what you know about it?"

There was no hesitation in my response. "I don't even get involved with billing. Miss Peacock handles all that."

"Would you know it if the Centre was over-billing a patient?"

"Not really, because she handles anything that has to do with the Centre's finances."

"Why don't you tell me about Darla Esposito?"

"She was fired from the Centre last fall, after an unfortunate situation involving one of the patients."

Conroy was getting riled, I could tell. He pushed his hair over his head with an open hand. "Would she be able to tell who was getting billed and who wasn't?"

"I don't know, because I don't get involved." I was in the

clear; they had nothing on me. "All I do is come in to work, and collect a paycheck every other week. There's not much to it."

"Do you know anything about Edwin Drea?"

"What about him?" I asked.

"Does he have schizophrenia?"

"I really can't say for sure, you understand."

Pennelton, who had been quiet, suddenly was struck by lightning: "Why don't you just answer the questions instead of being so vague?"

"Sergeant, I can't discuss the specifics of patients…it's called doctor-patient confidentiality."

They nodded—both were deflated. "It's the same confidentiality afforded to clients and their lawyers." They glared in my direction. "You're familiar with that rule, aren't you?"

"Sure, why do you ask?" Conroy plied.

"I'm not sure if it's a felony or a misdemeanor to break that trust. Any ideas?"

They glared for a second or two. "Why don't we ask the questions, and you give the answers?"

"I'm sorry gentlemen, if you have something against the Centre I suggest you take it up with the billing department. In the meantime, I hope we all play by the rules."

They both looked at me incredulously. "What's that supposed to mean?"

I shook my head, no. "I suggest we all play by the rules. Can we do that?"

"There's nothing more to it than meets the eye."

"Oh really? Did Esposito tell you something? How about Drea?"

"Dr. Ong, we'll be on our way." Conroy closed his little notebook and stuffed his pen into his sport coat. "Here's my business card…my cell number is on the back in case you think of something."

I'd think of a lot of things in the weeks to come.

Thirty-Six

THE FOLLOWING MONDAY I put on my best wool suit, packed my briefcase, and drove south to the home office of Atmantle Health and Casualty. The building was one of the nicer ones in downtown Lansing—perhaps ten stories tall—with one-way glass for all its exterior windows. It wasn't the "Smith Building," or the "Jones Complex." Nothing fancy, nothing auspicious. "Atmantle Health & Casualty" was just one of two dozen tenants listed on the building's directory.

When the elevator doors opened, the first thing I noticed was a security guard standing behind a wooden, chest-high countertop. He was the last resort between the offices inside and the general public. It seemed odd, I thought. *Why would an insurance company need an armed guard, for heaven's sake? Did they have something to hide?* It wasn't much of a first impression. It was hardly consistent with Atmantle's logo emblazoned over the metal doorway: "Insure With Confidence."

Employees were used to him. As I stood there, filling out the "visitor's questionnaire," several employees nodded in his direction before they swiped their employee badges through the electronic locks and made their way inside.

I really wasn't sure of the name I should use. Darvin told me that I should tell everyone that I was a financial planner. I suppose if someone really wanted to look into things, they could have discovered that James Ong was indeed a psychologist from Mt. Pleasant, instead of an anonymous financial planner. But what the heck, even if they did find out that I was there to see the top dog at the company, it didn't necessarily mean that I was there to treat the man. I could have been there for a job interview, or a consultation about employee morale.

One thing is for certain: Atmantle Health and Casualty liked their security. The guard asked me to have a seat in the lobby until someone from Darvin Wonch's inner circle came to pick me up. And the lobby wasn't much—just a handful of metal frame chairs circling a coffee table with issues of *National Underwriter* and *Fortune* on it. The guard had plenty to watch: monitors that tape-recorded the comings and goings of the employees in the parking garage, the cafeteria, the Information Technology Department. There would be little chance of stealing company secrets. So it seemed.

Before long, a very plain-looking woman in a drab business suit came to escort me to Darvin's office. "Good morning, Jim. We've been expecting you. My name is Lydia Davis, and I work with Mr. Wonch." She waved me inside, smiling half-heartedly. I gathered my briefcase and topcoat, and headed in her direction.

The guard handed me a visitor's badge: "Keep this on at all times, please."

Lydia had an employee badge of her own, dangling around her neck on a thin, cloth strip. They all did. I knew the metallic strip on the back would open the main doors by the security guard, but I had no idea what else it would do. The copy machines had receptors for the badges. I noticed a sign on every unit: "Don't forget the file's code."

Lydia was moving too fast. "Aren't you going to give me the nickel tour?" I asked her.

"Sure I can. This is our marketing department. They're in a meeting now, so that's why there's hardly anyone here."

"This must be the break room."

"Oh yes. Would you like a cup of coffee?"

"Sure. Thank you." She reached into the cupboard and grabbed a mug, shaped like an ostrich egg, Atmantle's logo across its face. I noticed a couple vending machines, each with their own receptors. "How does this work?"

"It's handy, really. Do you want cream or sugar?"

"Black is fine, thank you."

"You put your badge in here, and get whatever you want: chips, candy, soda. Whatever you want, really, without having to fumble with loose change."

She said "really" a lot but I wasn't sure why. "And how does everyone get paid?"

"The company takes it out of the employee's net pay, and pays the vendor for everybody's debits. It's on the employee's statement at the end of the month."

"Really?"

"Really. We use our badges for everything: copies, snacks… our security team knows our every move."

"What else?"

We were walking again, and her badge was working double time, opening doors between departments. "Before each employee logs onto the computer, they have to insert their badge so we can track where they go, what they do in cyberspace. The employees who have an expense account can use their badge like a credit card. Of course, it's auditable, and they have to justify the expense, really. At the end of the day the employees use their badges to get out of the parking garage, so we can keep track of when they leave, when they come and go."

"Why keep track of copies? It seems that you should be able to make a copy if you want to, without having to justify it."

She stopped, just a few feet from a rich-looking mahogany door. "That…you'll have to take up with Mr. Wonch." It seemed that Lydia knew her place, and it wasn't to disclose any of the company's secrets. She rapped on the door, much like a nurse would in a doctor's office. "Mr. Wonch, your nine o'clock appointment is here."

He turned from one of four computer screens and pronounced in a voice loud enough for half the building to hear: "Jim! How nice to see you."

Lydia shut the door. We were alone. "Ready to do a little investing?" I asked him.

"Ha, ha!" He chuckled. "What's the old saying, buy low and sell high?" He was laughing, confidently. "I'm doing quite well, on the investing front. Have you seen our stock? We're up to thirty-five dollars a share! It's almost unbelievable."

"That's great, Darvin. I'm happy for you."

"I just gotta get this damned B.K. off my record, you know what I mean?"

"I hear you."

"Did Lydia give you the tour of the place?"

"Oh, yeah. This is impressive. Your company. Your office is unbelievable."

"Thanks. You gotta impress people, if you're going to be in the business world, right?"

"What are these…twelve-foot ceilings?"

"Yes sir. That's cherry paneling, and the tin ceiling came from the Park Place Hotel in Traverse City. I got it when they did their restoration a few years ago."

"That's great."

But what was really impressive about Darvin's office was the wooden boat he had mounted on the wall above his desk. It wasn't a whole boat, but a half—cut down the center, bow to stern. It must have been close to twenty feet long—sleek and smooth, with rounded ends and a fin-like keel.

"What's up with the boat?" I asked him.

"That's not any ordinary boat, that's a Bill Loughlin '17,'" he said, proudly.

"Never heard of it."

"That's okay…most people haven't. It's relatively rare, even though I have one piece of it here and the other half up north." Darvin tossed his feet on the desk, cupped his hands behind his head and leaned back in his chair. "They were built back in the 1930s on Walloon Lake in Charlevoix County, if you know where that is. This one was made from Filipino mahogany, the spars from cedar. Hemingway summered on Walloon…in his youth, but he really wasn't into sailing." I felt like I was getting a history lesson. "He spent more time fishing out of a canoe. Smallmouth bass, northern pike, and of course he did a lot of trout fishing too in the nearby rivers."

"So, it's only seventeen feet long?" I asked him.

"No. Not at all. It had a single, hollow mast, and seventeen square meters of sail. That's how it got its name."

"Why would you cut one in two if they're so rare?"

"Because I never get up north to the cottage, and I never sail, but I sure like the looks of them… This way I can glance up at it and think about what might have been."

I shrugged off his musing as eccentric.

His desk was almost as impressive, but I didn't dare ask him about it. All I knew was that he was seated, which gave me the opening I was looking for. Before I left Mt. Pleasant, I packed the digital recorder in a padded brown envelope inside my briefcase. Only the microphone was visible. Once inside Darvin's office, I opened the opposite end of the envelope and pushed the record button. We were in business.

"So this is where all the magic takes place, huh?"

"That's right. This is my kingdom."

"This is your domain." I was buttering him up.

"It's really my whole world. This is my everything."

"What do you mean?"

"I mean I practically live here. This is my life…this company…this computer. Everything."

"You still like to gamble though, don't you?"

"Sure I do, but since you've got me on those pills I don't like to gamble as much."

"I told you it would work."

"I know it. The Xanax gives me a little buzz…a kick, just like gambling does."

"What was your prescription?"

"One pill, twice daily."

"And the Zyprexa?"

"Three a day. But I don't think that stuff works."

"You haven't been on it long enough."

"That's what she said. The trouble is, I'm almost out of Xanax."

"Really?"

"Oh yeah. That stuff is the best. It works better than a stiff drink at the end of a long day. I really like that stuff."

"They gave you sixty pills, right…a week ago? They were designed to last you a month."

"I know it but I had some issues come up and it helped me get over the hump, if you know what I mean."

"Sure…I know what you mean, but that stuff will kill you if you're not careful. You don't mix it with alcohol, do you?" Darvin stood up, and paced behind his massive, leather chair. Unlike the other times I saw him, today he was wearing a tailored, dark suit and a flamboyant striped necktie. He was mixing booze with his prescription drugs; I just knew it. "What kind of issues do you have?"

"I got issues, trust me."

"You don't want to tell me?"

"Not really. It has nothing to do with why you're here… with gambling."

"That's fine, but we still have an hour and a half to go in

our appointment. What else do you want to talk about? How's business?"

"Our business is doing well, and once we get things settled, we'll be on a roll. I can feel it."

"So everything is just great, right?"

"Pretty much, Chief."

"Why don't you tell me about your business…what's working, and what's not?"

He stared in my direction and made a funny expression with his face. "You mean like profit and loss statements?"

"Sure, let's have a look."

"It's all right here." He sat down at his computer, and swished an electronic mouse. In no time we were into the inner workings of the company's bottom line. "This is where we're at today…these are the company's assets, and this page represents the liabilities."

"Where is the premium trust account you were telling me about?"

He looked at me quite surprised. "I did?"

"Sure you did."

He pointed to the screen. "It's got its own line."

"And how accurate is that figure?"

"Never mind."

I shrugged my shoulders like it was no big deal. "That's fine. I hope you keep a backup of your files somewhere."

"Of course we do: claims, accounting, payroll, everything. We keep a backup; we keep a paper file on everything."

"That's probably a good idea." I looked at the file name: "p&l 1q." They apparently didn't use a lot of originality when it came to naming the files at the Home Office. We were in the first quarter, and we were after the company's profits and losses.

"We have all kinds of safeguards against lost information, against stolen items. The employee badges tell us everything we need to know. We don't allow any floppy discs, because it's too easy for an employee to walk out of here with one stuffed in a briefcase or purse."

"No kidding."

"Sure. Every one of our computers is monitored. We know exactly what every employee is doing, because they log in with their employee badges. At the end of the month we all get audited on what we did. We've got private investigators, too. They periodically check up on our adjusters to make sure they toe the company line."

"Why are you afraid of your claims adjusters?"

"I'm not, but sometimes we deny claims on technicalities, and I don't want the adjusters to blab to the wrong people. For the most part they've been pretty good."

Darvin paused for a second. "Oh?" I asked him.

"I don't want to bore you with everything, but our claims philosophy is that we pay the little stuff, but the big claims we deny. Since there's so much money on the line, it's worth it for us not to pay, and hope that the claimants just go away. It's not the adjusters' tails on the line. I'm the one who denies the claims."

"And that's what you're hiding?"

"That's right, the denials…the people whose claims were denied."

"Like who?"

"There are lots of them."

"Like who?"

"It really doesn't matter, does it?"

"Sure it matters, if you think about the lives you ruined," I said.

He hesitated for a second, and I thought that maybe he had a twinge of guilt. "I don't care about that. I don't want to know about them."

So much for that, I thought.

"You don't care?" I asked him again.

"No." He raised his eyebrows. "I can't even think about that."

I watched him intensely. The guy really didn't care about people, about his clients, about his employees. It was horrible. He was a monster.

All he cared about was money.

Just then my cell phone rang, as I had hoped. It was Rachel. "How's my timing?" She asked. "Call me later so I know you're okay." I shook my head, and tried to make it seem like I was perturbed by the intrusion.

"Sorry, Darvin, let me turn this thing off." I fumbled with the phone for a second, just long enough so it seemed like I was sincere.

"Now look who's got the issues!" He was laughing at me, like the shoe was on the other foot.

"I got issues, all right. We've got a couple of patients with severe paranoia. One thinks that we're trying to poison him, so he's taken to drinking water out of the toilet. The other patient insists that the government is out to kill him, and wants to be in protective custody. He's locked in a padded room, for heaven's sake, and he still won't believe us that he's already in protective custody."

"Oh god."

"Yeah, tell me about it. A really sad situation. That was Mary Cornwall...you know, the doctor who prescribed your meds."

"I remember her. She was a cute little number. How do I get her to give me some more of those pills anyway?"

"You can't get a refill until thirty days have passed."

"Can't I get a prescription from another doctor just like her?"

"Sure you can, but your health insurance company will send up a red flag. You ought to know that since you're in the business."

"If I paid cash nobody would know about it."

"You're right, but I told you before, that stuff will kill you."

"Hell, I could drop dead tomorrow, with my bad heart."

"You?" I questioned him. "A bad heart?" Darvin laughed. I had him softened up. The phone call had sewn the seeds of urgency back at the office. "Would you mind if I gave her a call? Maybe an e-mail? Just give me five minutes, and I'll be back in the game. Who knows, maybe she'll approve another refill if I ask her."

"No, certainly." Darvin conceded. "Use my office. I'll be outside. The rent's up on my coffee anyway."

"Give me five minutes or so, thank you." I handed him my empty coffee cup as he passed.

Darvin closed the door, and I jumped into gear. His computer sat there like an open book. I found the discs in my briefcase, rammed one inside, and began making copies. First quarter, last quarter accounting, P&L, claims. And last, the juiciest file of all: "pry and deny." It was wonderful.

A moment later Darvin's computer was back to where it was, and the tape recorder turned off. I didn't want anyone to hear the rest of our conversation. I would go on the offensive, and tread in waters that were less than honorable.

He knocked at the door, and asked me if I wanted more coffee.

"No, thank you."

"Suit yourself." He was back in his chair, tapping the handle of his mug with one of his gaudy rings. "Everything okay back at the ranch?"

"Yes, thanks for the use of your office. It was extremely helpful."

"No problem."

"You know, Dr. Cornwall approved a refill for you."

"Oh yeah?"

"Sure, we've got a little leeway when it comes to that."

"Thanks…that's what I like—a man that knows how to get things done."

"But before I give it to you though, I'd like you to tell me about the issues you had that made you want to take more Xanax."

"Oh that," he looked confused. "It's just my wife. She'll hardly talk to me anymore, even about our kids."

"You still love her, don't you?"

"Yes, I do, for some strange reason."

"Why do you say that?"

"Because she's moved out and everything."

"What would you like to see happen with her?"

"I'd like her to move home, to get back together with her."

"What does she say?" I pried.

"She doesn't say anything, that's the problem. All she says is, 'It's over, Darvin. Move on with your life.'"

"And you can't seem to come to grips with that?"

"I can't. Things are going so well at work that I want her to be a part of the reward."

"I don't get it."

"I mean that if the share price keeps climbing, we're going to be filthy rich. She can go and do anything she wants. Trips, fur coats, fancy cars. She can have everything."

"Maybe she doesn't want all that."

My proposition stopped him dead in his tracks. "What do you think she wants?"

"I don't know," I told him. "I've never met her, or know her, but I believe most women would rather have a great relationship with their husband more than anything else in the world."

"You don't know my wife then."

"Why don't you tell me more about her?"

Darvin loosened his tie. "I think I told you that she used to like to gamble with me. She used to be intimate, and all that."

"Keep going."

"The kids came along and her priorities changed. She's quite a bit younger than I am, and cut back her hours at the facility."

"What facility is that?"

"The rehab center in St. Johns. She's a physical therapist."

"A what?"

"A physical therapist. You know, after surgery or a car crash you need to work out to get back into shape. She helps people with all that."

"All right, I'm with you."

"What else do you want to know?"

"What's her name?"

He paused for a second. "Sharon, why?"

My heart skipped a beat. My tongue became a slice of rubber tire. I didn't know what to say. "I'm not sure I should say anything..."

"Come on, Chief."

"Didn't you say that she was a prude, and would never in a thousand years have an affair?"

"Yes, I said that. Not in a *million* years, why?" He looked at me impatiently.

I had to think fast. I had to tell him. Tactfully. "I think your wife may be on the Internet." I hesitated. "On a porn site."

Maybe it wasn't so tactful.

He roared with laughter. "You've got to be kidding me." He howled. "No way."

"Seriously. How many Sharons can there be from St. Johns, who work as physical therapists?"

"Show me." He stood up from his chair again, and held his hand toward a computer as if to say, "prove it." Judging by his body language, it was either show him what I meant, or get my face bludgeoned.

My mind was racing. I never did go to the website Warren

told me about. I never even thought about visiting it. And now I had to pull it out of the back of my head like a magician's rabbit. "That's okay...you can drive, Darvin."

He sat back down again, his peculiar-looking fingers at the ready. "Let's hear it, Chief." He was daring me to be wrong.

"Okay, try this..." It was on the tip of my tongue. I was drawing a blank. "Home cookin' dot com."

His fingers rapped the keys, confidently. "Oh my," he said. "'*See what these amateurs are cookin' up.*' Oh that's just great." He turned the screen in my direction. The website was written in a thick red font, perhaps to look like lipstick. "Where to, Chief? There are hundreds of them. I don't see anything yet, and I'm not used to looking at this stuff. Wait till the auditors see this at the end of the month." He laughed.

"Look for a gallery called Bare'n Sharon."

"What? Are you kidding me? It can't be her. I don't even see it." Seconds inched along. He scrolled down the list of galleries. There were dozens of them, each with their own saucy name. "Here we go...Bare'n Sharon, right?"

He clicked one more time.

His life would never be the same.

The first image was harmless enough, of an attractive brown-haired woman who appeared to be in her mid thirties, wearing a nurse's outfit that barely covered her swollen bosom. The caption said it all: '*Sharon is a mild-mannered physical therapist from St. Johns, but when the day is through, she's hardly a saint...*'

Darvin's posture slumped. His hands covered his face; his eyes peeked through the cracks. "Oh god...it's her." He clicked the arrow button, and Sharon's chest was only inches away from the back of Warren's head. '*Sharon's been known to give special treatment to her favorite patients...*' It was like a slide show. Click. Warren's hands cradled her breasts, still holstered in a red, lace bra. His tongue was at the back of her neck, his nose wedged under a brilliant diamond earring. "Oh god," Darvin muttered, the jealousy mixed with astonishment. "I paid good money for those earrings."

Click. "You bitch." He squinted, painfully and turned the monitor so only he could see.

Click. "Oh Jesus."

I watched him suffer. I saw the grief on his face, the horror that must have been pulsing through his veins. He was crying. Sniveling. He had been a fool, and I was there to administer the venom. How satisfying indeed.

Revenge is a wonderful thing, Virginia, a powerful emotion.

Darvin collected himself, slightly, or at least that was what he wanted me to believe. He blew his nose in a monogrammed handkerchief, got up, and walked to the window. He stood there for a moment or two, wiping his nose, then wiping it again. I didn't say a thing. It was painful to watch; it must have been torture to endure.

"Sometimes," he started, "when I'm all alone in here and the place is quiet, I think about the mistakes I've made in my life." He drew a deep breath, held it in his chest, and eventually exhaled. "I never thought that marrying Sharon was one of them." His voice was almost inaudible. "I thought that she would always be true to me." He put his hands on the marble sill, and bowed his head in shame. "Until now."

His office was deliciously silent.

"Well, I guess that takes care of that," he said.

"Of what?" I asked him.

"Of me and Sharon, that's what." He marched back to his desk, and pressed the button for the intercom. "This will only take a minute, Chief, sorry. Lydia…will you please get me Mr. Brian on the phone?"

"Right away, sir."

"Oh, and have marketing get their asses up here right away."

"What are you doing, Darvin?" I asked him.

His finger left the intercom. "I'm filing for a divorce, that's what." His little cry was short-lived. The hurt feelings only lasted a minute. It was time for revenge. He tugged on his lapels, confidently, then pulled out a bottle of medicine from his desk drawer. "This is one of those times when Xanax comes in handy." He tapped the edge of the open bottle into the palm of his hand, then stuffed the pills in his mouth. I got the feeling that if it had been afternoon, he would have swallowed the pills with a splash of scotch from his crystal decanter.

"Yeah, but why are you calling in marketing?"

"I'm going to have 'Bare'n Sharon' on every billboard in Lansing, that's what. That bitch. Nobody gets the better of Darvin Wonch." He laughed. "That slut will have to hide from everybody. She'll be run out of town!"

"What about your kids? How do you think they will react to seeing their mother's image up there?"

"I don't care about them. They'll have to deal with the fact that their mother is a tramp, that's what! She's the one that should have thought about it." He had steam billowing from his ears.

The phone beeped on his mahogany desk, and Lydia said that Mr. Brian was on line three.

"I guess this means that our appointment is over?" I asked.

"Sorry. We'll have to do double time next week." He fiddled with the top button on his oxford and straightened his tie.

He was pacing, irritably.

Out of control.

Out of his mind.

"Did you want those refills for your prescriptions?"

"Yes. Thank you."

I gave him one for Xanax, one for Zyprexa, three and fifteen milligrams apiece.

Three times the dosage that Mary Cornwall prescribed.

Thirty-Seven

GLEN MORRISON WASN'T especially happy to see me later that week when I clanked the bronze doorknocker on the front of his two-story colonial. His wife answered the door and invited me inside, making small talk about the snowstorm that had dumped almost a foot of snow on mid-Michigan. "Glen," she cried. "It's Jim…" I think she forgot my last name. It didn't matter; the voice up the stairs had a tone that was less than friendly. "Let me take your coat," she said. "He's upstairs, tinkering with his clocks." I smiled at her. "You can just go up there yourself. Turn right at the top of the stairs…second door on the left."

Glen's house was a monster. Built in the early 1900s, it may have been owned by one of a thousand lumber barons who stripped Michigan's North Woods of her white pine. The stairway must have been eight feet across, with steps that were at least fifteen inches deep. Its handrails were as dark and rich as ten-year-old bourbon. When Glen's daughters were old enough to date, the stairway alone must have made quite an impression on the young men that came calling. Even if they were the biggest sluts in town, they must have looked like princesses when they waltzed down those stairs.

"Is that you, Jim?" He asked.

I cleared my throat.

"What can I do for you?" He never looked up from his desktop, covered with an olive green dish towel and what appeared to be a thousand pieces of a clock's bowels. "Strange… seeing you out on such a miserable night." He wore a set of dentist's magnifying glasses strapped to his head, and sat under a hundred-watt light bulb. I took a seat next to his desk, adjacent to a speaker that was uttering classical music.

I sat there, waiting for an opening.

Carrie had told me about Glen's passion for clocks. Throughout his career he had spurned country clubs and golf outings in favor of antique shops and flea markets. The extent of his obsession was never more evident than on that snowy evening a few weeks after the holidays.

His hands were busy…filing the teeth on a spindle the size of a quarter. "I come up here most nights just to putter. It relaxes me after a long day at the office," he said. "My wife likes to watch 'Jeopardy,' or read a damn book after dinner, and talk on the phone all night with our daughters." He sprayed the spindle with brake fluid, then rubbed it down with the tattered remnants of a mottled tee-shirt. "It's kinda relaxing up here…tinkering, puttering…all by myself. And when it's all done, you've got something to show for it." He kept his head and his eyes on the task at hand.

"Glen," I said. "I really want to talk to you about my investigation into Atmantle Health & Casualty."

He wasn't biting.

"They're a horrible company, Glen."

He raised the spindle to his lips and blew a puff of air.

"I got all kinds of evidence, Glen. I'm inside them now…a cancer."

He never did look up from his work.

"I got a case against them that's watertight. If you want, I'll put a nice, big, red bow on it for you."

"Can't we talk about this at the office?" He asked, finally.

"No, we can't."

"And why's that?" He asked.

"Because they're on to us. They've got your office bugged."

At last, he put down his work and looked my way. "Who?" He yelled with his eyes.

"The attorney general, that's who. And how about the insurance commissioner's office?" He gestured like I should keep going, so I did. "The governor. They're all involved….and I got the proof."

"Nobody bugs a god-damned lawyer's office! That's against the law."

"Glen, I know they bugged it because I set a trap."

"You what?"

"I did. They took the bait. I'm telling you they've bugged your office."

Glen flipped his magnifying glasses on his forehead. "What the hell have you done?"

"You told me to look into this mess and that's exactly what I did."

"You haven't been looking into this mess, you've created one." He was getting louder. "The governor? For Christ's sake man! Have you lost your mind?"

I didn't say a thing. I crossed my arms, stood up and shut the door. "Do you want me to show you what I have, or do you want me to go to another lawyer?"

Glen put down his work and swiveled in his chair. "Just show me what the hell you've come up with. I don't believe it." I opened my briefcase and pulled out my laptop computer. He sighed impatiently.

"This," I said, "is everything you need." My computer's

drive was humming. "This file is called 'pry & deny' and explicitly details the way the company pries into a claimant's history, with the intent to find information that will establish cause for a denial."

Glen crossed his arms. "What are you trying to say?"

"Okay, sorry." I opened the file, and it was all laid out in front of us. "The company issued health policies with minimum underwriting, but denied their claims based on preexisting conditions."

"It's okay to do that, I think."

"Yeah, but look at the preexisting conditions they've come up with...the cause for the Abbotts' denial: 'allergies.' The Andersons': 'diabetes.'"

"Diabetes is a valid reason, right?"

"You'd think, but look at this column." I pointed to the screen. "The guy wiped out on his motorcycle and needed surgery to repair his broken ankle."

Glen shook his head. "What does diabetes have to do with a motorcycle accident?"

"Exactly," I said.

I handed him the computer. He scrolled through the list alphabetically; his eyes panning left and right. "Carrie's in there, Glen. I already looked her up. They denied her cancer claim because of a cyst she had on her ovaries."

"How long ago was that?"

"When she was fourteen!"

"Jesus."

"Look at this column. They've got doctors on staff that earn bonuses for digging up this stuff. They're paid to establish the relationship between preexisting conditions and a denial. They've got a stable of private investigators to take pictures of claimants raking their yard, when they should be laid up in bed, just to bolster their denials. It's incredible."

"Holy hell."

"I'm telling you, Glen. It's only the tip of the iceberg. There must be thousands of them." I reached into the side pocket of my computer case, and pulled out a spreadsheet Kathy and I put together. "Here's a list of the people in Michigan who have filed a complaint with the insurance commissioner's office against Atmantle. They're all ready to file a suit. Almost all of them have said that they'll pay you five hundred dollars apiece to get the ball rolling. If you haven't looked into the firm's escrow account lately, there's almost twenty grand sitting there. These people sent in their money without being asked. We only asked them if they'd be willing. They want to move on this lawsuit. They're okay with a fifty-five percent contingency. And this is only one state. I got Indiana too, and Illinois in the works."

He looked at me with angry eyes, flipped through the pages and shook his head.

Suddenly the clocks weren't that important. He stood up and began pacing when I told him about Atmantle's connection to the attorney general, the governor, and the insurance commissioner.

When I showed him the accounting files, and the column entitled "deviation," he opened the door and yelled down the stairs: "Carol, will you put on a pot of coffee? We're going to be here a while."

When I told him about Taren, and the exterminators who planted the bugs at his office, he rolled up his sleeves and clenched his teeth. "Those bastards. They can't do that."

I showed him the story from the *Lansing State Journal*, with the picture of the insurance commissioner pictured in her swimsuit at Atmantle's condo, pina colada in hand. The headline said it all: "Commish: high on the hog."

By midnight we had everything laid out on the living room floor. Glen liked it that way...in a heap. A mess. Our case against Atmantle lay there like the gears, the motors, the hardware of a Swiss grandfather clock. All we had to do was put it all together.

And put it together we did.

I was surprised with Glen's resolve. There was no insecurity. No second-guessing. "Here's what we're going to do," he said. "Here's what *I'm* going to do. *I'm* going to send them a letter, short but sweet, indicating my intent to sue." He was pacing again, waving his index finger. "And I'm going to give them a week to think about it. That's it. If they want to talk between now and then, we'll talk; otherwise I'm going to punch their ticket with a heavy-duty lawsuit."

"I'm glad to be a part of this."

"Nobody gets away with stuff like that. One way or another, they're going to pay."

Thirty-Eight

RIDAY MORNING I woke up early and finished my research on stock options. Even though it was a complicated subject, I did realize some important facts. The first was that the option doesn't always expire on the third Friday of the upcoming month. It may be many months into the future, depending upon what you bought. I could have bought options on Ford Motor Company in March, or April, or September. The second feature was that the further into the future the option was written—and consequently the better the odds of collecting on it—the higher the premium.

I had no intention of buying options on Ford Motor Company or any other company; it was Atmantle or nothing. And there were options all right. With only six days to go before the third Friday of the month, and the stock now over forty dollars a share, most of the options listed through my online broker were for 'calls.' Everyone believed that shares of AHC would go up in value. Everyone assumed that the latest Initial Public Offering would scream its way to two hundred bucks a share. They'd call it a steal when it was only forty-one dollars. Shares of AHC had more than doubled since its initial offering. Who's to say it wouldn't do that again?

Somebody did. After scrolling through the list of 'calls,' I found several dozen options for 'puts.' The terms appeared to be reasonable enough: a thirty-six hundred dollar premium, with a strike price of thirty-eight dollars. There were scores in the neighborhood of three thousand dollars and thirty-five dollars. They even had some long shots: sixteen hundred dollars and thirty-two dollars.

It was relatively easy to figure out what kind of money I would make if Atmantle's stock met every one of the three strike prices. My ten grand in premiums would gross over a hundred thousand dollars. Not bad.

I knew that Atmantle's stock was going to tank. I knew that it was headed south. There was no doubt in my mind what would happen. The only question was when.

Virginia's seventy-five thousand dollars was sitting there, accruing interest at a piddling two percent, compounded annually. It would take years to turn it to a hundred thousand.

The time to move was now.

What kind of man are you, Jim?

I sat in front of the computer screen forever...reviewing each option, scratching down numbers, figuring and refiguring. I jotted different risk-taking scenarios: conservative, moderate, and foolish. The warnings at the bottom of the computer screen seemed sincere: I could lose all or part of my investment. Back and forth I went. Round and around.

Finally, I placed an order. Then another, and another. When the dust settled on my online gamble, I had spent about fifty thousand dollars on options that were due to expire in either ten days, or a month and ten days. I was probably too conservative when it came to my orders, even though stock options are a risky proposition. If I had more confidence I should have bet the house, bet the farm.

At least I wouldn't have to wait long to find out how the first round of orders would fare. Ten days isn't long at all. If Atmantle's stock hit my strike price on every option I placed, I'd clear about seven hundred thousand dollars. Not bad at all.

In a way, I felt like a gambler. Like I was the one with the addiction. A lot of people would have said that spending that kind of money was silly, or stupid. "You should have kept it in the bank," they'd say. "Be conservative, frugal." In a way, I could see their point. Then again, life is full of risks and rewards. The risks were substantial, but with the plans I was concocting, it seemed like a shoe-in that Atmantle's stock was going to drop like a stone. I couldn't see how I'd lose.

Investors don't like uncertainty. They don't like it when bad things happen. What I had in store would certainly give them reasons to worry.

And I had my own set of worries. Since this whole thing started I was the one throwing the punches; I was the one firing the jabs. It's always more fun to play offense, to be in control. I knew that the goons at Atmantle would come after me eventually. I knew that the two guys from the state police would too…probably sooner rather than later. They must have figured out that the shrink they talked to regarding the Centre's overbilling was actually the lawyer they bugged the week before. Maybe they realized the mistake they made. Maybe they realized they were too quick to investigate Darla Esposito's claims, instead of listening to the trouble lawyer Jim Nunnelly was stirring up.

What really worried me was if the guys at the attorney general's office talked to Darvin Wonch, my goose was cooked. I still had one more appointment with him before the options on Atmantle's stock expired.

Anyway, I patted Toby on the head, donned my long, wool topcoat, and headed out the door for another day at the office. The snow around the Centre was still a brilliant shade of white and coated everything like the frosting on a birthday cake. I heard the snarl of snow-blowers and the obnoxious grind of snowplows scraping the Centre's many parking lots. I walked down the path to the sidewalk, where the head of the maintenance crew was sitting in an old Dodge pickup, snowplow bolted to its front end. I stopped to say hello, but ended up talking with him for several minutes. He was a nice guy, and wasn't complaining about the snow. In fact, he called the snow "job security." I laughed at his optimism, then watched him drive away. I wished that more of my clients and patients would look at the snowfall in their lives as "job security" instead of a miserable, depressing by-product of winter.

The old Dodge may have been a good truck for plowing, but it needed lots of tender loving care. After it rumbled off, I looked down at the parking lot and saw a saucer-sized puddle of antifreeze.

It was a little after seven when I made it to the office. The place was just beginning to stir. I opened the mail, booted up my computer, then checked the answering machine. The voice on the recording didn't need an introduction. I recognized the slurred lisp right away: "This is Jerry DelBanco up in Traverse City, and I wondered if you still wanted to talk to me about my dad, Joe." I listened intently. "Please give me a call, maybe we could get together this weekend or maybe tonight sometime. My number is...."

It was good to hear from Jerry. *Shwell,* I thought.

It would be good to find out about his dad. At last. I checked my schedule on the computer and realized that my last appointment was at three that afternoon. I gave him a call and we made plans to meet at his restaurant in Traverse at about seven that evening.

For the rest of the day my mind wandered to the drive ahead of me. Two hours up, two hours back. In the dead of winter. I had to go, I had to meet him.

That's not to say that I wasn't a good shrink the rest of the day. I listened. I cared. Nobody noticed that my mind wandered to the big drive ahead of me—to the answers to the questions that surrounded Joe's morbid confession.

Shortly after quitting time, I let Toby outside, then fed him a scoop of food. I told him to watch the fort as I headed for the Jimmy that would take me to the mighty death trap, M-115.

It was about then that my cell phone rang. "Jim. They're after you. They're going to kill you." My heart turned to sand. It was Taren. "We got a letter from the Security and Exchange Commission...a follow up, on a letter they got from a god-damned lawyer named Jim Nunnelly. It's about that Atmantle stuff."

"Taren, slow down."

"No...you slow down. You've got about three flippin' lawyers and an investigator here who want to see you hung out to dry. I'm serious, Jim. They're coming after you."

"Who?" I yelled.

"Them. All of them."

"Who is it, Taren? Tell me."

"The state police. The governor's security detail. Us."

"When?"

"Now, I tell you. They're after you. I can't talk long. I'm on a pay phone outside. It's freezing!"

"Is that it?" I asked.

"No...hell no."

"What is it?

"They're inside the Centre. They've got tapes and cameras in there. They're going to contact your clients. They're going to give away your clients' secrets."

I didn't know what to say. It was unbelievable. They wouldn't tape record the most sacred of relationships. Or would they? I looked down at the speedometer, and realized that I was only going forty-five miles an hour. The news took the wind out of my sails. It took my mind off the road. Cars sped by. Some of them honked their horns. Others gave me the one-fingered good-luck sign. I had to make time if I was to be on time to see Jerry. I stepped on the gas just as the third-lane passing lane ended. The van behind me sped up, matching my speed.

It was them.

"Taren, you've got to do something!"

"What? I know that something needs to be done, and you know it, but it's all got to be done in the right order."

"Bring in the feds." I was doing sixty then sixty-five. They were still on my tail. "Tell 'em that Nunnelly is harboring a fugitive. Tell 'em that you need backup. Anything...but don't tell them your name."

"I'm scared, Jim. I don't know what to do."

"You're scared?" My little Jimmy snorted. I was doing seventy and they were gaining on me. The car that had just passed me minutes ago was only sixty feet in front of me. We sailed by the deer carcasses, the crosses, and the side roads that angled at forty-five degrees. "I'm the one they're chasing. I'm the one they want to kill."

"Please be careful, Jim."

"I'd better fly."

I hung up the phone and riffled through my wallet for Detective Conroy's business card. It was nearly dusk. The crows had left their carcasses. I noticed the sign ahead of me: "Next passing lane three miles."

I called Rachel on her cell phone. She was always so upbeat. "What's happening?" She asked.

I wasn't a wimp anymore. There was no time for minced words. "I love you" poured from my mouth as if it would be my last words on earth.

"You what?"

"I love you."

The phone was silent. "What brought this on?" She asked.

"I've been meaning to tell you that for some time now."

"Wow…that's quite a revelation. Is everything okay?"

"Just peachy." The two heads in the van behind me had to be Conroy and Pennelton. "Can't wait to see you again."

I hung up the phone, and dialed Conroy's cell number. Another passing lane approached. The row of traffic readied for a race. At once the cars ahead of me punched the accelerator. I was behind a white Chevy Monte Carlo…was it Richard Petty, or Jeff Gordon, or Earnhardt? Didn't matter. He was the perfect draft for Conroy and me. All three of us were doing eighty on a three-lane highway. Slower traffic hugged the right lane. Some of them slowed slightly and took the side roads gracefully at forty-five. A semi-truck loomed ahead. Everyone wanted to get ahead of it. It was crazy. I pressed the 'send' button on my phone. It rang once and Conroy answered.

"You might as well ride with me, detective…you're practically in my back seat."

"What's your point?"

"Get off my ass," I said. The semi loomed ahead. We were flying. "Tailgating is unbecoming of a law enforcement officer."

The Monte passed the semi, but stayed in the left lane. I saw the "merge left" sign just ahead.

A side road just beyond.

The timing was perfect.

I stayed with the Monte, drawing Conroy along the semi's flanks. There were cars everywhere. He was pinned. The semi turned on its blinker to merge left. Conroy was trapped. I slowed, slightly, but then dashed ahead of the semi, cranking the wheel to the narrowing right lane. The semi bellowed its horn, veered to the left, pushing Conroy into the oblivion of oncoming traffic. I had to slow down, the side road was just ahead. My Jimmy caught the edge of the shoulder, skidded slightly, but managed to keep its track. I was home free on the gravel road, sailing safely on the back roads near the Muskegon River.

I picked up the phone and listened to Conroy scream for an instant. Then the phone went dead.

My heart was still pounding. Hammering. I was out of breath from the adrenalin pulsing through my veins. My hands still clenched the wheel as if it was the reins on Hot Tamale.

They were after me.

It was horrible.

I've never been so close to death, so close to a close call.

What's more, I never had the guts to stand up to a bully the way I did.

I collected myself, gradually, and limped my way on gravel roads north by northwest toward Traverse City. I called Rachel again and apologized for the suddenness of my admission.

"You don't need to apologize," she said. "You sounded like you wanted to get something off your chest."

"I did," I said. "I just had to tell you that."

"That was a nice thing to say," she said. "Unexpected."

I changed the subject suddenly. "I'm afraid that I can't stay at my house anymore," I said apologetically. "This thing with Atmantle has gotten way out of hand. Would you mind going to my place and picking up a few things for the weekend?"

"Sure. What do you mean by 'way out of hand'?"

"These people are out of control. They're after me. They just tried to run me off the road. I can't stay at my house and that's why I need you to pick up a few things."

"Like what?" She asked.

"Toby…for starters."

"I can do that. Then what?"

"I don't know," I said. "Can I give you a call back when I come up a plan?"

"Sure."

About an hour later I made it to Jerry's restaurant on the south end of Traverse City. It really wasn't a restaurant, more a diner, with the menu printed on a grease pencil board over a row of swivel chairs at the counter. "Jerry D's" was the name of his establishment, and featured a fried fish dinner every Friday during Lent. A rather attractive cherry pie sat on an elevated tin, a handled lid over both. We were, after all, only a mile or two from Cherry Capitol Airport in the heart of Michigan's cherry country.

I sat in a booth closest to the kitchen, in case Jerry had to run to the kitchen, or a couple of thugs stormed inside, guns blazing.

My waitress was nice enough, a pregnant-looking twenty-year-old with dishwater-blonde hair. I asked her what kind of fish they had.

"Cod, Pollock, whitefish, and northern pickerel."

"Oh my," I said.

"Beer battered or pan fried," she sighed.

"I'll have the whitefish—pan fried—and please tell Jerry that Jim is here to see him."

She nodded, then went to the marker board and crossed whitefish off the menu. Apparently I ordered the last of the last. Business must have been good.

A few minutes later Jerry swung open the kitchen doors, a stained apron around his midriff. He was carrying a plate, piled high with fish, coleslaw and hash browned potatoes. "Here's your dinner," he said, with that peculiar lisp.

"Thanks," I said. "Wow, I'll never eat all that."

"We were expecting you, and figured that you should have the works...a little of everything," he said. "We like to call it Jerry D's smorgasbord." He laughed, approvingly.

So did I, but for an entirely different reason. "Shmorgash-bord" was a mouthful.

"Wow...thanks," I said. "I'm starving."

"How was the drive?"

Jerry D's smorgasbord was one of those "roll up your sleeves" kind of meals. You don't pitter-patter around your plate, admiring the garnishes, the presentation, or the atmosphere. Dive in, head first. Chow, man, chow. "It was a little scary until I hit the back roads near Marion."

"No kidding. Somebody said there was a bad accident there."

I picked up a filet and waited for more details.

They never came.

I didn't ask.

The fish was delicious, even though I had no idea what "northern pickerel" was.

"I really want to thank you for having me up here like this," I said. "I had kinda written you off as a lost cause, considering that so much time had gone by since the funeral." Jerry just sat there, watching me pick through the filets, plunging each piece into tarter sauce.

"There's your whitefish," he said. "We have it shipped in here fresh from the fisheries in Leland. Everyone loves it. Do you know where Leland is?" My mouth was full, but I was able to nod. I held up my hand to make the shape of a mitten.

It seemed that Jerry didn't want to talk about his dad, but I didn't drive two hours to hear about where he got his fish, either. I kept quiet, and ate like a man possessed. Maybe he was waiting for me to finish.

"Did Joe like the whitefish you served?"

"Oh yeah. Everybody loves it," he said. I nodded, hoping that there was more to the story. "He used to come up here a lot, just to visit. He and mom both." I stopped eating, and watched him wipe his broad forehead with a napkin. "Until she got sick…then everything went down hill fast." He paused, and I felt like I had to prime the pump.

"She had cancer, right?"

"Yep. Blood cancer."

"That must have been horrible."

"It was. The doctors were nice and everything, and seemed like they knew what they were doing, but it's just one of those things that you can't help. One of life's nasty twists."

"Her death must have been hard on your dad."

"The worst."

"What happened, Jerry?"

Our waitress brought a pitcher of water, and filled my glass. He played with the silverware, anxiously. "She was suffering, so bad. Just in pain, day after day." He was getting choked up. "We felt so bad, watching her with no dignity. She was my mom for christ's sake." He blew his nose in the napkin.

"What happened, Jerry?"

His chin quivered, and in a quiet voice said, "She killed herself...at least that's what he had the cops believe."

I watched him squirm. "*Who* had the cops believe? Jerry?"

"Dad...Joe...whatever you want to call him."

"Your dad killed your mom?" I asked him.

"That's not really how I like to remember it."

"What do you mean?"

"Dad ended Mom's suffering. She wasn't in pain any more. He took her life, but her life wasn't worth living." He blew his nose again.

I nodded, and found myself making gestures with my hands. I had a delicate question to ask. "When did your dad...?"

"Go off the deep end?" He asked.

"Right."

"After the funeral. After everyone left, and he went home to that same old farm where they lived all those years." I nodded my head. "He never woke up. He couldn't deal with the guilt."

"That's horrible...and I am really, really sorry about what happened." Jerry looked at me and could see the forgiveness in his eyes. "Why didn't you visit him more often at the Centre?"

"I thought about it, but the nurses all told me that he couldn't talk, that he was all doped up. I did stop in a couple of times on the weekends, but he just sat there."

"I saw your name on the guest registry…once I think." He shrugged his shoulders like the nurses didn't write it down the other times. I wasn't sure if I should believe him or not. "How long between the time she got sick and the time she died?"

"About a month or two."

"Wow….quick."

"I know it. They did a few tests…diagnosed her…and that was it."

"Didn't she have chemo or radiation?"

He shook his head no. "The doctors weren't convinced that it would work. They wanted to send her to Mayo Clinic but Dad's insurance company denied the pre-approval."

"What did Joe do for a living? Wasn't he in sales?" I asked.

"Yup. Windows. Had a big territory, was on the road all the time when I was growing up. I never really developed a bond with him. He was never around much, and when he was, he'd complain about his bills. All the time: bills…bills…bills." He laughed.

"No kidding."

"Yup. He was behind the eight-ball all the time. Couldn't keep up with them. I guess there wasn't much money in windows."

I nodded, wiped my mouth with a napkin, and took a drink of water.

It seemed that the mysteries surrounding Joe were solved.

"Or benefits…" He continued. "He had to buy his own health policy. He hated it. Thought it was the biggest rip-off ever, the way they jumped his premiums. When they denied Mom's trip to Mayo, he almost went postal." Our waitress visited again, and asked me if I wanted a piece of cherry pie for dessert. When I told her no, she ripped the paper check from the stub, and left it on the table.

I looked at Jerry and the way he was talking. *Curious…his lisp*, I thought. I found myself wanting to talk just like him, just like I would after talking to someone from another country or a different part of the nation. Southern drawls, Irish burrs, even people from the west end of Michigan's Upper Peninsula have an infectious way of speaking. *Jerry'sh wash no different,* I thought.

"Why did they deny her trip to Mayo?"

He waited for a second or two. "I forget the reason…but it wasn't very good. They said something about her bad prognosis didn't justify the means. And that was the other thing, they wouldn't give us an answer for three weeks." He picked up the check off the table. "She had one foot in the grave by then. They waited so long to give us an answer it was too late. I've been telling everybody who will listen what a crummy deal we went through."

"Horrible," I said.

"The Mayo Clinic may not have saved Mom's life, but it was worth a shot. If only the company didn't wait so long to give us an answer."

"Who was the insurance company, Jerry?"

He hesitated, "It was an oddball name, something I never heard of."

"Do you remember what it is?"

He hesitated again, "It was…Atmantle something."

I stopped dead in my tracks. Another ruined life. "That was the name of the company?"

"Yup…Atmantle. Dad bought a major medical policy. Had them for four or five years before Mom got sick."

"Did you do anything about it?"

"What do you mean?" He asked.

"I mean did Joe file a complaint against them or did you talk to a lawyer…?"

He shook his head no. "We thought about it, but figured that it would have been more anguish than what it was worth. We figured that that's how things are done…it was our bad luck that she had a preexisting condition."

"What was the preexisting condition?"

"Parkinsons. She was in the early stages, why?"

It was almost unbelievable.

I explained to him that Atmantle was about to be sued for their handling of hundreds of other cases just like his. "That's great. Somebody better stop them. I hope they get hung out to dry."

Jerry was right. Somebody had to stop them.

About ten that night, Rachel met me at a rest stop near the confluence of US-131 and M-46, on the west side of Michigan's Lower Peninsula. Toby was first out of her little pickup truck, and walked rather casually over to greet me.

Rachel looked frazzled. Whipped.

I gave her a hug and asked what was wrong.

"It's that dog of yours," she said. "I found the key to your house and let him outside, but he's been throwing up all over. I had to stop once or twice on the way here." Toby looked okay. His tail swished merrily as it always did, and he was quick to push his muzzle under my hand.

I gave Rachel a kiss and apologized for all the trouble I had caused.

She was scared. She didn't like the idea of trouble, or retribution, or cover-ups. But most of all, she didn't like the fact that I could be in danger.

"What are you going to do?" She asked me, "keep running away from things? You can't do that, can you? Don't you have to work Monday?"

"Yes, of course I do."

"Won't they find you then?"

"If they get to me Monday it'll be too late. All I have to do is make it until then."

"Why?"

"Rachel, please. I can't tell you now, but I promise to tell you about it soon."

"You're worrying me, though. What are you going to do, hole up in a motel until then?"

"Don't worry about me. I'm going to catch up with an old friend in Muskegon, and get a motel room somewhere. There must be a motel that allows dogs—even sick dogs—with access to the Internet."

"What are you going to do?" She was crying, half-heartedly. I could see her breath, smell her perfume in the crisp winter air.

"I've got some work to do. We are so close, Rachel. Then you'll see. I'll have a big surprise for you, and trust me, you'll really love what I have in store."

"After Monday?"

"After Monday...I promise."

"I'm worried about you...driving around in this."

"Why?" I asked her.

"There was a bad accident up 115. Some off-duty police officers were either hurt or killed in a car accident."

I shook my head. "That's bad, but I'll be fine...really."

I gave her another kiss. On the lips, on the forehead. I hugged her tight. As tight as I could.

Even though I was keeping secrets from her, even though our hug was through layer after layer of clothes, I never felt closer to her.

And somehow through the madness of the situation, and its uncertain outcome, I knew that Rachel was growing closer to me, too.

Thirty-Nine

BY MONDAY MORNING Toby was a wreck. He threw up many more times over the weekend. He was lethargic, sullen, and horribly weak. He'd pick at his food, but would throw it back up a few minutes later. And it wasn't the garden-variety vomiting, either. His were the kind of heaves that were working from the depth of his bowels, like he was trying to yank his tail through his throat.

I knew that he needed help. There was something wrong. I picked him off the motel bed, and loaded him into the front seat of my Jimmy. He whimpered slightly, the same way he does when I accidentally step on his toes. It was horrible. I hated to see my old pal suffer. I hated the sound of his cry, his moans of pain.

So I got on the cell phone and tried to find an animal clinic in Lansing that would be open first thing Monday morning. My plan was to drop him off on my way to see Darvin Wonch at his office. The drive from my motel room on the outskirts of Grand Rapids to Lansing was uneventful, other than I saw several bill-boards in the Lansing area with the image of Darvin's wife on it.

"Bare'n Sharon" stuck with me. It was a reminder of what I had done wrong, of the confidence I had broken with Warren. It was also a reminder of Darvin's sense of bitter retribution.

The people at the vet's office were nice enough. They wanted to know all about Toby...how much he weighed, his medication, his age, and whether or not he may have been poisoned. It never crossed my mind that he may have been poisoned. I thought he was sick.

My mind wandered. When he was a puppy I took him to a friend's cabin on the outskirts of Gaylord. While we were cooking steaks on the grill, Toby helped himself to a container of mouse poison my friend left in the corner of the garage. And he didn't just have a few nibbles of it either...he dove right in.

I didn't take any chances with that escapade. I took him right to the vet's office, and they made everything right.

Then I thought about the puddle of antifreeze in the Centre's parking lot, and what a convenient snack it may have been. I should have told Rachel to watch him a little more closely. I should have asked her to put him on a leash. Suddenly I was feeling guilty for his horrible condition, and for dragging Rachel into it.

All in all, I spent about twenty minutes there, giving the doctor all the information I could. They said they'd give me a call on my cell phone as soon as they had any news.

The timing of Toby's illness couldn't have been worse. I was going to see Darvin Wonch in a few minutes, and didn't want to be distracted. I needed to have a clear head. Since the first day I met him, he seemed to be one step ahead of his adversaries. He stayed ahead of the regulators, paid off the authorities, monitored his employees, and dared his customers to file complaints.

And when people made a fool of him, he plastered their image on billboards across their hometowns.

I had quite an appointment ahead of me, and it all came

down to how much Darvin knew. If he knew that I was the one planting the landmines, I was doomed. If he knew that I downloaded his company's documents, I was in trouble. If he understood that I had anything to do with Glen Morrison, the stock options, or the tape recordings, my goose was cooked.

It started off okay. The security guard recognized my face, and gave me a visitor's badge without a second thought. Lydia met me in the lobby again and escorted me to the break room, where she poured me a cup of coffee, black. A man in an oversized oxford was heating up a sliced bagel in the toaster. I looked at his badge…Kevin Schultz…the guy who low-balled Mrs. Denton's car claim. I felt like punching him right then and there, but decided the better of it. *You'll get yours, mister.*

Darvin seemed pleased to see me. He shook my hand as if we had a business deal pending. The small talk carried on for twenty minutes…about the weather, sporting events and the business climate. I held my own on all fronts. After glancing at one of his computer screens, he was proud to announce that the price per share was now at almost forty-five dollars. "Just incredible, when you think about it," he bloated. "Our company's bottom line has never looked better. We've already started to put the shareholders' capital to work, and are getting our technology and marketing departments cranked up."

"That's great, isn't it?"

"Sure it is. It's the American dream, right here in little old Lansing, Michigan."

I acted supportive. "How's all this going to play out?"

"It's business. Anything could happen, so I'd hate to make predictions."

"What do you think will happen?" I asked him.

"I think our stock price will continue to climb. The sky's the limit."

"Isn't that what they call a 'forward looking' perspective?" I asked.

"Well, sure it is. That's my job—to lead this company into the future."

I tossed him an oddball question. "How's your gambling addiction?"

He looked at me like I was a skunk at a picnic. "Why do you want to talk about *that?*"

I laughed. "*That's my job*—to make sure you're on the road to recovery. I've got a judge that wants to see your progress. You didn't think that we were going to spend an hour or two chit-chatting about your insurance business, did you?"

He stood behind his desk, tugged on his lapels, and paced. He glanced at the stock monitor, then turned to the window, under his auspicious wooden boat.

"I bet that you still have a gambling problem," I said, chuckling in a taunting way.

He chuckled too. "What are the stakes?" We were making light of a heavy situation.

We both did.

"You know, I've got enough money today to pay off all my creditors. I'm seriously thinking about it. I could be rid of you—no offense—the banks, the lawyers, everybody."

"None taken," I smiled, facetiously. "Why wouldn't you?"

"Because then I'd have to sell my shares in the company, and I don't want to do that."

"Why not?"

"Because today it's worth…forty-five-something a share, but tomorrow it'll be worth- who knows—two hundred?"

"It could go the other direction too, right?"

"It could…but I doubt it."

"Hasn't it already dropped today?"

He looked at the screen. "It's dropped a few cents… big deal. We're a good company, with great connections. We'll be just fine."

I nodded my head in agreement. He was a step ahead of me

again. For now. "How will your stocks affect the divorce?"

"I don't know yet, but my lawyer said I'll have to pay her fair market value, even after what she'd done…"

"The billboards—I saw a couple of them."

"Isn't it great!" He laughed, triumphantly.

"Does that make you feel better, posting her photos up there?"

"Hell yes, it does. Nobody tramples Darvin Wonch and gets away with it."

"Nobody?"

He stared at me, incredulously. "Do you have something to tell me, counselor?"

"Like what?"

"What's the old saying about begging forgiveness is better than asking permission? Have you got something you want to tell me, Chief?"

I didn't say anything, but I had a hard time maintaining my cool. I lost eye contact. I lost my nerve. "No…" I said, rather feebly. "I don't."

"Who the hell is Morrison & Nunnelly?"

I was silent again.

"You don't know anything about it?" He was loud.

I shook my head. "It's a law firm up in Mt. Pleasant. That's all I know."

"Of all the damn law firms in Michigan that have to stir up trouble, we get one in your back yard. Don't you think that's a little odd?"

I shrugged my shoulders. "I don't appreciate the tone in your voice. I have nothing to hide, Darvin. I have nothing to do with them."

He reached into the top drawer of his desk and very calmly pulled out a handgun. It was good-sized, heavy looking.

"Whoa, whoa, Darvin. What the hell are you doing?"

"What's wrong…do I make you nervous?" He picked up

his gun, and slammed back the action. "Now, how about telling me some secrets of your own?"

"Put that damned thing away," I told him. "I have nothing to say. I have no secrets." My heart was racing. He was bluffing; I just knew it. "Why do you have that thing in here, anyway?"

"I started bringing this piece of metal in here about a year ago, after we had a problem with one of the claimants." He set it on the desk, and tapped the barrel with his odd-shaped fingernails. "Just the sight of a gun can be rather intimidating, don't you think?"

"Sure it is." I said calmly, as calmly as my racing pulse would allow. "A guy might think that you're trying to coerce a confession out of somebody."

"Let's hear it then."

"I have nothing to confess, Darvin."

"You're lying." He picked up the gun.

"Whatever you tell me stays between us."

He sized me up. He looked me over. He glanced at the computer screen. "Jesus."

"What is it?"

"Our stock's down two bucks already." He thumbed his watch. "And the market's only been open a half hour."

I breathed a sigh. "It'll come back, right? You're a good company," I said, somewhat cheerfully.

"Sure we are, but that's a big jump for one day."

"Don't the optimists call it a 'buying opportunity'?"

"Hell if I know, Chief. It's my job to make sure it goes up."

"It'll be up by the end of the day, you'll see." I tried to smile.

I couldn't distract his attention from the monitor. He pulled out a remote control and pointed it at a television screen in the corner. It was tuned into the stock channel, the one with the twenty-four-hour stock prices crawling along the bottom of the screen. "Let's see if we're still the darlings on Wall Street."

"What happened to our counseling session?"

"I'm sorry, Chief. Let me turn it off." He sat back in his chair, but continued to be distracted. The guy couldn't pay attention. He couldn't think straight. He reached for the intercom. "Lydia, will you please get me our liaison in New York? Lydia?"

Lydia wasn't there.

He marched to the door, opened it wide, and looked rather impatiently down the hall. "She must be in the rest room." I should have grabbed the gun. I should have run, but I sat there, watching the spectacle.

"What's wrong?"

"I'm on damage control, that's all. We need to get out some positive-sounding press releases to cut off the free-fall. I can't have our stock lose ten percent in the first hour of trading."

He looked at the screen again. "Christ! This is horrible."

I just sat there.

"Lydia!"

Darvin pulled out a bottle of pills and stuffed a small handful into his mouth. "What are you doing?" I asked him.

He took a drink of coffee. "If one pill is great, then half dozen is even better."

"Darvin, that stuff will kill you!"

"Oh bull. These things are harmless. They're no worse than alcohol, or gambling."

Just then, we heard a knock at the door. It was Lydia. "Mr. Wonch…"

"You're back!" His voice had a disappointed edge to it. "Get me our liaison in New York," he barked. "Our damn stock price is falling like a stone. And get marketing up here…"

She didn't move. Her arms folded across her chest. "Mr. Wonch, there's a Mr. Jones from Muskegon to see you, and he says that you two have some unfinished business…"

Darvin threw his hands to his head. He pulled back his hair

so his eyebrows stretched. I couldn't believe his reaction. It was intense. He loosened his tie, and winced the wince of a man possessed. "Give me a minute."

She shut the door.

I asked Darvin if it was the same Jones who wanted to blow his head off.

He nodded.

"What should we do?" I asked him. "Call the police? Call security?" He was pacing…wildly.

"No, no. It would just infuriate him, make matters worse. I'll just pay him off, that's all. I'll have Lydia cash a check now for half of what I owe, and I'll sell some stock today. I don't care what it'll look like to the SEC or the board. It's about time I got that guy off my ass."

"What's the stock price now?"

"Holy hell, this thing's falling! Thirty-five. And the volume! Everybody's pulling out."

I shook my head; the guy was crumbling before my eyes.

"It can't be!" He pulled at his hair again. He waived his arms. "I can't do this counseling thing."

I nodded.

He was a mess.

Out of control.

I watched him place the gun under a folded copy of the *Wall Street Journal*, with the barrel facing my seat.

I gathered up my belongings, put away my briefcase and headed for the door. I saw Jones sitting in the waiting room across from Lydia's desk, waiting patiently. Just as he always had.

Darvin tried to put a positive spin on things. He tried to save face. "Thanks a million," Darvin proclaimed.

Thanks a million, indeed.

Forty

I BREATHED A SIGH of relief when I made it back to my truck. It seemed that I had wriggled through the hands of fate, the stranglehold of destiny. Darvin didn't have a clue that I was behind the pending lawsuit, the visit from Jones, or the fact that his stock price had just started its crash. Even if he had figured out that I had something to do with it, I really didn't think that Darvin had the guts to pull the trigger and actually shoot me. He would have had one of his goons meet me in the lobby, or follow me home, or he'd find a thousand other ways to abduct me. The gun was just a gambler's ploy, a tactic, a bluff.

And I called his bluff like an old pro.

The vet's office left a message on my cell phone, and the news wasn't good. Toby's condition had worsened. "The doctor believes that Toby has some sort of blockage in his digestive tract." My heart sank. "We'd like your permission to do an upper GI and if necessary a lower GI too. It'll cost about five hundred dollars for the procedure, and there's no guarantee it'll work."

The money wasn't the object; it was that my old pal Toby wasn't doing well.

I called them back and told them to "do whatever it takes, but please save my dog."

Poor Toby. He was all I ever wished for in a dog, all I ever hoped for in a pet.

I didn't have time to wallow in my grief. Taren Lisk called me and said that the two cops that were tailing me Friday night got into a bad accident on M-115. They spun out on the icy roads and wound up overturned and in the ditch. The department's press secretary told media outlets that they were off duty when the incident happened.

"One guy broke his leg, and had to be airlifted to Saginaw." Taren was upset. "The other guy is a lot worse, and they don't know if he'll make it. They said that they lost control on the icy roads and crossed the center line on M-115."

"Geez, Taren…I'm sorry about all that."

"Did you have anything to do with it?"

"No, I was just driving along, minding my business. If the department said that's what happened, it must be true."

"Liar."

"Taren! Watch it. Is that the only reason why you called me?"

"No, no. Hell no. Cripes. There's way more to it."

"Lay it on me then."

"This place is a zoo. The media is swarming outside. There must be twenty television crews here. Radio. Newspaper."

"Why?"

"They got tipped off that the governor and the AG are in collusion with your favorite insurance company. They've got word that there's some lawyer named Brian involved in it too. They've all been cheating the public for years."

"No way." I tried to sound sincere.

"You jerk."

"What?" I asked. "Do you think that I had something to do with this?"

"I know you did."

"What are they trying to prove?"

"If it's true. I guess."

"What about me?" I asked her.

"We've got one of our lawyers at your office right now, and he wants to ask you some questions about this whole deal. But I don't think he knows what's going on down here." She cleared her throat. "He wants to know what your role is in all this."

"What does he know?"

"That you've been impersonating a lawyer."

"Is that all?"

"As far as I know. Remember, I'm in another department… just an associate."

"Yeah, but you're still my lawyer."

She was quiet. "I'm not sure I should be in this situation."

"Taren, you can't bail on me now."

"I'm not, but I don't want to lose my job or jeopardize my career, either. I've got bills and loans. I need this job."

"I know, but what should I do? What should I say?"

"Don't say anything without a lawyer there."

"That will be easier said than done."

Less than an hour later, I was at the office. The Centre's office. Just as Taren suggested, a man was waiting for me dressed in a sharp gray business suit. But he wasn't alone. The personnel manager was there too, with arms crossed and an unpleasant look on his face. "Good morning, gentlemen," I proclaimed. "What can I do for you?"

The personnel manager introduced the suit as an investigator with the attorney general's office. He was rather blunt and not particularly friendly: "Got any legal advice?"

I looked at him and rolled my eyes. "I don't know what you're talking about, and I don't want to say anything without a lawyer present." The three of us stared at each other for a second, before I looked at the manager and gestured that I'd like to speak to him alone. We stepped outside my office and I asked him what was going on.

He was obviously uncomfortable with the whole situation. "They think that you're somehow involved with a conspiracy of some sorts…I don't know the details, and frankly I don't want to know, either." He was almost whispering, and he looked a little embarrassed. "They've got a search warrant for your house, too."

"Great."

"They've already been there, and were carting out your stuff all weekend…your computer, everything."

"Lovely."

"They found a hidden microphone in your office." He furled his eyebrows ashamedly, as if he was embarrassed by the whole situation. "The cord ran under the carpet to the back of your desk, but they can't find the recorder."

I shook my head, no. "*They* were the ones doing the tape recording. They taped my sessions. They bugged my office, and recorded it by remote."

The personnel manager looked confused. "This guy was?"

"No, not him, but somebody from his department. That's why I don't want to talk to him or anybody else from Lansing. They might be tape recording us right now." He looked around suspiciously. "Where's Steve anyway?"

"He's downtown…" I leaned on him with my eyes. "At the sheriff's office. They think he's been over-billing Medicaid. And they got proof…lots of it. He's in big trouble."

"Really?"

He had a disgusted look on his face. "That's right," he nodded. "You know, I really never liked him."

Sure you didn't, I thought. "Do you know anything else about this guy?" I asked.

"He's with the attorney general's office…one of their investigators…the higher ups. That's all he told me."

"This is just great. Tell him that I'll talk to him just as soon as I reach my lawyer."

"What should we do about your appointments today?"

"What do you think?" I asked.

He looked uncomfortable with making a decision. "We'd better reschedule, don't you think?"

"You're the boss."

"I'll take care of it."

Glen Morrison seemed to be waiting for my phone call. He had been watching the noon news broadcasts—the lead stories—from downtown Lansing. "The shit has hit the fan," he laughed. "I'll be right over."

When I hung up the phone with Glen, the vet's office called, and said that Toby's procedure went well. They found a sponge the size of a golf ball in his stomach, and asked me if I have any enemies.

"Why?" I asked.

"Because we often see sponges in the stomachs of dogs when someone wants them dead."

"Really..."

"Yep. It's a good way to kill a dog...quiet...without the mess. We usually see it when a dog bites a neighbor kid, but the owner doesn't want to euthanize the dog. The kid's parents can't worry about the kid getting bitten again, so they give the dog a sponge and the problem just goes away."

"I never knew that."

"If you had waited any longer to bring him in, he would have been a goner. After a dog swallows it, and tries to vomit it up for a few days, it'll eventually become lodged in the intestines, and that's it. If it blocks the digestive tract, it kills 'em."

"Yeah, but why would he eat a sponge?" I asked.

"That's where the enemy part comes in. They soak it in bacon grease, or hamburger fat, and feed it to him that way."

"Wow..." I said. "Thank you."

"We're going to keep an eye on him for a couple days if that's okay?"

"That's fine. Perfect, really. I'm going out of town for about a week, so I was going to board him somewhere anyway."

"We'll keep an eye on him. We'll keep him here until you get back in town."

"Thank you."

Before Glen got to my office, I pulled up the Internet at Miss Peacock's desk. Atmantle's stock had plummeted to twenty-two dollars a share. When he arrived, it had fallen to $19.46.

"That was a good year," Glen said.

"What?"

"Nineteen forty-six...the year I was born."

"I guess it was." I led him down the hall and out the back door of my office. We were in the courtyard, away from the microphones, the tape decks, and the trouble.

"What are we going to do?" I asked him.

"Nothing," Glen said, confidently.

"What do you mean...nothing?"

"We're not going to do anything. The guy here from the AG's office may be part of the cover-up. He'll realize it eventually, and stumble out of here with his tail between his legs."

"How can you be so sure?"

"That's just the way it is." Glen smiled and swirled his hand as he spoke. "It's obvious that someone from the attorney general's office, or the governor's office, can't investigate it. They're involved."

"Who will it be then?"

"The feds." He laughed. "Oh yeah. And you're going to be their star witness."

"Why?"

"You're the one that leaked the info, you're the one with the inside connections."

"There's one problem," I said, almost ashamedly.

"What's that?"

"Actually...a lot of problems." Glen rolled his eyes and sighed. "I haven't been a model shrink when it comes to all this stuff."

"What are you getting at?" He looked concerned.

"Like the stuff I showed you on my laptop...I never told you how I obtained it."

"I don't want to know," he said, wringing his hands.

I felt like I needed to come clean. "I got tapes of Atmantle's chief executive, admitting all kinds of horrible things."

Glen shook his head, and took several seconds to absorb what I just said. "Don't you understand, those tapes are your ticket to freedom. You're holding the trump cards. I'll cut a deal...your testimony in exchange for immunity. The feds won't care about prosecuting a shrink for penny-ante stuff like that...they want to collar the big game animals on safari. They want the AG, the governor."

"What about my stuff?" He looked confused. "They got a search warrant, and ransacked my house."

"They have to catalog it, and look through your records. It'll take a week or more. Did they get your computer?"

"I had one, but it was on loan from the Centre."

"What are they going to find?"

"Nothing at all. I kept everything related to Atmantle on my laptop."

"Like what?"

"You know," I said. "The letters to all those people...how we cataloged them. Even my stocks and options trading."

"And where's your laptop now?"

"In a locker at the airport in Flint."

"That was smart. Are you going someplace?"

"Yes—on vacation."

"When?" He asked.

"Tomorrow morning."

"Why would you leave when all this is going on?"

"I've had this trip planned for months," I told him.

"It's probably just as well that you're leaving. At least temporarily." He crossed his arms and paced. With each step the salt crystals under his shoes crunched painfully. "It'll take a week at least until the feds figure out that you're their star witness. I'll coordinate everything. I'll be the point man on all this."

"Thank you Glen. I knew this was going to work."

"Have you seen the news reports?" I shook my head, no. "Lansing is crawling with reporters. The place is clamoring. They got the AG and the governor involved in this collusion with our boy at Atmantle." He was getting caught up in the story. "The governor is part of an investment group...a major shareholder in Atmantle. And the AG looks to be in hot water too. He's given Atmantle *carte blanche* to do whatever they want, because Atmantle is one of their biggest campaign contributors."

All I could do was smile.

"Don't tell me that you had a part in all this?"

"Okay...I won't."

He laughed, wryly. "That's only the tip of the iceberg. They've handed out indictments against some slimy arbitration lawyer named Brian and the insurance commissioner too. The lieutenant governor has already bailed out. She's down there throwing gas on the fire of this thing."

"Really?"

"Yup. She's telling the media that 'this won't happen on her watch.' Stuff like that. She seems to think that the governor is going to resign, if not go to jail. I get the feeling that there may be a lawyer on the inside that knows half the stuff that you've been cooking up. The lawyer must have a hell of an informant behind the scenes to make sure the bosses get their due." He quit pacing. "Why don't you get out of here? There's no reason for you to stay. Pack your bags and go."

"Are you sure?"

"Hell yes, I'm sure. But before you leave, make sure you've got copies of those tapes hidden somewhere safe. Where nobody will find them. That's your ticket to freedom."

"Don't worry about that, Glen," I said. "I covered my tracks fifteen ways to Sunday."

Forty-One

BY FIVE THAT AFTERNOON, the investigator from the attorney general's office had long since left, and the personnel manager slithered back to his little office down the hall. The nurses and orderlies whispered amongst themselves and pointed fingers in my direction. I said my goodbyes to Miss Peacock and Mary Cornwall, but I never told them where I was headed, or with whom. They didn't ask, and I didn't volunteer a thing.

If the feds wanted to track me down, I wasn't about to make it easy for them.

I drove downtown to our favorite coffee shop and pulled up the Internet on one of the computers they have mounted on granite countertops. There were no urgent e-mails, no rhetorical fires to extinguish. At least for now all was quiet in my little world.

I felt a little guilty when I pulled up my online trading account. I had made an easy dollar, and quick bucks always come with a mental price tag of guilt. I didn't want anyone to see it; I didn't want anyone to be looking over my shoulder. It was difficult to act nonchalant; it was hard to act like I was pulling up the box scores from last night's hockey games.

But it was a big deal. A very big deal. The trading day in New York had ended; the markets had closed. All my options had met their strike price. Even the long shots. Although I still had a few days to go before I got paid on it, the first volley of trades were going to net about $535,000 in profit. It was just incredible. Although it was tempting to whoop and holler, I decided not to. After all, I didn't have the money yet.

It was just about then that my cell phone rang. I didn't recognize the phone number on the display, but recognized the area code as either Darvin's or the vet's office.

"This is Lydia Davis, Mr. Wonch's assistant in Lansing. He wants to know if you can come back down here this afternoon and meet with him?" I didn't answer. "He apologizes for cutting your meeting short today. We've got your visitor's badge waiting for you at the parking garage, and you know how to get to his office." I still didn't answer. She didn't say a thing. I didn't know what to say.

"Is this Dr. Ong?"

"Yes it is."

"Should I tell him you'll be arriving in about an hour?"

I hesitated. I really didn't want to see Darvin again. Ever. I should have told her that I was busy, or had other appointments. I wanted to ride off into the sunset and enjoy my vacation without the thought of the Darvin Wonch hanging over my head.

On the other hand, if Darvin was comfortable with his assistant making his appointment, perhaps it was his way of reaching out for help. Maybe this was the breakthrough I was waiting for. Either way, another appointment with Darvin presented an interesting proposition; especially with the way Atmantle's stock had gone in the tank. "Yes, that would be fine, but you'd better give me ninety minutes instead of an hour."

"Very well then, I'll give him the message."

I drove back to my house and finished packing for my trip.

The police didn't take my suitcases, or the travel documents I laid on the countertop with the stacks of bills. They were after incriminating evidence. They wanted the stuff that would tie me to the business at Morrison & Nunnelly.

My office at home was a mess. They had rifled through my briefcase, my file cabinet containing everything from my college transcripts to letters of recommendations. The box of diskettes was missing, as was the computer the Centre loaned me.

It didn't even faze me. I grabbed my suitcases, and found my summer clothes in the bottom of my drawers. It seemed odd to wear shorts, or white linen trousers with golf shirts. I was really looking forward to my vacation, to the warm weather, to the prospect of getting a sunburn.

The hour's drive from Mt. Pleasant to Lansing was a restless one. My mind bounced from the things I needed for my trip, to the meeting ahead with Darvin Wonch. It's one thing to wonder if you packed the toothpaste; it's a whole other matter to realize that I might be waltzing into some sort of trap.

It all seemed so well orchestrated, so well choreographed. The guard waved me to his little booth and handed me a visitor's badge…Darvin's invite, Lydia's courtesy, the guard…Was this a trap? Was Darvin going to use his gun on me, or were a couple of his thugs going to throw me down Atmantle's elevator shaft? I thought for a second about bailing out, about running off to the Bahamas and never looking back.

If "curiosity killed the cat," then curiosity was going to kill me too. I just had to see Darvin one more time. I was drawn to his office to see what he really needed. If he begged for help, I'd do my best. If he said he was wrong, I'd listen to his confession. I just had to see him. I just had to see him before I left for the Caribbean.

It was nearly seven but the offices of Atmantle Health & Casualty were still bustling. The cleaning crew was vacuuming the labyrinth of cubicles, and I could smell the subtle sting of cleaning supplies. Six or eight swollen garbage bags were stacked near a bank of shredding machines. The only paper that could leave the office had to be transformed into confetti.

I didn't exactly rap on the door to Darvin's office. It was one of those, "I'm a little bit scared" knocks that children use when they're not exactly sure of themselves. A voice inside mumbled something inaudible. I opened the door tentatively and saw Darvin Wonch slumped in his chair, feet propped on his desk. A quick look behind me revealed no men with guns, no thugs with brass knuckles. If Darvin's charade was a set-up then it sure was off to a slow start.

"Have a little drink, Chief?" His words were slow and slurred, his necktie three or four inches from his brisket. A half-finished bottle of Famous Grouse whiskey sat on his credenza.

"No thank you, Darvin, but you go ahead without me."

"Don't mind if I do." He reached for the bottle, but missed on his first attempt. His dexterity wasn't much better when he uncorked the lid and dribbled two or three ounces into his glass.

"Long day, Darvin?"

He barely had the wherewithal to acknowledge my question. "That may be the world's biggest understatement." I nodded, and pulled in the scene. His office was still. His computer screens were blank, the control room on pause. "Our stock fell ninety-four percent in one day." He chuckled pathetically. "We set a record on Wall Street for the largest one-day drop. It was horrible." He wiped a tear. "It closed at $5.22, Chief, because of all this stuff with the AG and the governor." I let him ramble. "The AG and the gov are backpedaling. They're on the hot seat. Their blood is in the water, and the media smells it. They want a body; they want a corpse." He opened the desk drawer and pulled out the handgun, and a bottle of pills. I watched him shake his head as if he was a brook trout with a Royal Coachman in its upper lip. "Can you imagine the taste of gun metal on your mouth, counselor?"

"No...why?" I asked him.

"Can you imagine trying to fit a double-barrel shotgun in your mouth, then reaching for the trigger?" He gestured with his hands, as if he was playing an imaginary trombone.

"Why do you ask?"

"That's what Hemingway did." Darvin reached for the pills, opened the lid, and poured fifteen or twenty into the palm of his hand. The pill bottle was now empty. "Blew his head off with his favorite Boss shotgun. Both barrels. Couldn't take it anymore."

"Take what anymore?"

"Life, I guess." He shook the pills in his hand as if they were dice at the craps table.

"Don't do that. Don't take all those."

"Why not?" He shrugged his shoulders. "Maybe I can't take life anymore either. My company's in the toilet, my wife's screwing some other man, and I just lost a fortune on the stock market."

"You have a lot to live for, too."

"Sure I do," he slurred, sarcastically. "My time is now. I'm just like Papa Hemingway."

"How, Darvin?" He had me leaning into the question.

"He wanted to die. Had depression really bad. Paranoia too...thought the FBI was tape recording him...reading his mail...auditing his taxes." He tossed the pills in the back of his throat, raised the whiskey to his lips and took a giant pull. "Ahhh!" Seconds passed. "They tried electro-therapy and medicine to stem the tide. Nothing worked. When they flew him from his ranch in Idaho to Mayo Clinic in Minnesota he tried to kill himself by walking into the whirling propeller of an airplane."

"Why did you take those?"

"Why not? What difference does it make?"

"You're in my care, that's why. I need to call for help."

"Go ahead. The doors are all locked. They'll never get up here without a badge. The cleaning crew will never hear them with the whine of the paper shredders."

I pulled out my cell phone and dialed 9-1-1. Darvin just sat there, finishing the glass of whiskey and pouring another. When I finished the call he laughed. "Maybe we should have had a toast…more pageantry…"

"To what?"

He shook his head. "Not to what, Chief, to whom…"

"Who then?"

"To Papa Hemingway and Cecil Armbruster."

"Who's that?" I asked.

"Our namesake."

I stared in his direction, confused.

"Captain Cecil Armbruster, of the *Atmantle*…one of the first steam-powered boats of the late 1800s."

"The *Atmantle* crashed, though. It sank." I was confused. "Why would you name your company after that?"

He laughed. "You've done some homework on us, haven't you?" More laughter. "How many shares did you buy? A hundred? A thousand? How much did you lose today?" He closed his eyes and slumped further into his leather chair. His arm stretched for the desk, but fell short, the glass shattering into a thousand shards. I didn't say a thing. He spoke without lifting his head from the chair, without opening his eyes. "Armbruster was a gambler, a risk-taker just like me. Bet on everything that moved." His laughter was forced, fake.

"He was an officer in the Union navy…and made a name for himself with his daring maneuvers during the Civil War." I listened. "After the war he bounced from ship to ship before the *Atmantle*. Then in September of 1895 he had a load of wheat and cotton aboard." Darvin's speech was slower still, even though he remembered plenty of details. The pills were in his bloodstream—playing tricks on his brain, racing his heart. "The weather forecasters were nothing like today's, but they said that the storms were really bad." He put his hand over his eyes, his nose, his mouth. The sweat poured from his pores. "The other boats decided to stay in port until the storm passed, but not Armbruster. One of the other captains bet him that he couldn't make it to Baltimore." His breathing was heavy, deliberate. "Who knows what the stakes were, but I'm sure they were substantial." Seconds passed. I heard the sirens wail in the distance. "Of course, you already know what happened to both the ship and good captain."

"I still don't know why you would name your company after a ship that sank," I asked him.

He laughed again. "Ever try to come up with an original-sounding name for an insurance company?" Laughter. "It's impossible. They're all taken. When I read about the *Atmantle* I liked the way it looked on the paper." His hand rose from the armrest, and his index finger made a few swishing motions. "With the tall letters in the beginning and the end, and short ones in between, it just looked good. It looked like a little ship on the paper." He chuckled. "'Atmantle Health & Casualty…Insure With Confidence.' What a joke. We're in the tank. We suck."

His hand fumbled for the gun.

The sirens were loud, on the street below. They were on their way upstairs.

He waved the gun as if it was a sixth finger.

"Put that thing away!"

"It's hopeless," he mumbled.

He pointed it at the television screen in the corner of his office, then to one of his computer monitors.

"Darvin, please!"

He turned the gun to his temple, and shouted, "Bang!"

"Give me the gun," I yelled at him.

He didn't flinch.

"Bang," he yelled again. I snapped. That was the last straw.

I jumped from my chair and leapfrogged over his desk, tackling him with all the force I could muster. The gun skittered across the floor, careening off one of his wooden desk legs. "You bastard," I sneered. My teeth were clenched in the fury of the moment, my forearm wedged under his chin. He tried to push me off but I had him pinned. He was dripping wet, flailing his arms, his legs. We were scuffling. The smell of whiskey was everywhere. He was a big guy, a strong man. It took everything I had just to stay on top of him.

The paramedics rushed inside, shouting, "Hello, who needs help?"

"Over here," I cried. "He just collapsed."

Darvin lay in a heap, his arms no longer flailing, his legs stiff. He had passed out.

Like a giant, dead bear.

They held a finger to his throat. "His pulse is racing."

I was panting mightily, myself.

"What's his name?" They barked.

"Darvin Wonch."

"Mr. Wonch, can you hear me?"

The cleaning ladies and the security guard were standing in the doorway.

He didn't answer.

"Mr. Wonch?" They shoved his desk aside, opened the little medicine bag, and jerked on their rubber gloves.

I backed away…slowly. My heart was racing too. Adrenaline was flowing like a raging bull.

The paramedic searched again for a pulse, probing his throat with frantic stabs. Nothing. "I got no pulse!"

The ladies gasped, putting their hands over their mouths.

I walked their way and shoed them out the door. "Come on now. Let's give them some room."

The paramedics shouted directions at each other.

It was hectic, horrible.

"Ladies, let's get those doors propped open. Hold the elevator!" They left with the guard.

The medics had Darvin's shirt ripped open and were zapping him with those paddles. They rolled him on a gurney, and yelled for some help. "Sir, take an end! Let's roll!"

A second later we were flying down the hallowed halls of Atmantle Health & Casualty, its commander in chief receiving CPR.

Some of the ladies turned their heads and gasped as we rolled along, a medic thumping Darvin's chest with rhythmic jabs.

When we made it to the elevator I watched Darvin, and his blank, lifeless, expression. The blood of life had left his cheeks.

"What happened?" The paramedic asked me.

"He took a handful of pills…Xanax. And alcohol." More CPR. "He just collapsed."

"How do we get ahold of you?"

The elevator door opened, and I handed him a business card.

They rushed to the back of the ambulance, tossed open the doors and shoved him inside. "When his wife comes to visit, you'd better watch him closely," I said, as they locked the gurney into place.

The paramedic shook his head hopelessly.

Darvin Wonch was dead.

Forty-Two

EVERYTHING FELL INTO PLACE. I caught the 7:35 A.M. flight from Flint, Michigan to Memphis, Tennessee. After an hour layover there, we were airborne again, and headed east by southeast to Nassau, Bahamas.

Everything went according to plan. The flight attendants were courteous and friendly, the turbulence was next to nothing, and my neighbor in the seat next to me didn't snore or hog the armrest. The captain announced over the intercom that the temperature in Nassau was "Eighty-three degrees, with southeast winds of five to ten miles an hour." The plane's cabin didn't exactly erupt with applause, but a subtle sigh of relief was surely detected.

After a seemingly never-ending Michigan winter, eighty-three degrees was going to feel like paradise.

Nassau's International Airport wasn't exactly the most organized, or teeming with modern conveniences. The flight attendants threw open the cockpit doors and a set of mobile stairs appeared. From there, we entered a plain cinderblock building that must have been ninety degrees inside. I had to admire the parents of small children in that setting. Moms cradled their perspiring babies in their arms. Dads held the hands of their grade-schoolers who were begging for something to drink. Everybody was hot and sweaty, so close to the end of their journey, so close to rest and relaxation.

All I had to do was make it through customs.

And it really wasn't a big deal. They merely inspected my driver's license from behind an elevated, glass cubicle. From there, I passed through a turnstile and a set of metal doors to the baggage claim. A group of four women—dressed in flowery, tropical dresses—greeted us with an upbeat, happy serenade. They swung their hips and snapped their fingers in unison, and boy, could they sing.

If the roar from the rapids on the Escanaba River was the sound of the cabin, then the pleasing gush of the Bahamian serenade was the sound of the honeymoon I never had.

The ride from the airport to the resort was also uneventful. Since Memphis, I had been in constant contact with a family from Kansas. The father wore a Kansas University t-shirt, and so did one of his boys. Both he and his wife looked to be a little older than I was, and by the looks of their wardrobe, more successful than me too.

Maybe up until recently.

On the shuttle ride from the airport to our resort she shook her head at the squalor that is life in the Caribbean. She was feeling the same guilt I was. Here we were—staring out of an air-conditioned vehicle, on our way to a three hundred dollar a night resort—while other people had to live in one-room houses without plumbing. It was painful to look at.

I was thankful for a lot of things…where I lived, where I worked, the vacation I was taking.

An hour later my luggage arrived at my room, compliments of a dark-skinned man with bright white teeth and a matching white shirt. "My name is James, welcome to the Half Moon Resort." I gave him a twenty-dollar tip, and said that I would look after him for the rest of my stay. He bowed like my dry-cleaner friend back home, and said thank you over and over again. I felt like spreading the wealth; I was in the mood to share.

My room wasn't really a room. It was more like a section of a house. Stucco-sided and tall, with round archways and black and white towels hanging on polished brass fixtures. It had black and white everything: bed spreads, tile floors, loveseats, and curtains. They didn't waste any space in the kitchen; it was none too large, with a refrigerator, two-burner stove, and coffee pot. My bathroom was really special, with its door-less shower, and garden Jacuzzi tub the size of an overturned Volkswagen beetle. The bedroom was huge: my king-sized bed looked like a twin, because it was surrounded by a table and chairs, a wet bar, several couches, potted plants, and a porcelain set of dominoes.

All the while, the ceiling fan quietly rained baby puffs of air.

As tiring as the trip was, I really wanted to see the sights. Outside my door, the ocean hurled waves on the beach. I stood there for a second or two and thought about which way I should go. To my right was a croquet course and stable; to my left, a fair-sized swimming pool, and a thatched-roof pavilion. It was almost four in the afternoon, and the sun blistered a hole in the cloudless sky. A strange-looking grackle fired an annoying *"kling-kling"* from the top of a palm tree, and a chameleon dashed across the black, seamless cart path.

It was too hot for a horse ride, too lonesome for croquet. I didn't really feel like going for a swim and it seemed too late in the day to start a good book. So I made my way to the overgrown pavilion and sat down at the bar. Nobody else was seated. I asked the bartender for a vodka tonic, then took a look at my surroundings. It looked like paradise. It was paradise.

A moment later, I pulled the straw from my lime, and pushed it to the bottom of my glass. I stabbed the flesh with my straw, sending tiny plums of citrus into the spirited mix. My glass was cold and tall, loaded with ice, and just what the doctor ordered on a warm afternoon, an hour shy of cocktail hour.

The couple from Kansas was seated around the kidney-shaped pool, trying to relax while watching their children swim with inflatable inner tubes on their arms. *She was remarkably pretty,* I thought. I like a woman with long legs, and a proportioned, healthy body. She doesn't have to be big-breasted, or thin as a rail. A woman that takes pride in her body has a natural magnetism.

She was all about taking care of her body.

"Did you need a bucket, sir?" I turned to the seat next to me, but the voice didn't need an introduction. It was Telpher Beaman, the man I hadn't seen since I spent the night in the woods in Michigan's Upper Peninsula. "Or would you rather drool all over your nice, new shirt?"

"What are you doing here?" I asked him.

"What does it look like?" He still answered every question with one of his own.

"Having fun?"

"Who wouldn't have fun at a place like this? It's like paradise." It was rather odd to see him without a tweed sport coat and a printed ascot wrapped around his neck. In the breezy heat of the Caribbean, he wore a set of Bermuda shorts, a flowery printed shirt, and a flat-soled pair of loafers. A quaint straw hat dappled his eyes in shade. "One of the best eye openers I've ever had."

"Eye opener? What's in it?"

"You've never had an eye opener?" He looked at me rather sarcastically. "Jamaican Rum and cold water."

I nodded my head but disagreed with his assessment. His drink needed something else.

"Must be the setting that makes it taste so good." He raised his highball glass toward the pool, meaning that he liked the view as well. "I wonder what her story is."

"What?" I asked him.

"If she's happy?" He pondered. "If she thinks of herself as lucky to be here, or if she's got a suitcase full of emotional baggage."

"I was thinking the same thing," I said.

"Is she happily married, or does she merely tolerate him?"

"I can't really tell."

He paused, "You can't really tell unless you talked to her, right?"

"That's right," I agreed.

"And if you talked to her, would you tape record your sessions?" I watched him raise his eyebrows and look at me disapprovingly.

"No, I wouldn't," I told him, sternly.

"Would you betray her trust?" He sipped his drink casually. "Would you use her to forward your own agenda?" He set his drink on the bar, and smacked his lips. "What's wrong, Jim, having a twinge of guilt?"

I couldn't say a thing.

He was inside my head.

"Shrinks aren't supposed to do that," he said. "You should have walked away from that whole situation. You should have told Darvin that he needed to get a new therapist." He wiped his mustache. "Revenge may be a wonderful thing, a powerful emotion, but forgiveness will give you peace of mind. Ever notice how often you say you're sorry?"

I nodded.

"Sorry isn't the same as forgiving. Until you learn to forgive people, you'll always have an unhealthy streak inside you." I took it all in. "You've got to learn to let things go, Jim."

Telpher was right.

He gestured to the pool again, and the woman from Kansas. "If you did talk to her, you'd ask her things that would be hard to answer, wouldn't you?"

"I might."

"You'd get inside her head. You'd make her think about stuff that she's never thought about, right?"

"Do you have to put it so bluntly?"

"Isn't it the truth?"

"That's what we do…sometimes."

"I don't think so. You wouldn't want her to think about stuff *all the time*, would you? Can't she just sit on her little lounge chair and think about what a wonderful vacation she's having?"

"Sure she can."

"Why don't we just forget about her then, okay?"

"That's fine with me Telpher. I was simply admiring how pretty she was, that's all."

"Me too," he said.

We spun on our barstools, so we were no longer facing the pool. We prodded our drinks with our straws, and watched the bartender wipe down the counter for the third time.

"Seriously," I asked him. "What are you doing here?"

He wouldn't look in my direction. "I'm having a drink with an old pal. What's wrong with that?"

"Is that what I am to you?"

"We're pals, aren't we?"

"You always show up at the most bizarre times though… Carrie's funeral, the time in the woods up north…"

"Don't forget about the hay wagon. Remember?"

"What hay wagon?" I asked him.

"You don't remember…the Haunted Forest? Joe's suicide?" I was drawing a blank. "I was on the hay wagon just as you were about to cold-cock that frat boy."

"Is it me, or some sort of coincidence that you show up at the most bizarre times?"

"I do?" He asked again.

"Yeah, you do," I said disgustedly.

"Coincidences are God's way of remaining anonymous," he said, confidently. "And I'm just along for the ride."

"I see, so does that mean you're my guardian angel, or just the guy who verbalizes my conscience?"

He looked at me like I had just painted him into a corner. "I told you, I'm just an old pal, catching up with a friend."

"Tell me, friend, now that Darvin Wonch is gone, and the people in Lansing are in hot water, is there anything else to the matter of Carrie's death?"

He smiled, and remembered our conversation from the day of her funeral. "I wondered if you had forgotten it, or chose to repress it all these months."

"Well, are you going to tell me?"

He shook his head, then toyed with the straw in his drink. I waited for an answer as he pulled the flesh from his orange garnish with his clenched teeth. "Let's just say: Many a slip, twixt the cup and the lip."

"What the heck does that mean?"

"What do you think it means? I can't tell you everything, Jim."

"I don't know, Telpher, now please tell me."

"Don't count your chickens until they're hatched."

I laughed. "There can't be more to it. I saved Carrie's honor." Telpher raised his eyebrows again, and I wasn't sure what he meant by it. His drink was empty, so was mine. "Let's have another drink and go for a bike ride around the grounds. What do you say?"

I waited for his answer, but it never came.

The bartender was waiting…"Another drink, sir?"

I smiled. "Yes, that would be fine. Thank you."

"Very well, sir."

Telpher was gone. He was never there. He was…but he wasn't.

I sat on my barstool for another hour; sipping drinks and watching a crew make the preparations for dinner. They wheeled out an enormous grill, and loaded it with charcoal. Before long I could smell the hickory smoke. It reminded me of the cabin.

Telpher never did show up for the barbecue buffet of jerk chicken, shark, and seasoned grouper. All fresh, all right from the resort's back yard. He missed the bike ride around the grounds, and the obligatory Cuban and cognac before bed. I guess I didn't want him to be there, after all.

At 10 P.M. I was still out on the patio, sipping my cordial and puffing my stogie, when I heard a knock on the door. "Housekeepin'," the voice said. I peered through the peephole, and saw a woman standing there, enshrined in a black and white maid's outfit. "Would you like me to draw your bed?"

"Sure," I said, curiously.

"One person or two?" She asked.

"Just myself," I told her.

"Very well, sir." She entered the room and went to the bed, pulling down one edge of the covers, so all I had to do was slide underneath. But there was more. She fluffed both pillows on my side of the bed, left a mint next to a candle on the nightstand, and a miniature doormat on the floor. Apparently there's nothing worse than getting up in the morning and having to put your feet on the "cold" Bahamian tile. Whatever. Even though I wasn't used to that kind of service, it was a nice touch nonetheless.

The following morning, I woke up early, showered, swam a few laps in the pool, then walked a half-mile or so to the main lobby where they serve breakfast. In the shade of palm trees, I ate crepes filled with fresh fruit and whipped cream. The coffee, the setting, the atmosphere, was incredible.

After that, I called for a taxi. Our first stop was the post office in downtown Nassau, Atmantle's home office. For the Caribbean, the post office was quite remarkable. It was clean and neat. Orderly. There were rows and rows of post office boxes, each with metal doors and the numbers engraved in black.

The place was bustling. Workers dashed left and right, shouting instructions, selling stamps, pushing carts, and sorting mail.

I saw men and women of varying shades of skin. They marched in—wearing business suits, their heels clapping the floor—getting the mail and leaving. I'm sure Atmantle's management company would be along at any time—if they hadn't already stopped by—to pick up the mail of their own. I had no reason to be there other than to have a look around. I bought a couple of post card stamps, and that was enough to satisfy my curiosity.

The Bank of Scotland was just as uneventful. It was just like any other bank I had been to. Nobody really asked me why I was waiting in the lobby. Nobody really cared. I exchanged a couple of hundred dollar bills for local currency. I knew that there was much more going on behind the scenes at the Bank of Scotland, but I really didn't care. There are crooks and crevices, loopholes and landmines everywhere. People will always find ways to beat the system, to railroad their agenda, and the Bank of Scotland was just one of those ways. And what the heck, what I did to Darvin Wonch wasn't especially honorable, or endearing, but I had my opening and took advantage of it.

Was I just as bad as he was?

Am I the ultimate hypocrite?

Enough was enough.

I had my fill of Darvin Wonch, of Atmantle Health and Casualty, of the whole festering mess.

I would teach myself to forgive.

I would learn to let things go.

It was time to move on.

"To the airport, please," I told the cabbie.

"No problem, mon!"

"Oh, and thanks for waiting for me." I reached over the seat and handed him a Bahamian fifty-dollar bill. He turned down the reggae, and smiled.

"Thanks, mon." His voice was scratchy and rough: smoker's voice. "Are you on your way home, or are you going to pick someone up?"

"Pick up…m'lady friend."

"Yeah, mon. Good for you."

I got the feeling that it was a really good tip because he sped through the villages and compounds with the moves of an Indy qualifier. We made it to the airport in plenty of time. It allowed me the chance to draw up a sign on the back of a cardboard box: "Miss America."

Ahead of schedule, Rachel's flight touched down and taxied to the terminal. I watched the passengers file down the stairs. The four women in the flowered dresses assembled behind the metal doors and began singing. A few seconds later, the doors swung wide, and the masses trickled out in pairs and family units. Kids were crying. Parents were frazzled. I kept waiting for her to appear. I kept waiting to see her pretty smile, and her wonderful gait.

At last, she did appear. She was radiant. And blonde.

She gave me a hug. A giant one. Then a kiss. It lasted for minutes.

"Is that you, Miss America?"

She laughed. "Today I am. I feel like it."

"You look like it too. Your hair." I touched it, and it slid through my fingers like holy water. "It's wonderful."

"Thanks. I figured that I couldn't come to the Bahamas as a brunette. It just wouldn't be prudent."

I took her by the hand and we headed for the baggage claim. The setting was warm and sweaty, just like her hand. "Weren't you a blonde when I first started seeing you at the Centre?"

"I think so, why?"

"It's marvelous."

"Glad you like it. How about the rest of me?" She twirled, showing off her brilliant red and yellow dress. Sleeveless. Endless. I noticed her tan legs and arms, firm and delicious—to match the scent in the air.

"I'm speechless," I proclaimed. "Just a few moments in the Bahamas and you're already tan!"

"I was thinking about my outfit. Don't you like it?" She mocked a little curtsy, drawing at the edges of her dress, a few inches above her burnished knees. "Don't I look like a tourist with my outfit and my fake tan?"

"You look great, fantastic. I'm so glad you're here. That we're together."

"Me too." She put her hand on my arm, and kissed me again. In front of all the other tourists, in front of the women in the flowered dresses. I could feel the heat from her face, taste the sweat from her lips. It was sweet—like potion. Love potion.

She wanted to know all about the resort. The cabbie raced along, with his reggae music, and the air conditioner. She put her hand on my knee, cupping it nicely. I watched Rachel view the scenery. She winced at the poverty, but rejoiced in the prospects of what fun we would have. I put my arm around her shoulder, and felt her sway with each bump in the road, with each turn of the wheel.

When we passed through the wrought iron gates at the entrance, she held her hand over her mouth. "Oh my god, Jim, it's beautiful." Her eyes twinkled. She was on the edge of her seat.

The cabbie raised his head, and I saw him look at the rearview mirror. He winked. "Back to the main lobby, then?"

"Yeah, mon," I affirmed.

Rachel slapped me on the thigh, apparently amused with my ability to speak the vernacular on such short notice. I wanted her to keep her hand there—on my bare thigh—for a second longer. Her nails on my skin sent chills down my spine; it tingled.

"See that building there?" I said.

She nodded.

"That's the spa, and I hope you don't mind, but I scheduled you for a massage and facial tomorrow morning." Our cab had slowed to a crawl, and two women on the stoop of a white bungalow waved in our direction.

"I've never had one of those."

"Me neither, but I thought it sounded like fun."

"What's the occasion?"

"No occasion, it's just that we're going out to a fancy restaurant tomorrow evening."

"What else have you in store for me?"

"Plenty." I winked at her.

The cab slowly came to a stop, and the bellhops threw open the doors. I told one of them my room number, then paid the cabbie. All three men had their hands full. Not only did Rachel pack three pieces of luggage, they were stuffed to the gills. She was ahead of me—into the lobby—absorbing the scene, soaking in the ambiance. The cement lions stood guard. "How many bags did you bring?" I asked her.

"Lots…we've got to get these furs to the tannery before freeze up," she told me.

I smiled, thinking that her comments were remotely familiar…

She smiled, provocatively.

I was still drawing a blank.

"Isn't that what Sacagawea told Lewis and Clark?" She giggled. We both did.

I put my hand in hers. "Come on, let's check you in, and I'll show you around."

The lady behind the counter gave Rachel a key to the room, a packet of brochures, and a handful of passes for the grand buffet breakfast. I took her by the hand and showed her the enormous patio where breakfast would be served. I told her all about the crepes, the watermelon, cantaloupe and papaya juice, and the wonderful coffee.

She marveled at the water, as blue and seamless as the sky itself.

We spent the rest of the day running around the resort as if it was our last day on earth. We played a game of croquet, even though neither one of us was any good at it. We rented a bike—a tandem—and stopped at every pool, just to see what they looked like. We considered going for a horse ride, and playing tennis, but decided to try it later in the week, in the cool of morning. Before dinner, we stopped at one of the shops, and bought a few items for the refrigerator: Red Stripe beer, "Ting" soda pop, bottled water, and wine.

"We should probably get some postcards for all our loved ones," she said.

"That's right," I told her, even though I had seldom heard her talk about who those people might be. "I've got stamps back at the room."

It was a slightly awkward situation when we decided to get ready for dinner. Her bags were in the room, next to mine. The bed suddenly looked huge again. It filled up the room like an examination table in a doctor's office. Aside from the budding prospects of intimacy, there was only one place to sleep. The inevitable was lying right there in front of us…calling our names, drawing us near.

We hemmed and hawed when it came time for the bathroom. She thought I should go first because she would tie up the bathroom longer. I told her that I could pour some drinks and write up some postcards. She acquiesced; I conceded. Back and forth we went. Finally, she agreed to go first, taking a glass of wine with her.

While Rachel bathed, I sent a postcard to Virginia.

> *Having a ball down here. The weather is excellent, the food spectacular, and have found someone special to share it with.*
> *I put the money to good use.*
> *Trust me.*
>
> *Jim*

Almost an hour later, we were ready for dinner. I wore a golf shirt and slacks. She wore an inviting v-neck, sleeveless number, and sandals; her blond hair clamped in a flowered clip on the back of her beautiful head. We caught a golf cart shuttle to the restaurant and I couldn't help but tell her how nice she looked, how nice she smelled. I put my arm around her, and caught a glimmer—just a glance—of her bra: chocolate brown, lacy, and snug.

"Do you like my sandals?" She asked me.

"Sure…they're nice. Nice nail polish too."

"Thanks. Do you know how hard it is to find sandals in Mt. Pleasant in the dead of winter?"

"No."

"Oh yeah. Most stores don't put out their sandals until Memorial Day. I found these in a little shop in the mall in Saginaw. I got four pairs for the price of three."

"Wow…quite a bargain shopper."

"I know, but the guy who sold them to me was a real weirdo."

"What do you mean?" I asked her.

"He was weird. He put his face right up next to my toes; I swear he was trying to smell them."

"Oh nice. Did he take your shoes in the back, too?"

"Yes…he did," she said. "Why?"

"It's a sure sign he has a foot fetish, that's why."

It had to be Maury. I just knew it.

"Oh great…" she said, puzzled. "Maybe we should talk about something else."

"Absolutely," I nodded. "I'm starving," I told her. "Let's hope that tonight's meal is as good as yesterday's."

"I'm sure it'll be fine."

The *maitre'd* was waiting for us. "Right this way." He spun, gracefully, and led us through the maze of linen-covered tables. I was so proud of Rachel, so enamored with her looks: erect, tan, and confident. I watched the men in attendance; they stopped talking and eating as they watched her pass. *Eat your hearts out, gentlemen.*

"Tonight's special is yellow-fin tuna…blackened, brazed or broiled." I watched Rachel and the way she looked up at him. She smiled, and her eyes sparkled in the twilight. "And served on a bed…"

My mind was wondering again…to the room…to her tattoo…the ultimate inkblot.

"It all sounds so good, doesn't it?"

"Sure does," I told her. *On all accounts.* "Why don't we get a bottle of wine to go with it?"

"Sounds fine, but I don't want to get all messed up."

"Why not?"

"You might not like me when I've been drinking heavily."

"Oh my. Don't tell me…you turn into Darla Esposito."

She laughed. "I thought you liked her?"

"I did. I liked what she did, at least."

"It was probably the gutsiest thing I've ever done in my life, even though there wasn't much to it."

"Don't be silly, you were wonderful. You sure fooled those crooked cops, didn't you?"

She raised her finger. "Do you have any regrets about what happened?"

"Why?"

"Why?" She gave me a stern look. "A lot happened there… Darvin Wonch is dead."

"I know he's dead, Rachel…but it's not like I killed him. I didn't force him to take those pills." Her posture went from tense to accepting. "The guy had a compulsive personality—an addict—and took too many pills. Mary Cornwall was on vacation, and Darvin was in a jam. Psychologists refill prescriptions all the time for their clients even though they're not licensed."

Rachel nodded, somewhat approvingly. "And there's one other thing," I started. "Since he's gone, there will be no other ruined lives." I reached for her hand across the table. "It's over. It's done."

Rachel nodded again. "Let's not talk about it any more, okay?" Our hands met at the center. "Can we just put that whole thing behind us now?"

"That's the best thing you've said all night." The wine arrived, and we both watched our waiter open the bottle as if it were some sort of exhibition. "Why don't we have a little toast?" I suggested. She sat up tall again, and raised her glass. "To," I hesitated, "The best days of my life." Our glasses met near the candle, and clinked gracefully.

Twilight turned to dusk, and the candles at our tables were glowing in their globe-like jars. The metallic din of steel drums cantered in my ears. We were a long, long way from home, the trouble, and the troubled past.

There was very little controversy through the rest of dinner. We chatted momentarily about all the folks back in Michigan and their lousy winter weather, about the surprise the vet's office will have when they first discover that Toby barks at his poop and whizzes in his bowl. The more wine Rachel drank, the more talkative she became. By the time they served us raspberry sherbet in little pewter cups, Rachel had a sandal off, and was talking a mile a minute. She ran her toes around the inside of my pant legs, and toyed with her bracelet on wrists as smooth and hairless as honeydew rind. *Multi-tasking*, I thought. We were laughing and carrying on like we were young and falling in love.

It felt like I was.

Instead of taking a golf cart back to the room, we decided to walk the beach. I'm glad we did because it was the most romantic setting I've ever encountered. We took off our shoes, and were ankle deep in the warm ocean. She held my hand like it was the towrope at Caberfae. I hung on to hers as if it was the end of Toby's leash. I don't remember what we talked about; I don't remember what she said, but when we made it to the thatched-roofed pavilion near the room, we decided to sit in the gazebo a hundred yards from the shore.

We sat there for quite awhile in the relative darkness—swinging on the bench, listening to the Caribbean's waves lap the rocks around us, hearing to the laughter of happy couples behind us. She saw a shooting star, but had a difficult time saying it without slurring her speech. I laughed at her expense; she smacked me on the thigh. All at once she put her hand behind my head and pulled me toward her. Our lips met, and we kissed. Like mad. I couldn't help but close my eyes and feel the heat of her breath on my cheek, the softness of her lips, the taste of wine on her tongue. The swing rocked slightly as I leaned her way, embracing her. We were locked there for a moment or two—her tongue exploring mine—her breast pressed against my shirt. My hand brushed her hair—silky, smooth—then moved to her sleeveless arm, her waist, her hip. She rolled my way and I felt the outline of her panties, the fertile playground of her bikini line. Things were really heating up. My lips turned to her earlobe, then her neck. Her perfume filled my nose...it triggered something primal. My hand traced the hem of her dress, the firm, polished skin of her tan thigh as soft as eider down. She didn't pull away or hesitate; she just held me close. I was lapping at her. Kissing her neck, her earlobes. I nibbled on her shoulders while she raked my back with her long, stiff fingernails.

My god, I thought. *This thing is getting out of hand. In public, no less. In front of God's green earth.*

"Rachel," I whispered. "Come on..."

"I'm with you, Jim."

"I want to do this right." I kissed her forehead, her cheek. She was panting. So was I.

I cupped her cheeks in my hand. At last she opened her eyes; they were mere slits. "I'm all yours." She reached behind her head, unleashed the clip and let her blonde hair fall straight and long. She pulled at my hand, and leaned back on the swing...She must have misunderstood me when I said, "come on." I wanted to go back to the room, but I believe she would have had me right there and then.

"No, no, Rachel," I whispered. "Not here. Let's go back to our room. I wanna peel these clothes from you. I wanna kiss you in places that'll make you scream."

She purred. "Oooo la, la."

"I wanna see you in that yummy chocolate-colored bra of yours."

Her eyes opened wider. "How'd you know that?"

"Come on, you." I pulled her off the swing…two-handed. She stood, tippy-toed, and gave me a jab to the belly.

"Race ya!"

In a flash, she was gone: down the boardwalk, under the pavilion, and scampering across the blackened cart path. I felt like a buck chasing a doe. In heat. She was moving fast, darting, and dancing the dance of playful love. I caught her at the threshold to our room, spun her around, and pressed her against the door. She was out of breath. So was I. We were giggling, hungrily. She yanked at my shirttails. She unbuttoned my shirt in seconds. I was stabbing her with kisses. "Come on, man. Open this door," she said in a feral growl. "I'm going to ride you like a rented mule."

"Hee-haw…hee-haw!"

I found the key in my bulging trousers, and slid it tenderly through the waiting lips on the electronic lock. The light blinked green, and we were backpedaling across the checkered tile to the giant bed. She let out a wail, a cry of delight. I was all over her. My shirt disposed, my pants discarded, I was ready to do the same. I rolled her on top of me—wildly. She let out an "Ooooo," but never stopped kissing me. The slide on the back of her dress was but a piece of rice. In an instant, I had her dress unzipped to the small of her back, my hands inside. I felt her skin, smooth and firm. She was rocking her hips, driving them into mine.

All at once she bounced out of bed and disappeared into the bathroom. "Where are you going?" I asked her.

She didn't answer.

When I got up to lock the door, I noticed that *both* sides of the bed were turned down and a mint was on each nightstand. How nice. The front desk must have notified the staff that there were two of us in the room.

I turned off the lights, pulled down the comforter, and wriggled under the sheets. I kidded myself that I looked rather sexy.

Anticipation is as much fun as participation.

I heard the bathroom door open and a faint glow filled the bedroom. It was Rachel, donned in her little chocolate underwear, carrying a fat black and white candle. She walked slowly like a bride down the aisle, one hand ahead of the flame. The light cast a heavenly radiance on her chest, her chin, her hair. It was like the first few rays of dawn, all fresh and new.

"Oh my," I whispered. "You're beautiful."

She approached the bed, lit a second candle on the nightstand, then backed away.

"What are you doing?" I asked her.

She posed for me, pawing at her thighs, wiggling her hips. I simply stared.

"Don't you like the view?" She purred.

I took her all in…she was incredible.

"I love the view, now turn around."

She obliged, spinning in a half circle. I noticed the long blonde bangs, the goddess-like profile, and the way her underwear cut slits through her smooth, scrumptious bottom. Her hands reached behind her back, unfastening her bra in one graceful motion. I watched her turn around again—exposing her breasts as tan and firm as Bahamian mangos. "Oh my," I gasped.

She didn't stop. Her thumbs slid under the face of her lace panties, fingers wriggling like a magician. She was teasing me, toying with me. Her breasts were sandwiched between her biceps, nipples dancing hypnotically. "What are you doing?" I asked her again.

"I wanna show you my tattoo."

I smiled; at last the secret revealed, at last the object of my fantasies. "Show me, Rachel."

Slowly she lowered the silk icing that ran around her midriff. It felt like I was watching the ball drop in Times Square. I was counting down the seconds. Inch by inch, wriggle by wiggle.

At last.

The secret revealed.

The tattoo.

The whole package.

"Would you like a closer inspection?" She cooed.

"Come here, you."

She placed one knee on the bed, then the other. She was crawling toward me, inching toward the last fulfilling plunge.

And when she came, it was like magic all over again….

We lay there for several minutes, out of breath, out of energy. We gave each other all we could, all that we had. It was awesome. There's nothing more satisfying than having the buildup, the anticipation, the carnal fire boiling inside you, and your lover meet every need. Rachel exceeded mine.

I thought about saying something funny, or witty, but the best I could do was "Welcome to the Bahamas, Mon" in my best Caribbean accent.

She reached for my hand.

"Mmmm," she purred. "I thought this was paradise."

Our fingers intertwined between our sweat-drenched hips.

"It is paradise, as long as you're here."

She squeezed.

"That was nice," she whispered.

I took a breath. "It's true. I think I've fallen in love with you," I said. Her head turned from the ceiling fan. "I know I've said 'I love you' to you before, but that was when I was getting chased by those goons." She rolled on her side, and propped her head up with a folded pillow. "The truth is that I've always had my eyes on you. When you first came to the Centre, and wore all those baggy clothes, I could see the beauty you possessed somewhere beneath the hardened shell…the wall of despair." She sniffled. "And last fall, when you really started to get better, I really took an interest in you. You're beautiful, plain and simple. I started having thoughts of you and me together. You were on my mind a hundred times a day." She reached for a tissue, but I didn't stop talking. "I'm so glad you asked me out. That you got the ball rolling between us." Rachel was in the crook of my arm again, her hand around my tummy. "That time at the pool up north…when you asked me 'what kind of man' I am…I wanted to scoop you up, kiss you like a madman."

Rachel was crying.

"What's wrong?" I asked her. "Don't you want to hear all this?"

"No, it's not that…you're so wonderful."

"What is it, Rachel?"

She squeezed me. "I'm the one that should be delivering the confessions."

"What could you possibly confess?"

I sensed that she was boiling over. "You've been so open and honest with me, and I haven't been that way with you…there's plenty."

"Tell me, Rachel."

She didn't say much, so I gave her a nudge, and it worked. "I had a part in all this."

"In all what, Rachel?"

"In the Bahamas…" She seemed to be searching for the words. "In sending you here." She sniffled. "In sending you the notes." Her words were getting louder. I bit my tongue. "There's something you should know."

"Tell me…please. Whatever it is."

She took a deep breath. "It all started over a year ago when we had a client come into our office." She sighed. "She was pretty and young, fresh out of law school, and recently married," she said.

My hand clutched her side. "Where did you work again?" I asked.

"It's called 'Advanced Directives of mid-Michigan,' in Mt. Pleasant…"

"What is it?"

"We work with lawyers, doctors, and sometimes hospices… for folks who know they're going to die, but want somebody to carry out their legacy, to make their last wishes come true."

"Like what?"

"It can be as simple as a living will, where you tell your family not to keep you alive in case you're brain damaged." She blew her nose in a tissue. "Or it could be something as simple as sending your daughter a birthday card every year that you're gone. We have hundreds of clients doing marvelous things for their loved ones."

"Keep going."

"Anyway, this young lawyer came into our office and told me all about her husband, and what a wonderful man he was. She told me all about the way she met him, and the romantic way he proposed. She told me everything. Everything Jim." More sniffles. "She also said that she was going to die…and her greatest wish was to send him on a vacation…to the place she went with her family many years ago."

"So you set all this up?"

"Yes…I did, but I never wanted you to invite me. Carrie hoped that you would go with somebody, a new love. She wanted you to have a romantic getaway. She wanted you to find someone…another woman."

Now I was getting a little misty. "Why would you feel bad about that?"

"Because…I came to your office under false pretenses."

"What do you mean?"

"Please don't be mad at me." She squeezed. "I scheduled an appointment with you just so I could meet you."

"You did?"

"Please Jim, don't be mad…I was never depressed. I never needed to see you…or needed to take Mary Cornwall's medicine. I've never been healthier mentally or physically." She was rambling. "I just had to meet you after what Carrie told me about you…she told me everything about you. I mean everything. She told me how much you liked her perfume, and how it would drive you wild." She reached for another tissue. "I'm the one that sprayed those letters with Black Cashmere. That's the kind of perfume she wore. Once I started seeing you professionally, I couldn't stop. You were as wonderful as she said, and now that I've gotten to know you, I can't stop having these feelings for you."

"Rachel, why didn't you tell me sooner?"

"I should have, but I was afraid that you'd cut off the relationship. Then I really would have been depressed." She buried her head in my chest. "I'm sorry, Jim. I really am."

I didn't say a thing. On one hand I felt betrayed…that Rachel kept the secret from me for as long as she did. On the other hand I felt honored that the two of them would go to the extent that they did.

Maybe I am a good man after all.

This was no time to hold a grudge.

It was time to move ahead.

Telpher's words echoed in my head; they oozed from my pores; they passed through my lips: "I forgive you." I wrapped her in my arms, and squeezed. "I forgive you, Rachel."

She sighed.

Relieved.

We both did.

Her hand brushed the side of my face. "I love you, Jim. Oh god, I love you." She suddenly came back to life, kissing my arm, my chest, my neck. Her secret revealed; she suddenly felt uninhibited. "I love you. I love you. I love you. I love you." She rolled on top of me, cupping my face in her hands, her breasts quenching mine. She smothered me in kisses, and a thousand 'I love yous.'

"Okay…okay Rachel, I believe you."

She didn't miss a beat. She was all over me. "Oh god, I love you."

"Rachel," I said, grabbing her arms at the biceps, "what are you doing?"

She stopped kissing me for a second; just long enough to peer back at me through her long, silky bangs. "The first time tonight was for fun. Now I'm ready to make love."

Breakfast the following morning was just as good as I told Rachel it would be. She marveled at the varieties of juices: papaya, cantaloupe, watermelon, and mango, to go along with the traditional favorites of apple, orange, grapefruit, and plain old grape. She stared at the ocean, the faces in the crowd, the ambiance, the spectacle of leisure in a first-class resort.

I was so happy to show her around, to introduce her to new things, and to watch her face light up with every turn in the road.

We sat there for quite a while—the way you're supposed to when you're on vacation, when there's nothing hanging over your head.

"Looks like another beautiful day in the Caribbean," she said.

"Not a cloud in the sky."

"What do you want to do today," she smiled "After my facial and rub down?"

I laughed. "I really don't care. We could play a round of golf or go for a horse ride. It really doesn't matter."

She had a stack of brochures from the lobby. "It might be kinda fun to go snorkeling, or deep sea fishing."

I nodded, and watched my girl. She was so pretty, so nice. I was the luckiest guy in the world.

"I'd better run," she said. "My appointment is in fifteen minutes. Why don't you look over the stuff and come up with a game plan for the rest of the day."

She dabbed the edge of her mouth one more time with a cotton napkin, pushed her chair back gracefully, and gave me a kiss on the lips. I watched her go, weaving her way through the tables.

I was so lucky, so happy. A man could get used to living in the lap of luxury, to the adulation of a young, beautiful woman.

The waiters came and went. They asked me if I wanted more coffee.

"No thank you," I told them. "But I would like a newspaper. *New York Times* if you've got it."

"Right away, sir."

I handed him a ten-dollar bill.

Minutes passed.

The family from Kansas walked by—the children several yards ahead of the parents. The mother hid behind her sunglasses and a wide-brimmed, straw hat.

The sun was just starting to heat up the grounds. It was going to be a beautiful day.

"Dr. Ong?" The waiter asked.

I nodded.

"Here's your newspaper. And a telegram."

"Thank you."

He held out his tray.

A small envelope sat on the large newspaper.

I wondered who would be writing. Glen Morrison? The vet's office? The authorities?

Not even close.

It was her.

> *Dear Jim,*
>
> *If you get this note I know that you've found someone special to join you. I hope she's pretty, and nice, and treats you well. But most of all, I hope that she makes you happy. That's all I had ever hoped to do while we were together.*
>
> *This is the last of the notes, the last of my letters. I'm so happy that you're moving on with your life, that you found someone to love. Enjoy your stay; enjoy the trip we never had. God bless you, Jim, and Happy Valentine's Day.*
>
> *Love, Carrie*